OLENA ꓠ

CW01081926

OATH OF BETRAYAL

THE CURSED BONDS
Book One

NOTE FROM THE AUTHOR

Dear Reader,

We appreciate that everyone has a different level of sensitivity and may be triggered by different topics. It is up to your discretion whether you can handle the content in our books.

The book is intended for a mature audience of particular interests in 'why choose' romance and contains a certain amount of coarse language, graphic sex scenes as well as elements of BDSM dynamic. You can also find scenes of death and physical violence and domestic abuse.

It is a work of fiction set in a world with different racial, cultural and social norms - none of this reflext author's personal opinions and is purely created as a plot device. Any resemblance to actual persons, living or dead, events or localities is entirely coincidental, and the names, characters and incidents portrayed in it are the work of the author's imagination.

This book is loosely based on Slavic/Eastern European mythology and, therefore, contains names and words that may seem unfamiliar. The glossary at the end of the book provides detailed explanations of those.

CONTENTS

SEREN FORTRESS

AURE'LANE

CARE'ETAVOS EMPIRE
(DARK FAE)

WIOSNA

DRWARVEN HILLS

KLINCH

KINGDOM OF LUMIVITAE
(LIGHT FAE)

LOWLAND KINGDOMS

ORDER OF
AETHERIC MAGIC

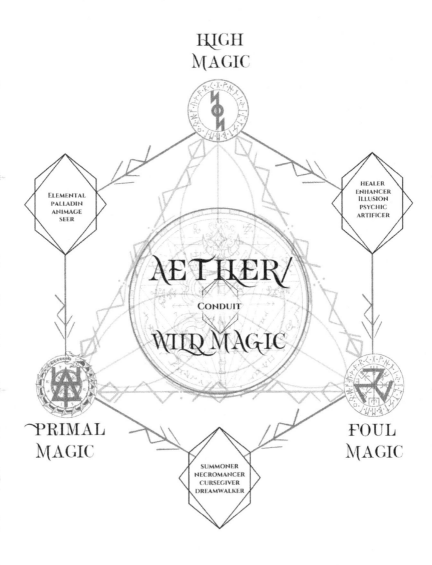

HIGH
MAGIC

ELEMENTAL
PALLADIN
ANIMAGE
SEER

HEALER
ENHANCER
ILLUSION
PSYCHIC
ARTIFICER

AETHER/

CONDUIT

WILD MAGIC

PRIMAL
MAGIC

FOUL
MAGIC

SUMMONER
NECROMANCER
CURSEGIVER
DREAMWALKER

PROLOGUE

ANNIKA

I woke slowly to the gentle caress of Talmund's fingers tracing patterns on my back. I cherished these lazy mornings, waking up sprawled across his chest, even if we were in a cramped tent with rough bedding and a pungent smell on this particular morning, the result of our long and arduous journey.

From where he lay on my other side, Arno's whispers interrupted my examination of Tal's chest and I frowned. 'We shouldn't be here, Tal. If my calculations are correct, the number of demon attacks here is abnormal, even for the Lost Ridge. Sending a rookie mage unit on their final year of training would be a joke if the situation wasn't so dire.'

Tal's sigh was so deep I felt my head move.

'You know it is our job, right? To deal with the Vel. You worry for no reason. They might be natural occurrences; wild magic is stronger near the Barrier, so it isn't surprising that they multiply here. We won't encounter the greater Vella on our side, so let's just try to enjoy using our magic together,' he said. When Arno didn't answer, Tal sighed again. 'You are such a ray of sunshine.'

'We are a specialised unit with a conduit mage. It isn't our job to fight common Vel. Those are for soldiers, dragon riders, or even hunters to deal with. They wouldn't send us unless they expected there to be a problem.' The angry tone of Arno's voice woke me up completely.

He'd been worried ever since we'd been assigned to guard a high-order mage as he investigated the increased number of Vel demons in the area. I shuddered at the thought of the strange, glistening wall so close to our camp. Some, especially the southern nobles, believed it was no longer needed. However, they hadn't read the accounts of those involved in the Necromancer's War and the Lich King's abhorrent experiments on the living—but *we* had, as a part of our training.

I'd had nightmares for weeks after reading of the torturous spells that turned people into greater Vella demons. I was grateful for this remnant of the war, the last defence against the Lich King's army. I was also a little intimidated by the fact that it had lasted for five hundred years, a feat I couldn't even imagine replicating.

The mage we were guarding was an artificer of the High Order with a particular interest in the Barrier. He had been in the wilderness for years, but this was the first time he had asked for an escort.

No one knew why the number of Vel had increased. The official explanation given by the University Council was that a dissonance between the spell sustaining the Barrier and the rare incidents of wild magic allowed the demons to access this realm. Arno didn't believe it, and neither did I. Maybe someone overheard our discussion because the next thing I knew, we were in the dean's office being given this job by the royal mage.

The high-order mage had led us to a place near Varta Fortress. It was deemed safe, especially since the fortress and its dragon riders guarded the mountain ridge and the Barrier keystone's resting place, located somewhere deep in the mountain's heart.

The scholar had demanded protection because, as he'd said, '*I don't have time to deal with such petty annoyances.*' I suspected we'd have to fight a few strigae or—I shuddered—ghouls. We might even have to cleanse a few undead corpses from an abandoned cemetery, but I was more than ready for it.

'Precisely. They sent *us* because Ani here is a conduit who needs to build her experience. Besides, we both know she wanted it,' Talmund said, bending to kiss my forehead. 'You saw how happy she was when they offered us the chance to prove ourselves.'

'Oh, stop worrying and give me a kiss before the old twat wakes up,' I murmured, reaching for Arno without opening my eyes, and he happily obliged.

My magic blossomed under his touch, the physical expression of our synergy. Arno's healing abilities belonged to the High Order. Somehow, we had discovered that he had synergy with Tal's and my elemental magic of the Primal Order. 'Hmm, see, that's better. You don't have to worry. I can power your spells, and we can deal with the Vel,' I said, stretching as he kissed me.

I was slowly waking up under his languid caresses and Tal's wandering hands when something disturbed the aether flowing around us.

'Get out of the tent, you useless cunts!' I heard our esteemed leader yell and sighed heavily. The scholar we were supposed to guard was a royal pain in the arse, but we were under his orders. Rolling my eyes, I untangled myself from my men's embrace.

'Come on then, before he throws a fit again,' I said, and they smirked in unison. We hadn't undressed for the night so I only needed to grab my weapon before leaving the tent.

'Yes, sir. What do you re—' my voice died in my throat as I faced a horror I'd never expected to face in this lifetime.

A wlok.

How the fuck *do you defeat a pile of bones?*

It wasn't supposed to be here; it shouldn't even be possible. Such an abhorrent creation, a remnant of the old war, only existed on the other side of the Barrier, where the Lich King's touch corrupted everything and everyone.

3

That's why we had the impenetrable construct dividing the Lowland Kingdoms from the Barren Lands, and we weren't close enough to the Barrier for it to pass over our borders, even by mistake.

Unless the Barrier is failing. If a wlok was here, what else could come through? Are there more monsters? Fuck, Arno was right. The Barrier should stop anything with even a hint of foul magic, yet an immortal wlok was *here.*

The wlok was more myth than reality, or so we thought. Nobody had encountered one in living memory. It required certain conditions, a hefty dose of wild magic, and lots of unburied bodies—or a skilled necromancer ruthless enough to sacrifice a town's worth of living creatures in order to harvest their bones and give the construct a semblance of life.

Encountering a greater demon of the Vella was unheard of. I wasn't just out of my depth; I was drowning in the ocean, clueless and scared, while an immortal wlok stared me in the face.

Everything can be killed. I just have to find a way to do it.

I needed to believe in my unit because this monstrous evil couldn't be allowed into our world. It had no coherent thought, no intelligence behind its insatiable hunger and constant need to expand. Once released, a wlok rolled over fields and roads, searching for more—more life, more bones, just ... more. Human or animal, it didn't matter—it took anything and everything, stripping the flesh from bone and absorbing it to roll onwards, endlessly, constantly growing.

Wlok left no evidence behind, shredding and absorbing their prey without damaging the surrounding vegetation. They would be the perfect weapon if they weren't impossible to control. Everyone who encountered the monsters simply vanished, their bones joining those that went before.

It must have been the wild magic and potency of the Lost Ridge Mountain that had brought this one to life, because only a madman would release a wlok. And only a fool would try to fight one.

It was our turn to be those fools. The magical force majeure had surprised us in our sleep, rolling over the camp. Whoever had decided to send us here was as big a fool as us, and we were about to pay the price of their arrogance.

'Annika, look out!'

Talmund's voice echoed through the valley right before several rocks crashed over the ledge. I barely had enough time to reach for the aether and create a shielding glyph before they fell towards me, smashing into the invisible barrier. I shook violently, choking back my fear, before facing the wlok as it tumbled forward again while my men took their positions.

My gaze went to the man we were supposed to guard. I watched in horror as the mage tried to cast spell after spell aimed at the vortex of bones, each one hardly slowing the wlok as it reformed and attacked again.

But before I could form a coherent thought, he was engulfed, and that scream … the soul-shattering scream of pure agony still echoing in my ears, stripped away every rational thought.

He'd been ripped apart within seconds, and as I added my own scream of terror to the unfeeling universe, I realised the same rule that made a conduit mage leader of their battle group meant that I was now in charge.

Our small group didn't have a hope of escaping this alive.

'Annika, for fuck's sake, what do we do now?' Arno shouted from over the boulder, and I stood up, brushing away the debris covering me.

Talmund answered before I could. 'Run. I will hold it off for as long as I can. Go to Varta Fortress. Maybe the dragons can burn this bastard to dust.' He stepped up from his hiding place, sword held aloft, and ran a hand over his blade, setting it ablaze—a paladin mage ready to sacrifice himself to save others.

Although my conduit abilities made me the strongest mage, it was Tal who always led us and most often shouldered the burden of responsibility. He once again stepped up when I had frozen. Now, one of the men who was bound to me for life stood against the fiend like a hero of old.

5

'I will always protect you, Ani. I will be your shield, guarding your back when you do that insane thing with your magic.' I could still hear his loving whispers as we lay together, his breath caressing my neck. I loved him more than I feared the wlok, and I couldn't let him face this alone.

'You'll die if you do that. We're not leaving you behind,' I answered, and Talmund shrugged sadly, his expression forlorn. 'Unless you have a plan, we'll die here anyway. At least this way, the people in the valley will have some warning,' he said, and I knew he was thinking about his mother and sister, who lived in a town hardly three days' ride from here.

'Tal, I mean it, get the fuck away from there,' I shouted. As he braced himself for the nearing wlok's charge, I threw a hastily created fireball at the monster to buy Tal some time, but he didn't budge. To make matters worse, Arno stepped forward, heading towards the warrior, his arms outstretched and healing tattoo sigils gleaming on his palms, ready to support him.

My hands shook as I drew a fire sigil. I didn't have dragon fire, but with two Anchors, I was capable of fuelling a limitless spell, even if I wasn't sure how much of it my body could withstand. I knew Tal was right; one of us should run, but I couldn't leave them to their fate.

A sudden pull on my aether broke my focus, shattering the half-made sigil, and I screamed when Tal charged, drawing power from our bond. Blue flames of pure aether enveloped the outer edges of the wlok, burning its bones to cinders—but it was too big, too strong. For each stroke of Talmund's sword, another sharp edge of bone ripped a piece of flesh from his body.

More and more blood filled the air, scintillating like a red haze while Tal danced with his sword, eyes filled with pain. My paladin, my heart, my everything, unwavering in the face of death, was buying us time as the mindless truss of animated bones ripped him apart.

The pain I felt through our bond brought me to my knees, blinding me with its intensity. Talmund was drawing on my power hard, so hard I could barely contain the stream of aether, but he needed it. So I dug my hand in the dirt, focusing in order to direct the onslaught of magic.

Something swelled inside my chest, a pressure that caused Arno's gaze to snap in my direction. He could always sense me. I didn't need to look at his face to know the strain he was under, yet I did. He was pale, so bloody pale that I knew he was draining his life force to keep Tal alive for as long as he could. I took a deep breath and pushed some aether into my bond with him as well.

Maybe if I'd been experienced I could do more, but I was an untested conduit who could only use my skill to sustain their spells or fight the wlok myself. I couldn't do both. Worse, I suspected that even if I channelled all the aether of the Lost Ridge into their magic, it would only prolong our agony if they insisted on fighting this demon.

'Run,' Arno mouthed, but I didn't move. Arno—my gentle fae, scholar, and healer, the only man who could make me laugh when I was ready to rip the world apart. The man who kissed away my scrapes and bruises ... was standing his ground while asking me to run.

What life would I have without them?

If they were going to die, then I would die with them. The thought hardened my resolve, and I reached for the aether, feeling Tal's and Arno's spirits grounding me as I opened myself to the primordial power that sustained our world. The air shimmered as my mind seeped through the cold stone beneath my feet until I touched the pure, wild magic of the mountain. It blazed with power, and I took it in, moulding it to my will.

Tal's agonised scream broke through my concentration as the bedrock responded to my call. I saw the sharp bone piercing his chest, his eyes glazed with torment, when he stumbled towards me. He knew he was dying, yet he forced another painful step, reaching out to touch me.

A smile blossomed on his bloodless face when another bone pierced him from behind. He didn't falter but looked at me as if, in his last moments, I was all he needed. 'You can do it, Ani. I believe in you. I'll wait for you behind the Veil.'

Tears poured from my eyes as I shaped my magic into a spear of pure power, the mountain trembling when I released it. The only way to stop a wlok was to prevent its relentless tumbling, and I was going to bury it with us. The elemental force smashed into the cliff above the wlok, shattering the granite to send down an avalanche of stone and dirt upon us all, inseparable even in death.

Tal's family would be safe, and even if no one found our gravesite, it was the right thing to do. My magic raged, ravaging the mountainside, when I felt Tal's tether vanish from my core.

My unyielding heart, who had walked through life armed with an incorruptible code of honour, had died trying to keep me safe. Agony blasted through my senses and unbalanced my magic. I screamed and screamed, tears leaking from my eyes. I prayed for death to take me; losing Tal was unbearable.

Arno's eyes widened. I knew he felt the same pain I did and that he tried to take mine away, but nothing, not even his healing skills, could numb this wound. He whispered my name. I saw the desperation in his eyes and watched in disbelief as a man who valued life reached for death.

My healer cut his forearms, letting blood pour over his fingers in the direst of rituals to draw a sigil. Arno was no longer trying to heal me. Instead, he channelled foul magic, forbidden to his kind, tainting his soul in a living sacrifice in order to summon enough power to create a protective spell around me.

The avalanche crashed into us, and I screamed as the wlok tore Arno apart moments before the granite boulders buried them together. Arno's tether, too, vanished from inside me. I was left empty and numb to the world, cursing his name for condemning me to live while they both died.

Earth-shattering power still raged around me, as uncontrollable as my grief. With no Anchors, I was unable to stop it. I didn't even try, hoping that it would consume me or the protective spell keeping me safe from the rocks above.

The mountain shook again, its walls distorting, the ground rolling like the sea as an earthquake broke it apart. Aether mauled me like a dog that had finally turned against its owner. Blood flowed from my eyes and ears, my body shutting down, overwhelmed by the power tearing through me when a deafening roar penetrated my living tomb and the anguish in my soul.

Dragon riders. Our saviours had arrived to rescue us. My sobs didn't stop. I didn't care about their arrival. It was too late to save those I loved. I saw the rock wall crumble, but I didn't move, didn't call for help, hoping to find oblivion in death.

The enormous muzzle of a black dragon, its skin marked with blue stripes, appeared, eyes filled with compassion. My unbound magic reached for him, searching for a new Anchor, almost forging a connection, and his vertical pupils widened.

Exhaustion washed over me as the darkness enveloping me grew deeper, my breathing now ragged. When I took my last breath, I welcomed it, hoping that somewhere on the other side, I would meet my men again. They held the pieces of my shattered soul, and with their deaths, I had nothing left to live for.

I was ready to die.

CHAPTER 1

ORMOND

Ten years after the Lost Ridge incident

I rubbed my temples, attempting to focus on the soldier reading out today's reports. It was difficult, as a slew of sleepless nights had sapped my strength and ability to concentrate.

Since I'd taken command over the Lost Ridge five years ago, we hadn't had such a terrible year as the one we were facing now. I performed my duties with due diligence, and sleepless nights were no excuse to miss the morning brief.

My eyes watered as I fought a terrible headache, trying to hide a grimace at the pain to maintain the decorum expected from Ormond Erenhart, Lord Commander of Varta Fortress. There wasn't much in the report to capture my attention. It was the same rambling minutiae, day in and day out.

Undead ghouls, strigae, and remnants were swarming us, a never-ending stream of Vel demons created by foul or wild magic and violent deaths. Or at least I *hoped* it was wild magic because the other alternative was much more terrifying, meaning the keystone had cracked further, allowing the Lich King to gain more access to our lands.

What I really cared about was the report from Tomma, my lieutenant, who'd led a recent patrol. 'The last patrol behind the Barrier. How far did they get?' I asked my adjutant, grinding my teeth when he shook his head.

'Not far, sir. The spectrae were closer than ever. The dragons had barely flown across before they had to retreat behind the Barrier. We ... lost one rider. Tomma has gone to inform his family. That's why the report is delayed. Poor boy, no one noticed he had broken from formation until it was too late, and the spectrae had already latched onto his dragon, draining his life.'

I exhaled slowly, feeling the tension in my body increase tenfold. 'Fucking vampire ghosts. How many were there?' I asked when I was finally able to control my voice. I was worried because the spectrae rarely appeared alone. They were the main threat to dragons and their riders when we travelled over the Barrier to patrol the Barren Lands, and now they had killed one of my men.

'May I speak freely, sir?'

'Yes, what is it?'

'Why? Why are you trying to go deeper into enemy lands than the previous commanders have, especially with how dangerous its become?'

'Because I want to see Katrass and confirm that the former capital of the Ozar Kingdom is still the smoking ruin the war chronicles describe, but the spectrae always force us to retreat. Why do you think that is?'

'I don't know, sir.'

'Me neither, and I can't defend my people from what I can't see. None of those lazy bastards at court seem to be concerned with how dangerous the Lost Ridge has become recently.'

I made a mental note to train my riders in techniques used to deal with swarms of spectrae and began drafting another hopeless letter. Despite my countless pleas to the king and the Council of Mages alerting them to our plight, no one believed that the spell on the Barrier keystone was failing. I had begged them to send a representative to investigate time and again, all to no avail.

I had one decent mage, a few healers, and a bunch of criminals for soldiers, with no hope it would ever get better. Ever since the avalanche caused by a rookie mage had changed the topography of the Lost Ridge, creatures mad with bloodlust had been descending on the borderlands, and it felt like the Crown had simply abandoned us.

Everything had changed after the opening of the small crevasse on the border of the Barren Lands, becoming increasingly dangerous. My unit had been the closest when it happened, and my dragon, Vahin, had rescued the sole survivor. The woman he'd dragged from the pile of rocks had looked more like a rag doll than a person, too filthy to even identify.

'Tired already, Commander?' Alaric walked in with a predatory grace and an all-knowing smile before standing beside me. I felt the touch of his magic as his hand effortlessly slid over the back of my chair, only for his fingers to brush against the base of my neck.

He was the only one who knew about the headaches that plagued me. Of the frustration of having to use all my self-control to tame the wild magic in my soul to prevent it from rising and making me go berserk. It was a small, covert gesture he did every morning to check on me, and as much as it had felt strange at the beginning, I was used to it now.

'Ari. What are you doing here? I thought you were busy today,' I snapped, wondering what had brought the dark fae to the map room after he had refused breakfast. 'Shouldn't you be digging through old manuscripts trying to find a way to replace the keystone?' I grouched, still annoyed about the reports and our hopeless situation.

In spite of my attitude, Alaric simply shrugged, settling in beside me, unfazed by my outburst. *I shouldn't have taken my anger out on him*, I thought while my fist closed over the parchment before me, obscuring its bleak figures.

I'd really needed his company. He was the only person apart from my brother who made me feel like I could be myself without judgment. Just like I didn't judge him whenever he'd place a hand on his chest, his mischievous smile darkening before excusing himself to head to his workshop. It was just another of his mannerisms I'd gotten used to after so many years in his company.

My tone was harsh, my words petty, but I was grateful for the moment of distraction his presence had gifted me. I'd lost several men yesterday, but losing a rider and his dragon pained me the most. We didn't have many of them left.

Despite several attempts, dragons didn't want to bond outside of certain families, and the spark of wild magic needed to bond with the beasts seemed to diminish with each generation, especially since some men had begun to marry outside of families with known dragon rider ancestry.

'What set you on edge?' Ari asked, and I pointed at the stack of papers.

'That. If our losses keep piling up like this, I will have to ask for reinforcements before the regular draft. A request that will probably be denied,' I said, not even trying to hide the bitterness in my voice.

He must have sensed my tension because he slid his fingers to my temples, massaging them slowly.

'Close your eyes for a moment. You have a headache again?' He probed in a matter-of-fact manner. I nodded and followed his command, letting his magic soothe the gnawing pain while I thought about the future of the fortress.

I dreaded the idea of bringing more untrained men to this isolated region, but I doubted I'd have a choice. The mountain fortresses always had two types of men: dragon riders, who conducted aerial defence and patrolled the Barren Lands; and the regular army, for threats that couldn't be dealt with using dragon fire.

However, the quality of our ground forces had deteriorated year after year. I couldn't shake off the feeling that the Crown wanted us to fail. The farm boys being recruited as foot soldiers, or even the nobles' second sons sent here to 'become men,' were just fodder for the monsters.

The worst were the convicts—and keeping them in line added to my already tasking duties, but I couldn't refuse. Otherwise, I would get nothing.

So I took whomever was sent here, even if none of them could fight the way we needed them to.

They could manage in a dispute with ordinary humans, but what did the king expect them to do against foul magic and the vile creatures it bred? That, I didn't know.

'Thank you for staying with me in this godsforsaken place,' I whispered. Alaric's hands stilled for a moment before his calm touch continued. 'Ask for a mandatory draft. Maybe your brother could help—he *is* lord marshal, after all,' he suggested. Ari knew that despite the bleak responses coming from court, I was preparing for war.

'I can't. There would be a revolt. Our soldiers have always been recruited from volunteers.' It helped that they were each well paid for their five years of service to the Crown.

Except for the criminals. They had a choice between service ... or the gallows. The unlucky ones were sent to one of the fortresses, where they lived in a permanent war camp—albeit with the best food and alcohol this kingdom could provide.

It was a long time to spend in constant peril, and with the recent casualties, the large payout or chance of relative freedom had lost its appeal.

'I think that's enough, my lord. You look like you're falling asleep,' Alaric said in an amused tone. 'I came to tell you that I'm going to Grey Stone Valley. I saw mention of a high concentration of aether there in a manuscript I read recently, along with something about a lake and the unusual properties of the stones found in its depths. The manuscript also noted that the Barrier crystals were taken from the mine close to its location.'

Alaric's plans caught my attention, and I looked up to see the distracted expression he always wore when talking about his findings. I had asked the Council of Mages about the keystones the moment he had mentioned replacing the damaged one, and although they told me it wasn't possible, I trusted my mage.

'It'll take you at least two days to get there by horse. I will go with you. I need the diversion, and if we ride Vahin we'll be home before supper,' I offered, pushing the chair back so hard that it fell over with a heavy thud.

'Yes ... well, if you insist.' Alaric waved his hand in dismissal to the adjutant who'd waited patiently during our conversation. The man saluted and began gathering the day's reports and stacking them into neat piles on my heavy oak desk.

It always amazed me how easily my men accepted Alaric's orders. He wasn't in the army. He wasn't even human or from our kingdom; though his own kingdom—or rather, empire—was part of the Lowland Kingdoms, the coalition formed between all of our neighbouring territories after the Necromancer's War.

One day, Ari had simply turned up, stating that he was an emissary of the dark fae empress to our kingdom of Dagome. He had asked for permission to investigate the wild magic in the Lost Ridge ... and never left.

Initially, I'd suspected him of being a spy. But after several months of scrutinising his every move, which consisted of him either visiting the Barrier or reading ancient texts in the library, I had dismissed those concerns. I desperately needed a competent mage after the last one left for our capital of Truso, and he fit into life here so well that it seemed natural to offer him the position of fortress mage.

'After you, my lord,' Alaric urged with a wry grin, and I walked forward, heading towards the landing field.

From the outside, Varta Fortress might look like a gloomy castle, with its rough granite turrets and walls that seemed to grow from the mountainside; however, behind the imposing front was a mountain valley with a thriving town. The work of countless riders over the centuries, it had been a slow process developing the quiet trading post into the stronghold it was today, but it had flourished with a surprisingly pleasant atmosphere.

The granite ramparts housed a robust military presence, and the lower levels of the valley were full of barracks and training grounds supported by artisans. The middle held a large town with a central market square and all the buildings one would expect to find there: a tavern, healer's house, a few permanent shops manned mainly by retired soldiers, and, to my men's relief, a small but very popular brothel, which—thanks to the primarily male population—was a well-respected establishment.

Contrary to the rest of the kingdom, being a *lady of the night* was considered a highly reputable profession in the fortress.

Our permanent residents also lived at Varta Fortress.

Mated and unmated dragon riders, soldiers, and craftsmen occupied houses around the town square, which shared a corner with the landing field surrounded by rocky gardens. Here also stood the second-most-popular building in every fortress—the female boarding house, where unmated women lived during their yearly service.

On higher ground was the castle, carved directly into the side of the mountain. It contained not only the administrative buildings, the library, and a spacious courtyard, but also dragon caverns, a dungeon, and officers' chambers, with the upper floor designated for the lord commander and fortress mage.

The castle was a perfect creation of dwarven architecture, dragon flame, and human magic. It was as well-appointed as any palace, even if its luxury was wasted on the men who occupied it.

My heavy sigh caught Ari's attention.

'Come now, Orm. Try to put your worries aside for a moment. You look like you want to rip someone to shreds. Should I take you outside and teach you how to use that dagger on your belt?' Alaric had dropped his formal speech the moment we were alone, and I looked at my friend with a smirk.

'As if ...' I jested, knowing all too well he was deadly with daggers.

'Perhaps we could ask the local villages to increase the female population here even before Maiden's Day? As far as I know, none of last year's bond servants have stayed in the fortress. That could lead to unrest.'

I sighed again, shaking my head. 'Tell me, how am I expected to guard the ridge when half of my men are busy wooing new bond maidens, and the horribly unprepared soldiers the king sends are cowering under the kitchen table?'

'That barbaric custom never ceases to amuse me. Why do your kind insist on this yearly service for your women? Just marry them or lock the castle gates. One way or the other, they'll stay. Giving them a choice always ends badly.'

'So says the man who's never lived with an angry woman. We don't have enough females, and the riders can't stay in the lowlands to court any partners.' I shook my head, wishing he understood.

'Yes, I know, your dragon always comes first,' he said, exasperated, and I knew that without the bond, he wouldn't be able to understand why we lived this solitary life.

He was right, though. Our beasts came first, and although they could live anywhere, they didn't enjoy the lowlands or crowded places. They preferred high nests or deep caves and a vast sky to soar through. For the sake of our dragons, those who were bonded riders lived in the chain of fortresses so high in the mountains that the air burned our lungs. It was a dragon's paradise, and our voluntary prison. That was the price we paid for our soul-deep bonds.

'Ari, we don't have a university where riders can mingle like mages do. Once you are chosen by a dragon—at the ripe old age of eight—you are sent to a training camp, where all you have are your brothers and your own fist. *That's* why we have compulsory yearlong service for unmated females. It is an unfortunate, but necessary, evil. I don't like it, but if it's the only way for my men to meet a woman without resorting to despicable means, then I'll gladly accept the guilt of having the women work here as support staff.'

Deep in our own thoughts, we walked across the vast landing field—a silent testimony to when the castle had been filled to the brim with dragons and their riders during the war. Now, we were left with the skeletal remains of a once-formidable force. With so many problems stemming from the Barren Lands, I would not repeal the bondage law I despised.

I mentally called for Vahin, and my dragon descended from the sky with an ear-splitting roar, landing gracefully on the grass before us. He was a massive beast, yet still as agile as a cat, even managing to look like one.

His ink-black opalescent scales were flecked with midnight-blue stripes in a pattern similar to the tigers of the jungle in the Lowland Kingdoms. His short snout and blue eyes with their narrow pupils could convey various expressions, and right now, the massive bastard was in a mischievous mood, headbutting me playfully.

Our minds connected, and I felt his joy at flying free at heights too dangerous for his rider. In answer to my call, Vahin flashed an image of a frozen-solid dark fae on his back into my thoughts. 'Stop teasing, old friend. I need your help to get us to Grey Stone Valley,' I said as I avoided looking in Alaric's direction.

Vahin glanced to the side, a question forming in his mind. 'Yes, it was Ari's idea, but don't pretend you dislike it. We haven't flown together in far too long, and we both need it,' I affirmed.

'Don't make me beg. I promise to behave.' Alaric affectionately rubbed the dragon's snout. Vahin huffed a cloud of smoke at the dark fae as his eye roll sent my companion into a fit of wheezing laughter.

I couldn't blame the dragon. Expecting a dark fae to behave was asking for trouble, and Alaric was no exception. He was a prime example of his species in every way.

Tall and lean with well-defined muscles under silken light-grey skin and soft flowing white hair, usually braided or tucked behind his pointy ears, he was a work of art. Most remarkable were his eyes, which shone with a golden light that could shift into pools of crimson when he was angry or worked his spells. He was also a powerful mage, well-versed in both high magic and foul arcana, and, like many of his brethren, he was secretive and had a cold, cruel streak.

After my dragon's display of humour, we settled onto his back, enjoying the sharp gusts of mountain winds as we adjusted ourselves. Vahin's muscles coiled beneath us, and with a powerful beat of his wings, he shot into the sky, leaving Varta behind.

I exhaled slowly, letting my lungs adjust to the sharp, cold air before I settled into the familiar rhythm. Vahin manoeuvred between the mountain peaks, sometimes so close that the tip of his wing brushed the snow off the narrow cliffs.

I knew my beast did it to vex Alaric because I felt a wave of amusement each time the dark fae groaned after a sharp turn. Still, with Vahin's strength, it only took an hour to arrive at the edge of the large valley. As soon as we dismounted, he leapt back into the air, circling above our heads to scout the area.

However, instead of being pleased with our swift arrival, Alaric tensed and looked around with a deep frown.

'Hrae!'[1] he shouted through his clenched teeth, and the way he slid into a defensive stance as I heard him curse made me very grateful that we were armed and in the company of a dragon.

---

1. Fuck!

CHAPTER 2

ORMOND

Alaric rarely cursed. My hand fell to my sword as I looked around, but nothing appeared to be wrong. He pulled me towards the edge of the small lake glimmering in the rays of the morning sun. The valley looked peaceful, carpeted with verdant green grass dotted with mountain flowers that seamlessly blended into a forest wall.

'Something's ... off,' Alaric trailed off, his frown deepening. 'I found a manuscript that suggested the crystals here have a purity similar to the keystone and that they are able to refract the condensed aether because they are, in essence—the wild magic—in solid form. I think that might be the source of the recent disturbances in this area; but if the manuscript is right, they could be used as a replacement for the current keystone. I wanted to check how accurate the claims were, but something ...'

I nearly missed the startling revelation when Alaric once again fell silent. 'They can? Do you mean there's a real chance you could fix the Barrier?' I asked, hopeful that the mages in the capital were wrong and Alaric had found a way to replace the broken keystone.

Before he could answer, a sudden movement caught my attention. Someone bolted from the trees bordering the far edge of the lake, halting as she reached the water. 'Wal'vith hrae j'nesst!'[1] Ari cursed again. His eyes turned crimson as he gestured rapidly, creating an illusion spell that made the world misty and grey.

'What's wrong?' I asked, raising my sword.

'There is a disturbance in the aether. She's running from it. Oh... she's a mage,' he exclaimed, pointing towards the female.

We watched as the woman spun around, her left hand lifting to execute a series of practised movements as she created patterns in the air. The air in front of her solidified into glyphs, but I was more interested in what she held in her right hand.

Blazing with blinding blue fire, a falchion rested comfortably in her grip, and the way she held the sword looked neither panicked nor inexperienced. She was focused on her task, a determined look pinching her features into a frown.

The wind wrapped her simple peasant dress around her full feminine figure, and despite her relaxed grip on the burning sword, she didn't look like someone who fought often. The thought of a village healer or herbalist facing danger didn't sit well with me.

I stepped forward, mentally calling for Vahin, but Alaric grabbed my hand, shaking his head before I angrily shook him off. 'This is wrong. We can't let some hedge witch face whatever danger needs a drawn blade as well as magic. I won't let someone face peril alone. We need to help.'

'Wait, there's something about her ... I know you can't see it, but the way she ties the aether ... Please wait,' he implored, observing the female with quiet fascination.

'You can always step in if she needs you, but you couldn't be more wrong about this one. She isn't some defenceless hedge witch, not with that skill. Look at the glyphs, at how complex they are and how fast she's creating them.

---

1. Oh, for fuck's sake, woman!

I want to see what's coming, Orm. I need to know what she can do. Please trust me, brother.'

I ground my teeth but acquiesced. Magic was Ari's domain, and if he needed to see this woman fight I would indulge him ... to a point. However, I couldn't let someone, especially a female who could wield magic, get injured for the sake of his curiosity.

The stench of the undead filled the air when two ghouls and a striga rushed into the clearing, charging at the female. As they appeared, she thrust her free hand forward, activating the spell she'd been working on.

The first charging ghoul was set ablaze, screeching as the flames engulfed him. The second, caught in a different glyph, slowed down as if he were trudging through molasses.

As if realising the danger, the striga paused, but the mysterious mage rushed towards it, her sword swinging in a deadly arc that grazed its chest before she twisted to avoid the monster's claws.

Magic flared blood red on her fingertips as the woman slid across the grass and angled her sword between the remaining ghoul's legs, severing its tendons with surprising accuracy. With a bloodcurdling scream, the creature stumbled to the side—straight into the striga's slashing claws, the deadly talons stabbing deep into the ghoul's chest.

'Damn, I would love to duel with her,' Alaric remarked next to me, but I was too enraptured by the deadly mage in front of me to pay attention.

Unlike me, she relied on speed and flexibility instead of strength, and it worked in her favour. I blew out a breath I didn't know I'd been holding as she twisted her body and landed a fatal blow that took the ghoul's head.

I didn't think she could fight against three attackers for too long, and I was soon proven right. Her luck was starting to run low as the glow of her spell dimmed and she stumbled to avoid the striga's muzzle.

The hiss of surprise by my side dragged my attention back to Alaric. He held his chest, his eyes widening in astonishment.

'Gods above ... Hrae! Her magic is looking for an Anchor. She's a conduit!' he whispered in awe, but I'd had enough.

His curiosity would have to be satisfied with what he'd already seen. I almost barked the order as the next blow of the striga's elongated claws raked over the woman's sword arm, catching the leather vambrace and dragging her closer, 'She is tired. We've waited long enough. Let's go.'

'Why won't you die, bitch?!' the mage screamed. I could hear the anger and pain in her voice, but as I made to run towards her, a black shadow descended from the sky.

Just as the woman's hand connected with the striga's chest, blinding blue flames burst through the creature's body as my dragon ripped the monster's head from its shoulders, the lifeless skull bouncing harmlessly to the water's edge.

The fight was over. The mysterious mage stood there panting heavily, her body trembling while she eyed the dragon warily. Vahin only moved closer, gazing at her with unbridled curiosity.

'Are you out of your fucking mind? I could have hurt you,' she scolded the massive beast as she tried to catch her breath, and my mouth gaped open.

'Why isn't she afraid of Vahin?' I heard Alaric's fascination as he stared at her as if she were a miracle.

'There is a connection between them. Her magic ... I don't know how, but it's like she called out to him for help—and he answered.'

'Wait, *what?*' I'd never seen Ari so shocked, but my companion's face was the picture of confusion and wonder until he managed to rein in his expression. Before I could ask him what had happened, though, I had another riddle to solve.

Almost as if he couldn't control it, Vahin's thoughts so strongly radiated surprise and joy that my vision was superimposed with the dragon's sight. The strange phenomenon ended after a moment, just as the massive beast released a peculiar sound that was half growl, half whine, and flattened himself on the ground.

What? Did he just ... apologise?

The woman rushed towards Vahin, placing her hand on his muzzle before walking around him as if checking for injuries.

'There, there. I'm sorry, too. I didn't hurt you, did I, handsome? I'm sorry if the flames burned you. I was almost done with her, so you didn't need to intervene. What should I do with you now, huh? Are you hurt? Hungry? Where's your rider? Do you even have one? Gods, you look so familiar ...' she fussed, stroking the sensitive spot under Vahin's gigantic eyes, causing the dragon to relax and purr.

The pleasure that radiated through our bond, the contentment that Vahin felt from the female's attention, the pride at her actions, and the possessiveness that blossomed in my dragon's mind concerned me. Vahin was civil to strangers ... well, mostly. But *liking* them was another thing.

Did she put a spell on him? I wondered. I couldn't feel anything untoward in his mind, but I didn't know what tricks she may have used when she touched him with her magic, so I closed my eyes, commanding him to leave.

I finished sending my thoughts, but as I opened my eyes, I noticed Alaric had broken free from the illusion surrounding us. 'If I had a conduit mage ...' He paused for a moment before muttering, 'If she can respond to Vahin, she could potentially Anchor my magic. Orm, she could be the solution to our problems. We need to take her to the fortress. You need to grab her. If you don't, I will.'

Ari stepped forward before I was able to stop him, and I raised my eyebrows at his actions. *Someone else who has developed a sudden unhealthy obsession with this strange fighter.* I knew it was her magic that fascinated him, but we weren't savages who kidnapped females from the fields. Besides, I had doubts that this encounter was a coincidence.

I felt like I had seen her before. There was something strangely fascinating about her. Dressed like a countrywoman, with enough power to make Alaric envious and enthral my dragon, she was more than met the eye. I needed to assess what danger she posed before I could let her enter my fortress.

As my dragon continued to be stubborn, I sent Vahin another mental order to leave. Meanwhile, Alaric marched away from me through the grass with his usual decisiveness, his steps long and purposeful as he neared the mage. However, the woman was too preoccupied with stroking the dragon to pay any attention until he was almost upon her.

... Vahin refused to leave. My godsdamned dragon had ignored a direct order, twice. That was enough to make me second-guess the idea of trying to bring her with us.

'It's not every day that you get to see a lady stroking such an impressive beast, especially when surrounded by corpses,' Ari said, offering one of his charming smiles. The woman in question turned with the grace of a dancer and pointed her sword in his direction.

'Who the fuck are you?'

I could see her hand tremble and felt Vahin's annoyance radiating through our bond. Even more surprising, however, was how she positioned herself between the dragon and Alaric.

Is she seriously trying to defend a dragon?

As soon as the thought crossed my mind, I felt Vahin's amusement. My troublemaker of a beast wrapped his long neck around her, glaring at the dark fae as he released a soft growl. Seemingly unfazed, my friend only raised his hands in a gesture of surrender.

'My name is Alaric'va Shen'ra. I'm a mage, like you. I came here to investigate the legend of this mountain lake and the crystals that are said to grow within it. I'm not here to fight you, my lady. I'm simply curious as to your reason for being in such a remote setting without an escort?'

'Do I look like I need an escort?' she retorted, and my lips quirked as she straightened, flicking her hair back with casual arrogance. The smile she gave Ari was polite and confident, though not exactly friendly.

I watched my companion's body tense as the woman took her time studying him, making no attempt to hide her feelings, her expression unimpressed at what she found. After a brief glance at the dragon, the mage inclined her head towards Ari.

'Well, Alaric, my purpose here is to make the woods safe for travellers such as yourself. Did the council send you here to check on the Barrier? I'd thought they learned nothing from the last time.'

She grasped her kirtle and wiped her blade. 'You shouldn't journey alone. I suggest you bring an escort next time you come looking for pretty crystals. As for the lake, it is just a myth. If you'd attempted to dive in, you would have found the water freezing and the famous crystals nothing but pretty bits of ice crystallised on the lake bed.'

The woman didn't offer her name, nor did she disclose much other than the surface reason for her presence. Still, she had politely provided information that would prevent an unnecessary death from someone foolishly swimming in the freezing waters.

Of course, she might be lying, but Vahin wouldn't be so friendly to someone with malicious intentions. She was brave and secure in her skills, yet intelligent and evasive, which appealed to the soldier in me.

How would she react to me? came the thought, bringing with it a budding interest. *I should recruit her,* I told myself. I knew I was making things up to justify taking her back with me, but with a mage like her, our ground forces would likely suffer no losses. My internal strategist was already planning out how to incorporate the mysterious female into our army.

The stubborn expression she held as she looked at Alaric warned me that she was trouble, but trouble that would be worth keeping. I could appreciate such an attitude. If what Alaric had said was true, we needed to get her to the fortress.

I'd heard about conduit mages and their immense magic; after all, they were the power behind the mages that had initially raised the Barrier. At best, she could be the key to restoring the Barrier, but if not, I could still recruit her as a battle mage. She was clearly used to dealing with monsters and possessed fine combat skills.

Alaric seemed to be of the same mind as he continued to question her, his voice morphing into the sensual timbre that had seduced many women into his bed. 'May ask your name, my lady?'

Unfortunately, it fell on deaf ears as the mage rolled her eyes. And, as irritating as the situation was, I had to restrain my laughter at the expression on Alaric's face when he failed to impress her with his alluring charm.

'No, you may not. I don't know you. Your race isn't often comfortable at such altitudes, and you appeared out of nowhere *after* I finished fighting these creatures instead of helping me as a crown mage would do. So no, I won't give you my name. Though I *will* give you the benefit of the doubt and, with it, a little advice,' she said.

The smile disappeared from his lips, his eyes narrowing at the challenge in her voice. Unaware of her effect on him, the woman's gaze once again slid over his body, taking in his lithe masculine form, and sighed.

'If you're planning on further excursions, come better prepared. Bring a sword with you, and if you have magic as you claim, be ready to use it. This place is swarming with danger, from humans as well as monsters, and I don't have time to dispatch every threat. When you're done with whatever you're here to do, take the leftmost path to the town. It is safe for now, but do not linger for too long.'

Remembering myself, I tried again. *Vahin, get the fuck up!* I commanded, this time strengthening my order with a harsh push. The dragon grew restless, expressing his anger at Alaric for upsetting the woman, and I'd never felt him so agitated. I didn't want him to hurt either of them accidentally, though—much to my relief—he finally obeyed.

'I appreciate your concern, my lady, but I'm not taking orders from some nameless mage, no matter how beautiful or skilled,' Ari ground out through clenched teeth.

I couldn't blame him. He could easily handle a small army with his spells, yet she had lectured him as if he were an ignorant child who'd come looking for adventure.

'I also have a suggestion for you: with skills like yours, you should come to Varta Fortress. We could use a skilled mage to help defend the borders,' he offered, and she laughed in his face.

'If I wanted a man to tell me what to do, I'd take a husband. Goodbye, Alaric. I have enough on my plate without looking after clueless fools.'

I was right—the woman was trouble. Taunting a dark fae wasn't a good idea at the best of times and disrespecting them was even worse. Alaric was no exception. Before I could react, she turned away, sheathing her sword and walking back the same way she'd came.

When I finally joined him, Alaric's face was unreadable. He quickly removed the illusion spell he'd placed over me, but I saw how tightly his jaw was clenched, muscles rigid with anger.

'Ormond, she must live nearby, and she is unmated. During the next Maiden's Day, you will take her to the fortress. She might be a shrew, but she is a conduit, and I would sooner kidnap her from her bed than let a conduit mage escape us.'

CHAPTER 3

ALARIC

'No, please, Dark Mother, not again,' I sobbed, thrashing in my bed and clawing at my chest, knowing it was all for nothing. The dream, the one that had tormented me for the past five hundred years, pulled me under.

My mother's curse was merciless. It didn't matter how hard I fought; it always ended the same.

I lost.

My mind drifted back to the worst moments of my life ... and there I was, cowering on the floor as my father stood over me, whip in hand.

'You useless, weak child. I wish I'd left you for the wolves when you were born. Why do you continue acting so human when my blood runs in your veins? You are a disgrace to the Shen'ra name,' my father spat, raising the whip.

'What do you expect? You're the one who took a human as a mate,' I hissed through clenched teeth just before the lash bit into the skin of my back, but I had to endure. Otherwise, the terrified servant behind me would bear the brunt of my father's fury.

'If you didn't look so much like me, I would think your mother had spread her legs for the swine in the forest.' The whip cracked again.

Agony tore through me, but my eyes searched for the child hiding beneath the chair, and I smiled reassuringly as our eyes met. I would protect him from this injustice. All the child had wanted was to learn, and I was the fool who had agreed to teach him.

Again the lash fell, and again I refused to scream. My father would not break his son so easily, and I relished every moment I frustrated his desires.

'You think you can hold on? Fine. You wanted to teach the human, then teach him,' he snarled. A magical net squeezed my throat so tight that my vision began to waver.

Hrae! What irked him this time?

He'd been at court earlier to see the empress, and I knew he hated it. Each time he returned, he took his anger out on us, but it had never been this bad before. At least this time, my mother and sister were safe from his wrath.

'Lost for words, boy? Go ahead—teach him about Ozar. Tell him what happens to those who trust humans.' My father sneered, and I felt the silver strands of his magic tightening on my throat.

Will he end up killing me this time? *I wondered.*

'Cahyon Abrasan is one of the most brilliant mages on the continent.' I rasped. 'He is skilled in …' I dragged in another breath before continuing, my father smirking as my pause caused the net to squeeze tighter, my little student crying too hard to listen to the mockery of a lesson.

'He is skilled in transmutation and soul binding, making his golems incredibly powerful constructs as well as a source of free labour. This also made them unstoppable, which no one realised at the time. The gentle night-dwelling Moroi were so impressed that they invited him, a human mage, to the Kingdom of Ozar so that he could create servants to care for their needs during the daytime.'

'Please, stop, Father. You're killing him, please.' I heard my sister call out over the wailing of the child servant and silently cursed. Why did my Ro, my little sunshine, have to turn up now? I had drawn away our father's anger. She just needed to stay silent while I endured.

Outside of the horror I was trapped in, my struggling body wept, remembering the hatred I had felt at that moment—not for my abusive father, but for Ro, as she wrecked my efforts with her begging. My guilt from that emotion haunted me, and I wished I had fought back and saved her—saved us all—from my monstrous parent.

'Stop?' he laughed. 'Why would I stop when this is the perfect teaching opportunity?' my father replied. 'Continue, Alaric.' I followed his order, hoping to focus his ire on me alone, caring as little for my life as my father seemed to.

'Through subterfuge and the use of twisted magic, Cahyon gained the support of the day-dwelling races, and when his golems turned on their helpless masters, no one opposed it. Those here in the Care'etavos Empire were shocked when dishevelled refugees appeared at our borders, nauseated by their accounts of horrifying barbarism. Of how the king and his court, helpless under the blinding sun, were dragged out at midday and slaughtered. That day, Cahyon stepped from the shadows and took control of the country, beginning his reign of blood and terror.'

My final words were little more than a wheeze as I fought for breath, but I fell into silence, knowing that if I begged now, it would only make things worse.

'Don't stop now, half-breed. You were doing so well,' he jeered, enjoying my struggle.

'The Moroi could only submit or die. They were a gentle fae race, and that merciless human now known as the Lich King took them and corrupted their life-affirming blood rituals so that they felt only an unquenchable thirst, turning the kind people into monsters.' I took a breath.

'Within a few short years, the glowing cities of Ozar were cesspits of death and debauchery. The surrounding nations were horrified at such carnage, but they also knew to fear and refused to commit to a war they might lose. So they sent emissaries to negotiate with the new king and established secret negotiations with their neighbouring countries.'

My face was on the ground and my vision was failing, but I had finished, and no one else was hurt. I felt my sister's arms wrap around me, her voice cracking as she pleaded with our father, trying to use her own power to keep me conscious without realising she was prolonging my agony.

'There we are. Now, let me continue your lesson, boy. Our wretched frightened empress has decided to send me as one of those emissaries—I, Roan'va Shen'ra, will be a servant to that human's court,' he spit out. 'That's what you get when you let females rule. Truly disgraceful.'

The illusion darkened as my past self blacked out when my father's rage manifested in his magic, and for a brief moment, I felt a profound relief, even knowing it would soon start again.

Light flickered, my nightmare dragging me back into the memory. I fought its pull, sobbing in my frustration, knowing what was coming and cursing my weakness.

My father, in his infinite wisdom—or perhaps cruelty—took my mother and sister with him. Supposedly as a gesture of faith, to demonstrate our nation's commitment to peace and cooperation.

I opposed the idea, intending to speak to the empress herself about it, but Rowena asked me not to intervene. And after reading the letters she sent to me during their journey, I began thinking that it was fine that I hadn't, that my suspicions were unfounded. Ro's stories were filled with excitement and wonder, the lengthening intervals between letters not so concerning in light of that happiness.

Our father was welcomed with open arms and seemed to hold an honoured position at the new king's court. So I relaxed, believing that all was well. However, the tone of Rowena's writing soon changed, fear and anxiety replacing the bubbly mood of her words. She was increasingly afraid of Cahyon, and when she learned of his deal with our father to make her his queen, Rowena begged for my help.

Just as I was leaving for the empress' court to ask for permission to go to Ozar, I received a letter from our mother. Instructing me to sell her valuables and whatever else I could to finance an escape—not just from Ozar but from our own dark fae empire as well.

The empress ignored my pleading, pleased with my father's plan for a political marriage. But, consequences be damned, instead of following my mother's instructions, I wrote to my father. In the letter, I demanded that he abandon this insanity and send his wife and child home immediately.

Then, one day, word came of a new power in Ozar. Indeed, Cahyon Abrasan no longer reigned. Now, the kingdom was ruled by the Lich King, an undead monster who was even more power-hungry than his predecessor.

The memory blurred, and I felt my chest burning as my curse marked the next part of my torment. The scene sharpened, and I found myself in front of a sallow-faced messenger.

'Master Alaric, you are summoned to the palace,' the young man wheezed as I sat at my father's desk, writing—begging—my friends for help to rescue my mother and sister.

It didn't take long to get ready, and half an hour later, I was at court. To my surprise, I wasn't brought inside. Instead, the emperor consort—a mage and my mentor—intercepted me, gesturing for me to follow.

We walked through several dark corridors, the walls dripping with moisture and the air stale with the smell of mould. A sense of foreboding settled over me and I trembled with apprehension, my heart pounding in my chest. What was going on? Had I done something wrong?... No, if that was the case, I'd be in irons and stripped of my magic.

I couldn't think of a reason for this strange excursion and worried that someone had discovered my abilities despite the lengths I'd gone to to hide my strong necromancy in order to avoid my father's wrath.

'I'm so sorry, Alaric,' the mage said when we entered one of the summoning chambers, its wards strong enough to contain a powerful demon. Then I saw it. A casket. With a woman inside.

My mother looked so peaceful, as if in the midst of a gentle dream, but the signs of corruption were clearly visible, even if I hadn't been a necromancer and knew what to look for.

'Who ... who did this? Where is my sister?' I cried out through gritted teeth, fighting the tears streaming down my face.

'Your father. Your sister ... is still in Ozar, but I have to tell you—foul magic was used on your mother. Roan ... Your father sacrificed your mother for something wholly appalling and used her life force to transform Abrasan into the Lich King. The empress is furious and has stripped your family's titles and lands.'

The mage's words failed to penetrate the numbness that overwhelmed me. All I could do was stare at my mother, the tears still falling from my eyes.

'Your mother's body arrived with a letter to you and a declaration of war. I hid the letter from the empress, but... the Lich King is marching south as we speak, and you ... there are orders to lock you up. I will give you a moment to say goodbye; then you must run.'

'You'd go against the empress?'

'She is hurt by your father's betrayal and frightened by the threat of Abrasan. I refuse to incarcerate you for the sins of your father, especially since—unlike him—you honour our traditions and care for those weaker than you,' he said, patting my shoulder. 'I'll leave you with her. You have an hour before I return with the guards, and I hope I won't find you here.'

'No, he can't be that evil. No one could ...' I trailed off, remembering the abuse, and fell to my knees.

The next thing I knew, I was standing over my mother, purple aether flowing through me as I revived her, begging for the truth. I watched as my magic breathed life into the body, its spirit settling within the corrupt vessel.

It was then I noticed the tendrils of the blackest aether flowing over my wrists and sinking beneath my skin. 'Hrae!' I shouted. I'd forgotten to shield, had revived her without a single protection in place, but most importantly, I'd forgotten what my mother was.

She was a dreamwalker, a strong psionic mage able to influence other people, and in my semi-delirious state, I had no way to stop her. I watched in disbelief as I cut runes into my chest, weaving the silver adorning the corpse into my bleeding flesh. Then, I uttered the words of an unbreakable vow—a hideous blood oath, cursing myself to a life of misery until I rescued my sister or avenged her death.

With a blinding flash of silver light, reality came crashing back, and I screamed once again, feeling the pain of burning metal sinking into my skin. I was covered in sweat, and smoke drifted from my top as my marks seared both my skin and clothing, so I ripped the fabric away, tossing it into the fireplace.

With an unsteady hand, I grabbed a pitcher and tossed its contents over my chest, cursing. This night's dream had been the worst I'd ever had. I squeezed my eyes closed, hating the person I'd become.

The man who'd once braved a lashing to protect an innocent child was now someone who planned to Anchor an unsuspecting conduit mage and use her to kill the bastard who sired him, and—if the Dark Mother allowed—the one who stole his mother's life.

I couldn't tell Orm. He wouldn't understand, and he certainly wouldn't accept using the woman like that. He needed an excuse, something more worthy of such a sacrifice. I'd already told him I wanted to replace the damaged keystone, knowing it wasn't possible. Now, I had just added another lie, making him believe I could do it if I was bonded to a conduit mage.

I was a selfish, overtired fool bent on revenge, but what choice did I have?

Both my father's transgressions and my own mistakes condemned me. Even worse, I hadn't fled the room after being cursed, and I'd cut down the guards that arrived before finally escaping. I lived as a fugitive in my own country for years; penniless, unable to pursue my quest.

When war broke out, I was forced to fight for my life at every turn. By the time I had gathered the strength to face my torment, the war was over and the Barrier was in place, preventing anyone with foul magic from getting past it.

I spent years looking for a way to break through that impenetrable wall that kept me from finding and avenging my loved ones, then even more years trying to remove the curse I had been compelled to inflict upon myself. Pain, my constant companion, ceased to be a punishment and became almost a need ... because I had discovered that only the torment of my flesh could ease the pain that ravaged my soul.

'I knew I'd find you here.' Orm's voice cut through the clear mountain air, and I turned to watch him approach. I smiled at my friend but couldn't prevent the stab of bitterness from ruining my mood. 'Am I that predictable?'

'Since you came here nine years ago, I'd always find you here when you needed to think,' he said. 'The servants saw you sneaking out of your room before dawn, so I thought it likely you'd be here.'

Even if my reason for living here was a lie, the fortress had become my home. I had no place in my own court. As for the human kingdoms, I was a dark fae, a necromancer with foul, tainted magic. Not here, though. Here, I was who I wanted to be—a scholar and healer who held the esteemed position of fortress mage despite the human prejudice against my race.

'My workshop's been somewhat stifling lately,' I replied, shrugging to disguise my feelings. 'How was your correspondence with the chancellor?'

'Same old bollocks, of course. He says the king's too ill to make decisions. I feel we'd have more success writing to your empress,' Orm responded, joining me and dropping onto the weatherworn rock of the fortress wall to dangle his feet carelessly over the long drop.

I turned back to the panorama before me. The mountains created a ridge—a natural grey barrier that divided the Northern Lands from the Lowland Kingdoms. I could still remember the fortress as a trading post, built by the dwarves to protect travelling merchants and shelter their caravans from the unpredictable mountain weather. Those times were long gone, and what had once been a smallholding had become a military outpost and then a thriving town.

'He wouldn't be the first who enjoyed the position a little too much, forgetting that he was chosen to serve,' I said, and Orm nodded.

'What's bothering you? Are you thinking about the mage again?' my friend asked, moving closer. I felt his hand rest on my shoulder. Others rarely touched me. Most humans treated my kind like we carried the plague, but not Orm ... and I appreciated that. He'd probably never know how much.

'No, I was thinking about my sister, my old life,' I answered truthfully, and his eyes narrowed. 'She always looked so human, even though she is stronger in the dark arts than most of our kind. The Shen'ra line has always been deceptive.'

I rarely spoke about my family, but after last night's nightmare, I was struggling to picture my sister's face, to not forget her. All I could remember was our mother's golden hair surrounding Rowena's pale complexion. Then there was her magic, a combination of dreamwalking and necromancy that alarmed even me.

'Don't ask me to try that stunt again,' Orm cut into my thoughts. 'You almost died the last time I crossed the Barrier with you. The Rift might be growing, but the magic is still too strong for someone with as much power as you to cross.'

'No, I don't want to try again. Not on a dragon, at least,' I laughed bitterly, remembering the agonising pain of my attempt to cross on Vahin. The Barrier's magic had rebuffed me, ripping me from Vahin's back. Only the dragon's agility had allowed for my mostly safe retrieval before I became an ugly smear on the ground below, but the grip of his claws had left me bedridden for a month.

The Barrier knew the truth. My soul was filled with the foul magic and power of a necromancer, and that construct of humans considered me to be the same as their—as *my*— enemy. And there was nothing I could do about it.

'You still miss her?' Orm asked, frowning when he saw me rub my chest. He knew some of the truth. A sad family story about a dead mother, a lost sister, and the traitor who had triggered the rise of the Lich King.

The story was too well-known throughout the kingdom to hide it. That was all I'd told him when I had secured his help in my failed attempt to cross the Barrier. The rest I couldn't share, even with my chosen brother.

'Yes, in a way. I've been restless since meeting the conduit. Have you made any progress in finding her? Is there any news from the capital?'

'Progress?' he smirked. 'I not only found out her name and that she was the mage that defeated that wlok and caused the damage to the keystone ten years ago, but was handed the key to her geas directly by the royal mage,' Orm said in such a matter-of-fact manner, though his hunched shoulders and lack of emotion told a different story.

The geas was a magical shackle that forced the loyalty of the most powerful mages, involuntarily making them loyal servants to the kingdom and compelling them to execute the orders of whoever held the key. I knew that Orm, with his code of honour, wouldn't have taken it if the stakes weren't so high.

At least he had control of the one thing our little mage could never argue against. I hoped he didn't have to use it, but I needed her here. I needed her power.

'I'll have to bond with her to be able to use her magic,' I said, and he frowned, looking at me sharply. After a pause he ventured, 'If that's what's needed, then that's what we'll do. Just ... let's wait until we have a viable crystal before using the geas. She may even choose to bond willingly.' He squinted out at the mountains. 'I won't force her for anything less than restoring the Barrier.'

'What if I could offer another, more permanent solution? Replacing the keystone should temporarily leave an opening ... I could cross it, Orm. Depending on the synergy between the conduit and me, I would not only have the chance to kill my father and avenge my sister, but end the Lich King as well.'

'What makes you think you'll succeed where every other has failed?'

'They didn't have a conduit mage bonded to them. You saw what she did to the mountain when the wlok attacked,' I said, and he sighed.

'I know she's powerful, and maybe you and she *could* put an end to the monster, but there's an army between that bastard and anyone that wants to harm him. I don't want to lose a friend on the slimmest of chances,' he whispered. His voice sounded raw, and his hand on my shoulder tightened in a rare display of emotion.

'You knew my stay here was always going to be temporary. Orm ... I need to find out whether my sister is still alive. If she is, the only way to rescue her would be to destroy the Lich King.'

'I can come with you, *help* you, if you let me. If Rowena is alive, you will need speed to escape, and nothing is faster than Vahin.'

'Dark Mother, I almost wish she was dead. If she's been alive this whole time, while she's been held captive by those monsters ... Orm, the only way to rescue her would be to sneak in, and as a necromancer in the land of the undead, I would be perfectly safe. You and Vahin would only be a burden.'

I knew how cruel it sounded, but I was trying to protect the man who was like a brother to me. He mumbled something I couldn't hear and pulled away. From his tight lips, I knew I had hurt his feelings, but it seemed he'd accepted my explanation.

Orm was a strategist, taught to examine a problem from many angles and weigh each decision with logical precision. As a dragon rider, he was trained to keep his emotions on a tight leash. The wild magic that ran through riders' blood would turn them into berserkers without that training, so I used his iron control and analytic thinking against him.

'The life of one woman for the life of many, that's the dark price that needs to be paid. Give me the mage, and I'll do my best to fix the Barrier—but if you help me Anchor her, perhaps there'll be no need for the Barrier at all.'

'I see two problems with your plan. First, what if she doesn't follow you? Second, you're planning on taking the ultimate weapon right to the Lich King's doorstep and hoping she survives. It is not about the price, Alaric. It is about the likelihood of winning, so unless the odds change, I can't risk her in the Barren Lands.'

'She will follow me because conduit mages are loyal to their Anchors. I promise I'll try not to use her geas. I don't like it any more than you do. I'm planning to become her friend or seduce her if all else fails,' I said, matching his tone. 'As for the rest, I will ask again once she settles here. Even if I abandon my quest, I may yet need to Anchor her to restore the keystone.'

Orm's eyes narrowed, and his fist tightened until his knuckles went white. I knew why. Protecting women was beaten into a dragon rider's psyche at a young age, and I'd just revealed I would stop at nothing to gain access to her power.

After a moment, he spoke in his usual stoic manner. 'If that's what it takes to protect the kingdom, then I will bring you my own pillows to make up your bed in your efforts to seduce her—but only to restore the Barrier; with regard to the rest of your plan, my answer is no.'

Pretending to agree, I smiled at his jest, though I soon sobered with the realisation of how much he trusted me while I weaved an intricate web of lies and half-truths, telling him exactly, and only, what he needed to hear.

I am my father's son, I thought with bitterness, my lies tainting the only place I called home. I didn't want to throw that feeling away, but living with this curse when I could be free ...

I truly loathed what I had become; that's why I was pulling away from Orm. He came to me because he *cared*, and it killed me to see the trust in his eyes. Feeling his concern hurt more than the blood oath ever did, and I found no pleasure in the pain.

'Lost in thought again?' Orm's slumped shoulders belied the gently teasing tone of his voice, but he shook it off as he stood and looked at me with concern. 'You don't have to do it alone, Ari. Take my offer. I can cross the Barrier at any time. Just wait for me, and as soon as the Barrier's secured, we can fly to Katrass to face the Lich King together. Please, I don't want to lose my friend, and I feel like you are pulling further away with each passing day,' he said with sadness, and his words stabbed me in the gut.

Damn the man. Damn the warmth he brought into my life. I didn't deserve a friend like him, but I had no choice.

Since we'd found the mage, my dreams had become more violent, but worse was the voice ... A constant companion, an incessant seduction, it was full of fake promises and platitudes. It haunted my dreams, robbing me of rest, and I didn't know how long I could handle it.

'You have your duties here, Lord Commander. The rest ... even between friends, some distance is needed,' I said, and Orm closed his eyes, but not before I saw the raw pain hidden in their depths.

'If that is what you think is best, I will respect your decision.'

He walked away without another glance, an ache arising—so unbearable it took my breath away—that had nothing to do with the silver scars on my body.

45

CHAPTER 4

ANNIKA

Three months later

I turned to the side, pressing the pillow to my face before inhaling its verbena scent deeply. The familiar smell and shape of my small bed calmed my racing heart. I laid there, listening to the wind and morning birdsong, and let the day seep into my body.

It was barely past dawn, the air in my small cottage slowly warming after last night's chill, but my dreams had awakened me early. My sleep had been filled with images of the dragon from the lake since our chance encounter months ago, his piercing blue eyes looking at me with such understanding and compassion that I woke up crying every morning.

I knew that the beast in my dreams wanted me to find him. In truth, he seemed to share my loneliness and growing need to belong, to have my spirit joined with another in a bond so profound it would leave me broken if it ever shattered.

I hadn't considered such a connection in years. The mere thought of caring enough to go through that again filled me with fear and repulsion, but now ... now, I wanted to live again, to be who I once was. A conduit mage with an Anchor that sheltered my soul.

I didn't know why my subconscious was so obsessed with the blue-eyed beast. Maybe because it had been a dragon who'd saved me before, digging out my broken body from under an avalanche ... I remembered that much, even if I didn't remember my saviour.

What if the Council of Mages found out I'm alive and sent the riders after me? Every time I thought about it, a new theory came to my mind, but it had been a baffling encounter. I'd been curious and returned to the mountain lake several times since.

Still, neither the dragon nor the dark fae ever appeared, so I had been forced to accept that my questions concerning their identities and motives would likely never be answered.

Could a woman from an ordinary family become a dragon rider?

The thought amused me, but the question had its merits. I felt connected to him, and even without an Anchor bond, his presence had helped stabilise my magic. That itself had surprised me, as I was sure that only men of certain bloodlines could have an affinity with dragons, yet simply touching him had connected me to a strength I only felt when in the presence of my Anchor.

Was it because a dragon had rescued me while I was still connected to the primal source of the aether? Had he corrupted my conduit power, giving it the potential to bind the beast? Was that the reason my body recovered after channelling so much aether it should have killed me twice, and that I've survived without an Anchor for so long?

I knew that, sooner or later, I would have to form a new bond. Each day I postponed it, my magic became more challenging to handle. It was unnatural and dangerous for a conduit mage to live without at least one Anchor. Yet here I was, living unbound and defying the laws of magic.

Am I ready for a new bond?

I touched my chest where the shield and healing ivy marked my skin. The sigils of my Anchor bonds. They hadn't faded when my men died, their magic disappearing with them.

I reached to the nearby table, grasped the small hand mirror I kept there, and pulled my shirt to the side in my personal ritual. *Still there. You haven't abandoned me.* I traced my finger over the lines, feeling the tightness in my chest threatening to choke me.

'I know you'd both want me to bond with someone, to be happy, but how can I? How can I take another man when you are still with me?' I whispered before putting the mirror down.

Even if I was willing to try, it wasn't just my life at stake. If a conduit mage rejected the Anchor bond in their soul, both the mage and their Anchor would die.

So, for the last ten years, the first thing I did after opening my eyes every morning was to look in the mirror, dreading the day I'd see un-blemished skin. Every single day, it was the same. The shield and ivy wrapped over my heart lingered, protecting it.

I placed my hand over the marks again, pressing down until the ache faded and I could breathe again. I might dream about enticing dragons, but I knew that deep inside I was broken and afraid that if I allowed myself to touch someone's heart, mine would fracture again.

Dragons are immortal and almost impossible to kill, whispered the voice in my mind, awakening hope that would never come true.

It didn't bother me that he was a beast. I could always find a lover. I already took care of that basic need when required, the occasional tumble with a stable hand or local hunk to ease the tension just a bandage for a broken soul that didn't want to mend. A safe outlet that calmed my body but didn't touch my heart.

I bit my lip, the familiar sting of pain startling me from such dark reminiscence and impossible thoughts. I sat up. If I couldn't find the dragon, I couldn't Anchor him, so there was no sense in thinking about it.

And who said the dragon would even let me do it? Forcing the bond never ended well, and my life might have been different if the council hadn't tried to do just that so soon after I'd recovered and they'd ceased questioning me.

My annoyed huff echoed in the cottage as I recalled their words.

'You did the impossible, Lady Annika. Now it's time for you to take another Anchor. The royal mage's apprentice is the best prospect.'

Take another Anchor. I snorted at the thought. It had been the darkest time of my life. I couldn't sleep, and I couldn't eat. I woke up every single night calling for my lovers unless I drank myself into black oblivion.

To the council members, however, taking a new Anchor was like buying a new dress when your old one had torn. To make matters worse, they had pushed me towards Ihrain—an arrogant mage with an unhealthy obsession with conduits. I'd been at my breaking point when he tried to force himself on me, and I almost burned the bastard. *I should have.*

A day later, I found the missive—just a scrap of paper shoved under my door—warning me that the council might consider using my geas to tether me to him. I knew I had to escape.

It took me a week to stage my death, to burn everything I owned along with a body that a well-bribed undertaker had provided me from the city morgue. I let everyone believe my magic had gotten out of control and killed me.

That's how I ended up in Zalesie, forging my credentials and installing myself as their local mage, much to the displeasure of the resident hedge witch. The town couldn't afford a university-trained professional, but I didn't want their money, willing to work for food and board, preferably served late with plenty of alcohol.

I'd been pleasantly surprised at the quality of the food, and the work had been diverse and interesting. The local population had soon warmed up to me, and with that rapport came respect—as well as demands for love potions, then even *more* demands to cure their scabies and less noble ailments.

I fulfilled my duties, indulging in the occasional monster hunt when the ache for my past life became too much and, little by little, life became more than just surviving until the next day.

I needed very little magic to cull the Vel creatures, and even less to cure the diseases of the local humans and their animals. None of those spells required my conduit abilities. As I settled into this ordinary existence, I had slowly forgotten that I could rain fire from the heavens and shatter the earth beneath my enemies. This was what I had chosen. My Anchors died so that I may live, and I lived this life to honour their sacrifice.

Annika Diavellar, the rare and precious conduit mage, had died from unrestrained magic and a broken heart. In her place, there was now only Ani Jaksa, town mage and the woman who sorted shit out when and how she saw fit. As long as Tal's family lived safely in this region and Arno's surname was spoken in the same breath as my name, I could live on.

'I wish I'd never met you, my beautiful dream. I was content here. Now I ache for more than I could ever have,' I whispered, getting ready for my daily duties.

I had to focus on my work. Tal's family thought that the pension that came from the magistrate was a crown pension for their dead son. However, the government had long forgotten the fallen hero, so it was my duty to provide for them. They had moved two years ago to seek a better life in the city, and I was happy to see them begin to enjoy their lives again.

Nevertheless, even in their absence, there was certainly plenty to do—far too much for a single battle mage, but I knew I'd do it, whatever happened. As long as the town council was content, they wouldn't send a request for support, and I wouldn't have to worry that the Council of Mages would send a mage who might recognise me.

My reminiscence was interrupted by someone hammering their fist against my front door, using so much force that my entire cottage rattled. I frowned, ignoring it as I laced my kirtle, only to blink in surprise when the pounding resumed, shaking the door of my humble abode so much that the dust was knocked from the ceiling beams.

'I'm coming! I'm coming! Just stop the incessant banging or your guts will end up the strings of a minstrel's lute. What's so bloody urgent that you'd risk pissing off the local mage?' I shouted, adding nastier curses under my breath.

Although the surrounding mountains could be dangerous, the town itself was peaceful. I made sure of it, so what could have happened that they needed to drag me out of bed so early in the morning? Especially after I'd enjoyed several well-deserved drinks in the local tavern the night before.

I hope it's not that stupid woman and her prized chicken.

The mayor's wife owned a cockerel that she treated better than the fruit of her own loins, but the damn feathered hooligan spent its life trying to escape her loving embrace. Invariably, I was the one cajoled, bribed, and threatened with being shunned to return it to captivity.

I swore, promising that if that was the reason for the disturbance, I'd roast it and serve its carcass at the village tavern. *The joys of small-town life, I guess. Sometimes you fight monsters, sometimes you hex a chicken ... Smile and nod, smile and nod, Ani.* I thought before opening the door.

A flowery wreath woven from willow and the bedraggled remnants of the local wildflowers landed on my head as I opened the door. Startled, I instinctively swung my fist, punching the nose of my smiling assailant. 'Fuck!' he grunted, taking a step back and wiping his bloodied nose before he looked at me.

'Are you tired of living, you damned fool?' I snapped, fighting with the twigs and leaves that tangled in my hair. 'What in Veles' pit is this?'

The stubborn thing didn't want to come off. I pulled so hard that it ripped out a strand of my hair, but the monstrosity they'd put on my head didn't budge. I strongly considered hexing the lot of them just to show the visiting committee how much I appreciated such gifts.

'Ani, you've been chosen to stand with the maidens of our town to welcome the dragon riders. Please follow us,' the magistrate announced. The insufferable man stood there, blood trickling from his nose, smiling like he'd just offered me the greatest gift ever, and I wondered whether I was still sleeping or if he'd lost his mind completely.

Then I remembered.

Today was Maiden's Day, but what it had to do with me remained a mystery. Mages were exempt from bondage contracts.

Maiden's Day was a kingdom holiday that existed thanks to the dragon riders' annual selection of maidens. Owing to the fact that the wild magic needed to bond with dragons was passed on only to male offspring, the warriors were exclusively men, leading to a need to recruit women to live at the outpost.

Each year, they descended on a different town to celebrate Maiden's Day and, as per the king's orders, chose women who had to follow them to the fortress or risk a year in prison. So they followed without complaint, especially since those who returned after a year of service were significantly richer and always spoke highly of their treatment during their time away.

No one mentioned the fact that most of them returned with bellies swollen with child, especially since those children inevitably went to live with their fathers' families, leaving the women free to choose husbands with dowries hefty enough to make everyone forget the past year.

The riders selected those of the unmated women they were attracted to during a ceremony to get to know better at the subsequent party, giving both sides the opportunity to weigh the other and determine their respective willingness to enter the contract. However, if there were no volunteers—which had happened only once since the tradition had begun—the dragon riders were allowed to simply pick whomever they wanted, as long as she was unmated.

Regardless, no sane man would ever take an unwilling mage, especially not one over thirty years old who spent the long winter nights sampling the local male population. For all the gods' sake, some of those samples were standing in front of me right *now*.

There was a reason why the riders' welcoming committee had always been young, unwed maidens—often blushing virgins. They were a perfectly naïve and receptive buffet for the horny men who spent too much time with only themselves and their dragons for company. Those girls wouldn't even think to protest when confronted by handsome warriors willing to lay the world at their feet.

That's why I was so confused at the magistrate suddenly knocking on my door.

The idiot wouldn't stop smiling, and with the flowery wreath hanging crookedly off the side of my head, I gaped at the gathered men. Then, without another word, I stepped back and slammed the door in their faces.

'Ani! Please, you can't refuse, and you know it. I know it's a little unusual, but the chancellor's order came a week ago. He commanded *all* unmarried women to join the selection, even mages. Please, Ani. We can't afford to lose the protection of the outpost. If the commander learns we didn't do as we were told, that is exactly what will happen. I will have to inform the council of your refusal. You don't want us to take you to jail, do you?'

'I'd like to see you try,' I muttered, more disturbed by him threatening to alert the council than his trying to take me to jail. The obstinate man just kept thumping on the door.

'You know what dwells on the other side of the mountains. We need them, Ani, please. We both know you're too old to be chosen, so just show up, stand around for a while, and then go to the tavern for a free meal. We'll even give you a horse for your trouble.'

The magistrate wasn't an evil man; he was simply out of his depth. I'd had him in my bed once, and once was enough to convince me never to repeat the experience ... though his "little problem" hadn't affected our friendship. Until now, of course. Now, he was pleading at my door whilst simultaneously offending me with his reassuring platitudes.

'Really?! *Too old*? I'm not too old, you dimwit. I'm just ... unavailable. I wasn't too old when you stuck your ... Never mind, you know what? Fine, I'll go, but I want more than a horse. I want a new bench for my workshop, and that meal had best be accompanied by that special brandy you've been hoarding,' I shouted, willing to extort more from the little shit for calling me old.

Grumbling, I looked in the mirror. I looked *good* for my age. If I made a little effort, there weren't many who didn't turn back for a second, more appreciative look as I walked by.

My chestnut hair accentuated the hazel-flecked green eyes that always seemed to capture people's attention, and my body was trim from all the trekking I did on the mountain, even if life had added a little extra padding to my curves.

Just because I rarely did more than braid my hair down my back or in a peasant's crown, and preferred male clothes or a kirtle over delicate dresses, didn't mean I wasn't attractive. The hairstyles were practical, and it was easier to wash blood and soot from leather and linen, but something about his comment prickled my female pride.

Did I really let myself go so much that even a former lover sees me as 'old'? And damn it, why do I give a shit? Fuck it, I'll prove them wrong.

I knew that with a little effort, I could lure any man to my bed, especially in a small town like this. Put me in front of the isolated dragon riders, and I doubted any would turn me down. I just didn't want to try.

Yet something in the magistrate's words bothered me immensely.

It appeared that I still had a shred of female vanity left. In fact, the foolish man had unintentionally touched on two things that could lure me out of the cottage: my pride, and my fear that if I refused, the repercussions might reach the Council of Mages, revealing my existence.

Once I'd promised to be in the town square by noon, the magistrate left me in peace—though he'd also left some men behind to ensure I wouldn't forget our arrangement. Another insult, considering I'd never gone back on my word in all my years of living here.

After several moments of tugging and swearing, the wreath finally gave up its hold on my hair, and I threw it onto the nearest table. I didn't care how important the tradition was—I refused to wear such an ugly monstrosity; it would have to be enough that I'd dress up for them.

Chapter 5

ANNIKA

Once I'd decided to show them the class and style of a crown mage, I found it was easier said than done.

Digging into my wardrobe, I realised that for the last ten years, I hadn't purchased a single dress suitable for such a show. After taking a moment to rethink my choices, I opened the trunk holding the mementoes of my previous life, pulling out my old ceremonial battle mage uniform from its depths.

Looks like it'll still fit.

The thought made me smile, and, with more enthusiasm, I put the dress on. It was a simple design, as—despite the decoration—it was tailored for fighting. The mossy green velvet was cut close to avoid catching on one's surroundings—or a stray weapon—and the stiff collar was designed to ward off the teeth and claws of ghouls and creatures of the night. Even the gold braiding was there to deflect an attacker's edged weapons.

Out of habit, I strapped two daggers to my thighs and added a cincher that squeezed my already narrow waist and enhanced the fullness of my hips and bosom. After a moment's hesitation, I pinned a small ornament, a circle with three stars joined in the middle, to the collar.

If any mage saw it, they would instantly realise that I was a conduit mage with Anchors; and even if that were no longer true, with my Anchors' marks still on my skin, it felt right to wear it.

I braided my hair on the sides of my temples, letting the rest of my unruly tresses fall down my back before I sauntered to the market square. Deliberately taking the long way around, I allowed the citizens of Zalesie the pleasure of the once-in-a-lifetime sight of their Ani dressed as a battle mage.

'*Too old,*' *my arse*, I thought, enjoying the covert and *not*-so-covert stares until I came to the floodplains.

Another of the joys of mountain life, the extensive field was covered in lush and vibrant green grass after the spring floods, the warming sun melting the alpine snow and creating a temporary lake at the town border. However inconvenient it may be, it was a great boon for the farmers, as the fresh grass that grew here after the waters receded kept their animals well-fed.

It was a long walk, but I hoped to see the dragons on my way to the town square, maybe even the blue-eyed creature that haunted my dreams.

A powerful gust of wind surprised me and I had to shelter my eyes from flying debris until it died down. Only then did I notice the cause: a familiar-looking dragon. With black scales glinting and blue markings capturing my attention, the magnificent creature settled down, and my heart stuttered with awe as I watched.

My dragon was here. Whether it was my wishful longing or pure luck, the subject of my dreams was right before me, folding away enormous wings and shaking the moisture from his head. Once he was finished, the dragon turned to me, his vertical pupils widening before he lay his head on the grass, making the strange growling-whistling noise he made the last time we met.

'Oh, hello, handsome. I was hoping to see you! I think it's time we had a little chat.' I grinned, raising the hem of my dress and marching towards him through the soft grass. It was strange how seeing him made me so ridiculously happy.

A warm breeze caressed my skin, and the soft murmur of a babbling brook made the moment feel surreal and illusory. I'd seen dragons a few times at university, but never in a field full of flowers, and never one I'd felt a connection with.

During our schooling, all battle mages worked with various military formations to learn how they fought so that we'd be more effective and accidental casualties could be kept to a minimum; that education also included the legendary dragon riders and the theory of fighting spectrae.

I still remembered the uproar when two of the beasts and their riders had landed in the university yard to facilitate that training ... It was safe to say that both mages and the young riders enjoyed the educational exchange in more ways than one.

I had already joined with my Anchors and was more interested in the creatures than their riders by then, and my eagerness to learn earned me a few strange looks. However, I'd learned that dragons were knowledgeable, sentient beings with their own personalities and thoughts.

Most of them still soared through the skies, unbothered by other races. Occasionally, they bonded with humans in a similar way to a battle mage unit. As for their thought processes, most of our knowledge was secondhand, as we had to rely on their riders for communication.

I always treated them with respect but had never felt the desire to get too close; I didn't know what was so different about this one. I should have been afraid, or at least wary, instead of charging towards the dragon as if he were my long-lost sibling.

'Who are you?' I whispered, leaning towards the beast while he nuzzled his snout into my hand, rubbing the polished scales over my palm. The dragon was so gentle, barely moving and observing me with such focus that I had to hold myself back from throwing my arms around his neck and embracing him. His warm breath enveloped me like a caress, making me sigh. I closed my eyes, feeling a strange sensation blossoming in my chest.

Happiness. It took me a moment before I realised it wasn't just me who felt it, but the impressive beast as well. It was exactly like my dream—the sensation that he missed me, the feeling of belonging once again.

Is this how dragon riders feel? Is this why they're ready to sacrifice their freedom to be with the dragons who choose them?

With those thoughts came another ... *Why do I feel like this?* Women couldn't bond with dragons. It just didn't happen. Besides, I suspected this one already had a rider. Otherwise, why would he have landed on the floodplains on the outskirts of town during Maiden's Day?

When my hand slid towards the corner of his eye, something inside of the beast rumbled, and I gasped, stepping away. I didn't get far before being pushed closer by the tail that had somehow coiled around me.

The dragon gave me a long stare as if he was trying to say something, and then he pressed his head closer, closing his eyes. He clearly knew what he wanted, but I had no idea. Hesitantly, I touched him again, and when he didn't instantly bite off my hand, I chuckled.

'Is that all you wanted? Do you like me stroking you? I didn't know dragons could be so gentle ... and so needy,' I said as he pushed harder into my hand. 'You are worse than a tavern cat. I wish I could keep you, but I suspect your rider would strongly object,' I cooed while petting him, and he rumbled again.

'What's this noise you're making? Is it good or bad for you, my lovely? Gods, I wish we could talk,' I murmured, lost in the moment, trailing my hand over the bumpy, raised ridge of his brow.

'He is purring for you, my lady,' a deep voice answered from behind me. My hand stilled, and I cursed myself for allowing anyone to sneak up on me. I turned quickly, meeting the gaze of a gigantic man.

He wasn't just tall—he was *massive*, and the wet linen of his shirt hid nothing of his physique. Broad shoulders, firm thighs, and a torso covered in scars that were clearly visible under the see-through shirt. Wherever I looked, there were muscles—nothing but a wall of oversized, bulging muscles.

The stranger's eyes shone with amusement when he noticed my wandering gaze. He ran his hand through the wavy jet-black hair that fell to his neck—clearly freshly washed—leaving a few strands plastered to his forehead. Most impressive were his eyes, their slightly upturned corners and irises a deep mossy green speckled with gold flakes.

He stood tall and proud, almost ... posing, *cheerfully*, during my inspection. That kind gaze, with its hint of curiosity, made me feel comfortable, giving me time to compose myself. Once I had settled, the corner of his mouth tilted, and he stretched his hand towards me.

'My lady, may I?' He said, reaching for my hand.

The dragon wasn't at all disturbed by the male's presence, which, along with how relaxed the man was, must mean they were a bonded pair. Out of sheer curiosity and maybe influenced by his smile, I let him take my hand.

For a moment, he didn't do anything else, just waited until he was sure I was comfortable, and I admit, his restraint charmed me. I was being held gently by the calloused hand of a warrior and couldn't have felt more powerful than I did at that moment.

As a smile teased my lips, the rider guided my hand to the dragon's eye, sliding it over the scaled ridges. 'This is the most vulnerable place for a dragon and one of the few spots they always strive to protect. Blinding a dragon is the easiest way of incapacitating them. I'm surprised Vahin let you touch him here, but he is an excellent judge of character. For some reason, it seems he is fond of you,' he murmured, again trailing my fingers along the ridges of the eyelid towards the corner of the eye, and the great dragon rumbled louder.

'Stroking the eyelid is one way a rider can soothe their dragon, and it's a source of great comfort to them both,' he continued, his body so close to mine that I felt the warmth radiating from his skin. Yet, he didn't touch me in any other way than holding my hand.

I knew he was here for the Maiden's Day selection, but I couldn't bring myself to feel hostile towards him. Maybe it was because of the dragon or because he was providing answers to questions I hadn't even known I wanted to ask, all while guiding my hand over the dragon's vulnerable eye.

The physical contact between us felt natural yet intimate, as if the pleasure of the moment was weaving its own special kind of magic. I couldn't remember the last time I'd touched anyone without wariness or lust ... it was a simple, joyful moment, being held in a way that seemed to comfort us both.

Then I realised he had given me the name of the dragon.

Vahin. That fits him perfectly.

'Nice to meet you, Vahin. I'm glad I finally know your name,' I whispered, and the beast opened his muzzle ever so slightly. A long, forked tongue slipped out to lick my cheek. I felt the dragon's saliva left behind, but the strange gesture didn't repulse me; it called to something deep inside my chest. My magic responded as if awakened from a long dream, but it didn't reach for Vahin. Instead, it stretched towards the man who held my hand.

I froze.

What the hell-what's going on?! Why him? Why now?

My heart hammered so hard that I felt it in my throat as I snuck a glance at the stranger's face and hesitantly resumed my movements. Aether poured through me, wrapping around him like an ivy, craving to take him.

I felt as if everything I had known about being a conduit, about Anchoring other mages, was pure nonsense. Nothing I'd read or learned had ever mentioned the possibility of bonding with a non-mage, yet his touch had awakened my conduit abilities.

I have to stop it before it goes too far.

I jerked my hand from the rider's grasp, avoiding his eyes as he looked at me with confusion, unaware of my internal struggle. 'I think Vahin has had enough of me petting him like a stray cat,' I commented, trying to deflect attention from my awkward reaction.

'That's not what he's telling me. In fact, he's been enjoying it so much that if I did what Vahin wants, I'd already be throwing you onto his back to fly us straight to the fortress. I must admit his suggestion has merit,' the rider answered with a playful smile.

He spoke about kidnapping me so casually, but the implications of his words hit me like a hammer. I wasn't ready for this. I had barely *thought* about it and it was suddenly here, smacking me in the face.

Feeling a connection to the beautiful Vahin was one thing—feeling tiny prickles of magic teasing my skin as I stroked his scales was so very appealing—but this man ... he was dangerous. The scars covering those unyielding muscles told the story of a warrior ready to fight at the slightest provocation, willing and able to take what he wanted.

Unfortunately, it appeared what he wanted right now was *me*.

Though my blood ran cold at the discovery that my magic responded to him, I could not blame him for my reaction. I couldn't fault him at all. Even his last remark was clearly meant to be teasing. He was friendly, and while he had certainly misunderstood the cosy little moment, he didn't make me feel threatened. The rider didn't even react when I pulled away without explanation.

'I have to go,' I said, calming my thoughts.

I took a step back, distancing myself from the man and his dragon. I had somewhere to be, and I didn't want to disappoint the magistrate with my late arrival. The only thing left to do here was to apologise for the misunderstanding and ensure that he knew I didn't want to be chosen. He seemed nice, and I wanted to spare us both any embarrassment if he planned to ask for me in front of the townsfolk.

'Would you grace me with the pleasure of your company tonight, my lady?' he proposed before I could speak. I took a further step back, and the dragon growled his displeasure, tail thrashing, ripping up clumps of grass from the soft soil until the rider laid a hand on his snout. The man kept looking at me, and his eyes narrowed when I shook my head.

'I understand the magistrate told you that you cannot refuse, my lady.'

The change of attitude was the perfect antidote for my unwillingness to hurt his feelings. He was no longer the gentle giant who looked at me with kindness but just another man who had tried to force my hand. Luckily, I'd had a lifetime of practice dealing with arrogant pri... men.

'Yes, he told me, but I doubt you will have any pleasure forcing yourself on an unwilling woman. Let's just keep pretending you are nice and can take "no" for an answer while I remember the enjoyable time I had with Vahin. Anything else will make the situation awkward.'

I turned towards the dragon and moved close enough to press my cheek to his snout. He was warm, and I wished I could embrace him because something in the enormous beast spoke to my soul, releasing feelings I'd buried ten years ago under the rocks of the Lost Ridge.

'I hope I'll get to see you again, Vahin,' I said, inhaling deeply before turning towards the rider. 'Good luck with finding a maiden to take home,' I offered, noticing his smile widen as he rubbed his hand down the dragon's side, inclining his head politely.

'We look forward to seeing you again, my lady. Would you tell me your name? I feel I've earned that privilege, at least. Or should I convince Vahin to roll over so you can rub his belly to be granted the honour?' He pressed, quirking an eyebrow.

'You don't need my name,' I answered, but the image he planted in my mind made it a struggle not to chuckle. I'd expected anger and petulance, but not humour. I had to give it to him. The man had charm.

'Clever. Men normally use cats or dogs to get my attention. By using Vahin, you certainly have an unfair advantage, but this is my final warning. You are kind and handsome. Don't waste your time on me when the town square is full of eager women who are much younger and easier to charm. I don't think you'd need to show them your ... dragon to get their attention.'

It was my turn to jest, but still, I gasped when my words were answered with a plume of smoke and a deep rumble that I could only interpret as the dragon's laughter. I didn't want to wait for the rider's answer, rushing towards the town square as if a horde of ghouls chased me, but I still heard the words that sounded like the peal of fate's bell.

'You can run away from me all you like, my stubborn mage, but I promise I'll always find you.'

CHAPTER 6

ANNIKA

I wasn't ready to join the welcoming committee just yet.

I needed to erase the vivid thoughts of the dragon rider still swirling through my mind, so I walked around town, enjoying the sunny day. I strolled for a while, smiling at the children playing in the streets while I tried to centre myself. I had to get him out of my head, especially after how my magic had reacted to his touch.

I couldn't deny that I had enjoyed his calm presence, the way he looked, *and how good his calloused hands felt on my skin.* I was so lost in my thoughts that I stumbled over a rock, hissing as I grabbed a painfully pulsing toe, noticing how close I was to smack my face on the gravel road.

'Bloody men with their perky ar ... dragons that can give a woman a broken nose or a year of bondage contract,' I complained, stuttering when I noticed I wasn't alone on the street.

Once the warmth of my cheeks had decreased, I headed towards my next ordeal, arriving only fashionably late. All the locals were already gathered, and as I sauntered in, the gawking townsfolk gasped. The relief on the mayor's face was the perfect balm to my wounded pride, making me snort with laughter.

We didn't get on, but the officious fool knew his job. The town square was beautiful, bedecked with wildflowers our blushing maidens had gathered from the fields, their scent lifting everyone's spirits. A centrepiece had been set up behind the platform for the town council, as well as a large white cloth embroidered by a talented, though not quite *literate*, soul.

Wlecome too Zalesie

The awful spelling made my teeth ache, but the beautiful artwork was impeccable. I didn't have the heart to point out the mistake to the proud matron standing nearby, whose broad smile and constant glances led me to believe that she or one of her daughters had made the banner.

I looked longingly at the tavern and the tables set up with refreshments and snacks for the evening celebration. The enormous barrel of mead I spotted almost made me forget that I wanted to be far away after meeting the imposing rider.

Thanks to the matrons' continued glances towards the maidens, I noticed that the crowd of young women was less colourful than usual. Some, rather than dressing in their finery to eagerly await the gallant riders, wore darker clothes.

They are mourning, I realised, recognising the daughters of several families who had lost their fathers or brothers after they'd gone to the forest lumber mill and never returned. I grimaced as a pang of guilt struck me, but I was just one mage; and even if I worked myself to the bone, there were too many monsters to combat them all.

I waved to Katja, our herbalist. I suspected she'd simply removed her apron before joining the crowd. For sure, the green-stained kirtle was a dead giveaway of her feelings towards the welcome party but seeing Katja here cheered me up.

She was the most down-to-earth female I'd ever encountered, always honest to herself and others, even if her way of expressing it was ... *slightly* brutal. *Why didn't I follow her example?* I berated myself. I stood out like a sore thumb, clearly overdressed for the occasion.

Most of the women gathered to the right of the small platform and the pompous town officials, the bench to the left bearing only two bizarre occupants: our muscular half-orc blacksmith Bryna, and old Helga, who last year celebrated her seventieth birthday.

Oh well, I thought, unable to process why they'd been dragged here—especially Bryna, whose attitude, impressive promiscuity, and frightening strength meant any rider foolish enough to choose her wouldn't be in a fit state to fight anything afterwards. *Gods forbid the poor soul runs out of stamina before she's satisfied,* I mused.

Bryna was more than capable of dragging as many partners to bed as needed to fulfil her desires, and they rarely objected. Despite her almost masculine figure and green-hued skin, she possessed a pretty face with a little perky nose; and, if that wasn't enough, an impressive set of breasts usually convinced even the most reluctant of men.

'Surely there must be better candidates ... Fuck, they must be desperate, dragging us here,' I mumbled to myself, bursting into laughter again.

'Ani! I see our illustrious magistrate managed to persuade you to join this ridiculous spectacle. *Wlecome too Zalesie*, where every woman has a chance for cock,' Bryna roared, her laughter startling several council members from their naps. With a friendly pat on the bench, the blacksmith invited me to join her.

'So, our beautiful mage, what did they bribe you with to ensure your attendance? The magistrate promised me a new forge,' Bryna said, waving her flask. I turned towards the penny-pinching bastard, whose reaction to my stare was the terrified flinch of a rabbit facing the arrow of a merciless hunter.

'You motherfu ...' I started, but Bryna's whistle stopped my tirade and likely saved his sorry arse from being fried. With a deep, cleansing breath, I turned to my friend. 'I only got a horse. I should have asked for a new house.'

'Yeah, well, you've never been one to bargain. Sit, Ani. We've got a front row seat to this spectacle, and I want to see the flying peacocks. Maybe one will tempt me enough to sample their wares later.' Bryna winked, gesturing towards the anxious women whispering between themselves. 'At least you're joining the sensible side.'

As soon as I dropped to the *'crones"* bench, Bryna pushed her flask towards me. 'Drink. You look like you need it,' she said, her casual scrutiny turning more serious.

Bryna knew my past; she and Katja were the only ones who knew I'd once been Annika Diavellar, the famous mage who fought an immortal wlok and 'won.' They also knew I had done nothing to deserve that fame and that my failure haunted me to this day. I'd let it slip one night after a challenging hunt that had left me stranded on a granite outcrop.

I learned three valuable lessons that day.

First, never chase a weregoat up a mountain unless you want to be carried back down like a baby by a half-orc. Second, if you take a numbing tincture that loosens the tongue, *don't* take it if you have a secret and the woman who's about to sew you up has a cheating husband. Third? Well, whether it's normal or not, a goat covered in orcish spices tastes *good*, especially if accompanied by the mead said earlier orc opened to celebrate eating the flesh of your enemy.

I took the flask from her hand, gulping down the rest of its contents. The sweet moment of eye-watering alcohol burning its way down my throat was brutally interrupted when old Helga bent towards Bryna and shouted in her ear: 'What's going on here? Where's my blanket?'

'Oh, Father of Fire, this isn't worth a forge. I'm not even fucking human,' Bryna muttered, shaking her head. 'You and I are just here to fill the seats. More importantly, your job is ensuring I don't burn this town down if I don't enjoy the spectacle, as Katja is clearly busy calming down our charming maidens.'

She trailed her gaze over me, taking in the dress and flowing hair before she shrugged.

'Are you sure you're not here to relieve a little tension? This new look of yours turned several heads when you arrived,' she commented, and I felt the warmth of an embarrassing blush spread across my cheeks.

Bryna was a good friend and as brazen as a cocksure sailor, but her remark still made me defensive. I'd wanted to prove that I wasn't some scruffy hedge witch; now I felt my efforts made me look desperate. As if I was trying to outshine my much younger counterparts.

To make matters worse, in my desire to prove the point, I had glossed over the fact that dragon riders weren't simple smallholders from a small town, hoping that my battle mage robe would fade into the other maidens' sea of frills.

Now, I was the one who stood out the most—and the last thing I wanted was for one of them to question what a single battle mage was doing in Zalesie. 'I'd better go home and change. I don't want to rob you and our lovely maidens of their chance,' I said, standing up to leave.

I didn't get far.

I went to tell the magistrate that I'd return after making a few corrections to my wardrobe. After he'd gone through the trouble to get me here, I didn't want the vindictive sod sending the town watch to drag me back, attracting even more attention to my dress. Besides, their uniforms were still singed from the last time they'd tried to manhandle me after I had punched Katja's now ex-husband for getting frisky in the tavern's backroom.

Unfortunately, before I could get anywhere near the magistrate, a murmur spread through the crowd in front of me, people shuffling to the sides to reveal our visitors. The squad of dragon riders marched straight towards the platform, cutting off my escape.

'My lady. I knew we'd meet again. The gods must be smiling down on me for such a beauty to greet us.' I knew that voice. The deep baritone, its smooth, velvety softness overflowing with amusement.

71

I opened my eyes, realising I'd squeezed them shut to avoid the inevitable confrontation, and looked up into the intoxicating eyes of Vahin's rider. The men had halted at some unspoken command, but the leader of the unit pressed on. Despite the mayor's wife waiting with a bouquet and the magistrate, who stood like a maypole with a hand outstretched in greeting, he walked straight towards me as if I were the only one there.

It was just my luck that in my chase for the dragon I had stumbled over the leader of the unit. His unwavering attention made me acutely aware that every single person in this bloody town was now staring at me.

The man in question clearly didn't care who was looking, and I struggled not to stare at him. If I'd dressed to impress, he beat me without even trying. He wore an imposing set of armour. Polished metal and leather gleamed in the sun as he took my hand, bowing and kissing the knuckles before he deigned to notice the city council.

Their reactions were comical; the women curtsied as if they were meeting royalty, and the overdressed men bowed so low that one man's feathered hat fell into the mud. The warrior's only acknowledgement was a casual wave of his free hand, the other still holding mine, his gaze not once leaving my face.

His military bearing and stoic demeanour while he stood before the entire town, his presence effortlessly commanding everyone's attention, reminded me so much of Talmund that my heart ached and my lips suddenly parted. I couldn't look away from him.

Then, his face lit with a such boyish smile that the atmosphere changed as the intimidating warrior released my hand, turned to the council, and greeted the assembled men. He lightly flirted with the mayor's wife as she gifted him the bouquet she'd been desperately clutching, and the poor woman fluttered around so much she'd almost fainted.

I saw his lips twitch when I laughed at the mayor, dragging his overly eager spouse away from the rider. I couldn't blame her. The man was a sight to behold. When he'd stood before me in the meadow, he'd dwarfed me, but he'd not been frightening. Now, he looked as though he ate demons for lunch, and the collective awe on the council's faces told me they were well aware of his strength.

I kept my own appreciation tightly leashed because each time the commander of the dragon riders looked at me, it felt like the festivities were pointless. There was kindness in his eyes, but also a steely determination—as if he'd already made his decision, and I was smack-bang in the middle of his plans. As understanding widened my eyes, he smirked and nodded before turning back to his conversation.

He could pass for the god of war himself, but if I'd wanted a powerful man to make my choices for me, I'd have stayed in the capital. I braced myself, ready to cut him down to size and storm off—free horse and bench be damned—when the mayor stepped down from the platform and stood beside me.

'Do you know each other?'

'We don't. Now, if you'll excuse me? I should make room for the ladies that want to be chosen,' I snapped, turning on my heel, but the warrior stepped in front of me.

'That is a regretful oversight on my part. However, as per tradition, I must insist on rectifying my mistake and getting to know you before making my choice. Let's start with your name, my lady,' he commanded, and the mayor's attention instantly snapped to my darkening expression.

There were only so many times a woman could rebuff a man before she suspected an ulterior motive.

Did he recognise the battle mage dress and want a mage in his service? Or maybe the dragon is behind this? I knew so little about dragons, but I understood that they communicated with their riders and I wondered if Vahin had told him we were connected. There were no other reasons for ignoring my desire to leave and then declaring his intent in front of the entire town.

Was this whole meeting an elaborate charade? Organised with its new rules to strip me of any chance for a polite refusal? Worse, if the magistrate had received the order from the court, did it mean that the mages in the capitol knew I was living here?

What if the rider was ordered to deliver me to the council?

A sudden wave of fear and the flare of my magic swept over me, almost as if the aether had reacted to my distress. I *hated* being manipulated, and the feeling of being trapped was suffocating. If the capital mages knew I was here, I had to run before they dragged me back to complete the Anchor bond with one of them.

Surrounded by the entire town and a flight of dragon riders, I struggled to keep my composure as I searched for a way to escape. I was going to tell the brazen warrior *precisely* what I thought of the entire situation when the mayor gleefully leapt into the conversation.

'Oh, my lord, this is Ani Jaksa, our town mage.' He turned to me. 'Ani, could you try being *nicer*? It's not every day you meet Lord Ormond Erenhart, Commander of Varta Fortress.'

Fucking patronising prick. I'll show you nicer.

Anger joined the fear in my mind, fuelling my unhinged magic. My hands clenched into fists as I fought to contain my power. It threatened to unleash itself on the gleeful man, but the mayor didn't have the sense to 'read the room.' But as an arrogant smile blossomed on his face, I lost control, sending red aetheric strands in his direction.

'*Fuck!*' I muttered under my breath, instinctively reaching for the Anchor bond, gasping when Ormond caught my hand and spun me around without seeming to move. His swift reaction doused the rogue spell, but not before the suddenly pale mayor fell back, thankfully unharmed.

As I stared at the warrior, shocked by the audacity of his gesture, I found myself with my hand pressed against his breastplate.

'It is a pleasure to make your acquaintance, Lady Ani. Please, call me Orm.' He lowered his voice, 'I'm sure we both hope that today will end agreeably, without either of us becoming fodder for the local gossip.' Orm stroked my hand, acting every inch the man who had found the woman he fancied.

'You aren't hurt?' I whispered, drawing a shaky breath when he shook his head, keeping his expression polite. He had effortlessly taken control of the situation, turning a near catastrophe into something that resembled a warm welcome, all while maintaining his calm demeanour.

It made little sense. Not only did my magic not hurt him, but his touch had broken through my distraction and centred me enough to regain my control. I'd been gently but sternly disarmed by a man I didn't even know.

My magic never behaved that way, and I stared at him, tense as a bowstring. *Who is he?* This rock—an unfeeling, unmovable, perfectly polite piece of granite—made me feel like I'd injure myself if I even tried to fight him. Ormond must have noticed my confusion, because he bent to whisper in my ear.

'We have much to talk about, but right now, you're scaring the young maidens. The mayor may be a little inept, but there's no need to spoil the atmosphere for everyone else.'

'Fine,' I whispered back, schooling my expression into one of false contentment. I needed time to think and understand what he really wanted before my fear drew the conclusion ... but not while I was pressed to him in the middle of the bloody town square.

I knew I would have to push through this welcome ceremony, but I hoped if he insisted on taking me because of Vahin I could try negotiating.

What if I tell him I'll come, but as a battle mage? With the recent Vel attacks, this could be a reasonable compromise and maybe even the reason he wanted me in the first place, I thought, setting the plan in my head.

I could come with him as an asset. Surely it was a better alternative than fighting an unwilling mage who could set his arse on fire? All I had to do was smile and nod, endure the evening, and talk to him tomorrow. Then he'd be free to choose one of the other women patiently waiting for our little drama to play out.

That would be the best solution for everyone, I assured myself, relaxing my stance, surprised by the prickle of uneasiness that came with the thought. *Oh, for fuck's sake, get a grip,* I thought, taking a step back before addressing the man.

'The pleasure is all mine, Commander. I hope you find Zalesie to your liking. As for knowing each other better ... now is not the best time. I would like to return to my companions, and I'm sure your compatriots would like to meet our local beauties instead of standing around waiting for this greeting ceremony to end as well,' I said loudly enough to satisfy the onlookers.

Orm frowned, as if it had only just occurred to him that he was keeping his men waiting.

'Of course, my lady,' he replied, bowing his head before turning towards his riders. 'Be at ease, men. Enjoy the celebration.'

Orm observed his men as they approached the young women, the poor girls suddenly becoming very shy, only answering with polite greetings. He watched for a while, seemingly assuring himself all was well. Once the first of the girls had smiled, the commander turned back to me, but I was already sitting between Bryna and Helga.

My friends would be the perfect shield until I could think of a good argument so that tomorrow, the commander would accept my plan. I knew one thing, however. Vahin and his touch had awakened not only my conduit magic but many painful memories, and with my power playing tricks, I didn't want to be sober tonight. I elbowed the blacksmith to get her attention.

'Do you have any more alcohol? I need so much more than a sip to survive today,' I muttered, making her chuckle.

'Ask the commander. I'm sure he'd love to satisfy your ... thirst,' she commented, 'If an attractive hunk looked at me like that, I'd have my trousers around my ankles before he could say hello and let him have his way with me as many times as he pleased,' she finished, roaring with laughter as I rolled my eyes.

'Knowing you, it'd be the man losing his trousers after you ripped them off him and stole his innocence,' I retorted, shaking my head. I didn't need her ribald jokes right now. I was already painfully aware of the way I reacted to him.

Ormond stood where I left him, exchanging pleasantries with the town officials before the innkeeper and his helpers began carrying out food for the feast. Dragon riders were well paid, and this feast must have been their doing, as there wasn't a single sour expression on the officials' faces.

The innkeeper brought out the best produce from his basement, together with several barrels of beer, wine, and mead. Soon, the town was more interested in eating and drinking than in the dragon riders' presence, so I took the opportunity to quietly observe the gathered crowd.

Time passed quickly, and I relaxed a little, watching Ormond entertain several women. I was happy he hadn't returned to my side or tried engaging me in conversation. I still couldn't understand what had happened in the town square, and it worried me. My magic seemed to be drawn to him, like it had a mind of its own, but I refused to be a slave to its urges.

As expected, none of the riders approached the crones' bench, and—contrary to my previous reservations—I enjoyed being a part of the gathering. Bryna had already slipped away in order to, as she put it, 'sample the wares,' leaving me with a bottle of wine and a sleeping Helga snoring beside me, but I didn't mind.

These last few months, I'd felt under siege. Monsters had appeared with no rhyme or reason, as if the earth had spit them forth, and I was tired from my relentless pursuit to hunt them down. As I was already as drunk as a proverbial log, I decided that tonight both Zalesie and I needed a bit of joy.

As dusk settled over the celebrating citizens, in a gesture of good-will—and well-laced with alcohol—I conjured a few small fairy lights. They danced in the air to the music of the band, brightening the evening and adding a romantic splendour to the event. Just as I started drifting into a relaxed stupor, a tall, imposing figure paused in front of me.

'Ani? I believe I've given you enough time. Would you do me the honour of joining me for a stroll?' The commander stood in front of me, patiently waiting with his hand outstretched in my direction.

'Don't you have to look after your riders? What if one of them gets overenthusiastic before they're given permission?' I said out of sheer defiance.

'The Maiden's Day Choosing is only meant to find women to work in the fortress, not enter any man's bed. No rider would force their touch on a woman without her consent. That's why I'm asking instead of throwing you over my shoulder and taking you somewhere quiet to talk.'

I choked on my wine.

'What?' I coughed before taking a deep breath. 'Let me guess, you won't take no for an answer.'

'You're an intelligent woman, Ani. I can see you don't want to be chosen, but that creates a dilemma for me. I need you to come with me, and I would prefer you came voluntarily,' he said, and I sighed, feeling the walls of a trap closing in.

Orm must have noticed my stubborn expression because his gaze softened. 'I don't bite, Ani. On the contrary, I want to earn your trust. I'd like to propose a contract that will benefit us both, but that involves disclosing things that should not be overheard in a crowd. So, my lady, shall we? Or should I behave like the brute you clearly expect me to be?'

I had to remind myself that I'd hoped for this chance to negotiate, but I also felt like I had to prove I wasn't a fool. 'I don't consider you a brute, Ormond. If anything, you are unnaturally calm, and that proves you are a dangerous man. I can see you like to be in control, but I'm not some simpering child who wants to hang on your every word,' I smirked.

'This town means a lot to me, and I suspect you had a hand in intimidating the town council. They think disagreeing with you will incur your wrath, stripping this place of the dragons' protection if they don't do everything you ask.'

Seeing his appreciative nod, I knew I'd guessed right. Ormond was the reason for my forced appearance. Still, if he thought he could play me, he was sorely mistaken.

'You want to talk?' I continued, 'Fine, we can talk. But this time I'll do the talking, and you'll listen,' I said, standing up, though my regal pose was spoiled as I swayed from too much wine. I'd been sitting for too long on an uncomfortable bench, and my muscles protested. My legs wobbled, and Ormond grabbed my waist, pulling me close with effortless ease.

'You're doing it again. Why did you help me earlier and ... how ...' I said before a hiccup forced me to stop.

'You looked ... startled earlier, and I didn't want you to suffer. I admit your power had a bite to it, but I'm no stranger to pain. As for the rest, I promise to listen.'

'You haven't so far. You just keep giving me orders,' was my retort, and he sighed.

'Is that how you see it? I'm not trying to intimidate you, but I'm a military man who's used to plain speaking. Would you prefer that I insult your intelligence by muddying the waters and whispering sweet nothings in your ear? I could do that if it would make you happy or more compliant, but we both know it would just make you angry,' he said, still holding me close.

'What ...?' I flinched when he bent to my ear. His breath caressed my skin, warming it against the chilly evening breeze. 'I can be very persuasive when I choose to be, so tell me if I'm wrong. Do you want me to be ... persuasive?

Or can we continue with reasoned discussion?' he went on, pulling me even closer and inhaling deeply.

'I saw the way you looked at me in the fields, Annika. I'm not immune to this, so if you want me to seduce you, I can. There is no means I wouldn't use to bring you to the fortress. You will join me tomorrow, but I will let you decide whether you'll come willingly as my guest or under the geas as my ward. I don't want to order you around. The way you treated Vahin ... the way you talked to me ... I'd prefer your cooperation, Ani, so I ask, as humbly as I can: please, will you talk to me?'

Geas? Did he say he had my geas?

He continued speaking, but all I could think of was the geas. Gods, how I hated that word. My body was trembling in his grasp, and for once, I was grateful, as I suspected I would have collapsed if not for his support.

If he had my geas, he knew exactly who I was. The only way he could have gotten it was by appealing to the royal mage. I looked up to find that his dark green eyes expressed nothing but concern.

'Annika?' He placed a hand on my cheek. His simple gesture centred me enough to break through the initial panic. He was still holding me, but as I pulled away, Orm reluctantly let me go. If he genuinely knew the words of my geas, I was trapped, and we both knew it.

'Do you really have it?' I asked quietly, and he nodded. 'Fine, my lord, you win. Let's talk. I will meet you at the floodplains. There's an old light-ning-struck tree nearby. Just wait for me—' I stopped when he raised his hand.

'We will go together. I'm sorry, but I can't let you burn your house again. It took a lot of effort to find you after your first *disappearance*,' he said. When I bristled, Orm gently tucked a stray strand of hair behind my ear as the wind blew it across my face.

'I'm not your enemy. I am, however, the commander who protects these lands, and you are a conduit mage sworn to defend the kingdom. I wish we'd met under different circumstances, but the fates rarely give us favourable choices,' he said. I saw regret flashing in his eyes before he exhaled slowly. 'Let's go, my lady. It is time we had that talk.'

CHAPTER 7

OR☾OND

I couldn't believe how much meeting Annika complicated my plans. The task was simple: come to Zalesie, find the mage, and use the geas to make her come to the fortress for whatever Alaric needed her to do.

Since learning Ani was the mage that had caused the avalanche ten years ago, the same person that Vahin rescued right after the incident, I'd been unscrupulous in ensuring she would have no choice in following my orders. However, Ani was nothing like I'd expected.

I couldn't shake the impression that I'd just sparred and lost, despite holding all the cards. She'd done it so skilfully I wasn't even disturbed by my loss. And her appearance ... The uniform she wore made her look dangerous and professional while accentuating her femininity and softening the righteous indignation she wielded like a sword.

She was also very drunk, glaring at me each time she stumbled, almost as if blaming me for the uneven cobblestones under her feet. 'Slow down, there's no rush,' I said, once again grabbing her arm to prevent her from falling.

My sigh as I wrapped her hand around my forearm earned me another murderous glare before I saw a flash of surprise in Ani's eyes, but something felt off. It was almost as if it wasn't me she was seeing until, with a quick shake of her head, my companion recovered her senses.

'Fine, we can slow down, so you can let me go.'

'No,' I answered, realising as I spoke that I enjoyed having her beside me. I expected my companion to protest again, but whatever she'd wanted to say died in a huff as she stumbled, gripping my arm tighter with a quiet grumble.

The woman was a contradiction, reasonable yet volatile. I'd almost burst into laughter, realising her unassuming allure was what had made me change the plans I'd meticulously implemented over the last three months—and all she had done was caress my dragon.

The search for the elusive mage from the lake had been challenging. We knew next to nothing. Just a physical description and that she was a conduit. So it had been a relief when Alaric came up with the idea of checking the royal records for living conduit mages, only to find one matching the description whose *death*, albeit recorded, was flagged for an unknown reason. By coincidence, it was the rookie who caused the Lost Ridge incident.

'How did you find me?' she asked as we walked, and I smirked. I couldn't tell her that I had followed her trail like a bloodhound. That I had sent my men to all towns within walking distance of the lake to bring me the names of the resident mages. Still, I felt I owed her some explanation.

'Your name, and the fact that Alaric—my fortress mage whom you met at the lake—sensed you were a conduit. There are few conduits in the royal register, and no high-class mage decides to live in the borderlands. Yet here in Zalesie was Ani Jaksa, who miraculously appeared just under ten years ago. It also helped that her surname was the human version of *Jah'aksai* ... the name of the fae healer who was recorded as one of a dead conduit's Anchors.'

She looked at me sharply before her shoulders slumped. 'And I thought I hid so well. So ... the strangers that kept coming to the town ...'

'Were my men. You have a talent for disappearing. I knew I couldn't leave you alone despite your connection to this place. You are a weapon, Annika. A weapon I desperately need.'

I couldn't take any chances, so I had posted men to monitor Annika Diavellar. Some of them tried to approach her with my invitation. Unfortunately, every time she saw a stranger, Annika wouldn't even give them the time to speak. They'd returned to the fortress with gaps in their memory, so I'd come here expecting to find an arrogant mage lording her status over the local population. Only to find a foul-mouthed but caring and respected member of the community.

Interestingly, I'd also discovered that she was also the reason we never received requests for soldiers or an increased dragon presence here. Ani was culling the monster population around the town like they were pests, and knowing how well she knew these mountains, I wanted to ensure she stayed where she was until Maiden's Day.

'How did you get my geas and ... order for the mages to take part in the Maiden's Day circus?' she asked, still slurring her words.

'Family connections. My brother is Lord Marshal of Dagome.'

'Of course, you're able to change the law when it fits you,' she huffed, and I sighed.

Her response stopped me from divulging that the royal mage had granted me the geas the moment he'd learned whom I'd found. He could barely believe she had survived without an Anchor or without causing a catastrophe for so long, and he made me swear I'd find a way to tame her magic.

The old man's hands had trembled when I told him who I'd discovered. There were only a few conduit mages in the kingdom, and it seemed Ani had faked her death to run away from the splendour of court before her geas could be activated, refusing to be bonded again. It was easier for everybody to believe she'd died than admit there was an uncontrolled power so close to the Barren Lands.

I was more than happy to sweep their mistake under the carpet, so I came here thinking I knew exactly who I would have to deal with, determined to drag her from this town by force if necessary. Then I met her on the floodplains and realised I knew nothing. Not only might I have misjudged her character, but I also didn't foresee how I'd react to the encounter.

We walked together in silence until I noticed Ani curling her hand into a fist, rubbing her fingers together, and I covered her hand with mine. As I suspected, it was cold, but I enjoyed the sensation of her magic prickling my skin as she tilted her head and looked at me with a frown.

'What are you doing?'

'I'm warming your hand. It is cold as ice,' I answered. I didn't stop her when she pulled away; we were almost at the floodplains anyway. 'Tell me, what's so special about this town that you moved here?' I asked to break the tension, but the rigid set of her jaw indicated I had asked the wrong question.

'Fresh mountain air and friendly citizens, of course. Why else would a conduit mage settle in an isolated town, filling her days with making love potions and chasing ghouls and chickens?' she answered.

Troublemaker, I thought, feeling annoyance mixed with amusement. I tried to ease the muscles in my neck, wincing as Ani jumped at the crunching sound. She was skittish, and as soon as she'd learned of my status and the geas, Annika had become more prickly than a thistle.

'Chickens?' I asked against my better judgement, and she pursed her lip.

'Of course. They are an important part of the local culture. Ask the mayor's wife. She'll tell you all about it, and in great detail. In fact, you *must* ask her about it, as their frequent disappearance is strongly related to the fading of the Barrier. At least that's what she thinks.'

'What?' I stopped and grasped her hand. The abruptness of my gesture made her stumble into me. 'What are you talking about? What do chickens have to do with the Barrier?' It sounded like nonsense, and I realised it was when Ani's lips twitched. *Brazen witch,* I thought, turning my face away from her to hide how much it pleased me.

'Nothing. On second thought, *don't* talk to the mayor's wife. No one deserves that conversation.' She laughed. 'Gods, the look you just gave me was so incredulous it was cute.'

I've been called various names—'unfeeling bastard' the one most commonly used within my hearing, but *cute*? That I'd never heard. My annoyance at her teasing ebbed into appreciation. Few dared to speak to me so disrespectfully; even fewer were bold enough to tease Varta's commander with crazed theories on fucking chickens.

She was the breath of fresh air I didn't know I needed.

We arrived at the tree she'd mentioned, and Ani instantly let go of my hand, leaning on the gnarly trunk. I could hear dragons snoring; Ani must have heard it, too, because she looked in the same direction.

'Do you think Vahin is there?' she asked. I nodded, quietly observing her. With the sound of music in the distance and under the soft light of the stars, her face had finally softened. I kept my distance, letting the peace of the night seep in until I felt she was ready to hear me.

'I like the night,' Ani whispered, turning her face towards the sky. 'It hides the monsters and ugliness of this world, letting you forget who you are and what you've done ... I sometimes wander outside to lose myself in the sea of stars and talk to those who can no longer hear me,' she continued, exhaling slowly.

The beauty of those words and the pain behind them stunned me into silence. I'd expected a fight. Instead, I stood beside a shivering woman who looked at the stars as if she could find all of the answers to her questions amongst them. There was unresolved grief hidden in her words, and I didn't know if Ani was purposely sharing this with me or if the alcohol had loosened her tongue.

'One day, I will take you to the stars if you'd like. Vahin can carry us both, and whatever you need to tell them will be heard by the gods themselves.' My offer was an impulse that I instantly regretted when she chuckled, shaking her head before turning her gaze towards me.

'Leave the sky for the dragons, Orm. If the gods want to listen to my ramblings, they'll have to come down to my level, but I appreciate the sentiment. You're making it very hard for me to detest you, so let's hear what you have to say. I know it is a strange place to talk, but whatever you need to say, it'll be easier to take here.'

As the silence stretched out, crickets, initially disturbed by our presence, resumed their melody. The air, filled with the perfume of night flowers, was the perfect backdrop for lovers, but not for the contract I was about to reveal. Yet, I couldn't stop thinking about how to soften the blow.

'Ormond, we can stay here all night, but at some point, I'll fall asleep. So please, tell me why you went to such lengths to entrap me,' she asked, and I cursed. Why did she have to wield her words like a whip every time I wanted to go easy on her?

My anger abated when she added quietly, 'Since I'm still here despite you knowing who I am ... don't you want to take me to the capital?' I shortened the distance between us, wondering how honest I could be and how she would take it when I announced to the town that she was my chosen maiden tomorrow.

She ran and hid here because she refused to take the Anchor chosen by the council. *Will telling her she has to bond Alaric to fix the keystone cause the same reaction?... I'll let him broach the subject. Let's see what she says if I offer my protection and the opportunity to do more than slay a few ghouls every once in a while.* My new plan had its flaws, but between the meeting on the floodplains and now, I hadn't had time to consider all the implications.

'The problem is here, not in the capital—and before you ask, only the royal mage knows you're alive.' She exhaled slowly, looking at me with a little less hostility. 'Tomorrow, I will announce that I have chosen you, and you will accept it without causing a scene. I know you don't desire that, so tonight, I wanted to explain why I must do it this way and why it's so important,' I said, and she pushed herself off the tree.

'Well, I'm all ears. I'm guessing you came here lured by the stories of my power, and the way we interacted earlier had you thinking you could kill two birds with one stone. Ugh, never mind, it's a starting point. Let's negotiate—but before I give you my terms, you need to know the truth.' The tone of her voice made me raise my eyebrow.

'What truth? Please, do enlighten me. I'm all ears.'

'You may have a body to die for, but I'm not interested in you. If you went as far as to obtain the geas, you know who I am and how far I can go to protect myself. Trust me, you'll not win a fight with me, so if you think you can force me to warm your bed, think again. You may rule Varta Fortress, but if you want a mistress, I'm not your woman.'

I smiled at the challenge in her eyes. She looked me in the eye, her expression informing me she wouldn't stand for any strong-arm tactics, and I enjoyed every moment, knowing she wouldn't slide from my grasp. 'Annika, I don't need a mistress. I need a weapon. Do you really think the royal mage would have just let you go once he learned of your existence otherwise?' I let the meaning of my words hang in the air.

'What did you promise him to get me?'

'I gave him my word that I would take responsibility for you,' I said, and she snorted a laugh.

'Well, then you are shit out of luck, Commander.'

'I don't believe I am, and I think we can come to an understanding. You are a contradiction, woman. In one breath, you tell me you find me attractive; the next, you find my touch repulsive. You wound me deeply if you think I'd force my attention on an unwilling partner, but rest assured, I wouldn't go through this much trouble just to get you in my bed. Though, if you wanted to join me, I could be persuaded.'

Gods, that came out wrong. I almost winced. I came here to acquire a weapon and had found a woman who loved the stars and who had a smile that could brighten the night.

That she would think I'd force her into my bed ... Her words wounded my ego, and I had lashed out without thinking. I didn't know what angered me more: the fact she didn't want me, or the fact she thought so little of me.

'I don't find you repulsive, but I don't like to be coerced or manipulated into a situation, and your attitude ... You've threatened me with the only thing I can't refuse, and you've done it here in my home. You have shattered my peace, Ormond. How did you think I'd feel about it? Do you know how it feels, after all these years, to still be seen as an unhinged mage who needs a guardian because I apparently clearly can't be trusted to live on my own?'

Ani inhaled sharply, fighting a losing battle to hold back angry tears.

'You know what? No, I refuse to be owned. So fuck it. Fuck the geas, fuck you, and fuck the king and the horse he rode in on. What can he do? Kill me? Officially, I'm already dead.' Ani's statement was spoken with quiet determination, accompanied by slowly building magic. The hairs on the back of my neck rose, and the coppery taste of fear coated my tongue as the destructive power of a conduit mage slowly surfaced.

'No!' I said, grasping Ani's arms, enduring the burning pain from the magic coursing through her body. I knew I had to stop her before she cast a spell in drunken anger. After a moment's struggle, the burning lessened, and her body softened in my arms.

I let Ani catch her breath, trying to ignore the now delightful sensation of holding her close. The tingling where our bare skin met was intoxicating, almost as if silken strands of magic were sliding over my flesh, binding us together.

'Annika, stop. I'm trying to give you a choice, one where you get to set your terms. Just give me a chance to explain. Did you really think the royal mage would let you go? I had to give him something.'

'You could have left me alone. And what the hell do you think you're doing?'

'Helping you contain your anger. I don't want to fight, and I don't want to hurt you if I'm forced to defend myself. Control yourself, mage, or I will be forced to control you. So, can I let go? Or does anger still cloud your judgment?' I argued calmly, noticing her cheeks redden at my insult, but at least she stopped struggling.

'Let me go, or my magic will do something we both regret. I was only trying to erase the geas spell from my mind before you could use it on me.' Her eyes sent daggers at me. *I won't be anyone's puppet.*'

I bristled at the comment but couldn't help admiring her defiance.

'It would kill you. Even I know that's impossible! I can't believe you're bold enough to have tried it. I was merely holding you down.' I paused. 'Your magic feels ... interesting. Tell me why it's wrapping itself around me,' I said, releasing her and backing up, my hands raised to show my peaceful intentions.

Ani stood motionless for a moment before sitting on the grass with a heavy sigh.

'Because I have no Anchors. What you felt was my magic trying to tether us together. When my emotions are high, the most primal part of my power takes control, and it only requires skin-to-skin contact ... You don't want to become a mage's Anchor, trust me,' she ended with a bitter laugh.

'Does it react like this to anyone?' I asked, unable to rein in my curiosity.

'No, but few dare try pinning me down against my will.' She lowered her head. 'My power has become more unstable recently. You saw for yourself in the town square, and ... thank you for helping me contain it ... it's become wilful and is trying to attach itself to any compatible being. That's what you felt, even if it shouldn't happen. I'm a broken mage, Ormond.'

I raised my eyebrow at her open honesty.

'May I ask why?'

'Why what? Why I refuse to be bound? Why I would need to be? Or do you mean why I would bind you?' she asked dismissively, clearly expecting me to know what she meant. However, whilst I knew some of Ani's history, most of it was a complete mystery.

'Any of those? All? You were kind enough to point out my ignorance, perhaps you should educate me.'

'I don't know why my magic wants you. You're not even a mage. Yet I feel ... something between us. I refuse to take another Anchor because I cannot let myself care for someone again. Why do I need to be Anchored? Because the amount of aether I can draw through my body is terrifying and unstable. Each time I cast a spell without an Anchor, I risk losing control and killing everyone around me, myself included.'

'How does it work? I admit I know little about conduit mages.'

'We are the access to unlimited power, like a dam on a raging river that can be opened and closed at will. Where a regular mage is like a goblet, able to hold a certain amount of magic, we can channel limitless magic. There is a danger, though. It is easy to open the dam, but to close it, one mage's will is never enough, and the stronger the conduit, the more Anchors they need to help shut off the aether,' she started.

'And the limitless magic ... the human body can only withstand so much. Each time a conduit's ability is used, it is euphoric, but the mage is left weakened for minutes or hours, sometimes even for days. At the same time, their Anchors, if they are close by, no longer need to use their reserves, and their spells become powerful beyond measure. The effect lasts for some time, even after the conduit closes the gateway to the aether.'

Ani gave me a look a defiance before continuing, 'Magic has conse-quences, and without Anchors, I'm defective—powerful, but essentially useless. You told me you came here for a weapon, likely because your mage told you about conduits' unlimited power, but you're wasting your time,'

I felt a soft, tender smile tease my lips. 'I think you're exactly the person I need.'

'Fine, tell me why I need to go to the fortress because *I'm* failing to understand,' Ani insisted, wrapping her arms around herself, gently shivering as she muttered something under her breath. I removed my riding cloak and wrapped it around her shoulders. Its fur lining would keep her warm. Annika appeared surprised by my gesture yet again.

'You are cold. Don't read too much into it,' I said, answering the unspoken question and ignoring the frown on her face. When she didn't respond or return my cloak, I sat next to her.

'When you first met Vahin, you also met my mage, Alaric,' I said, to which she nodded, acknowledging my words. 'At the fortress, we not only fight Vel demons, but also patrol the border, even going behind the Barrier to the Barren Lands to ensure nothing threatens the Lowland Kingdoms.' I stopped for a moment to let the information sink in.

'The problems with the Barrier began before you created the Rift. However, now that the Rift is growing, there's been more and more trouble. Alaric thinks there is a way to replace the keystone; that's why we were at the lake. Since meeting you, he's convinced that with the right crystal and your conduit abilities, he would be able to fully restore the Barrier.'

'Pray tell, how could I manage that? The archimages of legend created the Barrier, and all of them were part of the High Order. I'm an elemental mage of the Primal Order with no talent for artifice,' she asked, rolling her eyes and pulling my cloak tighter around her body.

'For that, you'd need to speak with Alaric. But I'll share something with you that may help you decide. With the growing breach in the Barrier, the casualties from each skirmish have increased. Fathers, sons, brothers—*good* men. They are dying because they were never trained to fight monsters.' I explained.

'We don't get the elite here. We get the unemployed, the unskilled, and farmers who've no idea which end of a sword goes where. Not to mention the criminals who just don't care. *Those* are the types of people being sent to the most hostile place in the country.'

I couldn't stop myself from going on; she had to know what I'd be bringing her into. 'There are rumours that the king is … not fully in control and has alienated the other rulers of the Lowland Kingdoms. It doesn't help that the southern countries think the monsters here are our problem; and since there is no war, they are no longer obliged to contribute.'

I huffed a breath, my annoyance and desperation simmering under the surface. 'We are alone here, Ani … And the Rift is spreading. You are my last thread of hope in a world of increasing attacks. Vel demons are breaking through every day—minor demons for now, but it's just a matter of time before something bigger forces its way through. Do you understand? That's why, if there's even the smallest chance you can help, I have to take it.'

'Ask the royal mage or the chancellor for help. If you have enough power to access my geas, you can ask for someone more competent than me to help your mage seal the Barrier. I'm not the only conduit in the country,' she argued.

'And I told you, my magic is unstable. Frankly, I'm no better than a hedge witch. I want to help, but you need a hero of old, not some disgraced mage who spends her evenings drinking herself into oblivion,' she insisted, but I sensed the tentative acceptance in her voice.

'My predecessor asked, and the high mage who came here was killed by the wlok. Others have tried, but all of them have said it was hopeless. I wish I knew more about this, but all I know is that Alaric said that your power resonated with the keystone.' I hesitated.

'There is also another minor detail … All of them refused to work with a dark fae and, as they said, *be tainted* by his magic.' I felt the anger seep into my voice and stopped myself before I made the situation worse.

I was glad I opted for the truth, though. While Ani's frown was still present, it was now directed elsewhere, and the look she gave me was filled with concern and empathy.

'Ormond, you've been lied to if you were told I'm strong. You've heard of my fight with the wlok and think I saved the day. All I did was lose control and … Trust me, I'm the last person you need. But if it will make you feel better, I'll go to the fortress and talk to your mage. I don't care if he's dark fae, orc, or something the cat dragged in. I will do what I can, but don't count on me making a difference when so many better than me have failed.'

I couldn't help the twitch of my lips. Annika cared for those around her and unflinchingly faced danger, setting her own terms. She just needed a little nudge to make the right decision.

'I need more than that, Ani. Give me a year. The more I talk to you, the more I'm convinced you can help. If, after a year, you still haven't found a way to fix the Barrier, you will be free, and I swear that no one will come after you ever again. Annika Diavellar will disappear for good. Your geas will be destroyed, and you will have my family's protection—not that you need it,' I quipped with a smile.

'The same applies if you restore the Barrier earlier. You will be free, Ani. Freer than anyone could ever hope to be.' She turned to look directly at me. The little crease on her forehead deepened, and somehow, her thoughtful expression made my smile widen.

'You know, when you're not threatening to fry my rear end, you're quite the reasonable woman. I've heard about how you fight the Vel without Anchors. You're obviously not afraid to face danger, even alone and outnumbered. What I wasn't expecting was for you to face me, especially armed with your geas … I'm impressed.'

'Then you're easily impressed,' she muttered.

'No, I am not. After fighting the Lich King's demons for so long, there is little that impresses me. Yet you've captured my attention. *You*, not your power. Though I confess I came here to retrieve a mage, maybe I can leave with ... a friend?' my voice trailed off as my need for her acceptance surprised me with its intensity.

'If I agree to this, it will be as a mage ... not as a bound maiden.' Ani's voice was barely a whisper, but what gave me pause was the smile that briefly ghosted over her face. The first smile that lacked any of her previous tension, and gods, it was beautiful.

'Of course. You will join us as our second fortress mage, and you will receive all the honour such a position deserves.'

'Fine, then I'll go. Just make sure your men know I'm not available,' she acquiesced and wrapped my cloak tighter around her body.

'Not even for those who understand you don't want a commitment?' I asked. Her smile gave me hope, and I couldn't resist teasing her a little.

I understood she didn't want to come as a bondmaid—a mage entering a bondage contract was a humiliating prospect, but her firm refusal of any encounters only sharpened my interest. As I looked at her suddenly solemn expression, I knew the first step to discovering Annika's secrets was to find out why she was so eager to place a wall between us.

'My magic doesn't understand noncommitment.' The calm bitterness of her tone was stinging and sobered my jesting mood.

'Annika, the offence you are afraid of is punishable by death. We protect women, having so few of them. It brings my men much joy to respect and cherish those who come to live with us. If anyone dares to touch you, no matter who they are, I will wring their necks myself,' I said, seeing her eyes widen.

To offset the harshness of my words, I added, 'Still, wintery nights in the fortress can be lonely and challenging; there'd be no shame if you sought comfort in such situations.' She huffed in annoyance.

'I don't need your pity, Lord Ormond, and I'm perfectly capable of defending myself,' she said, sounding offended.

'What if I'm the one asking for pity?' I don't know why I blurted it out, but as I did, I realised I wanted her to know how I felt. I'd revealed her secrets and if I was asking for her friendship, it was time to reveal some of my own. Even if it was a small admission, I hoped it would even up the scales.

'I rarely talk with anyone as an equal, let alone a beautiful woman, and while I can't deny that my misconceptions of your character made this encounter difficult, I find myself drawn to you. Whatever your magic was doing to me, it felt right, but I understand you feel otherwise. I simply wanted you to know that I am not averse to becoming close to you. A year is a long time to brood in a mountain fortress, but it doesn't have to be that way. Life is well lived behind our cold granite walls, and I wish to share it with you. Let me be your friend, Ani.'

'Hm ... friends ... Are you trying to make the world better for everyone or just for me?' she asked, turning her face to the side. I could see the pain she tried to hide before lowering her head and whispering, 'How can I be your friend when you are so much like Tal?'

'Tal?' I asked, surprised when Ani flinched at my question.

'One of my former Anchors. You remind me of him.' The tight smile she offered me didn't reach her eyes as she spoke, 'I don't know if I can be your friend. All I can promise is to try to be the best mage I can be.'

I already knew that Ani's Anchors had died the day she damaged the keystone.

It wasn't my fault that I reminded her of the past. Regardless, my lack of malicious intent didn't make me feel like any less of a heartless bastard. Somehow, whatever I'd said came out wrong, and I didn't want to hurt her feelings more. It was time to wrap up this conversation.

'Good night, my lady.' I bowed to take her hand, but she stepped back, shaking her head. I straightened.

'Until tomorrow.' There was nothing more to say.

CHAPTER 8

ANNIKA

My late-night conversation with Orm had taken the word 'disturbing' to a brand-new level. My world had been turned upside down when the commander had decided to recruit me, and the worst thing about it was that I felt attracted to him—not just his physique, but the calm he projected.

It was only me who felt that way, apparently, because everybody else was terrified of the man who could impose his will on the town council whilst maintaining a polite kindness. Amidst my wildly differing reactions, my magic had made a grab for his soul, picking the most unlikely of men as my next Anchor.

What the fuck is wrong with you? He isn't even a mage. I tapped my chest as if the primal force within could hear me. *I've made a deal with a demon. A handsome, calm, but ruthless demon,* I thought.

But I had to give it to him: Orm had me exactly where he wanted me. Between having the key to my geas and threatening to reveal my secret, he had manipulated me flawlessly into the situation. What angered me was that I *understood* his actions—and in his place, would have done exactly the same, likely with less grace and consideration.

He's wrecked my life with class and style, and still I'm excusing his actions. I barked a short, bitter laugh. In the grand scheme of things, disturbing the life of a town mage had little significance, and I understood that all too well.

I huffed, annoyed at my argument, unable to deny that I liked him a little.

Ormond, even with his demands, was kind and had tried to comfort me with his small gestures. He reminded me so much of Talmund that if I closed my eyes, I could easily pretend it was my lover who stood there and not the commander. Maybe that's why I felt so confused in his presence. But Talmund was gone, and I would never Anchor someone just because he reminded me of him.

It hurt to enjoy his company, and the old wound festering deep inside me reopened, robbing me of sleep.

I dealt with it the only way I knew how: I drank myself into the blackest oblivion.

The morning welcomed me with the clattering noises of town life, and as expected, I woke up with a hangover, puffy eyes, and a mood so sour it could spoil milk. I was also late for the announcement, not that it mattered. As we had agreed, I was going as a mage, and as soon as I was given my promised horse, I would be leaving for the fortress.

As I was running late, I made little effort to get myself ready. Still, I needed to see him. Lateness was one thing, but I thought it best to arrive before they sent a search party. Even if only to give Orm back his cloak.

I dressed in comfortable clothes, trying not to think about my upcoming trip. Zalesie to Varta Fortress was three days of solid riding over rugged terrain, and I wasn't looking forward to the arduous journey.

You can do it, Annika. Whatever comes, as long as you restore the Barrier and free yourself from the geas, it will be worth it. Valiantly battling nausea, I walked towards the floodplains.

The sight of several dragons almost cheered me up, but Orm's smug grin instantly brought me back to reality.

'Good morning, Ani. Vahin is quite strong, you know, so you didn't need to pack so lightly.' The commander's words didn't penetrate the fog around my thoughts, and all I could manage was a grunt in reply.

'For a moment there, I thought I'd need to remind you of our deal, especially after you missed the announcement. It was quite spectacular, the magistrate nearly fainting when I declared my choice.'

'Oh *no*, how could I have missed it?' I answered, the hand to my forehead and exaggerated acting expressing just how I felt on the matter. 'I told you I would be here, but I never promised to be in good shape,' I said, passing him his cloak.

I didn't want to tell Orm that my thoughts of *him* had resulted in my current state. It would have made that satisfied grin worse, and I couldn't face seeing it. Instead, I turned back to admire the waiting dragons.

The enormous beasts were all the colours of the rainbow, vivid and beautiful. However, it was Vahin who drew my eyes, those jet-black scales streaked with a blue pattern that reflected the rays of the sun like a mirror. 'Gods, look at them. They're gorgeous,' I whispered, my hand unconsciously falling onto Orm's forearm.

'After you leave, I'll go see the magistrate. He owes me a horse for joining in with your little play. I'll make sure he gives me one that's fit to make the journey to Varta. Once I've packed a few items, I'll head out, so have the welcoming committee in front of the fortress gates in three days,' I said, remembering why I was there.

'You intend to ride to Varta? By yourself?' At the disbelief in his voice, I turned to look at him.

'No, with a horse,' I said, rubbing my temple. Stinking headaches always made me snippy, but if Orm wanted answers, he could deal with it. 'Of course, I'm going alone. Unless you want me to bring along the freshly kidnapped maidens.'

Orm's confused glare made me think something was amiss. 'What?' I asked, feeling more and more defensive the longer he stared. 'Just tell me.'

'You were going to ride ... on a horse?' he questioned again, and I nodded, stepping away when he threw his head back and laughed.

'What's so bloody funny? And be mindful of your answer because I'm seriously considering violence,' I said, squinting my eyes, his booming laughter a dagger stabbing my hungover brain.

'You, Ani, and how you're planning to travel. Three days on the road with your backside rubbed raw on a saddle compared to flying there with Vahin in less than a day,' he said, and I felt the little blood left in my face drain away. 'You make the most interesting jokes. Besides, we don't have time to dally, and as much as I wish to trust you, we both know that, left to your own devices, you tend to disappear in a plume of smoke.'

'No,' I said, putting my hands out in a defensive gesture. 'We had an agreement, and I'm here ... I'll go to the magistrate now, and I'll be on the road before Vahin opens his wings,' I said, turning to leave, but Orm grasped my forearm.

'I don't have time for this and don't trust you enough to let you go by yourself. I understand that the first time on a dragon's back can be unsettling, but you'll soon get used to it. I promise it will be a pleasant flight and smooth enough to satisfy anyone's idea of comfort,' he grumbled, pulling me towards the dragon.

'I said *no!*' I dug my heels into the dirt, provoking a few surprised stares from the gathered citizens.

Here I was, hungover and angry in such an idyllic setting, making a spectacle of myself. I hated it, and I hated him in the moment.

It was a beautiful morning, with the sun shining brightly and wisps of mist curling around our ankles from the dew-touched grass. The mountaintops glinted with sparkling snow, and the valleys below were green and vibrant. Still, no one enjoyed the enchanting panorama as the gathered people were more interested in the scene I was making.

Of course, no one could drag their eyes away from the drama unfolding before them. The gasps of shock were drowned out by the sighs of yearning as Orm turned and, without pausing, encircled my thighs and lifted me over his shoulder.

'Ani, I will accommodate any reasonable request, and I promise I'm not trying to make your life difficult, but from now on, and for the next year, you will listen to me and *do as I say*,' he said. My ability to argue with the barbarous warrior was hampered by the contents of my stomach attempting to reappear over his beautiful, fur-lined cloak.

I reached for the aether, intending to fry his sorry arse, mortified at the laughter and cheers from the crowd, but before I knew it, we had stopped in front of the dragon. As the men's jibes encouraged Orm to take his 'bride,' Vahin's tail smashed into the ground, silencing everyone.

Fucking traitors, and I cured their warts for years, I seethed, and as I lost my grip on my magic, I changed tack and blasted Orm with my anger.

'You demented brute. I'm not some sack of turnips to be tossed around!' I shouted, clenching my fists. 'Let me go. I won't fly, and if you try to put me on Vahin's back, so help me gods, that will be the last thing you ever do.'

Orm simply put me down, his face expressionless. I wasn't sure whether to admire or kill him for it. His unnatural calm was so unsettling that I took a step away after he released me, stumbling back against the dragon. I turned towards the beast, noticing his tilted head and frown as he observed my outburst.

'Vahin asks if the thought of riding on his back offends you.'

'What? No, of course not!' I said, taken aback by Orm's statement. Nothing could be further from the truth, and I couldn't allow the sweet, gentle dragon to think I detested him. As much as I hated to admit my weakness, I had to reveal the truth.

'I'm not upset with Vahin. I'm refusing to fly ...' I said, biting my lip, 'I'm sorry,' I reached towards the dragon's muzzle, letting the simple touch centre me. 'I'm afraid of heights. I feel dizzy and terrified even on a high ladder. It's not your fault I ... I just can't do it.'

Orm cursed quietly behind me.

'I didn't realise. You seem so dauntless that it never crossed my mind. There is a way around it, Ani. Vahin can help you. Dragons have a way to calm the mind,' he offered, releasing a deep sigh when I shook my head.

'We need to fly because I have to be at the fortress by eventide. We lost several soldiers near the old dwarven mines, and the survivors reported a monster in the tunnels. I'll have to investigate as soon as we arrive. Otherwise, we will never find the replacement crystal in time.'

I thought about it for a moment. 'You know, the mines are on the way to the fortress. I can be there by tomorrow and even do the investigation for you. You can't descend to the mines on a dragon; and for me, it would just be another job,' I suggested, but he shook his head.

'No, I've lost ten fully armed warriors there already, and I'm not letting you go by yourself. I promise you won't even have to look down, and Vahin will glide on the updrafts more than usual so that it will feel smoother. He also asks for you to trust him and offers to make one quick attempt so that you can judge for yourself how safe it feels,' Orm said with a gentle smile, but there was an air of finality to his words—the implacable leader having to go down a hard path to get the job done.

'Please, don't force me to use your geas.' He had me again, and I wondered how often that threat would hang over my head.

Like all others, my geas was controlled by the three words uttered in the midst of a delirium caused by a blood-loss-induced spell. That spell, nicknamed *the bloodbath* because of the reddish tears it forced from its victim, also ripped all memory of the ordeal from those compelled to use it. While I didn't remember my own experience, I had witnessed a young psionic mage suffer through the torture of a failed geas spell that turned him into the Broken—a mage unable to access the core of his power, and I still had nightmares about it.

Afterwards, the words are recorded and forever locked in the royal vault with the mage's name on it. The geas shackled a mage completely, making them do whatever they were told by those who knew the words.

Being a crown mage, as those most powerful of us were called, came with prestige and several advantages. But if those envious of us knew the price, few would relinquish their freedom for the power we could wield.

I stared at Orm, knowing he didn't realise the crippling effect his threat had on me. *For him, it's simply a tool to get what he wants,* I thought bitterly.

'If I fall and die, I will haunt you for eternity—both of you.' I pointed my finger towards the dragon, who rumbled, presenting an impressive set of teeth in what I assumed was a smile.

'When are we setting off?'

'In a moment. Stay here, please. I have to ensure all the chosen women are properly secured, that their families are content with the arrangement, and that Zalesie's town officials are satisfied with the ridiculous amount of money we poured into their pockets. Then we will leave.'

Orm headed towards the mayor and his cronies, and I leaned against the dragon's shoulder, unsure of what to do. I was hungover, in casual clothes unsuitable for a journey, and worst of all, I knew as soon as we left the ground, my mind would blank out in sheer panic.

'Ani? Are you all right?' Katja asked, and I jerked in surprise. I was so preoccupied with my thoughts that I hadn't seen her coming.

'Yes, as well as I can be,' I answered with a sigh, and she nodded. 'I heard your conversation. I think everyone did. So I brought something for you, and later, if you wish, I can poison the bastard.'

'What is it?' I asked when she passed me a vial. 'Your morning's best friend. My famous hangover cure. You look like you were drinking all night again,' she said, and I snatched the bottle from her hand.

'You were sent by the gods themselves,' I praised her after downing its contents. 'I'll still lose my mind when we fly, but at least I won't puke on the dragon ... hopefully.' As if on command, the dragon behind me nudged me gently, and I yawned, blinking rapidly as I struggled to keep my eyes open.

'Katja, what did you ... fuck, what was in that ...?' I wondered, sliding to the ground as the world spun around me.

'You were scaring the other girls. It's just a sleeping draught, I promise. You'll be fine,' she said, observing me for a moment before walking away. I vaguely felt Vahin curling around me, his warm scales encircling me protectively while his body rumbled with a growly purr.

Katja's elixirs were potent, and she hadn't even diluted this one from the looks of it. I'd drunk it without a second thought. I was so done for now. If Orm decided to throw me around like a sack of turnips, I wouldn't even be able to curse him, let alone argue.

Of course, it was too late to worry about it now. I was floating away on a cloud of welcome oblivion. Since Orm had proved he could throw me over his shoulder, he could handle my unconscious body during the flight.

'What the fuck is going on here?' The angry voice intruded on the lovely dream I was enjoying, and the rumble in Vahin's body increased in volume.

'What do you mean, she drank something? Who poisoned her? For fuck's sake, unwrap yourself from around her, you big dolt. No, I will not punish her or her friend. Why would you think I'd do that?'

The one-sided conversation was bizarre, but it made me feel warm inside. Vahin cared for me; that was clear. I stroked his scales, feeling him slowly unfold. I almost fell on my face, not realising I'd still been leaning on the dragon, but Orm caught me.

'You are so strong, and I'm your turnip,' I muttered when I felt him brush the hair from my face. His face blurred, transforming into one from the past, and I raised my hand, stroking his cheek.

I'd always preferred Tal with a beard, but the slight roughness of his skin told me he'd shaved. That didn't stop me from caressing him, though. When I slid my finger across his lips, they parted, and still not fully aware, I hooked my finger over his bottom teeth, using them to pull him to me.

The face before me swam into focus, and I grimaced in pain. *'Why* are you so much like Tal? Gods, it hurts to be around you,' I murmured.

Orm's eyes widened, and for a moment, his lips closed on my finger. I smiled. It almost felt like a kiss. He grasped my wrist, tugging my hand away and placing it on my chest. 'Focus, Ani. We need to go,' he said, lifting me into his arms. I felt us moving until I suddenly landed astride Vahin's back.

'There you go, now wrap your arms and legs around me,' he said, my vision filled with the vast expanse of his chest moments before I was pulled in closer. My thoughts were so sluggish that it took me a moment to realise I was facing Orm instead of the head of the dragon, and even as I tried to focus, the position felt unnatural.

'I sat wrong,' I muttered, but Orm pressed my head to his chest. 'No, you sat right. It's this or the basket. I told you I'd look after you. Now relax and hold on to me. You can even fall asleep if you want,' the commander said, wrapping his cloak around us. I frowned when the world disappeared under a dark curtain that smelled of clove oil and musk. The potent scent, masculine and appealing, felt so welcoming as I trembled against him.

'It's all right, just trust me,' he crooned, his cheek pressing to my temple. '*Fuck, she feels so right,*' I heard him mutter, and the barely audible words made me smile again. I rested my head on his chest, focusing on the scent and the powerful arms holding me tight, but most of all, on the slow, steady beating of Orm's heart that soon sent me into an uneasy sleep.

CHAPTER 9

ANNIKA

I don't know how long we'd been flying, but when my eyes fluttered open, I could feel the wind buffeting my back and knew it was far from over.

Whatever Katja had given me had worn off enough for my sluggish thoughts to latch onto that one fact—*I was flying*. I clutched Orm's body, digging my fingernails into whatever part of him I was holding.

The moment I felt Vahin move beneath me, my legs spasmed, squeezing with every ounce of strength I possessed. With my mind screaming incoherently, I couldn't understand why it was so quiet; then my chest started burning, and the panic worsened. I couldn't *breathe*.

'Shhh, Ani, you're safe. I have you. Concentrate on my voice and let yourself trust me. I promise, I'll protect you. Do I really remind you of Tal? He must have been a remarkable man, I'm sure. Intelligent, talented, and I'm guessing incredibly handsome,' Orm said.

The little joke and the amusement in his calm and reassuring voice distracted me, and the tightness slid away. I managed to draw breath, and I tried to convince myself that my sob was a laugh at Orm's joke.

'Yes, he was handsome and remarkable, a true paladin mage—but just because you're both bossy and feel entitled to tell me what to do, doesn't mean you're the same. As for the intelligence, he was at least smart enough not to force me into a year of servitude,' I snapped and felt his deep sigh.

'I didn't force you. I used persuasion to help you make the right decision,' he deadpanned, and I huffed.

'Riiiiight, "*I have the king's geas, and I'm not afraid to use it*" is using "persuasion"?' I argued, and he averted his eyes as he shrugged.

'It worked.'

'Yes, it certainly did. Now you have a mage you can't trust, and I have a collar on my neck that you yank every time I try to express myself. Why didn't you just ask? Why not give me a chance to agree? I'm not stupid. I know what's at stake if the Barrier fails,' I said quietly, but Orm shook his head.

'Stupid, no. But stubborn? Most definitely, yes. Need I remind you that Alaric tried and you wouldn't even give him your name? I've even sent men with invitations and you sent them back barely able to remember their time in Zalesie. We spent three months searching for the conduit mage with a fiery temper, learning how crafty you were at disappearing. You did a good job of covering your tracks. Admit it, Ani. You wouldn't have given me the time of day.'

I couldn't help it; I tensed because I knew he was right. And I felt sorry for those men I had drugged with Katja's draughts, but seeing strangers asking questions and issuing invitations triggered my deepest fears. I was so afraid to be found out and brought back into service that I treated any stranger asking about my magic as a threat.

'I thought they were from the council ...' I attempted to argue, but he looked down at me, shaking his head.

'Yes, and I thought you were a belligerent mage. We've both made mistakes. I'm a dragon rider, schooled and bred for war. I don't take chances. All my adult life, I've been a leader, having to calculate the odds for success and account for our losses. Accosting you during Maiden's Day gave me the best odds for success. I do what I must because we are already losing the war against the Lich King, and he hasn't even breached the Rift. The gods save us if he ever does.'

'I know, but ...'

'No buts, Ani. For hundreds of years, the Barrier has been the only thing protecting the Lowland Kingdoms. We trusted it would last, and we were lazy. Look at what's happening in the south and fae courts. They don't even think they need to man it anymore. I'm fighting a losing battle, and it took only the tiniest of rifts to show us how weak we were against an undying enemy.' Orm's arm tensed, pressing me harder to his body before he exhaled, shaking his head.

'Right now, we are just dealing with Vel demons, but if I'm right, soon even a tainted human or a Moroi could pass. Do you know what would happen to Zalesie if a corrupted Moroi appeared?' I felt the shudder he tried to suppress.

My frown almost became an angry retort, but once again, I knew he was right. Those of the Moroi corrupted by the Lich King's magic, if they broke through the Barrier, would spell the death of everyone they encountered.

'So instead of coming directly to me with a reasonable explanation yourself, you arrived blowing your trumpets, scaring me badly enough that I almost cooked the mayor with aether. Then there's that bloody geas. *Gods!* It makes me feel like a disobedient dog, with you as my owner who keeps yanking my chain.'

'I should have let you cook that prick. I would have, if you hadn't looked so distressed,' he said with amusement in his voice. I thought he would leave things that way, but after a moment, Orm uncovered my face and looked at me.

'I know you find it hard to believe, but I'm an honourable man. I'm not proud of the way I did things, but my first duty is to the people I was entrusted with to protect. I will hold my post to the bitter end, but finding you gave me hope. As long as you work with Alaric, I will provide you with everything you desire and never bring up the geas again.'

There was a ring of truth to his words that I couldn't deny. What caught me off guard was the way he looked at me and the slight smile full of longing that appeared on his lips.

'I can be a good friend Annika, if you only give me a chance. I enjoy talking to you, even if you have this annoying manner of not fulfilling orders and disagreeing with most of what I say.'

'I'm not questioning you, I just don't know if I can be the friend you desire,' I finally said with a sigh. I understood his reasoning. We were both indoctrinated into the roles we'd been born into.

I remembered my sixteenth birthday when my conduit abilities had manifested. One moment, I was just a silly girl celebrating the beginning of her adulthood … The next, I was dragged from my parents' house, tied to a post in the temple of rituals, and bled until the torment of slow death made me recite the oath. No money my father offered could buy my freedom, and eventually, my parents stopped trying.

We continued the flight in silence, but I felt the hitch in Orm's breath several times as if he were trying to talk to me once more.

'Just say it, I don't bite,' I snapped, finally.

'Why did you stay in Zalesie all this time? Mages like you are much sought after. You could've gone anywhere, could have lived in a majestic fae city or even the steppes of the orcish kingdom and have had Anchors from amongst the best of your peers instead of haunting the mountains like some ghost.'

'Yes, I'm sure mages there would gladly have adopted a conduit who could enhance their own power to limitless levels. Maybe I would have even had a month or two before someone tried to force the Anchor bond. What do you know about Anchoring, Ormond?' I asked, and he had the grace to blush under my scrutiny as I continued.

'Anchoring requires taking a piece of your spirit and embedding it into another person's soul, taking theirs in return. It binds you in a way that can perhaps only compare to the bond you have with Vahin; but, contrary to the way you tethered your dragon, it requires skin-to-skin contact. The easiest and least painful way is through intimacy. You can ask healers for more of an explanation, but if you are in the throes of passion, the pain of splitting your spirit and having another joined to yours is ... well, more acceptable once you have accepted them into your body.'

He looked at me sharply, and I laughed at his baffled expression.

'That sounds ... inconvenient. What if you don't want to do it that way?'

'Don't be such a prude. It is still possible, but from what I've heard, all conduit mages prefer to have their Anchor *pierce* them in more than one way,' I teased with a chuckle.

When he frowned, I added, 'If one side, or both, don't fully accept the exchange, it can kill them, and if you can't accept your chosen one's touch, how can you accept their soul? To take an Anchor is to connect with another person on such an intimate level that there is no room for doubt. You bare yourself, giving them all you are for a piece of their soul in exchange.'

'So the Anchor must first be a lover?' he asked, and I shrugged. 'Or be enthralled, or under a spell, possibly even just a person you trust and accept completely. In the past, some mages would tie themselves to anyone who offered the power they craved, but it never ended well. In dire circumstances, I could do that. To make a deal, shackle myself to a stranger, and hope we survived the exchange.'

My sigh was deep and filled with an emotion I didn't want to share.

'I don't crave power, and I refuse to bond to ... That's why I ran from the capital. My Anchor gets not only my magic but also my heart,' I said, turning to blink away tears; my heart was gone, buried beneath the mountain.

'I think I understand now,' he said, and I sniffed, rubbing my nose.

'I doubt it. All you need to know is that I don't want you in my bed because years ago I decided that I would walk the rest of this life alone; and I won't let anything—not even my magic—force me to change that.'

113

'You didn't answer as to why you chose Zalesie,' he said after a moment, and I shook my head. 'That's all I'm willing to share. The rest is my secret to keep,' I said, and I felt the arms holding me tense again.

I felt surprisingly good in Orm's company, and I was spilling my guts despite not knowing him well enough to bare my soul.

Wait ...

Something was not quite right about this inner calm and the trust I showed Ormond.

'Why aren't I freaking out?' I asked after a moment of silence. I'd forgotten I was sitting on a dragon's back at high altitude without screaming my lungs out thanks to our heartfelt discussion.

'It's Vahin. That's why you're not riding in the basket. He assured me you would be fine on his back. Dragons can project their thoughts and feelings onto people they feel connected to, and right now, he wants you to feel happy and to trust he can keep you safe while you enjoy the ride. If you want, you can turn around and see the view. It is rare to see so many dragons flying in formation.'

Orm's words explained my sudden trust in not only the dragon, but also his rider. The mind trick may have forced out a few unnecessary confessions, but I supposed it was a small price to pay for not losing my mind.

After a moment's hesitation, I peeked out. 'All right, I'll try,' I said, shuffling my rear, twisting and turning until I was facing towards Vahin's head, thankful for Orm's hands steadying me with a vice-like grip.

'You have the spirit of a warrior, Ani. It is difficult to conquer such fears, even with Vahin's help,' he said, and I turned to look at him.

'Spirit of a warrior? You think that because I can look down without passing out thanks to a dragon's help, I am a warrior? I'm a battle mage. Not because I can sit on the top of a flying lizard, but because I fought and bled and *earned* my position,' I said, daring to look down.

The view took my breath away.

We were at the rear of the formation, a sea-green dragon leading the way. Four dragons on each side protected more of the magnificent beasts, each with a basket attached, likely containing petrified women. With the sun lowering below the horizon, its rays reflecting on dragon scales, it felt like we were flying behind a rainbow.

'Point taken. I meant no offence. I'm simply impressed that you're willing to face your fears,' Orm said, resting his chin on my shoulder as he pointed to the massive cliff on our left. 'We should be home shortly. It took longer than normal because Vahin used updrafts to smooth the flight rather than using his muscles since we didn't want to cause you more distress than was necessary.'

'How are you so calm, even when I snap at you?' I asked. Orm was like the heart of a mountain: unmovable, no matter how hard I tried to shake him.

'My anger was beaten out of me a very long time ago,' he murmured.

I frowned. 'What do you mean?'

'The reason only males of certain bloodlines can bond with dragons is the wild magic they carry. Some say the first riders were the descendants of dragons. Others say that they were dragons themselves who remained in human form. Nobody knows now, and the dragons haven't confirmed either theory. All we know is that around the age of eight, a kernel of wild magic manifests in some of our male children. It causes violent outbursts, destructive behaviour, and possessiveness beyond measure,' he explained.

'Mine was discovered after I almost killed my cousin when I bashed his head against the castle wall because he had played with my wooden sword. If not controlled early on, the magic turns us into feral and dangerous beasts; and it can only be tamed by rigorous training and bonding with a dragon.'

I hadn't known that.

'When my magic manifested, my parents brought me to the Cave of Binding. They left me there, where I wailed—alone, with no food or bed—until Vahin heard my cry. I climbed on his back, and he took me to the training grounds. I spent a year there—living in a nightmare where the smallest sign of disobedience or aggression was punished with a whip, starvation, and isolation until I learned to control my feelings.' Orm spoke without a hint of emotion as I stared at him in pure horror.

'Gods, who would do that to a child? Is that why all riders are so calm and polite ...?' I whispered, and he nodded.

'The day I lose my temper could be the day I kill us all,' he said, his chin returning to my shoulder. 'But you don't have to worry about that because I know a certain mage won't goad me just to see how long it takes before I snap,' he said, and I rolled my eyes.

'And you're telling me this *now*? I can be quite vexing even to the people I like, and you ... you're not as bad as I thought you'd be, but you should let people know. Maybe wear a sign on your armour with "Don't anger me," or "I bite," or something.' I chuckled.

His lips quirked into a coy smile. 'No, I'm not bad at all, and I don't bite unless I'm asked ... and even then, I prefer to nibble.'

I liked men who could appreciate my humour, and Orm, stern and domineering as he was, was also honest and straightforward. I could sense the mischief in those dark green eyes. As long as we weren't fighting, I, too, enjoyed his company.

'You are also not what I'd expected,' he offered. I swatted his forearm with another chuckle as he looked down at me. 'Do you like beasts that bite ... like dragons?' he asked, and the innuendo in his voice made me turn my head to avoid his eyes. As I did, a dark cloud on the horizon grabbed my attention.

'What is that? Why is it drifting against the wind?' I asked, pointing at the thing, gasping when Orm's body stiffened.

'Fuck. Spectrae,' he muttered before shouting a command to his riders. 'Brace for evasive manoeuvres. Fire on the perimeter. Spectrae are coming!'

CHAPTER 10

ORMOND

'Spectrae? That's not possible! Spectrae can't cross the Barrier. No greater Vella can. Are they ... oh gods, are they *swarming*?'

Ani's voice shook with fear and disbelief.

My reaction, however, was filled with the anger I'd assured Ani was under firm control. It didn't help that she'd pointed out something genuinely terrifying.

How the fuck could a swarm of spectrae have crossed the Barrier without being noticed?

I knew the Rift was growing, the keystone's magic fading little by little, and we'd encountered more Vel demons sneaking through. It wasn't even a matter of numbers now, though; their magic was stronger, too.

Ghouls and strigae were physical beings almost mindless in their hunger with little magic of their own, and were surprisingly adept at slipping through the Barrier. Spectrae, however, didn't have physical bodies. The foul magic that fuelled them had always been successfully blocked by the Barrier ... until now.

Does this mean that Alaric can join our patrols? I wondered, dreading a repeat of our first experience.

We weren't equipped for this kind of attack. Our unit was carrying civilians with a small protection detail, so we couldn't perform the evasive manoeuvres required to escape a spectrae swarm. The hard truth was that people, and likely dragons, were going to die today—and there was almost nothing I could do about it.

Still, if there was someone I could save, it would be the mage who'd give us a chance to restore the Barrier and prevent full-scale war with the undead.

'It's not the best time to discover they can cross to our side. We haven't had a single spectra in the kingdom since the end of the war. We've only ever fought them during patrols on the other side, but it appears our time of peace is over.'

'The baskets?' she asked, and her gaze instantly followed a crimson dragon, which I'd learned earlier sheltered the female who had drugged her.

Can I tell Ani the truth and risk her panicking?

The wind wrapped Ani's braid across her neck with a powerful gust. I took the silken chestnut hair in my hand, unwrapping it gently, and was surprised to find that she didn't pull away from my touch.

She trusts me, I realised.

It was time I earned that trust, especially since she was a trained mage who might know how to help with our situation. 'Most of us will probably die here. This swarm, its size, is unlike anything I've ever seen. It will be an impossible fight. If you have any spells that can help, I will be eternally grateful. And if we survive, I swear to treat you like royalty and kiss the ground you walk on.'

I clenched my teeth as I watched my squadron move into formation, assessing the size of the swarm as they approached. I'd faced smaller groups during patrols beyond the Barrier.

We patrolled regularly, even more so in the last three months, both to train the riders and to monitor events in the Barren Lands. When we'd encountered the spectrae, I'd taken the opportunity to train the men in the ancient technique used to handle the creatures I'd found in an old manuscript from the Necromancer's War.

It was simple, yet deadly.

Vahin took on the role of bait, luring the spectrae to feed off his life force. At the same time, the other riders would use their dragons to destroy the monsters. Still, looking at the swarm before me, I doubted if even Vahin could withstand their devastating touch.

The spectrae were the Lich King's answer to dragon riders.

They were a malicious creation formed using foul magic that ripped out the spirits of living creatures, using their suffering to fuel a ravenous hunger. Mad souls locked between life and death forever cursed to swim in the streams of the aether, they were incomplete and therefore unable to cross the Veil to eternal peace.

Their semitranslucent bodies had no solid shape and drifted like clouds until they found a host to feed on. They fed in order to regain corporeal form and finally find peace, but there was nothing, no amount of life essence, that could make them fully whole again.

There was only one way to destroy the spectrae, and it was only possible while they fed. Once the spectrae had stolen enough life essence, they would become solid enough to be vulnerable to spells, enchanted weapons, and dragon fire.

Any living being could be a victim, but a dragon's life force drew them like moths to a flame. If not eliminated, after the malicious spirits had tethered themselves to a dragon, they would siphon its essence until the dragon fell from the sky. That's why Vahin was always the bait. He was the strongest dragon at Varta Fortress, but I always felt the echo of his torment as the spectrae latched onto him.

I looked around at my comrades-in-arms, seeing their trust in my leadership whilst knowing I was about to send many of them to their deaths. This battle would not be about victory but about limiting our losses and keeping one person safe.

I sent Vahin a mental command to hold back and I heard the question in his mind, but what stunned me were the actual words that came from him.

Why, Orm? I can hold on the longest.

I knew dragons could communicate via *thoughtspeech,* a manifestation of wild magic that allowed them to speak into their rider's mind if they were close enough. I'd read in the old volumes that they could even talk naturally, although their words always had modulated hissing sounds. Vahin had never spoken to me before, though—only used feelings and images to communicate. Having my dragon speak in my mind had startled me, and it took a while to compose myself enough to answer.

Because of Ani. Alaric is confident her magic is the key to restoring the Barrier. I can't risk her life if there's a chance to fix it, I answered. Our bond deepened, revealing Vahin's disapproval of my reasoning, but he understood. I didn't mind risking our lives, but not when he carried such precious cargo.

I will have to withdraw my protection of her mind to focus on the others. She will be terrified, Vahin said.

Despite the upcoming battle, I marvelled at his willingness to talk and hoped it would continue. Since meeting Ani, Vahin had clearly changed, seeming more and more aware and interested in the world around him every day. He had even begun seeking my company instead of soaring the skies, descending only when called. And now, with a voice of his own, he felt more like a fellow warrior than the beast I rode.

'Stay back,' I told him, this time aloud for Ani's benefit.

She wheezed in a breath when the dragon rumbled in response, and I felt a tremor run through her body. That was how I knew Vahin had stopped projecting his calming aura. I tightened my grip around her waist, feeling sorry but impressed that she was holding her own.

'How can I help?' she gasped, leaning forward as the swarm of spectrae came close enough to see each individual enemy floating on invisible winds. 'You can't, unless you can somehow make them physical before they touch the dragons.'

I gestured to my second-in-command to take on the role of bait. Tomma's dragon wasn't as strong as Vahin, and I prayed to all the gods that he could withstand the assault while we attacked the spectrae.

Tomma saluted, and his dragon roared in challenge, surging forward to meet the threat. But my heart stuttered when I saw the lieutenant's face; there was no hope in his eyes, only the determination of a man ready to die to keep others safe.

I knew the pair would fight to the bitter end to buy us time to destroy the enemy. If they survived, I would do everything I could to reward them appropriately, though looking at the size of the swarm, I knew our chances were slim.

'Before you ask, I wish we could outfly them, but we can't. The spectrae will follow the dragons to the fortress, and that would endanger everyone there. I'm so sorry, Ani. I should have let you travel by horse.' I inhaled her herbal scent, knowing I'd likely have to sacrifice my men for her today.

'When the spectrae attack, Tomma and Rahsul will draw them in, flying a figure of eight to lure them all. When they latch onto his dragon ... It won't be pleasant to watch, but if he occupies them long enough, the squadron might be able to incinerate them while they feed. That means we'll have to fly fast and hard in order to dodge any stray spectrae and use dragon fire to destroy those attached to Rahsul. Our only chance lies in disrupting the swarm's connection. If we kill enough of them, they may retreat,' I finished, feeling Ani's breath quicken.

'I know, don't worry about me. But the rider ... Orm, he'll die. I've read about it. The bait dragon almost always dies.'

'We don't have a choice. We have no other means of fighting them. Our only weapon is dragon fire and sacrifice.' I wrapped one arm around Ani and placed the other on Vahin's neck.

'Brace yourself. We're going in,' I shouted, seeing the swarm cloud split apart at the edges to release a single spectra that drifted towards the squadron. At the same time, the rest headed towards the single, weaving dragon.

I grimaced as Vahin beat his wings forcefully, surging towards the periphery of the formation. The howling wind in my ears couldn't drown out the agonised screams. The spectrae attack had begun and crackling red aether pierced the dragon's midriff, pulsing in time with his steady heartbeat.

The sickening sight shone against the darkening sky, its ghastly crimson hue so reminiscent of blood that I almost looked away. The parasites feasting on Rahsul became more solid with each bright pulse, and I couldn't help but snarl in disgust and hatred. When their forms were solid enough to block the last rays of the sun, I commanded the squadron to attack.

'Now!'

Vahin roared, evading a stray tendril and tilting to the left as intense heat erupted from his mouth, bathing Rahsul's scales in coruscating flame. Muffled cries cut through the sounds of battle as the terrified women in their baskets panicked. Unlike them, Ani gasped but didn't scream. Her heart hammered so hard I could feel it through our clothing as she bent forward to flatten herself against Vahin's back while holding the saddle's pommel with trembling hands.

We almost collided with the squadron's youngest rider as he slipped out of formation, his dragon succumbing to an aetheric tether. The frantic beast was trying to burn itself free while his rider leaned down to stop a panicking woman from jumping from her basket. I directed Vahin to attack the spectrae to release them from the choking strands.

After aiding the rider, I joined the others circling Tomma, burning our enemies with unyielding determination—but there were too many, and they were relentless. Despite moving in a well-executed formation, more and more dragons broke off into solitary battles, fighting two or three enemies, leaving them unable to assist in the main attack.

Vahin manoeuvred with the agility of a swallow, but I could sense his agitation and guilt, especially when Tomma's dragon shuddered, dropping several metres.

'They are dying, Orm.'

Ani's voice sounded so strange, flat and devoid of emotion. The woman who'd been plastered against the dragon's back, whimpering during the rapid, wrenching manoeuvres now sat up as if she had a steel rod fused to her spine.

'We're all going to die,' I snapped, unable to control my frustration because I knew we were losing.

'I won't let it happen again. Ask Vahin if he'll let me Anchor him,' she said, and I frowned, unsure what she meant, but before she had finished speaking, an ecstatic roar made me shake my head.

Yes! Tell her I said yes!

'He said yes, but now's not the time ...' I started, the words dying in my throat when she turned to look at me.

'Fly forward and take Tomma's place,' she demanded.

Vahin instantly changed direction without my command. When I tried to protest, Ani placed her hand on my chest. 'You don't have enough dragons to fight them all, but you have me. I won't let good men die. Not again. It is time for you to see what I'm capable of.'

It wasn't the frightened request of a soldier or a lowly town mage. No, death and vengeance stared into my soul, and if I'd been able to retreat from its scrutiny, I would have.

Instead, I thanked the gods her ire was aimed towards my enemies and watched Ani continue.

I will give you the stars you pray upon if you can save us now, I thought, watching as Ani leant forward and placed her hands on the warm scales of Vahin's neck.

I barely knew her, but the wild magic, the darkness I caged in the depths of my soul, awakened, stirring in response to her courage and flooding me with the most unexpected feeling of desire. I wanted to kiss her—*so fucking much.*

As my hands tightened around her waist, Ani murmured words I couldn't understand, and the battle was drowned out by Vahin's roar. I felt my dragon's shock and pain as a power beyond any I'd ever witnessed burned into his mind, forging a magical tether.

Through my own connection with Vahin, I could see and feel each moment, wishing I could help, as magic tore into his spirit and then withdrew, taking a shard of his soul and leaving a piece of hers behind. Ani gasped when they fused, but something felt wrong—the process was causing them both immense pain.

Vahin's body quaked beneath me, short gasps of pain broken by eruptions of fire, and I could feel his confusion even as he allowed forces I couldn't understand mould him in new and frightening ways. All the while, Ani's body grew hotter with each passing moment until it felt as if I was holding a burning torch against my chest.

'Ra'shina'ta Vahin.'[1]

Ani's voice thundered with a pulse of power that hit me like a hurricane. As if on command, the spectrae stopped, and I watched in disbelief as even those connected to the furthest dragons withdrew their tendrils, rushing towards Vahin as if pulled on an invisible leash.

Tomma's eyes reflected shocked relief while the other riders chased the oblivious, half-solid forms of the spectrae, burning several to ash. I had never heard or read about anything like this. All of my instincts told me to fight, to

---

1. *I give you Vahin.*

force Vahin into evasive manoeuvres. But Ani had asked for my trust—so I held back, even as dozens of monsters swept towards us.

I could feel the power surrounding us, crushing the air from my lungs. Could see the distorted faces of the spectrae coming for us, their endless suffering dragging tears from my eyes. Pity mixed with fear as I watched on, helpless, wishing I could erase the existence of the man responsible for this abomination. The Lich King. The one who broke fate's contract to prolong his life and his reign, destroying everything he touched.

Vahin jerked, roaring in pain when the first tendril pierced his chest, then another and another. It looked like hundreds of spears were peppering his armoured body, the assault coming from so many directions that I couldn't follow them all. I knew what to expect, had braced for the pain from our shared connection. This time, however, it wasn't a dozen but *hundreds* of tendrils latching onto the dragon's vital force. Our bond was wide open, and as much as I tried to ease his suffering, to share it, I felt my strength melt away under the relentless assault.

'Ani ...' I croaked through a suddenly dry throat, but the woman in front of me was rigid and unresponsive. Doubt crept in, but it was too late for that now.

Thunder crashed, deafening everyone, while unnatural, crimson lightning blinded us, burning the air left in our lungs and the skin of our bodies. I clenched my teeth, trying to hold Ani in place as I fought overwhelming weakness.

Fuck, we're going to die.

Vahin's heart stuttered. Ani took one hand from the dragon's skin, raising it in the air. Somehow, miraculously, I heard her speak, her voice as gentle as a summer breeze, whispering a single word that set the world ablaze.

'Išãtum. [2]

---

2. *Burn.*

Though I didn't recognise the word, my body did: it was etched into every fibre of my existence. A living flame was unleashed upon the undead. A wave of cleansing fire erupted from the surrounding air, consuming everything it touched. I looked down, expecting to see my body turned to ash, but the fire flowed past, warming my skin as it connected with the spectrae's tendrils. The flames poured into the monsters' ethereal bodies, incinerating them almost instantly.

I could feel Vahin's pain ease with each passing moment, but his concern for Ani rose as she swayed. *Tell her to let me in. She can't control the fire without me. Tell her, Orm!* He shouted in my mind as Ani's breathing became so shallow I could barely feel it. I reacted to Vahin's fear and tried to call her back from wherever she had gone.

Vahin's panic grew as the skies cleared. The last of the spectrae disappeared into nothingness, revealing the bruised light of dusk as I held the unmoving mage in my arms. Then everything stopped, and the silence that replaced the thunder was just as deafening.

It was as if the attack had never happened. I still had an entire unit; maybe one slightly dishevelled, but I hadn't lost a single man, dragon, or passenger. Even if Ani wasn't able to seal the Rift, she was a godsent miracle; the first mage since the Necromancer's War who had fought the spectrae on dragon back.

Orm, hold her.

Vahin's voice rumbled in my head, and I instinctively tightened my grasp on Ani's waist. She fell back to my chest bonelessly, the ending of the magical spectacle seeming to have cut all the strings that had held her up.

'Ani?' I asked, gently touching her cheek. She was still burning up, the heat radiating through her clothes, but the hands resting on my thighs were ice cold. 'Ani, please talk to me. What is going on, Nivale?'

The word had slipped out so naturally, the nickname fitting the woman I held so close. The *nivale* was a flower that only grew on the highest mountain peaks next to the unblemished snow. They had iridescent, white petals streaked with veins that shone like fire, their leaves prickly and hard to grasp, with tiny needles that irritated the skin of whoever touched them.

Despite their rarity—or possibly because of it—the plant was highly sought after. Sometime in the past, it was discovered that the roots, bitter and difficult to swallow, could lessen the pain of those beyond salvation, easing their steps into the afterlife.

I felt the hope that Ani had given me twisting, becoming something I couldn't describe, but the prickly miracle before me was silent and pale. Only her shallow breath and burning body reassured me that she was still alive, and I knew I couldn't lose her.

'Fly to the stronghold as fast as you can!' I ordered the riders, and we surged forward. The fortress wasn't far, but the woman in my arms didn't look like she had much time left ... and I had no idea what to do.

She is fading from my mind, Orm. Talk to her. Give her something to hold on to. She still can hear you.

'Can *you* hear her? Can you talk to her?' I asked because as soon as he had mentioned her presence in his mind, I had thought about the dragon rider connection.

No. If I could, I wouldn't ask you to do so. The Anchor bond is not complete; something is preventing the connection from solidifying—Orm, she channelled dragon flame. I accepted her. I can feel her in my soul, but she didn't take mine. She will die if the bond fails.

The flames that played under her skin, creating a darkening pattern, and the tone of panic in his voice set me on edge. 'Ani, please open your eyes. Vahin needs you to let him in. Please, allow him to help,' I begged, noticing her eyelids flicker at the sound of my voice.

'You did it, you stubborn woman. You saved us all. Your friends are safe, so you can't give up now. We are so close to the fortress. Just hold on. Don't you dare leave me with a life debt I cannot repay. Don't you dare leave me ... Ani, please.'

I knew I was talking nonsense.

I searched her face for a hint of consciousness while the wild power inside me raged, thrashing with fear and anger in its cage. I wanted to protect her, but I couldn't, and it drove me *insane*. I was going to lose her; and my sanity—because I had never been so close to breaking, to going berserk. All because of her. 'Fuck,' I groaned, my arms pressing her hard to my chest. I had *failed*—failed to protect her.

I've failed my woman.

Vahin rumbled his approval at the term, and I felt his mental touch lessening the strain I was under.

Yes, ours. Keep talking. She likes the sound of your voice.

So I did.

'You know, we have an impressive library in the stronghold. The place is so old that several archimages have frequented it, meeting with the dragons before they'd enter the Barren Lands. Some say the original spell that created the Barrier is hidden somewhere within those dusty tomes. I will show it to you; or if you don't like books, I will take you to the summer falls. The lake is too cold to swim in, but it is so beautiful there. I'll show you my favourite place—a mountain peak that shimmers with mountain flowers. I will never force you again. I'll burn the geas. Just *live* for me, *please*.'

Ani's eyes flickered open, and I felt her hand tighten over mine.

'Promise?' she whispered, and I brushed away the hair that had been plastered to her forehead by the wind of our passing.

'I promise, Nivale. Just don't die on me and I promise I'll set you free,' I affirmed. I continued to tell her all about the fortress and the people who lived there while she held my hand as if her life depended on it. And maybe it did, because her skin kept growing hotter despite the buffeting wind.

I sighed with relief when, after what felt like an endless flight, I saw the sturdy walls of my home. Ani lost consciousness a few moments later, drifting into a delirium despite my best effort to keep her awake. I felt Vahin's strength fading fast alongside hers, as if the broken connection was draining them both.

'Go to the lair and feed, old friend. If I have to worry about you, too, I won't be of any use to Ani. I'll send extra provisions when we land,' I said as we passed over the exterior wall, but Vahin rumbled in disagreement.

I won't leave her.

'I promise to stay with her. You can sense her through me, but you need to heal as well. You just withstood an attack that should have killed you. Alaric will help her. He has the best chance of understanding what is happening.'

He is not a dragon, and he knows nothing of dragon fire.

'But he *is* a mage and knows about Anchoring. He's studied Ani and conduit mages every day since he discovered her gift. Why, when you finally get your voice, do you have to argue with me?' I asked with growing irritation. We still had to get Ani into the castle, and her breath had started coming in laboured pants.

She is not the only one who is changing because of the Anchor bond, and I don't want to lose this feeling again ... the awareness she awakened. I was asleep for too long; I have lost centuries, drifting in the streams of time. Fix it, Orm. Make sure she knows she won't lose her Anchor again. I'll fight for her. Tell her I didn't abandon her, he said, landing heavily on the grass.

'I will, and Alaric will find a way to connect you.' Vahin nodded, looking at me with sadness in his intense blue eyes.

He must. Otherwise, we will both die.

CHAPTER 11

ALARIC

'Hrae! What is *taking them so long*? They should be here by now.'

The impatience in my voice echoed through the empty library, mocking the calm I'd hoped to gain in the quiet chamber. The snarl I aimed at the mocking sound left me feeling childish. Orm had been gone for three long days, and despite trying to complete my research on the conduit mage, I'd spent the entire time pacing the library like a caged beast.

The squadron, with its precious cargo, had been due back hours ago, and the feeling of dread I'd had since luncheon refused to give me a moment's peace.

A sudden surge of magic so powerful it made the sky turn crimson left me gaping. The silver marks responded, burning themselves deeper into my body. The moment I could breathe again, I rushed to the overfull shelves, dragging tome after dusty tome down, desperately seeking some insight into the phenomenon.

What the hell just happened? I wondered, still pacing between the shelves, worrying that something terrible had ruined all my plans. As I caught sight of my reflection in a darkened window, I stopped, taking the time to smooth away the frown marring my features.

After glancing at the finery I'd donned to impress the conduit mage, I brushed away an imagined speck of dust. My black damask outfit was embroidered with intricate silver patterns, most especially around the collar and sleeves. They complimented the simple silver earrings that accented my sharp, pointed ears, fully uncovered since I'd braided my hair.

Orm had likely told her I was dark fae, and if I couldn't hide the fact, I wanted to show it off. During our brief meeting, she had given me the impression of a woman who refused to back down from danger, and I wanted to show her just how dangerous I was.

Annika Diavellar had dismissed me when I had tried to charm her, and I still felt the sting of failure. But from the information I'd gathered concerning her past, the mage respected strength and cherished intelligence. Both of her Anchors had been assertive men with potent magic, and only Annika had considered them kindhearted.

The roar of landing dragons was a heavenly melody—the sound of slamming doors and the heavy panting of the messenger who arrived shortly after that, however, felt like someone had thrown iced water down my spine.

'M-my lord ... The commander ... requests your presence in his quarters immediately,' the messenger stuttered, out of breath, and I frowned.

His choice of words was bizarre. *Why in Orm's quarters?* I mused. *This has to be related to that aether storm still reverberating within my chest. Dark Mother, protect them.* Pressure built in my chest, and the worry that my friend—or the mage—were injured nearly overwhelmed me.

We had healers here; mostly low-class or non-mage, suitable for the fortress. They were necessary for both the garrison and the town, and I was only called in the direst circumstances.

'Come with me and tell me what happened.' The menace in my voice had the messenger backing away as I rushed towards the door.

'The commander brought in an unconscious woman. There was an attack on the journey here, and her ... She didn't look good.'

'*What?* Get out of my way,' I snarled before bolting for Orm's private quarters.

She can't die, not now. I can't be trapped in this torment forever.

Jumping two stairs at a time, the images racing through my mind chased all rational thoughts from my head. I'd searched for centuries for this chance, and I'd be damned if I let her die now that she was within my grasp. I didn't even slow down as I reached my friend's chambers, smashing the door open with a pulse of magic, the hard rock wall chipping from the impact.

Orm's rooms looked the same as usual—a warrior's lair with unpainted stone walls and large stained glass windows overlooking the mountain ridge. The place revealed the personality of its owner. Soft woven rugs covered the floor, and animal pelts on the walls and furniture highlighted the ancient weapons placed at strategic points throughout the room. The space was lit by candles that created more shadow than light, with an antlered chandelier hanging in front of the massive bed.

None of those details escaped my notice, even as my attention focused on the fevered, thrashing woman that Orm was attempting to hold down as gently as possible. His face was stricken with such worry and helplessness that it hollowed his cheeks and tightened his lips.

'Help her! I don't know what to do. She saved me. She saved us all, but something happened between her and Vahin ... he's in pain, and she is burning from the inside out. I can feel it through the bond. If she dies, I don't know what will happen to him.'

I had never seen him so close to losing control. His voice was roughened and raw while a yellow glimmer lit his eyes from within. Then came the realisation. Orm wasn't asking for my help; he was commanding it, and it was an order I couldn't refuse. My friend didn't even look at me, his attention solely focused on Annika's face. That in itself told me that whatever had happened on the journey was enough to shatter the stoic commander's composure.

'Move aside so I can examine her and tell me exactly what happened. This was supposed to be a straightforward Choosing.'

'Nothing is straightforward when it comes to this woman. We were wrong about her, so fucking wrong. She *saved me*, even after I threatened her with the fucking geas.' He snorted a joyless laugh. 'She called me a bastard, rattling her chain. And fuck, she was right—but what else could I do?' He didn't move. Instead, his arms wrapped tighter around Ani's body.

'Orm, I need to examine her ...' I wondered whether this would be the moment I saw his walls crumble. He looked at me as if my calm offended him.

'You don't understand. Why didn't you tell me she could bond with a dragon? When the spectrae swarmed us, she did something that burned them all. The entire swarm died when she took Vahin's flames and ... *fuck*, it was amazing.' He threw his head back and laughed. 'I witnessed a fucking miracle today, sitting there like a damn idiot as she did this to herself ... and now she's dying.'

'She Anchored Vahin? Wait—spectrae attack? That's impos ... Dragon magic is raw and primal. It can't be Anchored,' I stuttered, utterly confused as I placed two fingers on her wrist. '*Hrae!*' I hissed, pulling my hand away before my skin could blister to cast a barrier spell on my body.

Her skin was burning hot, her pulse was so erratic that I knew she was burning alive. The magic ... the aether surrounding her sparked, hissing with power—the chaotic, destructive, all-consuming power of dragon fire. I'd never seen anything like it, and I would need to know more before even attempting to add my own magic to the mix. With no other ideas, I opted for the simplest of methods to help her.

'I'll open the windows. We need to undress her and cool her down. Hopefully, that will buy us enough time for me to think of a solution.'

'I will call for the women,' he said, but as soon as Orm moved, I grasped his hand, pointing to the blackening fabric of the bedding. 'Her power is out of control. I can protect myself to a certain degree, and your bond with

Vahin protects you from dragon fire, but any maids or servants will burn if they touch her skin. This isn't the time for false modesty, Orm. Do it, now!' I commanded, and his eyes narrowed.

'It's not about modesty. My touch ... Ani's magic wraps around me whenever I touch her bare skin. Or at least it did. I can't feel it anymore. She didn't want this, and I promised ...'

'What are you talking about? Did she try to Anchor you?'

'I don't know, but she didn't want me to touch her.'

'Orm, focus! Do you think she'll suddenly wake up and think you're trying to fuck a half dead furnace just to Anchor her? Trust me and just do as I say, or I'll do it for you,' I snapped, too concerned about the woman to watch my words. If Orm still refused, I would do it and hope that my protection spell would be strong enough to withstand the full force of Vahin's flames.

'*Watch your tongue*, fae. She saved my life, and you will talk about her with *respect*,' Orm shocked me with the yellowish glint of wild magic in his eyes and the threatening tone of his voice.

'Then do what I told you to do, and we can both meekly apologise later. I want her to live. *That's* my priority, not worrying about fancy words,' I answered harshly because Orm's words stung, but I couldn't allow them to faze me.

His muscles tensed, but he gently sat her up, leaning her against his chest before he undressed her. A brief sob shook her body when he reached for her blouse, and Ani threw her hands around his neck, pulling him into a tight embrace.

'Talmund, how did you survive? I thought I'd lost you, I thought I'd lost you both ...' she mumbled, resting her forehead against his neck. I saw Orm stiffen, his hands pausing. I cursed quietly as her magic became even more unstable with the voicing of those words.

'She said I reminded her of her Anchor,' he told me, uneasiness in his voice. 'I've never tried to ...' I felt how weak and thready her pulse was. I turned towards the door and shouted for buckets of ice-cold water and towels.

'I know, but we can use that. Calm her down. Be this Talmund if you must.'

Orm seemed torn. I knew deceiving her went against what he considered honourable, even if he was doing it for a good reason, but I felt no remorse. The entire castle could burn if we didn't get this under control before the dragon fire destroyed everything in its path.

As the servants dropped off water and ice, Orm finally peeled the last layer of clothing from of her body, exposing her delicate skin that was lit from within by the strangely dancing flames. She was filled with fire, and for the first time since I'd walked into this hell, I realised it might not be possible to save her.

'Vahin said she rejected his Anchor,' Orm commented, and my gaze slid to above her left breast, where conduit mages wore the symbol of their bonds. It was the physical manifestation of the tether, the mage's interpretation of the magic. She had one, but it looked nothing like a dragon. 'She still wears the marks of her dead lovers,' I said, grinding my teeth.

What kind of will or love could have kept their magic tethered to her body after they had died? What depth of grief did she harbour to cause it? I didn't have an answer, but it was clear why she had rejected Vahin's spirit.

Those symbols should have disappeared when the magic that had created them ceased to exist. Yet the shield, wrapped in healing blue ivy, was still there, sitting firmly over her heart. The flames were concentrated there, the faint shape of a dragon blazing from inside—seeking a way out, fighting to overcome the current symbols, and failing.

'She will die if the ritual isn't completed,' I said, placing a wet, cold towel over her chest and abdomen. The cold water hissed, sizzling on her skin. When I added ice over it, Annika cried out in pain, reaching for Orm. He caught her hand, soothing her and murmuring sweet nonsense. When she calmed, he looked at me quietly for a moment before reaching for a dagger with cold, grim determination.

'Would cutting out the marks help?' He held the knife ready, and I looked at him in horror. 'No, this is just her mind's manifestation of her bond. We have to cut the attachment to her lovers, her memories, not her skin.'

I was out of my depth. I'd healed my fair share of patients, but the woman burning on Orm's bed had Anchored a dragon and was wielding its flame while still being tethered to the spirits of her dead lovers.

Her attachment was almost unbreakable, and deep within my heart, I ached with envy. I'd begged, prayed and cursed my mother in order to remove the marks tying me to my family and here was someone who had defied death to hold those she loved near to her heart. Still, I knew that for Ani to survive, I had to break that bond.

'You are really not going to like this ... We have to use the woman's delusion against her. You need to keep pretending to be Talmund and convince her to accept Vahin's mark.'

'I'm sure I look nothing like him,' he answered. 'I know, but Annika is lost to delirium and only sees *him*, not you. The university report said that he was a paladin mage, forceful but fair, with his own code of honour. Do you see how she could have made the connection?'

'Yes, but if I do this, how will she ever trust me again?' Orm gave me a grim look and positioned himself behind Ani, cradling her head when it lolled to the side before brushing wet strands of hair from her eyes. She moaned painfully, cuddling her cheek to his large palm, and his face softened.

'Annika, you have to live. How can I fulfil my promise if you go and die on me? I thought you were too stubborn to give in to death.' I watched as Orm weaved strength, tenderness, and a teasing tone into those words, and I realised that in the short time he'd been with the mage, he'd grown to care for her.

Without prompting, my friend leaned down and softly pressed his forehead against Ani's, his grip tightening when her body shuddered. Vahin's pained roar shook the windows until she quietened, and as the mage's eyes opened, a delicate smile blossomed on her lips. I don't know what she saw, but hope glowed in the depths of her eyes as she gazed up at Orm.

That was my cue to act, and I began creating a sigil with the swirling aether. I placed my hand on her midriff, pouring in as much of my strength and power as possible to sustain her failing body, feeling her spirit brush against mine.

It was painfully exquisite.

Flames roared uncontrolled inside her, and when I activated my second sight, the world turned grey save for the maelstrom of aether buffeting Ani's soul. She was a marvel, and I was captivated by the iridescent beauty of her magic. It was like staring at the source of all power through a silken veil, like knowing one faced destruction if that thin barrier was only swept aside.

For mages, our bodies were the vessels of our magic, and we spent decades learning how to contain more, but once we reached our limits, that was all we could achieve. Annika, though, was the glimmering shroud fluttering before the vastness of the aether, and I couldn't resist the urge to peel it back just a little. I wanted to become a part of it, to bask in the glorious power, the woman ignorant of her immense potential.

I rarely utilised my mother's abilities, but this time I embraced my imperfect psychic gift. The marks on my chest lit up when I reached for Annika's mind. I wasn't skilled enough to perceive much, but I felt her essence burning in dragon fire with no rest or reprieve in sight; yet she was unwilling to let her lovers go. She apparently preferred to suffer than to let the last vestiges of their connection disappear.

There was no other way around it. As long as she grieved, there was no place for another Anchor.

'Damn it all to—this isn't going to work, Orm. You need to use the geas to make Ani let go. I can't keep her alive whilst she's still resisting.' I was beginning to lose the last of my composure, so when Orm looked at me in shocked disapproval, I flinched, offering a hasty solution.

'I can make her forget you did it. I know it's wrong, but this isn't about hurt feelings; it's life-or-death. Please, trust me. If you could see the ocean of magic that is trying to push through, you would understand. Do it for her, and don't hesitate—I can't hold on much longer.'

I was unable to say much more. Sustaining her life was taking an enormous toll on my strength, and I couldn't keep splitting my attention. Smoke rose from the bed, the ultimate proof that we were heading towards catastrophe, when I finally heard a grunt from Orm.

'*Rahit va'car.*'[1]

While I waited, I managed to direct part of my attention to a shielding spell. The heat decreased, but it wouldn't last for long, and even being next to her was becoming difficult. We had to hurry. I grimaced in pain.

Orm's face hardened into unyielding resolve. He placed a soft, featherlight kiss on her lips, and when she moaned softly, her lips parting to deepen the kiss, he whispered, 'I've wanted to do that since I met you. This is probably the first and last time I'll be allowed.' When he straightened, all I could see on his face was steely, unfeeling determination.

'It is time to say goodbye, my sweet girl. You can't hold the spirits of the dead to this world. It hurts them, and it hurts you. They need peace, and so do you, but I will fill the void they leave behind if you'll let me,' Orm murmured, cradling her to his chest, rocking them both gently. I watched as my friend whispered something and then cleared his throat. 'Release your dead lovers and let Vahin in,' he commanded.

---

1. *Increase the shield.*

Annika's body arched, every muscle pulled tight as her eyes snapped open, wailing as an unseen force tried to rip her apart. The raw terror in her features chilled me to the bone. 'No, Orm. Please ... No!'

'Do it, Annika. Obey my command.'

Orm held her as sweat poured from Ani's body, the low keening from her lips tearing at our hearts. Tears of blood slowly tracked across her pale face as she fought the geas, but the marks that tethered her lovers faded from her skin. I could see the strain my friend was under as he held the suffering mage; I was close to breaking myself, but with the disappearance of the marks, Ani finally relaxed, her quiet sobs the only sound in the room.

'Do what you have to do, Ari. It can't be any worse than my crime,' he said, wiping the tears from Ani's cheeks. I was left speechless at the guilt in his gaze, the pained expression of a man who had descended into a nightmare of his own making. The stern commander I knew was not a man of sweet words and gentle caresses. Yet, here he was, comforting Annika after shattering her world with the words of her geas.

'Somnara te sarashi jare va'et. [2]

I dropped the shielding spell and directed my remaining strength into the words of the spell, letting the glyph sink into her skin.

'Why did you do that? I can barely remember their faces. How can I let them go? I can't let them fade away. My memories are all I have left. *Why* did you do this to me? You promised to free me, but ... My life was already hollow. Without their memory, it isn't worth living ...'

Annika's words drifted into silence as my spell softened the rawness of her grief, leaving behind only the mild ache of a love mourned long ago. Orm swallowed hard and placed his cheek against her forehead.

---

2. *Forget what was done to you and release your grief.*

'You will never be lonely. You have my word, Nivale. Let the dragon in, my beautiful, thorny flower, and you will never be lonely again,' he whispered, stroking her hair gently, rocking them both.

Ani's body jerked suddenly, shocking the guilt-ridden commander into looking down. Thankfully, though, she was no longer in danger from Vahin's fire. The unblemished skin on her chest began to glow as the bond with the dragon manifested, fire erupting over her heart, the ghostly image of a dragon rising from the flames.

Orm looked at me in panic, but before he could utter a word the mirage retreated, leaving behind the symbol of a dragon, wings aloft, surrounded by a ring of fire. Annika sighed with relief as the torrent of magic subsided. Strands of aether danced briefly around us before settling peacefully into their regular pattern. Finally, I could release the breath I didn't realise I'd been holding.

'Did she forget them?' Orm asked quietly, and I shook my head. 'No, I only blocked the memory of what happened in this room. She will remember her lovers, but without a tether to their spirits, it will be more like a memory from the distant past, lacking the rawness of grief. That's all I could do.'

Orm shook his head as if he still couldn't believe what had happened, and his next words cut close to the heart. 'We've taken a lot from her and have given nothing back. All for the sliver of hope she might help fix the Barrier,' he said, a pained catch in his breath.

He pulled out a crumpled piece of parchment from his pocket and held it over a burning candle. I watched speechless as the geas turned to ash, leaving the commander the only man who could ever tame Annika's roaring inferno. The challenge in his eyes was enough for me to nod my agreement.

'I will take the blame for it. Your duty is to protect the kingdom and its people, whatever it takes. This had to be done. She had to come here; and now she must never know what we did to save her. You need her as an ally, not as an enemy at your back.'

'Yes, but she is not just a tool to be used and discarded, Ari. Not for me, at least. Not anymore. Ari ... I've never known anyone of such courage,' he said, stopping when Ani's breath stuttered and her eyelids opened.

I saw the flicker of some unreadable emotion in Annika's eyes. As it passed, she stared at Orm with a suspicious expression, and my friend gave her a tense smile. 'It's all done. You are safe and in the castle. You kept your promise.'

Ani cleared her throat, raw and dry after her ordeal. Orm, suddenly hesitant, moved away and, after a quick look around, grabbed a goblet. He filled it with water and held it to her lips so that she could sip at its contents. 'Did anyone die?' she asked weakly, and I saw tears pooling in the rim of her eyes. 'Why does everything hurt so much?'

'You saved us all by Anchoring Vahin, but something disrupted the connection.' Orm stopped, then shook his head. 'I can't lie to you. You were dying, and I couldn't let that happen. We had to protect you. My beautiful soul, I'm so—'

'*Onire!*[3]

I shouted it before he could finish the sentence, and Ani's head dropped to his shoulder.

'No! I told you. She must never know, and telling her just to clear your conscience will only cause her pain.' I knew that if Ani learned of our manipulation it could prove disastrous. Orm was the only person she knew and trusted here, and I refused to let him destroy that.

After looking into Annika's mind, I understood what the wrath of a conduit mage could unleash, and one small avalanche ten years ago was nothing compared to what brewed inside her.

---

3. *Sleep!*

CHAPTER 12

ANNIKA

*W*hy does everything hurt?

I lay still, holding my breath, trying to collect my thoughts as if that would help ease the pain. It felt like I had the worst hangover ever, but I didn't remember drinking. I was lying on something hard and hairy, and the tickling sensation on my nose forced me to change position. The sun was obnoxiously shining in my eyes even after I moved, so I squeezed my eyes tighter in annoyance and pushed my face into the hard pillow, wincing at the feeling of knives stabbing my brain.

It wouldn't be the first time I'd woken up in the stables, cuddling whatever animal was confined there. Though, I'd thought I was past that dark period in my life. Clearly, that wasn't the case and I'd lapsed into old habits. I hated sleeping alone, but as with everything in life, I had gotten used to it. However, the heartbeat beneath my cheek reminded me of just how good it felt to not have to.

I remembered little from the past few hours, only fever dreams of fire and pain. I knew Orm had stayed with me because his voice seemed to be the one constant throughout the ordeal ... There had also been another man who touched my mind and soothed the flames—and a dragon.

Vahin! Oh crap! Did I Anchor Orm's dragon yesterday? The breath I dragged into my lungs didn't slow my racing heart, and when my pillow groaned and shifted, I leapt out of my skin so quickly my heart had surely stopped.

I'm lying on a man!

This was way worse than drinking myself stupid and cuddling the local wildlife. I opened my eyes the tiniest bit, dreading what I'd see.

I was lying on a muscular chest with a vast expanse of soft dark hair cushioning my cheek. I looked upward, needing to know where I'd ended up, and when I saw Orm's strong features, a strange emotion shivered through my body. I was glad it was him ... no, not just glad, I liked it.

Much to my confusion, it no longer felt as if my magic wanted to entangle his soul. This was a huge relief but small consolation in these circumstances. I was in bed with the man who controlled my geas, and even if I liked how it felt, I hoped the commander had a good explanation for why I was using him as a pillow.

Gods, please have mercy. I didn't invite him in, did I? Not after I so vehemently told him that under no circumstances would we end up in the same bed. I tried to pull away, but he only tightened his hold, murmuring something in his sleep before he patted my head like a bloody dog and nuzzled my hair, inhaling deeply. That gesture was a testament to an intimacy that hadn't been there before.

The bastard promised me, I thought, trying to rouse some anger, but it was hard to feel righteous indignation when his touch felt so right. *Focus, Annika, you also like drinking and hunting dangerous monsters, but that doesn't mean they're good for you.* I tried to recall last evening. I vaguely remembered Orm's voice and the reassuring feeling it had given me.

I didn't feel as if I'd been violated, but this wasn't right. Still, if I'd invited him, I couldn't blame Orm any more than I could myself. I raised my head to study the man cuddling me.

Orm's shirt was open, revealing more than a muscular chest. His body hair narrowed as it reached his stomach, the thin line begging to be followed, and he had a scar running from his left shoulder to his right hip, as though someone had tried to slice him in half.

I wasn't surprised by the scar. The commander was a man who lived by the sword, but when I looked back at his face, I noticed something that didn't match his overly masculine physique. His eyelashes were so long and delicate that every maiden who ever saw them would surely be green with envy, and the thought of some jealous lover trying to pluck them made me chuckle.

My mirth woke Orm up, and he looked at me with concern. 'How are you feeling, Nivale?'

The soft baritone, so filled with worry, disrupted my merriment, and I pulled away, but Orm's arms caught me before I could escape, pulling me in close again.

'What do you think you're doing?' I pushed back with my hand to his chest. 'I'm sorry if my invitation gave you the wrong impression. I don't remember what I said, but we should forget this happened.'

'All I'm doing is trying to rest. You kept me up most of the night; it's only fair for you to let me sleep now,' he said, rubbing his forehead. 'And you didn't invite me in. You just wouldn't let me leave.'

'You should go to your own bed then.' My eyes opened wide. 'Wait, *what?*'

'I'm already in my bed. Can we get some rest now? Please?'

'No! What is wrong with you? If I didn't invite you to my bed—I mean, your bed—then what the hell happened? Oh, and where *is* my bed so I can go there—preferably before I fry your arse for taking advantage of my drunken state?' I again pushed on his chest. This time, he let me go with a heavy, exasperated sigh.

'Last night was challenging for everyone, especially for you. After you Anchored Vahin, things progressed so fast. When you collapsed, I ended up beside you in bed. Once the danger had passed, you refused to let me go, so I thought you needed me and stayed. I owed you at least that much for saving us all.'

'What? I would never cling to you ... you're lying. Tell me the truth—' I hadn't finished when he sat up, causing me to fall to the side. With a sigh, Orm wrapped the blanket around my shoulders.

'We are both tired. Your questions can wait until after you rest. In the meantime, since the sight of me angers you, I will go find another bed. Get some sleep, please. It's still early. Once you wake, I'll have some food delivered; just tell me what you'd like.' He stifled a yawn.

'Also, Vahin sends his regards; and he said that if you leave the room, he'll track you down and hold you captive until you go to sleep.' The commander stood up, and when I tried to follow him, he raised his hand. 'Stay in bed. Don't waste your breath, I'm not even listening.'

He started tying his shirt but stopped, noticing the laces were ripped. 'I have to say, you are a persistent woman. Although, the next time you rip my shirt open, please just tell me you want to be held instead of growling that you want my heartbeat. With a mage of your class and power, it's a worrying statement to hear, Nivale.'

'W ... what? Why do you keep using that ridiculous nickname? I'm nobody's flower. Gods, *men*. And if you're so upset about your shirt, I'll get you a new one.' I was so confused, and the longer he looked at me with that glint in his eye and the smirk on his lips, the angrier I became. Until I snapped.

'I only wanted to know what happened, but instead of answering, you've accused me of assaulting you and are *telling* me how to spend my morning. Do I have any say in how I live my life? Or has the mighty commander already decided what's best for me along with what my name is?' Orm gazed at me, barely restraining his laughter. Something about what he'd said filtered through the fog in my mind and distracted me.

'What do you mean, *Vahin sends his regards*?' I asked, studying Orm's features to make sense of everything, my eyes narrowing at the crinkling at the corners of his eyes. The bane of my existence tapped his temple, and the corner of his mouth lifted into a mischievous smile.

'You broke my dragon. We've always been able to communicate with images and emotions, but since he's met you, he's started *talking*, and godsdamn, he hasn't shut up since. The short version of yesterday's events is that your spell worked, you saved everyone, and you are Anchored to Vahin after a very tense few hours of delirium. Now I've got two voices shouting at me: one in my mind and the other in my ear, so if everyone could just calm the f ...' Orm's deep sigh and now tightly closed eyes made me realise he wasn't just talking to me, and curiosity overcame my anger.

'Is he talking to you right now?' I asked, fascinated, and Orm nodded. Then, leaning into my ear, so close his breath gave me goosebumps, he whispered, 'And when it comes to your nickname?' His smirk returned as he continued. 'I call you Nivale because you are as special and as rare as the mountain flower. You have a strength and resilience that leaves me awestruck. I wish our circumstances were different—you have me mesmerized, Ani. As for your strange need for my heartbeat, I found it quite adorable.'

I couldn't even remember a time when a man would dare talk to me like that without fear, reverence, or hunger for my conduit abilities. And I felt like a fool because I was falling for it, so I decided it was time to cut him off and change the subject.

'I didn't know dragons could talk like that. When we met, he felt ... well, he didn't feel like a person.'

'He has always been a sentient being, but something changed after your meeting at the lake. Vahin's thoughts have become clearer, and we can communicate with the same ease as if I were talking to you or Alaric.'

Before I could ask more questions, his gaze grew serious. 'Ani, I owe you a life debt, and I don't know if I can ever repay you. I know you wanted to have defined boundaries between us, but I crossed them last night to save you. I don't regret a single thing, but it will be difficult to keep our agreement when I remember how good it felt to hold you in my arms.'

How in Veles' pit did I end up in such a mess?

I didn't know what to do with Orm's confession and certainly didn't want to tell him how I felt about it. I was too tired to deal with it now, but one thing I most definitely had to correct was that 'life debt' nonsense.

'I appreciate your words, but I hope you remember that I was in danger, just the same as everyone else during the skirmish. If Vahin had fallen from the sky, I would have died there, so I was just saving my own sorry arse. You don't owe me anything, Orm.'

He looked at me with amusement glinting in his eyes.

'My dear Annika, it is my decision on how I feel about my life debt and your actions. For you, it may not have been much, but having my riders and their dragons safe here at the fortress instead of injured, or worse—dead at the bottom of the mountain—is more than I could have ever hoped for. You may think you were saving yourself, but you saved my squadron and the women from the village. You almost died in the process. That is why, my sweet Nivale, I will decide how I feel, and there is nothing you can do about it.'

He looked at me with such intensity that I felt naked, even with the covers.

A slight draft from the window caused the candles to flicker as it brushed over my skin and made me shiver. I pulled my arms together for warmth, looking down to see goosebumps on my skin. With a slight frown, I lifted the cover and looked under the blanket.

I was completely naked.

My clothes were gone, and Orm's calloused hands had been resting on my body the entire night, warming my skin. At the same time, I'd ripped his shirt open in my delirium to cuddle his heartbeat. That was something that needed explaining. Right now.

At least now I understand why he appears so confident and casual.

'Care to tell me who did this?' I pointed towards my body while pulling the blankets tighter around me. I was sure I knew, but I wanted to hear it from him.

'That was me,' he answered, so nonchalantly that I grabbed the nearest pillow and smacked him across the head. My hit landed perfectly, but the next thing I knew, he'd grabbed my wrist and pried the pillow out of my hand.

'Let me go,' I said, but he only raised his eyebrow. 'I'm tempted to answer "make me" just to challenge you and see where it takes us. I enjoy touching you, and I certainly enjoy a woman who is not afraid to stand up to me,' he said with a voice so raspy and low that I gasped. 'Do you want this, Nivale? Do you want to make me let go of your hand?'

I bit my lip, fighting the flood of arousal before relaxing my hand and diverting my gaze.

He enjoyed a challenge? I wondered how he'd like me acting like a docile lady from court.

'Could you please release me and explain? Please also accept my sincere apologies for the unwarranted attack, my lord.'

Orm burst into laughter but let me go.

'You are impossible. I should be offended; do you so dislike my touch that you'll really resort to demurely submitting like a courtly noble-woman? It was amusing to watch, but you don't have it in you, Ani. You wouldn't submit to a man just because he is stronger. Gods, I wish we weren't facing war; I'd show you just how I like strength and courage—with that delicious dose of mischief. Alas, I will leave you to your rest. We can talk later,' he finished with a kind smile.

Orm was back to being in complete control, and the tension disappeared from the air. I couldn't help but smile back, even if I was still angry with him for my present state. 'Don't leave just yet, please. I need to know more,' I said, and Orm slowly exhaled before nodding in agreement.

'Very well. Your mind rejected the bond with Vahin, and you weren't able to control the dragon fire. Alaric was able to help you, but we needed to cool you down before he could devise a spell. The fire was consuming you from the inside, Ani, and only I could touch you because of my connection with Vahin. I couldn't let the servants get hurt worrying about your modesty.'

'Right ... Just tell me one thing: did I Anchor you, too? Or Alaric? Is that why you're acting like we ... are more than casual acquaintances forced to work together? Because we haven't ... we didn't, did we?' I heard the sharp edge of panic in my voice, and he must have noticed it, too, because Orm instinctively raised his arms in a calming gesture. Still, I couldn't think straight, frantically searching for Orm's Anchor in my soul.

'No, nothing like that happened. I only undressed you, and Alaric helped you accept Vahin. I wouldn't take you or Anchor you without your consent, and I wouldn't let anyone, even my best friend, do that either. I'm sorry if all this frightened you, but we couldn't let you die.'

'Thank you,' I murmured, still shaking. Orm smiled crookedly, but I didn't miss the frown flitting across his features. 'You shouldn't thank me, Ani. I did what needed to be done. Alaric's the one you should thank.'

The lack of emotion in Orm's voice confused me for a moment, but whatever was happening, he clearly didn't want to share it right now. With pursed lips, I looked away but turned back when the commander covered me with extra blankets and mumbled something to himself.

Heat blossomed across my cheeks, and I hoped the blush wasn't too noticeable. Nothing had happened. Orm was right. I didn't feel tethered to him. I could sense Vahin, but no one else, and that instantly calmed me down. Somehow, Anchoring the dragon steadied my unpredictable magic, and I could touch the tempting man without dire consequences.

'At least my magic is no longer trying to tie you to me,' I offered cheerfully. I reached out and touched his forearm, keeping my hand still for a few moments to test the theory. Orm observed me quietly, then he placed his hand over mine.

'I know what you are afraid of, and while I liked the touch of your magic ... I don't feel it anymore. Would you believe me if I said that if I had felt the pull, I wouldn't have stayed the night?'

'Strangely enough, yes.' I removed my hand before shaking my head. 'Still, it doesn't change the fact that I'm naked in your bed. That's exactly the *opposite* of what we had agreed to. I don't intend to renegotiate my position here, so please show me the way to my room. I promise I will eat and sleep as much as you want, but ... this is wrong.'

'What is so wrong about it? If you're afraid of gossip, I can ensure the servants won't say a word.'

'What? No, I don't care about gossip,' I scoffed, and he frowned as if struggling to understand my reasoning. 'I don't want to grow attached, and being around you makes it difficult to remember that. Somehow, even if I'm angry, you make me smile. This was just supposed to be a contract, a year of my life given to the man who holds my geas. I don't want to like you. I don't trust easily, and ... I don't really know you, and I want to keep it that way. So please, let's not make this awkward.'

As soon as the words had left my mouth, I saw Orm's eyes darken, their mossy green becoming so dark they were almost black, but I didn't regret what I'd said. My attraction to him, the comfort of his embrace, made little sense. I might have had a near-death experience, and he may be a handsome man, but he was also the one who could always command my obedience.

'There are things in my life that I regret deeply, Ani, but bringing you here is not one of them. I misjudged the situation and should never have threatened you with the geas, but what's done is done. I wish you'd understand that I'm not your enemy and don't want to be the owner of your contract—Ani ... I want ...' He reached out, but I pulled away when I saw something dangerous flash in his features, an emotion that made his handsome face frightening.

Orm noticed my reaction and closed his eyes, inhaling deeply.

'I see. Nothing I say or do will change your mind.' His face reverted to that emotionless mask. 'We'll do it your way. You will stay here until you recover, and I will have your room available for you tomorrow ... I will give you some time alone now, but don't expect me to stay away just because you are afraid to like me.'

Orm stalked to the door but then halted, looking back at me. His gaze took me in before he brushed unruly strands of midnight-black hair from his forehead.

'You will get used to my presence, Annika. And although nothing happened between us last night, I can't promise that nothing will in the future. I didn't expect this ... pull, but it is what it is, and I'm just a man, Nivale. A man who refuses to deprive himself of your company.'

CHAPTER 13

ANNIKA

'**M**y lady, please wake up ... My lady, the bath is ready.'

The strange voice intruded on my dreams, and I pried my eyes open with an expression that made the owner of said voice flinch. My initial confusion, however, quickly gave way to embarrassed understanding.

I was still in Orm's bedroom, but now the smell of herbs and meat filled the air, making my stomach rumble. I focused on the bravely smiling face of a young girl with blond braids and eyes as blue as the summer sky. She wasn't from Zalesie, and she clearly didn't know me, judging by how vigorously she kept pulling at the covers.

'Who are you?' I asked, and the girl's smile widened confidently. 'Your maid, my lady. You've been asleep for several hours, and the lord commander told me to wake you and draw you a bath. He is busy with Master Alaric, but he sent some food from the kitchen and made me promise to make you eat something before the night's rest.'

'Night's rest? But it's barely morning.'

'You slept through the day, my lady. The lord commander took good care of you, then Master Alaric came, but unfortunately, they both had to go.'

I looked towards the corner where a tub large enough to drown two grown men in sat filled with steaming water. 'Right, of course. Well, let's try this again. How about we start with your name? Then you can explain why I'm not bathing in the communal baths and why someone was forced to carry this monstrosity up here.'

'My name is Agnes, my lady, and I will be your maid—your *personal* maid,' she said, emphasising the word 'personal' and bouncing with excitement. Anyone would think she'd been given a noble title.

'We have a large and well-equipped bathroom, but Lord Ormond said you needed comfort and privacy. Besides, it wasn't the servants who brought it here; the soldiers and riders did. And Master Alaric cast this weird spell that made everything so quiet.'

I rolled my eyes so hard I thought they'd fall out. Orm's idea of privacy came with an army parading through my room while I slept.

'Fine, thank you, Agnes. I'll take it from here. You may go,' I said, but she only shook her head. 'No, my lady. The commander was insistent when he told me I *must* assist you in everything you need.' Determination flashed in her eyes.

'What was your previous job?'

'I worked in the kitchen, but I've always wanted to be a lady's maid.' My shoulders fell at hearing that. It was a significant advancement for Agnes, and it was clear as day that she would do precisely as the lord commander instructed whether I liked it or not. I was stuck with a maid I didn't need unless I threw her out.

'If you insist on staying, then you must call me Ani. I'm a mage, not a lady.' I gave the maid a stern look and stepped out of bed. I cursed in surprise when my legs refused to hold my weight and almost sent me crashing to the floor. Agnes caught me with a strength I didn't expect from someone so slim and slowly guided me to the bathtub.

'I can only call you Ani when no one's watching, alright? The lord commander would kick me out penniless if I disrespected you. You know, he's never had a woman in his chambers. He mostly spends his free time with

Master Alaric, and we all thought that ...' She made an obscene gesture while blushing heavily before slapping a hand over her mouth. 'Ohh ... I shouldn't have said that.'

'Said what?' I enquired. Distracted by my weakness, I was unsure what she was alluding to. I climbed unsteadily into the tub, still wondering, when she continued. 'Well, we thought that Lord Orm and Master Ari were ... but now that I'm thinking about it, Master Alaric never came here, either.'

The girl was a gossip, but I loved the idea of having such a rich source of information.

'So you assumed Alaric was Orm's lover, and now you think *I'm* his woman?' I teased, my mischievous smile making my new maid blush. 'But you are his woman, my lady ... I mean Ani. How can you be so indifferent about it?'

'His woman? Did he tell you that?'

'Well, no. But you're here, in his bed. It is the first time the commander has chosen a maiden, and he rushed you to his bedroom. Then there were those noises ... If you'd heard him when he told us to serve you—even the cook got scared. So I thought you were his. There was talk amongst the riders that he calls you his *Nivale*,' she said, wide-eyed.

I couldn't fault her logic. Everything she had mentioned pointed to that conclusion, and I closed my eyes in defeat. *I will never live this down.* With a deep sigh, I sank lower, trying to let the verbena-scented water ease my muscles and wash away my embarrassment.

'How am I expected to work with the fortress mage if he thinks I'm here to warm Orm's bed?' I asked, and Agnes chuckled. 'It's not good to be at odds with Master Alaric. He can be mean to those who wrong him or the lord commander ... *You know* ... the sounds that sometimes come from his room, the voices. Some say he is possessed and that the dark fae is blackhearted.'

'Yes, well. I will have to explain this somehow, preferably before the poor mage hears that I was naked in Orm's embrace. That won't give him a good impression of me, and I can't risk breaking his black heart.' I winked. Agnes burst into unbridled laughter before positioning herself behind me and lathering my hair with scented soap.

'You are not what I expected,' Agnes ventured, her nimble fingers making me moan as she massaged my scalp. 'Yeah, I've been hearing that a lot lately,' I murmured as I felt myself floating away on the perfumed steam. Before I knew it, Agnes had me in a pleasant stupor with her gentle ministrations.

A soft knock, followed by a draft from the open door, made my eyes snap open a moment later. 'Is she ready, Agnes?' asked a melodic, masculine voice, and I found myself turning towards the agreeable sound.

'Ready for what?' I inquired, submerging myself further until nothing but the top half of my head was visible between the floating herbs.

'Ah, Annika, it is a pleasure to see you awake. I need to examine you. After all the trouble you gave me last night, I'm here to ensure my patient is recovering,' the dark fae said. I sighed, blowing bubbles before lifting my head slowly. It seemed everybody was dead set on seeing me naked.

'As you can see, I'm in the bath. Come back later,' I snapped, but he was already halfway into the room. 'Should I bounce a fireball off your head to stop you? I said come back later.'

'If you're worried about me seeing your body, darling, that ship sailed last night.' He smirked, coming closer, and I crossed my arms over my breasts. 'Yeah, but as I haven't seen *you* naked, you shouldn't make yourself too comfortable in my room.'

'That can be easily rectified if you'd like.' A mischievous grin lifted the corner of his mouth. 'Although I don't usually strip for my patients, the idea does pique my interest.'

'Good grief, what is wrong with everyone today? Shouldn't you be dark and broody? I can't believe I have to work with someone with a *sense of humour*,' I huffed, pulling myself to the opposite edge of the bath.

'You demand a lot from your poor healer—dark, broody, *and* naked? I'm not sure if I can sacrifice my sunny disposition even for such a cause.' I rolled my eyes.

'Oh, cut it out. What do you want me to do?' I gave in because the bastard had made me involuntarily smile and the mischief hadn't left his eyes.

'Right now, I only wish to examine you. There is a lot to talk about, much more than we can cover today. I trust Orm told you that we need to replace the crystal to fix the Barrier? Its magic is decaying faster than expected, and the incident with the wlok unfortunately sped up the process significantly. I'm afraid that your role in all this involves spending time with me and additional training in transmutation and artefact construction,' he said, and I pulled a face.

'Fine, I can do it. Anything else?'

'Judging by your expression, I assume you haven't done that since your university days. There is another way, in which I perform a spell using a conduit mage connection; however, that would necessitate you considering me as your second Anchor. It would make things much easier, but as it is not a decision to be hastily made, we will talk about everything later.' He reached out towards me. 'Your hand, please.'

I was still mulling over his statement as I reached towards him, placing my hand in his. While Alaric checked my pulse, I couldn't help but wonder if Orm had told him how physical the Anchoring was because his request felt so impersonal. Once he'd finished, the dark fae handed me a small vial.

'Here, drink this.'

I stared at him until he raised an eyebrow and smirked. 'It's just a revitalising draught. Drink up, or I'll call Orm,' he threatened, and I huffed in annoyance, reaching for the liquid and gulping it down in one go. What followed was a moment of pure bliss that left me moaning and slowly slipping beneath the water.

Alaric chuckled as he grabbed my chin and supported my head until I regained control of my body. 'That will help you heal and rejuvenate your energy. We will start our lessons tomorrow. Until then, Agnes will provide you with anything you might need,' he said before I pulled away. He'd saved my life the other night, but I was irritated by his constant commands.

'Your name's Alaric, yes?' I asked just to antagonise him, and when he nodded, I sat up straight, brazenly exposing myself. 'Thank you for saving my life, but even your "sunny disposition" won't be enough to convince me to Anchor you. I'm sure you know that already. Also, you aren't my teacher; I will be your partner, a second mage for the fortress, and you will treat me with all due courtesy. That means you can't come into my bedroom uninvited when I'm in no fit state to receive a guest—'

My tirade was halted by the sound of banging and crashing outside.

'Don't try to stop me, you bastard. Where's Ani? What have you done with her?' The muffled, angry voice made me stand up, barely registering that Alaric had hastily grabbed a towel and wrapped it around me. He positioned himself in front of the door with a dagger in his hand right before it burst open to reveal Katja as she fought with a soldier.

'The commander said our lady should not be disturbed while the healer is with her!' the man bellowed, and my eyes widened in shock. Somehow, over the course of the day, I'd advanced in rank without even knowing it.

'She is not *your lady*. She is Ani, *our* town mage, and *I'm* her healer! Why does she even need a healer in the first place?' Katja fought like a mountain lioness, and my mind finally registered that I should say something.

'Alaric, tell them to let my friend go and that if anyone else touches her, they'll regret it,' I threatened. The soldier instantly let the feisty woman go, bowing to me. 'Lady Mage, my apologies. I was instructed to ensure your privacy.'

'Go. Lady Annika is safe with me,' Alaric said, and the guard bowed again before leaving and closing the door behind him.

I gestured Katja towards the table where Agnes had left food and drink while I put on a white nightgown. Despite its simplicity, the fabric was soft and smooth, luxurious to the touch. I hadn't expected to find such finery in a mountain fortress, so it only added to the place's appeal.

As soon as I was dressed, Katja was by my side.

'How are you? And why is this dark fae claiming to be your healer? Ani, what is going on? One moment we're flying here, stuffed in those damned baskets like market goods; the next, the sky was burning, and everyone was saying you did it. Then I found out that the commander had locked you away in his bedroom! ... Are you a prisoner? I thought riders never forced their women.'

Alaric's snort earned him glares from both Katja and me. 'After that display of magic, I doubt anyone would dare try forcing Annika to do anything, or did you miss the guard's reaction to her threat?' He snorted again, and my glare darkened.

'Of course they'd never force a woman. How dare you even suggest such a thing? And ... and ... The lord commander is the noblest of them all!' Agnes bristled, adding her thoughts to the discussion. For a moment, I thought she might have even smacked Katja with the serving tray.

'There's something you should know ...' I interjected warily, and both women looked at me, forgetting their quarrel.

'Spill it, sister, because I know that look. Your magic ... that wasn't something a small-town mage could manage, even if she was university-trained.'

'Katja, I ... I deserted the Crown Mage Corps before I came to Zalesie. Orm—I mean, the commander—obtained my geas to bring me here; but after a little negotiation, I agreed to come—*not* as a maiden, but as a mage. I know what it looks like, but this irritating fuc ... *fae* here claims I can help him stop the Barrier from failing.' The words came out in a rush.

Alaric gave Katja an exaggerated bow when she looked at him sharply, and I continued. 'So, for now, I'll be staying here. Even though I need to stay near the commander and the fortress mage, I swear I'm safe,' I said, not giving Katja all the details to avoid another of her famous lectures.

'Can you really do it?' she asked quietly. 'That would help so many.'

'I don't know, but Alaric believes I can, so I have to try.'

Katja turned around, her gaze sliding over Alaric's relaxed posture with such judgement that he smirked when she was done. 'I hope you like what you saw, or are you another woman determined to see me naked?'

'No one wants to see your pasty body!' I snapped, looking for something to throw at him, but the exchange seemed to calm Katja. She chuckled slightly, looking around.

'Well, I'll leave you to your life of luxury and irritating men. Just don't forget about those of us crammed in the female boarding house. I'll visit tomorrow, and if I can do anything, let me know. I don't want you to struggle when I'm available to help.'

I loved her for that, for trusting my judgement and for accepting the situation without overdramatising or making life difficult. When she left, I turned towards Alaric. 'It's your turn now. I don't want you here,' I ordered, scowling when Alaric came closer, still wearing that arrogant smirk. 'Would you prefer someone else? I can call you-know-who if you let me stay and watch; you were so keen for his company last night.'

'Master Alaric, let my lady rest.'

Agnes's timely intervention saved the dark fae from a well-deserved slap, and I watched with a satisfied smirk of my own as she grabbed Alaric by the collar and marched him out of the room like an unruly toddler.

I was *definitely* going to keep her. A gem like Agnes could not be wasted peeling carrots in the kitchen.

Happy to be left alone, I dived under the blankets, sighing with pleasure when the masculine scent of cedarwood and leather filled my senses. I was in Orm's bed, and I was sure that my host hadn't been prepared to share, as the linen—albeit clean—still carried the scent of his body.

No one is watching, whispered the voice in my head. After a moment of hesitation, I grabbed a pillow and buried my face in it. Orm's scent was like a safe port in a heavy storm, and I allowed myself a moment to enjoy it, internally promising to put the pillow back in its place in a minute ... only to crush it to my chest and fall asleep with it in my arms.

CHAPTER 14

ANNIKA

The view before me went unnoticed as I stood on the granite walls of the fortress. The harsh mountain wind tugged at my dress, wrapping it tight around my legs. I wish I'd gone to see Vahin the moment I woke up instead of listening to Orm and staying in bed.

That damn man had used my recovery to fly to the mines without me. I knew why he'd done it, but being away from my Anchor felt *wrong*. Besides, I had proved I could help with the Vel when I had dispatched that swarm of spectrae.

Why couldn't he have waited for a few more hours?

He'd need to explain himself because I didn't intend to let this go. Especially since, in his absence, I wasn't sure what I should do. I'd spent the last few days aimlessly wandering around, with occasional visits to the town with Alaric as my only company.

'Are you feeling restless again, Ani?' I hadn't heard him approaching, but Alaric appeared by my side, seemingly out of nowhere. As a warm cloak landed on my shoulders, I turned my head to the side to smile at the dark fae.

After our rocky start, he had done his best to keep me entertained; but with Ormond and Tomma gone, he was left in charge—and the local population was giving him enough trouble to take up most of his time.

'A little. I tried to read the book you showed me, but I'm desperate for a break and needed to feel the wind on my face.'

Alaric had explained the situation the second I had noticed Orm's absence. Just before the commander came to Zalesie, the court had sent a letter and a group of miners, finally granting his request to reopen the old dwarven adit. However, he was only given a week to ensure the mine was viable and that the men were safe there. If the place was not secure in time—or empty of crystals—the workers had to return to the capital.

Orm had sent a contingent of soldiers to escort the miners and ordered the search for a replacement crystal within moments. Unfortunately, he'd received reports of an incident so had left to investigate at the first opportunity. The wounded soldiers sent back to the fortress had told Alaric that the search had been unsuccessful thus far, and constant fights with Vel demons had delayed the operation.

I tried to make myself useful, helping Alaric, ignoring how awkward it felt without Orm's presence. My days were consumed with researching how to link magical artefacts. And in the evenings, I would put aside my worries and enjoyed the dark fae's company.

Except for that one time in the bath, Alaric hadn't mention Anchoring me, and I was grateful for that small mercy. I was even more grateful when he explained his other idea to me, and we focused on something he called the 'tethering glyph.'

It was still a work in progress, but—in theory—it could replicate the Anchor bond. As a conduit, I could help by describing how the flow of aether was influenced when Alaric experimented with the lines of the sigil or the wording of the tethering spell.

There was a problem, though. The glyph was meant to be created with high magic, and not just any form of high magic—the *highest* order of descriptive magic; and even during my university days I hadn't come close to understanding the subject.

Alaric could do something similar with the blood sacrifice of the Foul Order, but it would only allow him to draw from me, and the one-sided link didn't fit our purpose. To say I disliked the idea of attempting to learn such a complex topic at my age was an understatement.

Once, when I'd thought I'd grasped the concept and had added my own lines to the construct, something in the drawing changed, and the next thing I knew, I had been zapped by a string of red aether so hard it had thrown me against the opposite wall. Dazed and angry, I had cursed up a storm while a laughing Alaric healed my scrapes. 'Calm down, my lovely apprentice. There's a learning curve, for both of us,' he'd said with a laugh.

I smiled at my reminiscence before I heard him say, 'If you need a break, then you shall have a break. Still, standing here won't make them return any sooner.' A gust of wind raised dust from the floor. I blew out a breath, squeezing my eyes, and Alaric stepped in front of me, sheltering me with his body. 'Don't worry, Ani, Orm always returns. It doesn't matter how difficult the situation is; he will prevail.'

'You're assuming I miss Ormond, but the one I'm waiting for is Vahin,' I retorted, raising my head, unwilling to admit I was waiting for them both, only to see that all-knowing smirk again.

'Of course, Ani, if you say so. How about we go to the waterfall, and you can miss the dragon there? Or we can return to the library—but instead of studying, I could read something for you. I've noticed several books about star-crossed lovers in there ... We could even recreate some of the more interesting scenes.'

Here we go again, I thought. During these few days in his company, I had learned that Alaric's mood was often unpredictable—fluctuating from serious to mischievous, from brooding to outright seductive. I never knew where I stood, but I could say I'd never been bored.

Alaric knew that the library had become my favourite place. If I'd known Varta Fortress held such a wealth of knowledge and ancient texts, I would have hiked up here years ago. That was why he proposed it now, while we stood overlooking the breathtaking landscape. Of course, I couldn't let his teasing go unanswered.

'Recreate ... *really?*' I rolled my eyes. 'Unless you mean the scenes where the hero dies a tragic death and the heroine becomes the sole queen of the kingdom?'

My companion threw his head back and laughed. 'Well, I would prefer scenes where the hero loses himself between her thighs, but I can play an incredibly good-looking corpse if you desire.' I sighed, pretending to be offended by the suggestion.

'I don't want to go to the library, but if you are up for a walk, we can go to town,' I suggested, and he nodded, extending his arm. I rested my hand on it, and as we strolled down the weathered steps, I asked the question that had plagued me the last few days. 'I know it's not my place to ask, but the servants' gossip, and with me still sleeping in Orm's bedroom, I just have to know for sure.'

'Let me guess. Someone told you I'm Orm's lover.'

'Well, yes. So ... are you?'

'No. I'm his friend, and we are close, but not *that* close; and even if we were, it wouldn't cause any issues. What do you know about the dark fae?' he probed, and I shrugged.

'Next to nothing. Your race isn't exactly open to sharing knowledge or welcoming visitors, and since the Necromancer's War, diplomatic relations between our kingdom and yours have been ... well, strained would be underplaying the situation.'

'Indeed. Then let me tell you why I'd be comfortable sharing a woman with him if we were together. Dark fae women—our *dominae*, as we call them—are rare and precious, and they rule our society. They choose who they mate with, and that includes how many at any given time. Dark fae males like to serve their lady, and the more powerful the woman is, the more elevated the status of the male; but just as the king in your country needs more than one guard or advisor, dark fae females need more consorts. We like to share, and sometimes bond not only with our females but with each other.'

'You mean, like ... intimately?' I asked, trying to calm my racing heart and the unexpected flood of yearning.

'Yes, although it doesn't happen often; but the households in which that harmony is achieved are envied by the rest of dark fae society. My father couldn't stand the power women have, so he chose a human mage for himself—and was considered an abomination for it.'

I felt my cheeks warm as I recalled my past and how I had chosen my Anchors. Cautiously, I broached the subject that had caused Tal and Arno no end of difficulty. 'But Orm isn't a woman or a dark fae.' Alaric laughed.

'He certainly isn't, but one day, he will choose his mate; and if we were together, I would most likely share him with her—well, if they didn't mind. I would enjoy it, Annika, having a family like that, having people I could trust.' The last words were said quietly and with strange vulnerability.

The moment passed, his usual mask slipping back on, and a casual mischief replaced the longing I had glimpsed in his eyes. 'Still, if you're worried, why not move to my room?' he added, biting his lip when my eyes widened at such innuendo.

'Will you stop this endless flirting? All you'd get from me visiting your room is a critique of the décor,' I said, because we'd entered the town square. 'It will be better for everyone if you don't see me as a woman you could both enjoy.'

'I know, but you are mistaken. I see you as a woman who could enjoy *us* both ... not the other way around,' he asserted before placing his hand on mine.

'Ani, when—or rather, if—our miners find a replacement for the keystone, I will ask you once again to consider Anchoring me. Even if we succeed with the glyph, it may still be needed in order to draw enough power for the spell to work. I know you're drawn to Orm. I just want you to know that bonding with me doesn't mean you would need to choose.' Alaric didn't bother to lower his voice, and I saw the curious stares of the citizens as we passed, noting the gleeful look in his eyes as he tested my patience.

'But it would be ...'

'A sacrifice, I know. I'm dark fae, after all. Mages wouldn't want the taint of my power touching them.' His tight, crooked smile exposed his feelings. I saw the flicker of pain that flashed in his eyes before he smirked. 'Still, I can guarantee our intimacy would leave you asking for more. My kind know all the sweet and perverted ways to please their women.'

'What? Gods! You are a menace, a bloody menace,' I snapped, and he laughed. 'You asked about dark fae customs. I just wanted you to know about our hidden skills. It is your decision what you do with that knowledge.' He said.

'Oh, really? I'll tell you what I'm going to do: I'm going to go to the tavern and drink enough mead to scrub what you just said from my mind. How does that sound? Yeah, you know what? That's the best idea I've had all day.' I headed for the second-best place in the fortress as Alaric strolled behind me.

'Splendid, give me a tankard of wine, and I will tell you about our mating. It is quite spectacular, unless you're repulsed by blood,' Ari teased, and I shook my head in disbelief.

I'll give him a tankard, or even several, just to shut him up.

He enjoyed goading me far too much.

We returned to the castle late; at least, *I* did—Alaric had to be carried back by two soldiers. Much to my amusement, his capacity for holding his liquor didn't match his boastful attitude. However, the dark fae was interesting and entertaining while drunk, even if I occasionally caught him looking at me as if he saw something precious but out of his reach.

I couldn't remember a time I'd laughed so much. My good mood, though, was washed away when an irate Agnes complained about my unladylike manners as I headed straight to bed. It seemed I would never be able to live up to my maid's expectations.

I hoped the copious amount of alcohol I had ingested would bring me some peace and not another unsettling night. I still didn't know how Vahin had been affected by our rushed and traumatic bonding, and I desperately wanted to talk to him.

All I knew was that the pain of losing my Anchors had eased, and I guiltily realised that for the past few days, I'd barely thought about Tal and Arno. Their marks had disappeared from my chest, replaced by a striking dragon.

That itself didn't bother me, but their faces fading from my memories and our love fading into a bittersweet ache did. I didn't want to lose them to the distance of time, yet those overwhelming emotions I'd held close all these years now seemed to be replaced by a welcoming, diffuse sadness. Like time had finally healed my festering wound.

Despite my worries, I slept like the dead until a presence in my dreams called me back to awareness, and I heard a quiet growl that made me shiver. I realised I was holding Orm's pillow, and I clutched it to my chest even though his scent had long since faded, replaced by the smell of verbena.

The flowers filled a vase beside me, and the light of the dying flames in the fireplace lit the source of the noise. A man was sprawled on the chaise lounge, snoring lightly. I recognised the commander by the unruly hair hanging over the headrest, and I knew he would regret sleeping there later.

A tugging sensation in my chest diverted my attention from him. The presence that had—I now realised—woken me, pulsated and called for me. Vahin was here, too. He was unsettled, and in his distress, was calling for me.

Murmuring a quiet spell, I attuned my eyes to the darkness, the translucent glow of swirling aether lighting my surroundings.

The chill floor made me gasp when my feet touched the stones. I wore only a nightgown, and I grabbed a woollen blanket from the end of the bed, wrapping it around my shoulders, clutching the quilted duvet with my other hand before going to where the pull led me.

I briefly stopped in front of Orm. I shouldn't have missed him, but I had. With sleep easing the constant frown, his face looked so peaceful, softened by the flames in the fireplace. I reached out, stroking his cheek ever so slightly, resisting the urge to trail my finger along his lips.

He was a handsome man—and a kind one, despite his rough exterior. I wished I'd gone with him to the mines. I'd felt the call of the hunt burning inside me for some time, and it would have been the perfect opportunity. I was going to grill him to find out what happened during his investigation, but that could wait until tomorrow.

I carefully placed the quilt around him. 'Shh ... rest,' I whispered, freezing when he murmured in his sleep, but when he didn't wake, I left.

I wish I hadn't given Agnes my boots to clean because now they were nowhere to be seen. I trembled each time my bare feet touched the polished stones of the corridor, but I kept walking, unable to resist the call of my Anchor. Endless dark passages lit by aether and the occasional torch led me down through the castle. With each step, the pull grew stronger, as if I was approaching the end of my journey.

Finally, I stood in front of a staircase. The steps disappeared into the darkness, looking more like a bottomless pit than an ordinary spiral stairwell, but I knew I had to go down. With a moment's concentration, I conjured the pulsar light that swirled around and washed down into the depths, lighting my way, and I took that first difficult step, smiling when nothing grabbed me as I kept going.

The steps were so slippery that it had taken forever to get to the bottom. Now, in the belly of the beast, I couldn't help smiling as the familiar pattern of Vahin's scales moved before me. The dragon's enormous head turned in my direction, and nothing could stop me from jumping forward and embracing him.

'Vahin,' I whispered, fighting back tears. My cheek rested next to his, and I breathed in the heavy metallic scent of his body. I knew that touching him would make me feel complete. Gods, it felt so good to be around him.

'Hello, Little Flame. What are you doing here in the middle of the night? And how did you sneak past Orm? He was so frantic to see you.' The deep voice, soft and rich like molasses, with a slight hiss that prolonged the last vowels, rumbled in the air.

'I could feel your need, a pull on my soul. You called me,' I said, feeling awestruck at hearing Vahin speak.

'My dreams … they … I'm sorry, but the aether currents are strong tonight. It always sets me on edge.' His vertical pupil narrowed, gazing at my feet. 'You came here barefoot? You are shivering, come here.' The commanding tone of his voice had me stepping closer until, with a gentle nudge from his snout, Vahin pushed me towards his leg. Then, with another, less gentle push, the dragon encouraged me to climb up.

'It's lucky you're so beautiful,' I mumbled, following his command.

'Agnes took my boots to clean, and I wanted to see you,' I said a little louder, nestling against his warm body. 'Vahin, I'm sorry I made you my Anchor in such dire circumstances. I didn't even ask whether you wanted to be bonded to me. Alaric said it was a punishing night because I refused to let you in. I didn't mean to. I'm sorry.'

I sighed with guilty pleasure as my feet warmed up. Vahin's body felt like a polished rock heated by the sun, and I promptly snuggled in, trying to absorb as much warmth as possible. He watched me, and I felt his amusement radiating through the thought bond.

'Don't apologise. It was harder for you than it was for me. Plus, I'm delighted, Little Flame. The world is so much brighter with the light of your soul within mine. Would you like me to cover you?' he asked, but before I could answer, my body was sheltered beneath the soft membrane of his wing. I shifted a little to get more comfortable before peeking over to look back at the dragon.

'I was worried. Our bond shouldn't have happened like that, but I didn't have a choice. I'm so sorry I took away your decision.' A deep rumble shook me and my snug perch.

'Why do you think I regret it, Little Flame? I should thank you for bringing my voice back. For awakening the part of me I'd forgotten existed. You brought me back from my slumber, and I forbid you to ever apologise for it.'

I was confused, but Vahin seemed to be overjoyed at becoming my Anchor, so out of sheer curiosity I asked, 'What do you mean by "awakening?"'

'You gave a beast back his personality, his identity. Dragons live for millennia. I've seen many races rise and fall. I have witnessed the advancement of humanity. I've carried countless riders and have lost them all; one after another, they've passed through the streams of time. It is easier to be a beast—to not think, not remember. To only feel a little and soar through a sky where time doesn't exist. When a rider dies, their dragon feels it all, and it breaks our hearts every single time. So we hide. We let our minds slumber and give control to the men on our backs, almost as if we were nothing more than winged horses. You touched the part of my soul that lay asleep for centuries, and it feels good to see the world in all its glory again.'

What Vahin said was surprising but made perfect sense. When I lost my Anchors, it almost killed me, and for years, I'd lived on as an empty shell. Now, it felt like a faded nightmare, most likely thanks to this wonderful being becoming my Anchor.

Had I, too, tried to hide all these years? Did bonding with Vahin finally bring me back to life? He must have lost untold riders. I could understand why he preferred not to feel or think.

I stroked the skin of Vahin's wing, trying to comfort both him and myself. I needed to touch him, and I knew that no matter what, I would not sleep alone tonight. 'I'm glad that I could help,' I murmured, and his body rumbled again.

'And I'm glad that I could help you. Now rest. I'm not letting you return barefoot and shivering—Orm would rip my scales off.'

Now, it was my turn to laugh, but I nodded sheepishly.

'Pfft, no one could move me from here. I'm sleeping with you, and I don't care what anyone thinks. For the record, I can't believe the spectacular Vahin would ever tremble before the human commander,' I teased, and the dragon laughed.

'Wait until you see him angry; *then* you can make fun,' he retorted, and I buried myself under his massive wing.

'Do you know what happened after I Anchored you?' I asked quietly.

'No, all I know is that I was exhausted after the spectrae attack—so much so I couldn't communicate with you, even when I felt some part of you rejecting my presence,' he offered with a quiet rumble. 'I felt my fire burning through your body, and I could do nothing to help. I was afraid, Little Flame. I was afraid for us both.'

'I'm sorry.' I whispered.

'It's all in the past now. I have you, and you will never lose me. I will give you my all—my fire, my magic, and my life. Just stay with me. I don't want to dwell in the dark again.'

I had so many questions, but more importantly, I just wanted to be with him. Even if I had Anchored him in an unorthodox way, I felt like he was the best thing that could have ever happened to me. Conduit mages choose their

Anchors carefully, knowing that they would possess a part of their soul. One touch of Vahin's spirit, and I knew I'd happily give him it all.

He was mine, and I belonged to him: my mighty, scaled guardian, the one who called to me in his dreams.

CHAPTER 15

ORMOND

I am never, under any circumstances, going to the mines again, I decided.

The pain of every joint creaking as I stretched felt like my body screaming in agreement. Dwarven mines weren't built for men over five feet, and as I was closer to seven feet tall, I'd spent the entire time bent in two. I would definitely be forgetting how many times I'd had to catch my balance only to put my hand into something slimy and foul-smelling. A week's worth of baths couldn't rid me of the smell.

That our search yielded nothing made me wonder why we fought for so long or as hard. The mines we could access were empty of even the tiniest shards. The one tunnel with even the slightest hint of crystal resonance was swarming with Vel and flooded. I'd returned to the fortress tired and angry. Even having Ani here wouldn't help restore the Barrier if we couldn't replace the damaged crystal.

The headache I'd gained from smacking my head on countless stalactites must have left me unable to think because, right after I took a bath, I had walked up here instead of falling into the nearest unoccupied bed.

I just needed to see her. I never thought I'd desire a companion. I'd thought my friendship with Alaric was all I needed but waking up next to Ani had changed my perspective completely. Now, I was paying for it, but I couldn't bring myself to regret anything.

When I approached the bed, seeing Annika there—so peaceful as she slept—had eased the pain of my headache. A serene expression on her face, her chestnut hair was unbound and unruly, her skin blushed pink in the firelight. Before I knew it, I'd placed my hand on her cheek, unable to resist the urge to touch her.

She was an irresistible paradox, strength and bravery mixed with a vulnerable, caring nature. I'd brought her here because it was my duty, to help end the danger posed by the damaged Barrier, but now ... now I wanted her for myself. I wanted to see the stubborn smile on her face and feel her sleep in my arms again.

This wasn't how I usually felt, and with the firm boundaries Ani had set, I didn't know what to do. My experience with women was limited to managing the servants, dealing with the few female soldiers the Crown sent us, or paying for a moment's pleasure. None of that applied to her, and despite my boasting that I could seduce her if I wanted, I was lost.

I considered leaving and sleeping in another room but sneaking away like a thief in the night somehow felt wrong. That would imply I felt guilty for being here. So, I slept in the chair, waiting until she woke up and threw me out of my own bedroom.

The thought made me chuckle, and I slowly opened my eyes, letting them adjust to the light before I looked at the bed to see if Ani was awake.

Only to find it empty.

When I arrived—so late I'd expected to hear a cock's crow—the woman had been sleeping peacefully, but now she was nowhere to be seen. I hadn't heard her leave. If anything, that showed how exhausted I was.

Did she leave because I was here? I wondered, jerking upright and letting the warm quilt fall on the floor. *Quilt?* I didn't remember grabbing that, yet the evidence that someone took care of my comfort was there, on the floor.

'Calm down, Orm, she is with me,' Vahin's voice in my head rumbled in amusement. *'When you come to collect Annika, bring her some clothes—unless you want her to parade around the stronghold in her nighty.'*

'What?!' I said out loud, and Vahin's laughter echoed in my head.

'And make sure to tell your mage to check on my Little Flame's health. She walked through the castle in the middle of the night wrapped only in a blanket, and she was freezing when she finally got here.'

'Your Little Flame?'

I wondered what Ani would think of this new nickname, especially when Vahin used it with such a protective tone. Or maybe he reserved that tone for me? My dragon's personality had blossomed since he'd Anchored Annika and I loved the change, loved working in concert as partners and not simply as rider and dragon.

'Yes, mine. For me, Annika is my Little Flame; for you, she can be the mountain nivale. She is a woman of many facets, and I'm sure Alaric will also find something that appeals to his dark soul.'

I frowned because I hadn't thought about them getting that close, and I had to admit it bothered me that my friend might want her affection. I knew Alaric planned to Anchor her. We'd discussed the idea in detail, and what we would do when we had both the conduit mage and the new keystone crystal. Once Annika arrived, he was going to convince her to perform the oath—and if that didn't work, I always had the geas.

The plan that, at the time, sounded so reasonable now felt like an abhorrent violation.

While we were searching for Ani, I'd petitioned the king to reopen the old dwarven mines on the southern side of the Ridge and supply the workers. The mines were famous for their crystals, but as I recently found out, the words '*were* famous' were more accurate than I realised.

Dwarves didn't abandon viable mines, and the one we had access to was empty—at least the part we could access. The time we were allowed in the mines was running short, much too short to explore the flooded portion, and the conditions set by the Crown made it obvious the mission was bound to fail.

My fists tightened at the thought that I'd have to beg the king and crown mages for their help. It felt like the dragon commanders were the only ones who still cared about the safety of the Kingdom of Dagome, but I knew my brethren were as tired as I was.

It's time to revise and adapt our misbegotten plan, I thought, but somehow, that didn't upset me as much as it should have. Not getting the crystal meant Ani wouldn't have to Anchor Alaric, and a small, selfish part of me rejoiced at the thought.

It hadn't bothered me before, but knowing what was required to create an Anchor bond, I felt conflicted. The Barrier was my duty, one I could not neglect, but did that mean I should give up the woman I'd begun developing feelings for?

Could Ani Anchor me in the same way she did Vahin? Was I ready to see her on the brink of death to avoid them being together?

'Fuck!' I grabbed the cup on the nearby table and hurled it across the room, watching it smash against the fireplace mantle before placing my hands firmly on the table, willing myself to calm down.

Annika was my doom. My darkness. The wild magic inside me, dormant and beaten down for years, had awakened under her touch, and it took a conscious effort to restrain my violent outbursts.

The gods must be laughing at my struggle. I had finally found a woman who was perfect for me, and I had to decide if I could let her fuck my best friend to save the kingdom. *There* has *to be another way,* I thought, analysing everything I knew so far.

Ari and I had talked about the Barrier so many times over a tankard or two that I even I knew more than most mages. If he was right, Annika had managed to kill the wlok and break the mountain because she had embraced the primal aether of the earth and it had accepted her touch. Unfortunately, he didn't think she could safely do it again without being Anchored to another mage.

I knew Alaric would do what needed to be done. I had seen the determination in his gaze when we had searched for the elusive mage, but deep inside—*gods forgive me*—I didn't want it to happen. Sharing her with Vahin wasn't difficult as there was no physical bond between them, but Alaric ...?

'Orm, you're thinking too loud. I need to hunt. Come and collect our sleeping treasure before I let her wander off and tempt all the men with her bare legs. I'm sure that will make the thoughts you are harbouring increase tenfold.'

'Vahin, don't. I'm not in the mood for your teasing, old friend ... Gods, if anyone dares to leer at her, I'll gouge their eyes out,' I snarled, pausing briefly when Vahin chuckled. *'Just give me a moment. I'll gather some clothes and come down.'*

I stretched again to relax my tense muscles, feeling my body protest. I needed a bed and a good night's rest, and that meant I would have to move Ani to her new chambers soon. The thought of it felt wrong, but again, it was something that needed to be done.

The rumbling in my stomach reminded me of Vahin. With the dragon's enhanced metabolism and his staying with me for the last few days, I knew he was starving, so I called for a maidservant, and Agnes appeared with a tray of food. The dainty canapés were more suitable as a lady's morning snack than a warrior's meal, but it would have to do for now.

'Find some clothes for Ani.'

'Where is my lady?' she asked with a frown, eyeing the bed before turning her gaze downward when she caught my disapproving frown.

'She went to visit Vahin. Unfortunately, her current attire isn't appropriate for walking around during the day. Is that enough of an answer, or will you test my patience further?' I snapped, pulling a change of clothes for myself from the wardrobe.

'No, my lord. My apologies, I was simply worried.'

I sighed. I hadn't meant to frighten the girl, but I felt every bone in my body, and hunger made me particularly short-tempered.

'It's all right, Agnes. I'm glad you take your duties seriously. Please ensure your lady's room is ready and move Ani's belongings there. If anything is lacking, ask the quartermaster to order it using my personal expenses. You must have learned what she likes by now, so make your lady as comfortable as possible.' The maid smiled, nodding eagerly.

She was the child of a dragon rider whose mother had stayed in the fortress. Her daughter had followed her lead, choosing to work here instead of trying her luck outside these granite walls. It pleased me immensely that she took to her new responsibilities with such enthusiasm.

'Buy yourself something, too. I will tell your father how content I am with your service.'

After Agnes disappeared to find some clothing, I quickly changed from riding leathers to more comfortable black trousers, a matching shirt, and a belt with two daggers, adding high boots and vambraces to complete the outfit. There was no need to carry a weapon inside of the castle, but I felt naked without a blade or two.

That done, I was ready to face the day. After I retrieved Annika from Vahin's cave, I'd have to talk to my officers about increasing patrols, but first, I needed to speak with Alaric. We'd made a worrying discovery during the battle with the Vel in the mines.

After fighting the nasty ant-like creatures in the tunnels closest to the Rift, we'd broken through into a vast cavern filled with luminescent mushrooms. As we stumbled through the entrance, our opponents fled, leaving us to catch our breaths in confusion.

What we had seen had everyone raising their swords in readiness—stood before us, was a vjesci.[1] The demon had looked like the textbook illustrations of the Moroi nobility, and when confronted, he had displayed manners that reinforced that impression. The vjesci had surrendered without resistance, and my men looked at me with wariness and distrust.

Despite that, I had them secure the demon and bring him back to the stronghold. I needed Ari, with his necromancer magic, to question him and discover how big a pile of excrement we'd landed in.

I couldn't remember the walk to Alaric's chambers, but here I was, standing in front of his door feeling like a fool. I felt the distance between us, almost like a physical wall preventing me from knocking. It left me missing our easy camaraderie.

Something had fractured in our friendship since we'd encountered Anni-ka; Alaric had withdrawn into his studies, and I didn't know how to bridge the gap. He was still himself, a dangerous mage with a wicked sense of hu-mour, but now it felt like a facade that hid some dark emotion I couldn't identify; and every time I asked, he refused to talk about it.

'Why didn't you just enter?' Alaric said. There was a hint of amusement in his voice. When I looked up, I saw the corner of my friend's mouth twist into a smile that almost made me flinch.

---

1. **Vjesci** — an undead demon that preserves the thoughts, personality, and body of the person it once was. After death, the body cools closely, and the limbs remain limber. The lips and cheeks remain red, and spots of blood often appear under the fingernails and on the face.

'I didn't know if I still had an open invitation.' I instantly regretted my words as his smile disappeared.

'It is your castle, and you are always welcome in my quarters. How can I help you?'

I clenched my fists. I wanted to simultaneously grab him by his fancy kaftan and beat him to a pulp until he told me what was wrong while begging him to abandon his plans with Annika. To leave her to me. Instead, I tried to break through Ari's silence.

'Is there anything I can do to help? You can lock yourself up in the workshop, but you can't hide from me. I know you too well,' I said.

'If you know me so well, you'd know you shouldn't ask,' Alaric answered calmly, and only years of conditioning helped me control my emotions before I reacted. I purposefully took a moment to relax my tense muscles before I nodded to him.

'I came here because I wanted to ask about Ani and tell you about the gift I brought back from the mines. A vjesci—one that looks like the old paintings of the Moroi. It likely crawled here from the Barren Lands. Maybe you can find out why he's here and how he escaped?'

Vjesci weren't an aggressive type of Vel. They had a sharp intelligence that seemed to suppress the mindless hunger of their fellow demons. They appeared to those who were about to cross death's veil, feeding on the fear their appearance awakened in their victims. That's why people call them *Messengers of Death*.

'Where is it?' Alaric asked sharply.

'Where else? In the dungeons, the cell closest to your workshop.' I said, and he nodded and ran towards the stairs.

'Should you not wait for Ani? She is a battle mage after all, and I'm sure her training included a few tricks we could use.' I rushed to keep up.

'No, I'll tell her about it later,' he answered. 'Where is she, anyway? Does she know about the demon?'

'She's with Vahin in his lair. Don't ask me why. She slept there for some reason,' I groused, and he laughed without humour.

'He is her Anchor. That is reason enough.' I frowned at the tone of his voice. Alaric seemed on edge, and I wondered if it was the vjesci or something else that darkened his mood.

We reached the basement quickly. I nodded to the saluting soldiers before we entered the warded cell where I'd left him. The undead demon was still there, calmly sitting on the stone floor. He turned his head as we entered, and I could clearly see the bloodless face and unnaturally red lips that confirmed his origins.

Alaric's eyes narrowed when he saw the creature, but before he moved forward, I touched his shoulder. 'Should I stay?' I knew he didn't like people seeing him use necromancy, as if the lack of witnesses meant it didn't exist. But I would stay if it would help, even if the stench of the undead could turn the strongest stomach.

'No, this won't take long. Go find Annika. I will join you shortly,' he said. The smile returned to his face, but I could feel how tense his muscles were under my hand.

'Fine, don't take too long, and if you have any trouble, we can do it together later.'

Alaric surprised me when he tilted his head, and for a moment, I saw my old friend looking back at me with those mesmerising golden eyes. 'Together? You volunteering to clean up the mess once I'm done?' His gentle chuckle and dark humour instantly brightened my mood. 'Go, Orm, I will be fine. Necromancy is my natural talent, after all.'

CHAPTER 16

ALARIC

After Orm left, I looked at the soldiers guarding the cell and gestured towards the door.

'Leave.'

They hesitated. Orm strictly enforced his protocols, and one of those orders was that no prisoner should be left alone with one guard, but this was no ordinary prisoner ... and I wasn't a guard.

Besides, I needed to be alone with him because as soon as I'd entered the dungeon, I'd felt my family's magic signature on the demon.

The vjesci stood up and looked at me. He was also waiting, which showed just how lucid he was after his corruption. The unblinking stare didn't disturb me, nor did the hypnotic swaying, the demon buffeted by the aether moving through the cell. With a guilty look at each other, the guards left. As soon as we were alone, I approached the prisoner.

'Speak.'

'Alaric'va Shen'ra, I have a message for you.'

A small bubble of bloody saliva splattered on his chin. Purple flames burst into life on my palm as I called on my necromancy, ready to destroy him if the message proved volatile.

It was unlikely a vjesci would be sent as an assassin, but I couldn't exclude the possibility. Before letting him continue, however, I asked, 'Did my sister send you or my father?'

'Lady Rowena made me, but I'm not her messenger.'

The creature licked his lips, taking a step closer. I could see the flash of anger in his gaze, but other than that, he didn't make any hostile moves. The blood oath on my chest throbbed. Its proximity to my sister's magic caused it to burn with urgency. I could feel the aether condensing around us, filling the space with the tension of an impending storm.

'Is she still alive?' I asked, unsure if I wanted to know the answer, as both possibilities were equally terrifying. 'Alive ... yes, she was alive,' the creature answered, tilting his head as if pondering the meaning of the words. 'She serves our lord now and wields significant influence.'

'Why did she make you?'

I refused to believe that my sister, the golden-haired, loving girl, kind even when causing mischief ... no. There was no way someone so full of life could create a vjesci. It took a skilled necromancer, one willing to perform the foulest of magics, to rip the life from someone whilst preserving the soul and mind so that it retained the ability to think and speak.

The only reason for her to have created him—other than the most dreadful—was that she did it to send me a message that maybe she'd found a way to escape.

'I don't know her reasons, but she made me and many others. Our lord asks, and she creates: strigae, ghouls, spectrae—she makes them all,' he said, turning the blood in my veins to ice.

I needed a moment to compose myself, and I turned my gaze to the wall, focusing on the droplets of water tracking their way along the granite. No matter how hard I stared, there was no escape from what I'd heard. It was true that vjesci were demons of bad tidings and death, because I felt that whatever he was going to say would be the death of me.

'Who were you?' I asked.

'Were? I am Tarant Sethan, from the noble House of Nightfall.'

For a moment, I felt pity for the being who still considered himself a part of a family wiped out during the Necromancer's War. The Moroi of the Nightfall clan were skilled in diplomacy and illusion. Tales of old spoke of the banquets they threw for foreign dignitaries, the spectacles so grandiose and full of light that everyone who witnessed them was spellbound by the power of Ozar and its culture.

'State your message, and I will let you find peace,' I commanded, and the vjesci's eyes turned milky white.

'Son of Shen'ra, you have something I want. You will bring the conduit mage to my court. In exchange, I will allow your sister to leave if she chooses. Fail to deliver the mage before winter, and I will send Rowena back to you one piece at a time.'

The voice that uttered its demands was different from the demon's. It was emotionless, almost monotone as if the Vel was reading a message burned into its mind. A wave of power washed outwards, forcing me back as the vjesci's face changed. It was the being who'd sent the message now in front of me, looking at me through the Vel demon's eyes.

'Oh no, you don't, you bastard. Possessing this corpse from such a distance won't allow you to influence me.' I quickly drew several sigils, pushing them forward, and purple flames wrapped around the vjesci like thorny vines, lifting the undead off the floor. It laughed, and the sound of it sent a shiver down my spine.

'Now, now, Alaric, don't you remember what happened to the last member of your family who defied me? Or was your mother's corpse not a strong enough message? You will be mine, boy. As will your new toy.'

Agony pierced my chest. Silver symbols crawled under my skin, burning with icy fire, and I felt like an open book while the Lich King looked directly into my very soul. *What have you done to me, mother?* I thought, dropping to my knees, clutching at my kaftan.

'*She screamed so beautifully as I tore her soul apart. When I was done, your father sent what was left of her, a corpse filled with a maelstrom of hate and magic, back to you. Do you know why? Even with her last breath, your mother begged me to spare Rowena, giving me you in return—and I did.*'

His gloating expression made my blood boil, but I silently stumbled to my feet to stand before the Lich King's effigy as he continued.

'*You're beginning to understand, aren't you, boy? Your mother sacrificed you to save your sister. That curse etched into your body marks you as my creature. The pain you feel now? It will be nothing compared to the inferno that will consume you when I touch your soul. Bring me the mage, or you will soon beg for the sweet release of death.*'

Fury so wild and consuming overwhelmed me and I screamed in anguish. As the last echoes of my despair faded, I sobbed. 'Why did my father not stop this? How did you corrupt him so completely that he forgot even the little love he had for my mother?' I asked the one question that had troubled me all these centuries. My father—harsh and cruel as he could be—had never hurt my mother, the only person able to calm his anger.

'*Fool. You think your father cared for that woman? Roan chose a human because he despised his kin. He didn't want to be one of those men kept as breeding stock like prize bulls. A sweet, innocent human would do as she was told and give him children to continue the bloodline before quietly dying once her usefulness expired.*'

I knew he hated fae women, but that my mother's only value in his eyes was as a broodmare? It explained many of my father's actions. I wished I could have kept the delusion that, at the beginning at least, she meant something to him. The revelations I was being forced to confront left me feeling numb inside.

Everything I believed in had crumbled to dust at my feet. I had loved my mother. Even after her spirit cursed me and forced me to take a blood oath, I still loved her, explaining away her actions. Yet now I knew she'd traded one child for another—the son who was the spitting image of the monster she married ... for the bright, shining star that was my sister.

I braced myself as I stared at the vjesci, its ghastly smile mocking the tightening purple flames around its body.

'*You have until winter. If the first snow falls on the courtyard of Katrass and you are not here with the conduit mage, I will see how much blood Rowena can lose before she joins her mother beyond the Veil. Then I will come tear down the Barrier and find you.*'

'We will strengthen the Barrier,' I lied, and the corpse laughed.

'*No, you won't. The damaged keystone weakens with each passing day. Do you seriously think one conduit mage can restore it? The Barrier will fall, it is* already *falling. The Rift is growing, just like my army, and when I flood your kingdoms with monsters, even your empress will bow to me. We will see where you stand when that happens: by my side, together with your father—or under my boot with the rest of them.*'

I'd heard enough. Despite the pain, or maybe *because* of it, my necromancy felt more potent than ever, and I used that strength to garrotte the talking corpse. The purple flames dug into the creature's flesh, dismantling the spell that animated it as they dismantled the vjesci's body. With one last grimace, the Lich King's visage disappeared, and I was left looking at the face of the proud Moroi once again.

'Are you going to destroy me?' he asked wistfully, emotion softening his voice, and I nodded, unable to prevent compassion from reaching my eyes. He was as much a victim of that madman as I was.

'Yes.'

'I'm glad. It's past time I rejoined my kin,' Tarant stated, looking me in the eye as I dismantled the magic tying the remains of his spirit to this realm. 'Don't believe anything your sister tells you.'

His last words haunted me, his remains falling to the floor with the final syllable, decomposing with unnatural speed when the ravages of time caught up with him. The muscles of my legs gave out as I released my hold on the aether, and I sat with a thud.

All these years, I'd had a purpose. A purpose that held back the few moments of self-pity I'd felt in my darkest days. Now I knew that everything I'd believed in was a lie, and there was no longer any way to pretend I was a hero saving the imprisoned princess.

The dead couldn't lie to a necromancer. My parents had betrayed me. Those who should've loved me the most had used me as a bargaining chip to save their favoured child, and I had stepped into the trap, willingly submitting myself to centuries of torment.

'I wish I'd never been born,' I said to the remains of the vjesci.

At least he could escape to the afterlife and join his kin. I had no one, and the only person I could call a friend I'd pushed away, knowing Orm's conditioning would prevent him from reaching out. Now, he was obsessed with his Nivale, and with his previous reluctance to let her go to the Barren Lands, I knew what his answer would be if I revealed what I'd learned today. I knew him well enough to realise he was falling for our conduit mage, even if he and the object of his interest were blissfully oblivious.

I recalled that first meeting by the lake and smiled bitterly. Annika Diavellar was the only person who'd quietened my curse, allowing me to breathe easier, whose magic was in perfect synergy with my own, even if she didn't know it yet. After that day, I thought Annika would treat me with scorn, like the rest of her brethren, but after a few days in her company, I knew I'd found a kindred spirit.

I sought her company not only because she eased the pain but because she let me hold her hand. I felt good about myself whenever I was near her, and for the first time since my father's betrayal, I felt a hint of pride at being a dark fae necromancer. And now the Lich King wanted to take even that from me.

I hammered my fist into the harsh stone again and again until I bled, but the vision of that demonic smirk demanding I bring Annika to his court refused to fade away. The dark cell began glowing eerily as my magic moved with a mind of its own, seeping into the bedrock surrounding me as I raged and mourned.

Not for my mother. She loved me; I know it, but how could she do such a thing to her own flesh and blood? Not for the bastard that sired me. The worst was the fact that I didn't even mourn my sister's fate.

I mourned for the waste that my life had become. All those years I'd lost, searching for a way to save my sister, to take some form of revenge. I'd learned to hide every emotion, painting a false smile on my lips when I was scorned by humans, just to gather knowledge or resources.

When the looks of disgust from mages for the upstart necromancer prevented me from gaining access to ancient texts, I'd learned high magic, hiding away yet another part of my blackened soul. I mourned the boy I was and the man he had turned into—the sad husk who craved pain because pain was the only thing he had left.

And I raged because, through all of that, I'd found a home. I found someone who had become my brother and a woman who gave me hope, but now the fates demanded that I destroy it all.

'No, I refuse to allow it. The only one destroyed will be you, Cahyon Abrasa. I will dismantle the immortality my father gave you and force you down Veles' throat if I must. Even if it means I die alongside you. That is my oath. I swear to the gods, above and below, I swear on the Dark Mother's tears. If I have to lose it all, I will take you with me.'

The Lich King was right about the Barrier, however. The keystone's magic was fading, and no magic could fix it. I had given Orm false hope because I knew the plan that I had formed in my head since meeting Ani was too reckless for him to ever agree to.

The only way to save the Lowland Kingdoms was to kill the Lich King. I needed Annika because, before the Barrier failed completely, I was positive it would be possible for me to force a way through despite the foul magic in my blood. I would fulfil the Lich King's wishes and bring him the conduit mage, but she would arrive Anchored and ready for battle.

She might, if we survived, even forgive my subterfuge that put her in danger. The bitter laugh that escaped at that thought forced a last, lonely tear from my eye, and I felt it slide over my cheek to fall silently to the floor.

For so many years, I lived hoping to remove the curse, but now ... Now, I would live for revenge. With one deep, slow breath, I centred myself, forcing a peaceful smile onto my lips. My heart and mind were in turmoil, but that was not for the world to see. I needed to play my part. I needed to be the Alaric they wanted to see: the charming man, the healer, and the high mage who had promised a solution to the swarming monsters.

When Annika finally trusted me enough to Anchor me, I would take her to the Lich King ... and her heart-shaped face will be the last thing he sees before I destroy him. I was not born a monster, but the Dark Mother willed it so. And I was done fighting my fate.

CHAPTER 17

OR𝖬OND

After leaving Alaric in the cell, I went to my office to wait for Agnes to bring Annika's clothes. That was soon forgotten when I saw a letter from the royal mage on my desk. After reading it, I struggled to rein in my temper, which had become a recurring issue this past week.

The bastard was sending one of his lackeys to ensure I'd Anchored Ani and had her under control, just as I had promised.

I wished I could throw the poisoned missive into the fire. Instead, I folded it carefully, intending to show it to Alaric later. My friend would take some time with his interrogation of the prisoner, and I knew better than to disturb him while he was using his ... *unique* skills.

When Agnes arrived with Ani's clothes, I was in such a daze that I didn't even acknowledge her presence, gathering up the dress and heading down to Vahin's lair, wondering how a half-asleep woman could have found her way to such a remote part of the castle.

As I neared the dragon's lair public entrance, I paused before snorting with laughter, realising I wasn't only carrying a woman's dress. On top of the bundle was a set of undergarments, and as much as I didn't care, the soldiers might get interesting ideas if they saw their commander parading around with female underclothes.

There was an alternative route, a hidden passage—or, more accurately, a hidden staircase—that led down to Vahin's quarters. I could only hope Ani hadn't used it; the injuries she could have incurred on the slippery stone didn't bear thinking about.

The view that greeted my arrival rendered me speechless. The fearsome dragon of Varta Fortress was curled up on the ground like a giant cat, his front paw held in front of him. In the crook of his elbow slept Ani, covered by an inky black wing, her creamy skin a stark contrast to the dragon's scales. I looked on, charmed by the enchanting and innocent tableau. In her white nightgown, Ani looked like a virgin bride sacrificed to the beast.

'*Beautiful, isn't she?*' Vahin's voice was full of pride, pleased with his prized possession. I watched as his head moved closer to her. His forked tongue slowly trailed over the sleeping woman's cheek before she swatted him away.

'Wake up, Little Flame.'

But instead of opening her eyes, Ani grumbled and pulled the membrane of Vahin's wing over her head, muttering, 'I don't want to. Let me sleep a little longer.' I coughed to cover my laughter, causing Annika to look over the edge of Vahin's wing. 'Orm? What are you doing here? How did you find me?' I smirked at her attempt to finger-brush her tussled hair.

'That overgrown bedspread you're sitting on told me. Shouldn't I be the one asking why *you're* here? If you intended to sleep on the dragon, you could have at least woken me so that I could have slept in my own bed. I assume you saw me, since I found myself covered with a blanket.'

I reached over to pass Ani the clothes. 'Please put those on before we return upstairs. The soldiers here don't usually see women running around half naked, and that translucent muslin might actually be worse. I don't want them getting any ideas.'

Ani scowled at me but snatched the clothes away before turning towards Vahin. 'Can you spread your wings, please? I need some privacy since the men here are *sooo* prone to getting *ideas*,' she huffed, and Vahin's laugh rumbled throughout the cavern.

'Of course, Little Flame. I will always protect you, though Orm is the last person I would suspect of having ideas. I'm afraid he is a man of stone, and even such a beautiful creature as yourself couldn't tempt him. Alaric, on the other hand ...'

'Could easily be tempted by such a gorgeous woman,' the soft baritone finished behind me, and I glanced over at him. Alaric had changed from the clothes he was wearing earlier. It was strange to see him here in his grey kaftan and matching trousers. He looked refined—and, I had to admit, dangerous—with the silver embroidery highlighting the natural light grey colour of his skin and the glint in his golden irises.

Annika's snort made me turn back, surprised.

'Well, as much fun as it is to have you two chase me around the castle dressed for high tea, I don't recall asking for assistance. I'm perfectly capable of finding the way upstairs myself,' Ani grunted as she fumbled with the ties on the back of her dress.

I couldn't help staring as the shape of her body became visible through the thin membrane of Vahin's wing. I was about to offer my help when Alaric stepped in. 'Let me help you,' he said when it became clear she was struggling.

'Really? What about you, Orm? Do you want to help? Was that the reason you visited me while I was sleeping? Poor Agnes will be so upset if you replace her.' I didn't take it to heart, expecting scorn after my impromptu visit.

I stepped closer to explain myself, but Ari smirked. 'Orm is only good at taking a lady's clothes *off*. I'm afraid he couldn't assist you prepare to face the world if his life depended on it. I, however, can do it with my eyes closed and with one hand tied behind my back. Besides, the privilege of touching such beauty should fall to the most handsome man in the room,' he said so confidently that it caught my attention.

Something felt odd in his demeanour. The elaborate clothes, the compliments as if he were trying too hard to impress her ... I stood to the side, observing him. He was trying to gain Ani's favour at my expense, but I didn't intervene, unsure why his attitude had changed. I watched the conflicting emotions rush across her features. In the end, she laughed, shaking her head at Alaric's playful expression.

'Let him help you, Little Flame.' Vahin's voice seemed to help her decide, and with a heavy eye roll, she turned her back towards Alaric, lifting her hair.

'Fine, but I demand two things. First, he has to admit no male, human or otherwise, is more beautiful than my dragon. Second, as soon as I get to my room, I'm burning this dress. I need something practical, not some elaborate court garment.'

'I will admit no such a thing. My dark fae beauty has been honed over centuries, and you're asking me to relinquish my crown to a dragon? As for your clothes, you can burn them or have them ripped off your body. Our tailor will be overjoyed to provide a new wardrobe, I assure you. I can even help you select the best practical designs, if you'd like.'

I didn't fail to notice how gently Ari held the laces, tying them slowly while his fingers trailed over her back. When he was almost done, my friend traced his fingers under the edge of her collar to straighten it. The move was slow and sensual, and despite a sharp pang of jealousy, it surprised me how much pleasure it gave me to observe his interaction with Ani.

She inhaled sharply when he brushed her bare skin and pulled away. 'Are you done playing around? Or do you plan on standing here all day?' She looked over her shoulder with a frown and I saw Alaric's mouth twitch with the hint of a smile that mirrored mine. Ani wasn't easily swayed, and knowing my friend, he took it as a challenge.

'You are ready. Shall we let Vahin hunt for his breakfast?' he said, pulling away before gesturing towards the stairs. Ani nodded, but before she stepped out of the dragon's reach, she bent over and kissed his snout. 'Thank you. For everything. I had a wonderful night.'

I felt waves of joy and pleasure radiating through my bond with Vahin. My dragon was happier than I had ever felt him being before. 'Any time, Little Flame,' he said, his voice almost a purr. The smile he received in exchange made me wish it was directed at me.

'Let's go, please. We can't let Vahin waste away,' I said, and Ani walked towards the exit before she stumbled, hissing and hopping on one leg. 'Bloody rocks ... Next time you bring me clothes, please bring boots too. This place is full of rocks.' She lifted the hem of her dress to check her foot.

I saw the blood smeared across her heel, and before I knew it, Ani was in my arms. It was a minor injury, but it angered me; I could have prevented it if I'd been thinking clearly. Then came the fear. She'd walked down here barefoot and could have fallen to her death with no one the wiser. *I could have lost her...* It was a startling thought, and what followed was a choking fear that I couldn't understand. As if on command, darkness rose from inside my soul, turning into a fury that I struggled to contain.

'How the fuck did you get here barefoot and barely dressed? You should be more careful, not acting like a toddler strolling around the place in their nightgown,' I scolded her, gesturing to Ari. 'Check her wound.'

'It was just happenstance. I wouldn't have come barefoot if I hadn't given Agnes my boots to clean. Next time, I'll take yours, since they were set out so neatly next to the door.' She rolled her eyes, unbothered by my outburst. 'Orm, don't be so ridiculous and put me down. It is just a minor cut, not a mortal wound.'

'No,' I said, tightening my grasp. I wouldn't let the cut get infected because of stupid pride. 'You are bleeding, and the cave floor is filthy,' Ari added calmly, taking on the role of mediator between us. I saw the bright hue of his magic wrapping itself lazily around his arm, changing from silver to green as he chanted a healing spell, weaving it together.

'You're healing me again. I know you're dark fae, but with your healing ability and all those glyphs … your power looks more like high magic than foul. There's no hint of purple. How is that possible?' Ani asked, leaning forward to observe Alaric. I used that as an excuse to press her to my chest, inhaling her herbal scent with its hint of verbena.

'My mother was human. I inherited both abilities, but I prefer to work with high magic than resort to my dark fae heritage. I don't think the citizens of Varta would like it if I started raising their friends.' He lifted her foot higher, and I frowned, noticing the scraped skin on his knuckles.

'I will tell you more later. First, I need to address this before Orm loses his patience with us. Judging by his expression, he's already getting testy,' he teased, and as soon as she nodded, his hand slid over her damaged skin.

'*Siltin o'goth.*'[1]

I felt his magic affecting me as well, the tiredness of last night vanishing and energy suffusing my body. Ani gasped, stiffening in my arms. She looked at Alaric with a deep frown, but his only response was a gentle smile.

'Yes, I didn't mask it this time, and I know what you felt. I didn't want to burden you, but from the moment I helped you deal with Vahin's Anchor, I knew that our magic was in synergy.' I watched the damage to her foot disappear, but Ani didn't pay attention to it or to me, her gaze solely focused on Alaric. 'That was more than synergy,' she murmured hesitantly. 'You shouldn't have hid it from me. Is that why you want to be my Anchor?'

'Not initially, no, but you have to admit it makes sense now.' He didn't even try to deny it. 'How many mages with perfect synergy is it possible to meet in one lifetime?'

I felt unease build in my chest. With no knowledge of magic beyond a basic education, I didn't fully grasp what my companions were talking about, but it seemed to have significant meaning for both of them.

---

1. *Heal the flesh.*

'I can't let you do it. It is too dangerous,' she said, disturbing my thoughts.

'It is far less dangerous than Anchoring a dragon, but I understand your objections. I'm willing to risk it, but it will always be your choice. Still, shielding you from my magic would make little sense in the long run. Sooner or later, you will see how compatible we are,' he affirmed, and Ani sighed.

'And you couldn't find the time to tell me earlier? In your workshop or in the library? I spent days in your company and you failed to bring it up. Why?'

'It slipped my mind,' he quipped with a roguish smile.

'Alaric!'

'I didn't want to pressure you. Trust is hard to earn, especially if one is dark fae.' He wouldn't look at her, and Ani reached out. I clenched my teeth but didn't move when her hand cradled his cheek, stroking him gently with her thumb until his gaze returned to hers.

'Stop beating yourself up with that chip on your shoulder. How many times do I have to tell you? You are who you are, that will never be a problem. I don't care what other mages think, and I'm not refusing because of who you are but because of what happened before.'

I felt excluded from the conversation. I'd heard of magical synergy: a rare occurrence when the power of two or more mages aligned so perfectly that they could connect and enhance each other's spells. Yet, both Ani and Alaric seemed to think there was more to it, and I had no idea what they meant.

It took all of my willpower to hide how uneasy I felt at seeing them so connected. That would always be something I couldn't give her. I didn't possess the kind of magic that could link us—yet another reason to let them find some happiness together, but even thinking about it stirred a wild inferno in my core.

'We should go upstairs. Alaric, I want to see you once I return from the barracks. We have much to discuss,' I said as calmly as I could. I was better than this, better than the mindless beast trashing in my core. I coughed, pretending not to notice Annika's questioning frown.

Annoyed by my lack of reaction, she wiggled in my arms. 'I'm all right now, so please put me down. I prefer people see me walking than once again being carried by the commander like some damsel in distress.' I shook my head, nodding towards her bare feet. 'You forget you're still barefoot, Nivale. How about we compromise? I will carry you upstairs, but as soon as we reach a level with clean and polished floors, you can walk to your heart's content.'

'You know, I could make you put me down,' she stated, tightening her lips to hide the smile I had still caught sight of.

'That is true, but then Alaric would be forced to avenge me, and we'd end up with a mage battle in the dragon's lair,' I said, feeling amused by her snarkiness.

She responded, 'And I could call a dragon for help.' Vahin chuckled in the background.

'Keep me out of this, Little Flame. Just let him do it. Let him experience carrying a human around like I've done for him for years.'

'Aha ... yes. Let me ride on your back.' The mischief flashing in Ani's eyes didn't bode well for me. Still, I tried to look as offended as possible when, with a deep sigh, she wiggled, wrapping her hands around my neck. Before I could protest, she scrambled over me to sit on my back in a truly uncomfortable position. It looked like I was going to be giving the stubborn mage a piggyback ride upstairs.

'Mush, mush, my noble stead, stretch out those oversized muscles of yours,' she said, patting my shoulder. Both Alaric and Vahin roared with laughter. 'How does it feel to be mounted like a dragon?' Vahin's voice reverberated in the air, and both Ani and Alaric snorted at his remark.

'You are much more comfortable, Vahin,' she called out, and I sighed, feeling utterly disarmed. 'Besides, he is not a dragon but a bear—a big and grumpy bear. Maybe I should start calling him Ursus, like the biggest bear in the stars?'

'You will be the death of me, Nivale. Bloody "*mush*"—as if I were a damn sledge dog. Even "giddy up" would have been better than that. Oh, and for the record: I hear one *word* of this from the servants, and my revenge will be swift and painful,' I threatened, a smile slipping from my control as I spoke. The woman who loved the stars had just named me after the biggest constellation in the northern sky. It felt as if the fates smiled at me.

Ani's defiant laughter told me how comfortable she was, and having her body pressed against me chased the rest of my worries away. My life was not a bed of roses. I ate when I needed to, worked until my eyesight blurred, and almost forgot how to smile. Yet here I was, laughing and carefree—all because my Nivale called me a bear and rode me like a horse.

'Thank you,' she whispered, placing her chin on my shoulder. 'For your help ... and the compromise, my Ursus.' I acknowledged her words, gently squeezing her thigh and followed Alaric as he created a light to ease the way.

I knew I needed to talk to Ari. About their magic, the synergy, and the Anchoring—because forcing Ani was no longer an option. Vahin was right. She was becoming important to us. I had to find out what my friend thought because, seeing the change in his behaviour, I suspected something was going on ... and as willing as I was to wreck the world for him, I wouldn't let Ani be put in harm's way.

CHAPTER 18

ORMOND

I stared at the report on my desk as if I could erase the words by sheer strength of will.

The mine was a bust. I'd need to clear the Vel from its depths or send a request to the other leaders of the Lowland Kingdoms to see if they had a crystal in their vaults. That would mean working behind my own king's back, which wouldn't end well—if at all—as my brother told me the king had called a meeting with the foreign ambassadors, reassuring them that the situation with the Barrier was under control.

My word against the king's. What were the odds?

'Fuck it all,' I growled at my thoughts as I hammered my fist on the desk, sighing when my knuckle left blood on the hard oak wood. I needed my control back; even my usually pristine and organised office was a mess now, with letters and orders cluttering every flat surface.

I felt like I was fighting this battle alone—well, almost alone. My brother was helping, and Alaric ... but my friend hadn't been himself lately. I knew he had nightmares and that they'd worsened. The only thing that seemed to make him smile these days was his time with Ani, and despite my own need to see her, I pulled away to give him the time he needed with her in his workshop or the library.

She was the only one who could make him smile. In her company, he became relaxed, and the mischievous, deadly man showed his gentler side. Still, we needed to talk, as the soldiers refused to train with him any longer. He fought so ferociously that they were being wounded far too often.

The problem was that I hadn't had a spare moment free to do it.

The other commanders reported that the Vel were raiding the villages closest to the Barrier. They called for a war meeting despite having no authorisation from the Crown, and I had to agree with them.

Even here, the attacks were growing more frequent, especially by the strigae and wind demons amassing near the roads. They were making travel in the region close to impossible without a heavy escort. I'd had to reorganise the entire patrol schedule, leaving soldiers to guard the roads and riders to assist them from above to deal with any casualties.

With everything going on, there weren't enough hours in the day to spend with Annika, and the nights ... the dreams that made me wake up hard as a rock wondering what she'd do if I knocked on her door ... *Would she let me in?* The image of her body wrapped in that damned white nightdress assaulted my senses, and I had to close my eyes, exhaling slowly, willing it to go away. *I should go to the brothel before I lose my last semblance of control.*

No, I wanted Ani, not just some temporary relief.

A knock on my door interrupted my turbulent thoughts, and I nodded to Alaric when he walked in. 'The envoy from the royal mage has arrived. He should be here shortly. I asked the officer to bring him via the more scenic route through the town so that we could talk.'

'Where's Ani?'

'I saw her in Katja's workshop furiously mashing some herbs. You should offer that herbalist woman a permanent position here. She is excellent at making tinctures and remedies. More importantly, she is a good friend to Annika, and your Nivale needs female company.'

A strange emotion flitted across his features as he rubbed his chest again, a habit that was growing more noticeable with each passing day. 'I will,' I answered. Another knock announced the arrival of the envoy, and Alaric positioned himself beside me so that we could both face the visitor. The man who followed my officer was dressed as a battle mage. His robes, however, were black, showing his status as both fully trained and a member of the royal household. He bowed his head respectfully towards me, but when his gaze slid towards Alaric, his only response was a raised eyebrow and pursed lips.

'Commander, I'm here to discuss your plans for tackling the recent Vel attacks. I have been given full authority by the chancellor to carry out an inspection of your preparations and disposition of your troops,' he declared arrogantly. I felt my fists tighten as I bit back my indignant response.

'I'm sure you already know my name but let me formally introduce myself. I'm Lord Ormond Erenhart. You may call me "Commander" or "Sir," as you choose.' I enjoyed seeing the mage rear backwards, his nostrils flaring. I gestured to my left. 'I believe you've already met our fortress mage, Alaric'va Shen'ra. Now ... who might you be?' I asked calmly while Ari looked down his nose at the envoy.

'I am Ihrain Zak, battle mage of the High Order and apprentice to the royal mage.' His gaze slid to Ari with open disdain. 'You are a fool if you employ a dark fae as your mage. They cannot be trusted.'

'You're right. We can't be trusted. Yet no one from the capital dares to come work at the fortress, so perhaps we can be trusted a little more than the commoners of the Lowland Kingdoms.'

I couldn't help but smile. This was Ari at his keenest. Within moments, he'd identified the envoy's weakness and eviscerated him. The envoy's surname was that of a family of ennobled peasants. That he'd thought to use the royal mage's authority as his own ... well, that told us everything we needed to know about his character. While I'd intended to use the knowledge as leverage later on, Alaric had decided to put the coward in his place from the start.

'You *foul* creature ...'

'Enough.' I slammed my hand onto my desk, and the envoy startled, falling silent mid-sentence. 'You will inspect the fortress if and when I allow it. Did your master brief you on the situation here?' I asked, and something akin to understanding flashed in Ihrain's eyes.

'You mean your intention to replace the keystone? That was a ridiculous idea from the start. If your mage had bothered to communicate with the university, he would have learned that the entire Barrier is failing, not just a keystone in the Lost Ridge. It is no longer about singular Vel passing through the Rift. All four fortresses have now notified us of an increase in attacks. Some have even sighted spectrae on this side of the Barrier.'

'Sighted? Lucky them, we fought a damn swarm of them. What is the king planning on doing?'

'His Majesty recognises the problem but decided that instead of war, we will try ... a different approach. Our mages were able to communicate with Katrass through a portal and received confirmation that messengers were welcome, so the king has sent our best diplomats to the Lich King's domain. Why fight the monsters when we can have peace with the man who controls them? The Necromancer's War was five hundred years ago. Times have changed, and it's time for us to change as well. The Barren Lands were once a thriving merchant hub with access to the Northern Sea, and it can become so again.'

'The empress tried that when Cahyon was still human. Have you learned nothing from her mistakes?' Alaric's voice was grim, but I had to agree with him. I wish I understood what was going on at court these days.

'Is that the reason all my requests for aid are being refused? Or why my army is now half-full of criminals instead of proper soldiers?' I hissed. The smirk on the mage's face was my only answer.

The king didn't care if the Barrier was restored. It explained the years of neglect and lack of response to my requests. Did he want it to fall? That could be the reason for the reassurances given to the foreign courts. Though one thing remained a mystery ... *Why had I been given Annika's geas?*

The meeting during which the royal mage had given me the parchment had been secretive to say the least, but I'd assumed it was because he couldn't admit to losing track of her for so long. Now it looked more like something else was afoot. Could Ani's disappearance have been orchestrated, or at least aided, by the royal mage? Was that secretive old bastard plotting against the king?

'You are getting the men you need, so what's the fuss? Political decisions are not for the likes of you to question, Commander,' he sneered, and I began questioning why the chancellor would send someone so stupid here. Before I could answer, the door burst open, and Annika strode inside in a cloud of herbal scent wearing a determined expression.

'If you think you can push me aside again, you are sorel ... ohhh.' Her tirade petered out when she saw the black embroidered robes of a battle mage and the man himself standing between us. She paled, swaying slightly, and I rushed to her side, but Alaric was there first.

'Annika? But you're dead!' The battle mage gasped out in disbelief, and I swore under my breath.

'Good morning, Ihrain,' Ani answered, now entirely under control. 'I'm sorry for disturbing your meeting. I will return later.' Her tone trembled a little towards the end, and she turned to leave, only to stop in her tracks as the battle mage snarled.

'Stop and explain yourself, creature.' The crackling sound of aetheric power being manipulated had everyone turning, ready to fight—none faster than Alaric, who'd already leapt forward, dagger drawn and thrusting.

'Creature?' she hissed, flames spitting from the ends of her fingers.

'You will speak to my lady with respect or not at all, boy. Choose your next words wisely. I would see you pay in blood for your insolence,' Ari threatened, pressing the point of his dagger to Ihrain's neck.

'Your lady? Can't you see, you fool?!' he spat. 'This is a doppelgänger, a latawica[1] pretending to be Annika Diavellar. Annika died ten years ago when she lost control of her magic after her Anchors died. She was promised to *me*, so I would know if she was still alive.' Alaric only pressed harder, drawing blood, and Ihrain finally paled. 'You're defending this demon?'

'Oh, cut it out, both of you. I didn't die, and I wasn't promised to you. I never gave my consent, and I ran away before anyone got any stupid ideas about using my geas. You *idiots* in the capital are so gullible.'

She approached the pair and took hold of Alaric's hand to ease the dagger from Ihrain's neck. 'They were bound to find out, eventually. I'm not exactly hiding anymore, am I? Ihrain will behave, or I will repeat our little tête-à-tête from school. Do you still wet yourself at the sight of fire, little Ihry?'

'You *bitch*! So it is you? Wait until the king learns of your survival. Who is your Anchor? You wouldn't have managed without one,' Ihrain demanded as he moved towards her.

'I am her Anchor,' Alaric said. Annika frowned briefly as she glanced towards him but didn't contradict his lie.

'A dark fae? Why am I not surprised?' Ihrain's gaze jumped between Alaric's and Ani's before his hatred focused on her. 'You took this foul mage when you could have Anchored the best in the country? The king is old and has no

---

1. **Latawica(f)/latawiec(m)** — shapeshifting wind demons that fly in currents. Their physical bodies are similar to large birds with sharp claws and colourful feathers, with human heads. They can shift into any human to tempt their victim with their song; and when they sing, those who hear it claw their bodies, ripping the flesh as an offering for the ravenous demons.

heirs, and I have the support of the chancellor. With your power, we could have taken control of the court. Who do you think will rule when he is gone?'

'Certainly not you. How you even become the royal mage's apprentice is beyond me. The old man didn't strike me as a person who suffers fools. As for your proposal? You tried to drag me into bed and force our bond. Consider yourself lucky that all I did was singe your little soldier for that crime.'

At Annika's revelation, both Ari and I pushed forward, but we stopped when she took Ari's hand and pressed it to her chest over her Anchor's mark. 'Dare insult my Anchor again, and I shall open up his access to the aether; *then* we'll see what happens to those who hurt the ones I love.'

Ani couldn't see it, but Alaric went ghostly pale, his eyes a swirling crimson as they stared at the woman who held his hand as if he were her lover. I cleared my throat to gain the battle mage's attention.

'Those higher than you already know about Annika, so dispense with your subterfuge. You are free to inform the king that Lady Annika is safely Anchored and will remain at Varta Fortress with her bonded mate. You'll be shown to your quarters now, and tomorrow you will travel back to the capital,' I said as calmly as I could manage, trying not to look at Alaric, who'd moved closer to Ani, embracing her as he pressed his forehead to hers, inhaling deeply.

'But the inspection—'

'Your inspection is concluded. You offended my hospitality, my mage, and my guest; therefore, you are no longer welcome in this fortress. If you try to resist, I have a squadron of dragons that would be happy to deal with you.' A mighty roar shook the windows, accenting my words. Vahin had eavesdropped on the conversation while linked to my mind, and he was more than eager to back me up.

Like most bullies, Ihrain was also a coward, and the sound of a dragon's roar shattered the rest of his confidence, so he followed my adjutant out of the office without further argument. As soon as we were alone, Annika turned to

209

Alaric with a big grin on her face. 'You were really convincing, but you can let me go now.' Although Ari did as she asked, his movements were hesitant. I could see he wanted to hold on longer.

'Let's hope it'll be enough. We have another problem, though,' I argued, and Ani looked at me with a frown. 'The king doesn't care if the Barrier fails. His compliance with my plans was a smokescreen for court politics. In his infinite wisdom, he's decided that opening the old trade routes through the Barren Lands will bring prosperity to the kingdom.'

'W-what?' Ani stuttered, taken aback. 'There is nothing left to open, and the monsters and pestilence make travelling through there pointless.' The disdain in Alaric's answering grunt was impressive.

'What he wants is eternal life. He's old and without an heir—you heard that buffoon's words. He may mask his desire as trade, but I've seen it all before. He's not ready to die, and he thinks the Lich King can help him cheat death just as my father helped Cahyon Abrasan.' Raw emotion roughened his voice.

'How can you be so sure?'

I could see Annika's distress, but I had to agree with Alaric. The king had withdrawn most of the mages from every fortress alongside the Barrier the year I took command and had spread misinformation about the state of the spell. Now the most qualified of the ones left were little more than hedge witches. Maybe if they'd had decent magical support, we'd have known about the entire Barrier failing sooner.

'I'm sure, Ani. People never change. The human hunger for eternal life knows no bounds, and the older you get, the easier it is to convince yourself that the price is worth it. The Lich King didn't start off as a monster. He was a powerful and skilled mage, and many envied him. But he wanted more—more fame, more riches, more life, and in the end, that was his downfall.'

'Then someone has to stop this madness. We can't let it happen.' I had learned enough of Ani's character to expect her words, but I shook my head.

'We can't stop the Barrier from fading, and opposing the king will only cause turmoil,' I answered, moving closer to them both. 'The only solution would be to kill the source of the problem, but no one can even get close to him. There is an army of monsters between the Lich King and us, not to mention his own immense power.'

'And that brings us back to the discussion we had a few months ago. The circumstances have changed, and ... I told you there is always a way,' Alaric muttered to me.

'No! Don't even think about it. We will do what we planned to do. I will find a bloody crystal even if I have to bribe, threaten, or steal the damn thing—and you will repair the Barrier, even if it only lasts another decade. That would give us enough time to train a decent army, at least. In the meantime, I'll talk to my family. They can rally the nobles to stop the king.'

'Orm, I'm sorry, I can't repair the Barrier—' Alaric started, but before he could say more, Annika interrupted. 'Why are you wasting your time? If there's a way to end the Lich King, we should do it.' Ani paced before stopping in front of Alaric. 'You've had an idea, haven't you? Tell me, I'll help.'

'No, all Alaric has planned was to sneak through the Barrier. He intended to free his sister and likely kill himself while trying to end the Lich King. The idea was insane when he first brought it up, and it sounds even worse now. We are not discussing it. I'm not losing a friend ... or you, to a suicide mission.'

'What if I find a spell to dismantle the Lich King's life? There must be a way to undo whatever is keeping him alive. Nothing is truly immortal. If sneaking in and doing the deed is the only way, I will do what's needed, Orm. That's why I'm here,' Ani offered quietly, and I slammed my fist, adding more blood to the desk's surface.

'*No.* The odds are so against us it's not even worth thinking about. Leave the strategy to me. We will wait, and when the Barrier fails, whatever we decide here won't matter. If it comes to that, Alaric and I will ride Vahin to fight. If we succeed, we will come back to you.'

'So you will take my Anchor and the man I consider a friend, but you'd make me stay here ... For what purpose? You brought me here to be a weapon, so let me be one,' she argued, and even knowing she was right, I couldn't stomach seeing her in danger.

'You will still be a weapon. You and Vahin's fire are our last line of defence, and I'm not letting our last hope fall into the hands of the enemy. I have to think like a soldier. There is no place for emotions or heroes in war, too many people could pay the price for reckless bravery. Unless the situation changes, you will stay in the fortress, and that's the end of it.'

I saw Ani's eyes narrow, and I braced myself when she tightened her fists, but nothing happened. Instead, she shook her head and turned to leave. 'We will see about that, Lord Ormond; and I'm not a fucking hero,' she huffed before slamming the door.

CHAPTER 19

ANNIKA

I couldn't sleep. Maybe it was the wind rattling the windows or the fact that nothing made sense. My argument with Orm kept replaying in my head. What did he want from me? What did both of them want? What did I want from them? My feelings towards Orm and Ari were beyond complicated.

To make matters worse, I'd encountered my university nemesis and found out that the reason I was at the fortress in the first place had become obsolete. Ihrain was an ambitious idiot who'd made my life hell after I'd rejected his offer to get together, but if he was right ... Gods, if he was right, we were doomed.

That fear tore away the last vestiges of sleep, and I jolted up, fully awake. It was then that I noticed it, a shift in the aether's flow that I couldn't identify. I felt malicious intent in the air, and then I heard it—a quiet but unmistakable whimper. At first, I thought it was just the wind or my ears playing tricks on me, but it came again and again. Finally, I grabbed a lantern and went to investigate.

The sound was coming from Alaric's bedroom. He and Orm were on the same floor as me, Alaric's room in the far corner of the long hallway. I hesitated at his door, but when I heard the sound again, followed by words filled with such heart-wrenching emotion, I frantically banged on it.

The door was opened by the ragged shadow of the usually flawless dark fae: Alaric, hair matted and unbound, swayed before me, his eyes a blazing crimson and his face tightened in torment. He was wearing the torn remains of his shirt and sweat-stained breeches, and I frowned at the lines writhing across his chest.

'What's going on, Ari? What are those?' I asked, feeling a creeping horror at the sight.

'Nothing. Everything is fine. Go back to sleep.' He tried closing the door on me, but I shoved my foot in the gap, hissing when the door slammed it, not letting him get away with his blatant evasion.

'Yes, of course it is. Everything is fine. That's why you look like something the dogs chewed up and spat out,' I said, pushing inside, and Alaric shrugged before grabbing a blanket to wrap around his body.

'It's just some old scars that bother me sometimes. Nothing you should be concerned about.' Alaric gritted his teeth, pulling away when I stepped towards him. That threw me off my stride—Alaric liked to touch me; throughout the time we've spent together, I'd become used to him taking my hand or placing his on the small of my back. For a moment, I just stared at him with a frown.

'Did you do this to yourself? It looks like you're bleeding. Let me get a proper look; maybe I can heal ...' As I reached out to brush away the blanket, he grabbed my wrist and threw me against the wall with a feral growl, pinning my body with his.

'I'm not that stupid. Hrae! Why do you even care about me? Why do my feelings matter to you?' he demanded, hammering his fist on the wall by my head. The anguish on Alaric's face broke my heart. I had never seen him like this, so violent and unhinged, with no way to ease his own suffering.

'Because you matter to me, Ari. Tell me what's wrong. I can see you're in pain. Please, let me help you.' I placed a hand on his cheek, happy to see his body relax a little, as if my touch eased something deep inside him. His ragged breath brushed over my ear when his head rested against mine.

'Nobody can help me. This pain will only stop if I bring my sister back from the Barren Lands,' he ground out, his fingers tracing along the column of my neck, and I swallowed hard. 'I'm a cursed man, Annika. Whatever I do, I'm damned, but you ... you should ignore this, ignore *me* and leave. Why couldn't you have been just another arrogant mage I could hate?'

Despite his words, Ari pressed closer, his hand trailing lower, tracing my collarbone, drawing lines on my unblemished skin, his thigh wedged between my legs. I felt the hard length of his shaft pressing into me. 'You shouldn't have come here,' he murmured as his hand slid over the side of my breast. His lips touched my skin, and I gasped when he slid the chemise from my shoulders. The world seemed to pause until Alaric faced me, his gaze finding mine before it slid away with a sardonic huff.

'The dragon's bond. I barely saved you that night.' I looked at the stylised dragon on my chest, releasing a shuddering breath as Alaric's fingers hesitantly caressed it. 'One day, my mark will join the dragon's, but not today. I don't deserve you yet. Maybe I never will.' I couldn't decipher the emotion darkening Ari's features, and he turned away before I could ask.

'Go, Ani. You are not safe with me as I am now. I need to be alone.'

I reached out, determined to understand. 'Why? Why are you speaking in riddles? Alaric, please, you are my friend. You know you can trust me.'

'I trust no one, not anymore. Go, Annika. Before I do something we both regret.' He exposed his sharp fangs and my breath hitched. Whatever was gnawing at him, Alaric was hell-bent on being alone, and I didn't want to discover the damage those fangs could inflict.

I looked for Orm to talk about what happened the next morning, but when I went to his office, I was told he'd left—called in by his brother—and had used the occasion to escort Ihrain to the capital.

I was concerned about the summons and the increased frequency of the patrols. It felt as if we were heading into a storm but were still unsure of which direction it was coming from, and this visit to the capital suggested the first blow could very well come from within.

Another thing that will have to wait, I thought. Fighting my frustration, I returned to my room and sat in the large bay window. The view that had charmed me so much on my arrival had lost its glamour. A tall waterfall cascaded from a high pass on the cliff, carrying ice-cold water to a small lake below. A river bounced and frothed exuberantly from there over jutting rocks with mountain flowers peaking from the cracks, the beautiful scene surrounded by heather and grass that swayed in time to the sighing wind. Still, I longed to be outside the fortress walls.

Alaric was expecting me to attend his workshop, but I needed to think. He said he couldn't trust me, and even if he'd said he couldn't trust *anyone*, it still hurt. However, this wasn't about my feelings but the pain I had heard in his voice. A pain I hadn't been aware of. I thought we were friends, but last night made me realise I knew so little of him.

What haunts you, my dark fae? What torments you so much that it leaves you close to violence? The question troubled me. As the days passed, I'd come to care about him, and I wished I could help soothe whatever bothered him. He was at least kind of mine—my Ari, my always teasing fae.

The knock on my door startled me for a moment before I answered, allowing my visitor to enter.

'Ani, why didn't you come to our session?'

Alaric walked inside as if nothing had happened. I wanted to talk, but a silent instinct warned me not to say anything ... He clearly wanted to play things that way, and I would let him—for now—until I had a plan for what to do about it. I smirked and waved him off.

'Go away. I'm not in the mood for another attempt to use our synergy. And don't bother with another lecture on high magic. If you want someone to mix potions, call for a servant.' Alaric looked like he was about to argue, so I rolled my eyes.

'No. Nagging won't work either, I think we established that last night. Why don't you show me some necromancer spells instead? We may need them when this place becomes overrun with monsters. High magic is so long-winded and boring that it's mostly useless,' I groused, unsuccessfully trying to hide my annoyance.

Alaric frowned. His pale, golden eyes narrowed, and a shiver ran down my spine. 'I apologise for last night, but ... boring? High magic is *boring*? Do you think *I'm* boring?' he smirked, and the flow of aether around him turned purple with necromancy. I shrugged, licking my lips and looking to the side. 'I ... No, you're ... I just need some time to think so ... please go.'

He grinned at my flustered response, moving further into the room. 'Oh, you need time to think when the mere thought of me makes your cheeks that pretty shade of rose?' His tone was a mix of amusement and challenge. 'Why would I ever leave you alone with those thoughts, my sweet lady? No ... I'm afraid that's not going to happen. You're doomed to spend time in my company, so you might as well see just what my magic can do.'

'Only if I'm willing to tie myself to a stubborn old mule who doesn't know when to leave a woman's room.'

'Better than being the silly goose who sits morosely in her room while a five-hundred-year-old mage is trying to apologise and teach her.'

'I don't need your teaching or apology. For the love of all the gods, how many times do I have to tell you? Has your memory failed with old age?'

'I don't know, maybe it has. Or maybe I can't resist the imperious look in your eyes that even the dark fae empress would bow before.' It took all of my restraint not to shoot a fireball at his head.

'Oh, just leave, you frustrating man.' His low, velvety chuckle sparked something in me.

'Make me,' he purred. As pure gold danced in his eyes, I swear he *purred*. He stalked me as he moved closer, his lips promising mischief.

'What?'

'If you want me to go, make me. Force this ancient "boring" mage with memory problems to leave. Show me you are stronger than me, beat me into submission, and I will do whatever you ask of me, but if I win, you'll owe me a boon.'

'First, that's not fair—we both know you are better. Second, what boon?'

'I haven't decided yet. You'll just have to trust that I won't ask for anything outrageous.' My breath caught at the intensity of his gaze.

This was insane, but I couldn't help feeling excited. There was no way I could overpower a mage with centuries of experience, but my interest was piqued. To see what Alaric could do, even if it was just a glimpse of his true power, was too good an opportunity to pass.

'Basic spells and no blades,' I countered, and he flashed me a deadly smile.

'Of course, my lady, but why place limits on our fun?'

'Because I don't want to hurt you. What would Orm say if I fried your arse?' I bluffed, hoping to distract him, acutely aware that he had slid into a battle stance.

'I hope he'd make you kiss it better. I wouldn't object if that was the price for losing. Besides, who said I'd lose so easily?' My imagination overwhelmed me with the lurid image ... I cursed, realising it was Alaric's magic and not my own mind that had conjured it. He was so much better at this game, and dispelling the scene took far longer than it should have.

'Oh no, you don't,' I laughed when he drew on the aether to create a shield.

Before it solidified, I attacked. Even though elemental mages needed sigils for almost every other form of magic, when they called on the basic power of the four elements already aligned with the nature of their magic, they only needed thought, intent, and will to perform a spell. I drew the aether into my grasp, transforming its energy into elemental magic, and threw a small fireball in his direction.

Alaric caught it, and I cursed myself. I should have foreseen his proficiency at redirecting the fireball into his spell to complete the shield, flashing his smug smile in my direction as he did so. I blinked in disbelief when Alaric drew another sigil quicker than thought. I watched it unfold, creating a silver spider's web that flew towards me.

The obscene gesture I offered Ari turned into silvery-blue daggers of ice that sliced through the net, damaging it, but I was forced to dive to the side as the tattered net repaired itself and continued towards me.

'What the fuck is that?' I yelped from the floor.

'Oh, this? It's just an old fae spell created with the necromancy you so wanted to see. A trap for careless wanderers. C'mon, Nivale. We both know you're better than this. I won't let you win without a fight. I want my reward too much to stroke your ego. Try harder or forfeit our duel,' he taunted, then drew more lines in the air.

The net grew, its strands reaching for me, but I was already on my feet, rushing towards the fireplace.

'Forfeit? I was trying to be careful, you silver-haired buffoon. But if you want to play hard, fine!' I cursed myself yet again for limiting our duel. Still, I would not give up. I reached towards the dying fire, grappling with the untamed heart of the flames. Ari could manipulate fire created by magic, but the true chaos of the element could only be tamed by those it called to.

Flames shot in his direction, smoke billowing out, covering everything in ash, but Ari leapt away so fast he was nothing but a blur in the smoke. Worse still, one tendril of his silver net glued itself to my ankle, tugging so hard I almost lost my balance. That frustrated me and presented a dilemma. I was out of my depth, and Alaric was much better at fighting in close quarters. His net spell was so precise and much less disruptive than my elemental spells. Frankly, I wanted to learn it.

Maybe I could have that as my prize if I won …

'You can't win this, Ani, but you shouldn't be bitter about it. I've lived a long time, fought and killed so many that I forget their names. Those mages were all more skilled than you. I could call on soul blades or turn the air into poison if our fight was real, but I would never hurt you.' Alaric stalked closer, his gaze firmly focused on my hand.

'You may be better, but you know nothing about me if you think I'd surrender so easily.'

Alaric's eyes widened when he noticed his mistake—I'd pretended to reach for the fire again; instead, the air answered my call. Alaric's golden eyes slowly turned crimson, but before he could stop me, the wind snapped the window open, ripping it from the frame. A high mountain storm burst through the gap and slammed into my opponent.

He withstood it. The power of my elemental spell blasted him backwards several feet, but he withstood it. I don't know how. My anger had magnified my power beyond anything I'd intended. I wanted to show him we were equal, but he proved me wrong with his next phrase.

'Plynn Ilta!'[1]

---

1. *Tie her!*

His voice reverberated through the raging storm, and suddenly, I couldn't move. While I'd been focused on the force wrecking the room, the silver strings of his net had crept closer and, following Alaric's command, fastened to my wrists and neck. There was something in the net, a barrier that blocked my access to the aether, and as soon as I was bound, my spell died. Only the now gently flowing aether within my bindings lit the room.

Alaric straightened and walked towards me. His clothes were torn in places, and unruly strands of hair had escaped his braid, giving him a wild, untamed look, but the most significant change was his eyes. They were full of crimson and power.

'Dark Mother! Ani, that was *magnificent.*' Alaric's voice was so husky it sent shivers down my spine. 'I've never been so close to losing a duel. Do you know how thrilling it is to finally find someone who can withstand my magic? How very alluring that feeling is?' I stood there, helpless before a predator, and I felt my tongue sneak out to lick my desperately dry lips.

The bindings disappeared, but the raw hunger I saw in his glowing eyes held me in place just as effectively. 'I've decided upon my prize. I want a kiss, Ani. I want to taste you.'

'And if I don't want that?' My voice trembled with emotion.

'I will accept it, of course. But ... I'll not duel with you again.' Alaric pulled away, but his gaze never strayed from my lips.

'Then kiss me. Claim your prize,' I said, my voice breathy and raw. I didn't even see Ari move, but the grip on my hair was firm as Alaric claimed my lips. The burning desire that rushed through my body only surprised me for a moment before I lost myself to the passion.

I yielded to his strength, gasping as my body ignited, seeking his touch. I wanted his hands to roam over my skin, but I was no meek maiden, waiting passively as my partner took charge. I exhaled softly, nipping at Ari's lip, savouring his response as he crushed my body against him. When his hands moved down, caressing my back, I felt Alaric's questing magic echoing his physical touch as it moved over my soul.

Before the pleasure of the dual sensations overwhelmed all logical thought, I stole a dagger from the sheath on his belt and pressed it to his throat. 'Yield to me, my dark fae, or must I spill your blood to cool your ardour?' I teased with a soft chuckle that startled him.

'Don't ... Hrae! Ani, I ... I like pain. You have no idea what you're doing to me,' he murmured. He was right. I had no idea what I was doing to him. I only knew the effect he was having on me, the power I felt as he towered over me, desperately holding himself back while his lips rested against my neck.

'Do you really want this? Would you take me as I am if I gave myself to you?' he whispered, and I knew our reckless game had turned into something more than either of us had expected.

I hesitated, suddenly anxious. Gone was the confident woman who embraced her desire, replaced by the feeling that I might be out of my depth in a game with rules I no longer recognised.

'Ye ... I ... I don't know. We were just teasing ... right?' I questioned.

'No, little wildcat, not since the magic in your heart lit the depths of my soul. You have no idea how much I've been craving you,' he breathed, his lips landing on mine.

Damn that man's voice. I was lost. The dagger fell to the ground as I pulled Ari closer, unaware of the blood that trickled down his neck. My magic soared, flowing over both of us, and my lips parted, our tongues meeting with a fervour that swept me away until the moment I cut myself on his fangs.

When I tasted my own blood, I pulled back with a frown, unsure what had happened. I couldn't think straight, couldn't look away from the swirling crimson in Ari's eyes. 'Your fangs,' I said, fumbling for something to say.

'You taste like the sweetest plum wine. *Hrae!* I wish I could devour you ... Anchor you ...'

His reply was too much for me. The room was suddenly too small, and panic squeezed my chest. 'No ... no, wait. It was just a duel, and you got your prize, but I don't want—I don't know ... I'm sorry, we shouldn't have ...'

Alaric pulled away, breathing heavily before regaining his composure. 'No, I apologise. You are right. It was just a duel, and I took it too far.' He licked his lips. 'I yield, my lady. Few can trick me, but you did it. You are formidable, both as a mage and a woman.'

I didn't know what to say. Apart from yesterday, Alaric had always been in control. Yet now he looked lost in a maelstrom of emotion—and so was I, because he was no longer the teasing fae I'd grown to cherish. Now, he was so much more ... and I found that I liked it.

'I'm sorry, but I need more time. I lost my ...' This was ridiculous. How could I expect Alaric to understand my feelings when I couldn't explain myself? It wasn't only about choosing to take an Anchor—I had warmed up to the idea—but about choosing the right one. Alaric was the obvious choice, and he said he didn't mind sharing, but the way I felt around Orm ... knowing the commander, I didn't think he was a man who would welcome such an unusual arrangement.

I wasn't ready to make such choices now. Not before I talked to Orm or understood what was happening to Alaric. With a deep, unsteady breath, I tried again. 'I'm afraid ... no, I'm *terrified*. I can't afford to make a mistake, not right now. Even after I Anchored Vahin, my heart rejected him, and we almost died. I need to be sure before committing to someone again and right now, I'm not,' I said anxiously, before Alaric gathered me in his arms.

'Shhh, Ani. It's okay, I understand. The way you stood up to Ihrain, the way you came to me when I needed you ... it gave me hope, that's all, but this was a mistake. C'mon, sweetheart, I want to see your smile, not your tears. I will wait for you, even if it takes a millennium. You're worth it. After all, you're the first woman to make me bleed.' He flirted so effortlessly.

'What? Oh gods, your neck! I actually cut you. I'm so sorry. Please let me check.' I made to pull away, but Alaric shook his head.

'It is not my neck I'm worried about. I can still taste you, smell you ... such exquisite torture ... so unless you want to adjust my cock, which is painfully hard at the moment, your touch won't do me any good.' He said it with such unbridled honesty that I forgot what I was going to say myself, and stuttered. 'Oh... I don't think that's a good idea.'

'I'd thought as much,' he teased. 'In that case, I'll survive. Gather some personal items and move them next door. I'll send some workmen and maids to repair the damage in the meantime.' He placed his hand on his chest and bowed. 'You won our duel, sweet lady. You're officially making me leave, so take some time for yourself today,' he declared as he straightened and shot me a quick smile.

When he left, I sank to the floor, manic giggles escaping my lips as I fell back to stare at the ceiling. 'That was the most insane, exhilarating, and intimate duel I've ever had,' I said to no one, still giggling, following a crack in the painted ceiling with my eyes. 'What a rascal!'

A loud gasp had me almost jumping out of my skin.

'Lady Annika! What happened here? Were you attacked?' Agnes slipped back into formal speech as she rushed in, grasping my shoulders and checking for injuries. Behind her, several workmen stood silent, looking on in disbelief.

I couldn't blame them. The window was shattered, and drapes and pillows were scattered all over the floor, mixed with petals and glass shards from various arrangements. There was ash everywhere, and I was in the middle of it all, laughing like crazy.

'Everything is fine. Alaric and I ... did a bit of impromptu sparring.'

'A duel? In the bedroom?' Agnes was so agitated that, by the last word, she was screeching. 'I will inform the commander about this. He'll put an end to this disgusting behaviour. I swear I'll not forgive him for this,' Agnes exclaimed, but as she turned to leave, I raised my hand, stopping her.

'Lord Ormond is still in the capital, and Alaric did nothing wrong. We were testing our magic, and things got slightly out of hand.'

'*Slightly?!* The window is destroyed, the entire room is ruined, and it will take several days to repair the damage. Where will you sleep, my lady?' she asked with righteous indignation, and I could only roll my eyes.

'There's plenty of space in the castle, and if I can't find an empty bed, I can always sleep in Vahin's lair. I'm sure he won't object,' I said, gathering my things and, like a coward, running away from her accusing glare. 'I'll be with Katja if anyone needs me. Stop worrying so much, Agnes. I've slept in worse conditions.'

I grabbed a shawl that had somehow survived the onslaught and rushed out the door before my bossy maid could berate me further.

CHAPTER 20

ORMOND

As soon as I left Ihrain at the capital, I had told Vahin to take us to my family's residence. Now I was waiting patiently in my brother's war room for Reynard to return from the court, wondering why the hell he'd called me this time.

I'd wanted to spend some time with Ani just to reassure myself she was settling in. But between the patrols, managing the fortress, and flying between the capital and the other two dragon rider strongholds, I'd barely had time for this.

That the burning need to see her now distracted me from my duties was disconcerting. *Why does it even matter? She's not for me.* The Dagome court's betrayal of our people stripped me of what little choice I had.

I looked at the map in front of me. The Dagome Kingdom was the closest to the Barren Lands and would likely take the brunt of any attack. Even with Care'etavos and Lumivitae—the dark fae empire and light fae kingdom, respectively—supporting us, most of the fight would happen on our soil, and that was always disastrous for the innocent.

Still, I had Annika; and if she could use Alaric's necromancy in a similar way to her use of Vahin's fire ... Even if it was an untested theory, the possibilities it opened up made the decision to pursue my own desires feel not only selfish but borderline treasonous.

If I could only move the fight to the Barren Lands, no one except the Lich King's forces would suffer. I thought, but it was easier said than done.

The dragons could fly at will, and with Annika on Vahin's back, we could go much further than skimming the borders. Once we gained a foothold, we could set up a permanent camp to secure the ground forces' arrival; and if other commanders could do the same or join ours, we could encircle Katrass and possibly even take the Lich King's capital. I moved the pins that represented my dragon squadron into the Barren Lands territory before realising the problem. We had three fortresses and only one conduit mage bound to a dragon.

'Vahin? How likely is it for a dragon to bond with a conduit mage if we find more?' I didn't need to wait long for an answer.

'I can tell you it is nearly impossible. The danger of dying if the bond is not accepted is not a small one. How many mages and dragons do you know who would accept such a risk?'

'Why did you accept her?'

'Do you remember when we rescued her from the avalanche? I didn't have to search the rockfall; the inferno of her soul called out to me. The way dragons see aether ... there are no human words to describe it. My race was born from the primal power that shaped this world, and when I saw her spirit—so similar, so bright and pure—I wanted to have it. I craved for it to be mine.'

There was so much possessiveness in his voice that a grain of uncertainty made me ask, *'Vahin, what did you do?'*

'Nothing except help her live, hoping that one day she would find me. You can't own someone's soul unless they gift it to you. That's why I'm almost certain no other conduit mage will Anchor a dragon, at least not during your lifetime.'

While that spelled the death of another plan, I couldn't give up on the idea of taking the battle to the Lich King. If we could coordinate the attack with

Vahin and Ani in the central position and join our forces, it might work. I have never heard of a dragon using thoughtspeech with a person other than their bonded rider, but Vahin could easily converse with Annika in his thoughts.

'*Can you talk to ordinary men? Or maybe other riders? I could use—*'

'*No.*'

I cursed silently. Our inability to attack from different directions meant I would have to concentrate my forces in one area unless I was willing to lose men and riders to the spectrae. Another issue with my strategy was figuring out how to move our ground forces across the mountains. After the war, the combined mage forces had destroyed every road leading to the former Ozar Kingdom; now, there was no known safe passage through the mountains.

'We'll have to widen the Rift's chasm to let the entire army pass; meanwhile, the undead bastard can simply flood us with monsters far more agile in mountain terrain than fully armed humans,' I muttered to myself.

'Are you trying to win a war that hasn't even started yet?'

I turned around and nodded to my brother. 'I prefer to be prepared. Why did you call me? Is anything new in court? Did the king rethink his decision, or did the chancellor convince him to drop this idiocy?'

'Nothing so helpful, I'm afraid. Since you are planning on winning the war, you can have my title of Lord Marshal if you want, along with what's left of the army.' Although his words were meant to be lighthearted, I heard the bitterness in his voice.

'What's left ...?'

'Yes, as it's clearly no longer needed since the king has maintained his position on the trade deal with the Lich King. It didn't matter that I and several other noble families objected. And the chancellor was as quiet as the grave. So now there are other things to talk about, brother.'

Reynard looked tired. I knew he'd never wanted the title of Lord Marshal of the army, but he was as diligent in his duties as I was in mine.

'You're going to rebel, aren't you?' I asked, and he nodded.

'What choice do I have? I don't care who sits on the throne, but the people ... Orm, we were given power, given an army to protect them. You sacrificed your life and your family to guard the borders, and now our hands are bound.' He said it with such vehemence I felt the need to ease the tension.

'Maybe we are both mistaken?' I said, not believing my own words.

'How? Don't tell me you believe in this talk of ... "*peace*?" Monsters don't change. They may mask their intentions and soften their voices, but it is all to lure you into a trap. So I will rebel if I must. I wish I'd noticed the rot spreading through the court before things got this far.'

'Who do you think is behind it?'

'I don't know, and therein lies the problem. All these ridiculous notions are pushed forward by the king, but ... where or how did he come up with them? He dances like someone's puppet, and I don't know who's pulling the strings. It was his notion to cut army spending yet again. The chancellor protested, albeit weakly, but both he and I were outvoted. I will have to dip into our family's reserve to pay the veterans. The rest can seek their luck elsewhere. I know what kind of soldiers you've received; if you can believe it, I sent you the best of those I was assigned. Untrainable dimwits or criminals ...'

He poured himself a generous measure of wine before continuing. 'Gods ... Orm, I believe that someone is dismantling our kingdom from within, and the war has already begun.'

'I will follow your lead, brother. If you want us to rebel, you have my support. I trust you. But as straightforward as it is to raise an army against a senile king with no heir, it's a different matter if someone is manipulating the situation from the shadows,' I said, suddenly uncertain about it all. It was so much easier to believe the Lich King was just a mindless monster throwing his spawn at us. The realisation that we might be doomed before any major blood was spilt was a heavy burden to bear.

'I have spies in the court and have reached out to the noble families that have voiced their discontent, but there are few of us. Anyway, leave it to me.

Just make sure you monitor the border—especially the Rift—as it is the only viable ground passage to the Barren Lands right now.' He nodded, passing me a goblet, and while I favoured mead over the dishwater so popular at the noble tables, I accepted it. 'I will send you a missive when the next messenger from Katrass is expected. Try to intercept him if you can.'

'Of course, but I can do more. I can go even further into the Barren Lands with Annika shielding my dragons from the spectrae. I was waiting until she settled in at the fortress, but I can start patrols with her as soon as I return home.'

'Annika ... Yes, your precious conduit mage. About that ...' The tone of his voice instantly raised my proverbial hackles.

'Yes ...?'

'After you asked me to retrieve the register of conduit mages, I thought it might be worth trying to recruit some of them. So I kept tabs on them, checking their whereabouts every now and again,' Reynard said, and I willed myself to remain calm, but I needed him to get to the point.

'And?'

'And I found that of the four conduit mages that were registered as "alive" in our kingdom, three have died due to illness or injury in the last few months, and one—a young female—is currently missing. Your Annika is the only conduit mage left, and likely only because no one knew she was still alive.'

'Fuck.'

'Yes, you drew the same conclusions I did. Of the three males, two were old, so their deaths weren't even looked into, and the other took his own life when his Anchors were killed in a tavern brawl.'

'*Fuck*! Ihrain—he knows she's alive.' I choked on my words, hammering my fist on the table. I couldn't say anything else, couldn't even move, my anger consuming all thought.

Fucking Ihrain. I should've killed him on the spot. If Ani's safety was compromised because that smarmy bastard blabbed, I'd never forgive myself.

Everybody would know that not only was she alive, but her exact location ... I looked at the map and crafted my plan.

Could I still take her on patrols? Would she be safe in the stronghold? Or with the ground forces? Taking her with me on Vahin would be safer, I supposed, but a stray arrow or poison dart could easily find its target in the heat of battle.

'The royal mage's apprentice? Well, that is inconvenient, but we can use it to our advantage. The easiest way to lure potential enemies is to offer them a juicy target ... Don't look at me like that, Ormond. I don't want her to get hurt, but if we know about the attack, then you can intercept the culprit and you or Alaric can interrogate them ... or their corpse. Then we will find out who gave the order.'

Reynard kept talking, blissfully unaware that I was internally fighting a losing battle.

When he approached me, placing a hand on my shoulder as if we'd come to an agreement, I lost it. 'What the *fuck* are you suggesting? How dare you propose using my woma—my mage as bait!' I roared in his face, stuttering at the end as the unfiltered words slipped from my lips.

'Your woman? You never mentioned ... Ormond, please tell me you are not falling for her. She's our weapon, not your—'

'I said *my mage*—stop trying to deflect the question. If Annika is the last conduit we have left, she must be protected at all costs—not paraded under the enemy's nose. What if something goes wrong and I lose her?' I snapped, trying to cover my slip of the tongue.

Reynard looked at me with a compassion I'd rarely seen. 'I didn't think I would live to see the day someone melted the ice shard you had turned your heart into. I wish there were a different path for those with wild magic in their blood. The loneliness you must have faced since the moment our parents left you in the dragon's cave ... I can't even fathom it.'

'I told you, she is not my woman, I can't ... All you need to know is that she is a mage with enormous power. Even if the possibility of replacing the crystal is gone, she should still Anchor Alaric to reach her full potential … or someone else of her choosing.'

'And you will accept it, whoever she chooses?'

'What say do I have in it? It is Ani's choice. I hope it will be Alaric. He is a powerful mage and a good man. He would never hurt her, and … she likes him. He makes her laugh, and I enjoy seeing her happy. How could I not? She saved my men, my life, so I can't let you use her as bait. Ask me for anything else and I'll do it, but not her.'

I hated seeing the understanding in his eyes. I shouldn't have said anything, but somehow, saying it out loud made the pain easier to bear. If she must choose a mage to fully stabilise her magic, let it be Alaric.

Reynard walked around to face me. 'I'm sorry, Orm, I didn't know. If you don't mind me giving you some advice … If your woman—I mean, *mage*—chooses the dark fae, what's stopping you from becoming her lover? She had two male Anchors in the past, and I don't think they were particularly chaste. We both know about the dark fae customs, of the lady of the house taking more than one partner. If they both accept it, why can't you carve out a little happiness of your own? I certainly wouldn't judge, brother.'

I looked at Reynard, feeling his hand on my shoulder. He wasn't much older than me, but sometimes he seemed wise beyond his years.

'I … I don't know if I can share,' I said truthfully, and he nodded.

'Then you are locking yourself in a prison of your own making, and you are the one holding the key,' he said, and with that, I realised I'd had enough of talking about my convoluted feelings for Ani.

'Did you forget I came here to talk about political affairs? Not confess my feelings? To be clear, I won't use Annika as bait, and she will stay in the fortress until we know it is safe for her to go out,' I repeated.

He nodded. 'Fine, but don't tell her why. If she starts looking over her shoulder, it will alert our enemies. I will send a few of my men to infiltrate your garrison and town. They'll keep an eye on anything untoward and warn you if needed,' he suggested, and I sighed heavily.

'How do you expect me to explain this to her without giving a reason?'

'That, my brother, I will leave to you. Nobody said life was a bed of roses. Also, please update the other commanders on the situation. I want them standing on our side when it comes time to confront the king.'

'Yes, Lord Marshal. I am, as always, at your command,' I replied with an exaggerated military salute, and his eyes narrowed at my teasing. 'You are such an arse, Orm, you know that, right?' He sighed, but I saw a smile ghosting the corner of his lips.

'So says the man who eviscerated my feelings, advised me not only to share but to lie to my wo ... mage before sending me to a ghost war.' He chuckled.

'Maybe I just envy you, little brother. You have your dragon, your fae friend, and the mage that is *"not your woman,"* while I have the court to deal with—and I assure you, it is a nest of vipers,' he joked with a bitter smile, but I felt the loneliness of his world.

We talked some more, mainly about army matters, before he asked for my agreement to use the family wealth to pay the soldiers, which I was happy to agree to. When I landed in my bed for the night, readying myself for an early morning flight, his words returned, robbing me of my sleep.

I had called her *my woman.* I don't know what had come over me to blurt it out to my brother, but I could no longer deny the attraction I felt towards Annika. It wasn't just curiosity or gratitude for saving my life. She interested me in a way no other woman had, but it didn't explain the visceral need to touch her, to hold her in my arms whenever she was near.

Could I be her lover?

The seed planted by my brother took root, and I couldn't stop thinking about it ... I wasn't sure if I could share, but the thought of her body next to mine awakened an irresistible need. I remembered her scent and the way her laughter filled Vahin's lair as she teased the protective dragon ...

I groaned, unable to shake off the vivid images. I'd seen Ani naked and she was perfect. Soft, with curves in all the right places, and even if I hadn't thought about it at the time—too focused on keeping her alive—holding her in my arms had felt so right. Her velvety skin was so soft against my calloused hands.

I remembered the touch of her magic when we first met and the sheer vulnerability in her gaze when I mentioned the geas, leaving me desperate to protect her.

Am I falling for her? What if she decides to leave after the year ends, as we agreed? What if she chooses someone other than Ari? Could I live with it? Could I share her affection?

The questions that flashed through my mind didn't stop the hand that slid down to my rock-hard shaft. Fuck, I wanted Ani so much—wanted to bury my head between her legs, owning her ecstasy until she begged me to take her hard. My body tensed, jerking as the idea threatened to overwhelm my senses. My hand worked faster to the image of Ani's back arching, her desperate pleas, and I felt pleasure building at the bottom of my spine; so close, but not there yet.

Another image intruded on my fantasy: the delicate, grey skin of Alaric's hands sliding over Ani's body, fingers pinching her swollen nipples. My eyelids fluttered as I tried to open my eyes, but I was too far gone to stop.

'*Make her come for us,*' he whispered in my mind, his eyes filled with crimson fire, and I came so hard my roar shook the walls of the room. The release pooled on my stomach as I lay there, panting, eyes squeezed shut, shuddering in the aftermath of a powerful climax, unable to believe what had just happened.

I'd come so fucking hard to the image of Alaric and I pleasuring Annika together.

And I felt utterly lost.

CHAPTER 21

ANNIKA

It had been a strange two weeks.

After returning from the capital, Ormond stopped going on patrol, leaving it to Tomma, and we spent a few days in each other's company. He felt different—as intense as ever ... but I kept catching him looking at me with a strange expression.

Today, for some reason, he asked me to help him manage the reports, and I quickly discovered that Ormond was a slave to routine and liked things done a certain way. Unfortunately, I only found this out after he'd taken the pile of documents I'd already spent hours organising and started putting them in their *correct* order. I couldn't help rolling my eyes.

'Why am I here? I mean, in your office. You don't need my help, and your adjutant twitches every time I touch your letters,' I enquired as politely as I could when Orm leant over me, pulling another parchment from my pile.

'Maybe I'm teaching you how to manage the fortress, or maybe I just enjoy your company, Nivale.' He played with my braid before I huffed and pulled it out of his hand.

'My hair is not a toy,' I said, and he narrowed his eyes as if pondering over something.

'No, it isn't, but I wish I could wrap it around my hand and pull you to my lips,' he murmured before letting his breath trail over my ear as he moved away. 'Just a thought, of course, to take your mind off this boring bureaucracy.'

We both turned at the sound of the adjutant's gasp, finding him blushing and trying to melt into the shadows.

After the unexpected exchange, Orm acted his usual calm and stern self, strictly adhering to his office rituals until it was time to head down for a meal. It still amused me that he was friends with the chaotic Alaric who couldn't follow a routine if he was bound hand and foot to it.

Later that evening, I found a strange package in my room. When I opened it, there were several dresses from my home and a falchion with a nivale flower on the pommel in a beautifully embossed scabbard. When I went to the dining area to ask about my unexpected gift, Ormond was particularly quiet; it was Alaric who spilled the beans.

The commander had commissioned the sword from Bryna before travelling to the capital. On his return, he'd picked it up, as well as clothes that the blacksmith thought I'd appreciate. As I stroked the beautifully patterned scabbard, a wave of homesickness and gratitude washed over me.

I approached him with falchion pressed to my chest, tiptoeing and placing a hand on his shoulder to support myself. 'Thank you,' I said, kissing his cheek, 'It is beautiful. You really know how to make a woman happy.' His eyes lit with joy before he schooled his expression into his usual stoic features.

'I wanted to give you something almost as unique as you are.' He said it so nonchalantly, as if a handcrafted sword was no big deal, before pulling my hand off his arm and kissing the palm. 'I'm glad you like it, Nivale.'

His lips caressed my skin, sending goosebumps along my forearm. I felt warmth spreading in my chest, and only Alaric's focused gaze stopped me from embracing the massive rider. Orm was playing a dangerous game, and I didn't know where it was heading.

I noticed the fleeting grimace on Alaric's face when Orm kissed my hand, but when I turned to him, he shook his head with an all-knowing smile. Unable to make them both happy, I went with my third option and excused myself, rushing to the dragon's lair to show Vahin my newest possession.

I was lounging on the dragon's arm, playing with my blade after Vahin had expressed sufficient elation over how beautiful it was when both men joined me. When I refused to move, they took it upon themselves to see who could make me laugh harder with ribald stories of their past adventures. It was a strange contest, but the joy was palpable, and I wished we could stay like that forever.

The next day, I woke up earlier than usual and went to the training grounds with the sword attached to my hip to find the commander shirtless and sparing with his men. When I taunted him for a match, Orm was initially eager and we spared for a good hour before our intricate motions began attracting attention. Then, many soldiers came over, asking to cross blades with me.

Orm didn't protest when I agreed, but after I defeated several of them and the veterans flocked to ask me to show them my techniques, his expression became more and more thunderous as the number of men surrounding me increased. He didn't intervene; he just observed my interactions with a grimace I struggled to decipher.

'Why didn't you tell me you are going on the patrol tomorrow? I can be ready by dawn. I'll join the regular soldiers since we get along well,' I said to him after overhearing a soldier boasting about it. His jaw clenched, and I faced a wall of stubborn refusal. I didn't care.

'I said nothing because I scheduled you to train new recruits with Alaric.'

'Then you can reschedule me.' The excitement from training still thrummed through my veins, so I grabbed Orm's hand, pulling him towards the castle. 'Come Ursus, I can see something is bothering you, and I think you will be more agreeable after a good breakfast. Sated bears are less likely to be obtrusive.'

The moment we entered the castle, Orm's arms surrounded me, and he buried his face in my hair, inhaling deeply. 'I'm not obtrusive, I just ... I can't ... it's too dangerous out there,' he groaned before releasing me and striding away as if a ghoul were biting at his heels.

I stood watching him go. Something was very wrong if the man who had hired me to fight monsters would rather lock me in a tower than let me face a threat whilst surrounded by an army.

Alright, Commander, I'll let you get away with this one, but if you stop me from going on the next one, I will find out what the hell is going on myself.

The opportunity to leave the fortress walls arrived sooner than I expected.

Two days later, I was training with the soldiers, cursing under my breath and trying to sweat out my frustrations. Orm and Ari had held a meeting with two other commanders, and after the Ihrain incident, both men had decided I should stay out of sight—at least until they knew where we stood with the rest of the dragon riders.

I was going through a complex attack sequence that involved both blade and a fire sigil when a messenger ran in shouting that a supply wagon was under attack on the road to the fortress. The Captain of the Guard was asking for assistance from anyone who could hold a sword or spear. I wasn't sure what exactly had attacked the wagon, but my muscles were warmed up and we had several men there who'd just finished their own routines as well.

'Gather your weapons! We are needed,' I called out, grinning like a madwoman.

'Under whose command?' one of them asked, but I only looked at him, raising my eyebrow before he lowered his head, muttering, 'Yes, Lady Mage, but we should inform the commander.'

'The commander is in a meeting, and the merchants won't mind who saves them as long as their skin is intact. I'm going, and you can shift your hairy arses and help me or explain to Ormond why you let me fight alone. Your choice. Whatever you decide, I won't hold it against you.'

I made for the gates. As I began running, I saw one of the veterans whisper something to the messenger, but I didn't turn to check as I rushed to the scene. I hadn't even broken a sweat by the time we made it out of the stronghold, but as we reached the edge of the forest, I saw several guards fighting a pack of werewolves.

'Vahin, there's an attack near the gates. I can handle it, but if you could check the perimeter of the fortress, I'd appreciate it. A pack of werewolves coming so close to civilisation is unheard of, and there may be more ...' I said through the link we shared, smirking at the surprise in the dragon's thoughts.

'Do you need me there, Little Flame?' he asked. I could sense he was concerned, but he didn't try spoiling my fun.

'No, you are close enough if I need to access the aether. I'm more concerned about other travellers and can't cover that much ground myself,' I answered, wishing Orm and Ari were more like him. A dark chuckle rumbled through my thoughts when I failed to hide my last mental remark.

'Oh, I can be possessive and overprotective too, Little Flame. I've just had millennia to learn that those feelings can ruin even true love. Orm's barely tasted the dark edges of his soul. No one taught him how to deal with his wild

magic; all they did was teach him to cage that part of him. Now it's rattling the bars, and he doesn't know how to handle it.'

I was too close to the skirmish for more conversation, especially when I saw one of the guards pushed to the ground as a rabid werewolf locked his jaws on his soft entrails. I grasped a stream of aether and shaped it with a quick incantation, pushing condensed energy into the beast's head.

A pain-filled screech cut through the noise when the power of my spell threw the beast backwards, but now the attention of the rest of the pack was solely on me.

'C'mon you sons of bitches, you know you want to,' I taunted, laughing and feeling the familiar heat of battle rising in my veins.

'My lady, you can't fight them all—the commander will have our hides if anything happens to you,' muttered one of the veterans while the others attempted to form a wall of shields around me.

'Oh yes I can, and I will. Gather the wounded and guard the wagon. Don't let the mutts bite the merchants. The rest of you ensure nothing jumps on my back. If the commander says anything about it, I'll tell him to kiss my arse,' I barked.

The men dispersed, but not before I heard one of them mutter. *'Oh yeah, he would absolutely love that.'*

It took effort to keep a straight face, but the attacking werewolves soon sobered me up, and before I knew it, my sword caught one in the chest. I felt at peace. The group was too small to be a serious threat but big enough to keep me interested, and I sank into a recognisable routine.

Aether tingled on my fingertips, and I wove it into spells. Cut, parry, combat sigil—a dance as familiar as my old boots. I ploughed through the pack, and the beasts that didn't fall to my blade were swiftly dealt with by the rest of the soldiers.

I wasn't sure how much time passed. I was so focused on my task that it took several moments for me to realise someone was roaring my name. Dark obsidian blood splashed across my face as my sword sliced my opponent's body open before I turned, expecting to see someone needing my help, only to find Orm, unarmed, wearing only a shirt and a pair of bloody linen breeches.

I gaped, watching him plough through the fray, tearing apart anything that came close. The savagery was terrifying, but as I saw my bear of a man go berserk with my name on his lips, my body reacted, not with fear but with exhilarating desire.

I held my breath, grasping the aether when a beast pounced, but my magnificent warrior caught it midair, twisting its neck effortlessly. Orm roared as the body fell from his grip, but as he cast around for more enemies, I noticed the sudden silence surrounding us, our enemies dead or crippled on the ground. As I hastily cleaned my sword and sheathed it, I moved slowly towards the snarling warrior, watching him warily.

The moment I noted recognition in Orm's eyes, I rushed forward, jumping into his arms and kissing him passionately. 'Did you see? Did you see your men fight? After just a couple of days of training, they fought like veterans. We can do so much more if I keep training with them. For the victory!' I rejoiced, and before I realised what I was doing, I kissed him again, just like I always did with Tal after we had won a battle.

Orm gasped, his arms tightening around me with enough force to lift me off the ground as he returned my kiss with wild abandon. My paladin mage had never kissed me that way. Tal's kisses were always joyful and loving, leaving me laughing and happy, but Orm ...?

Orm possessed me.

The world disappeared in a cloud of lust. His tongue pushing past my lips, Orm acted as if my kiss had opened the floodgates of desire and nothing mattered more than this moment. The cheering of the surrounding soldiers barely registered as my passion and magic thrummed through my body, the swirling energy sparking and biting at Orm's chest.

In a swift jerking move, Orm swung me around, breaking the kiss before he groaned, his features distorted with pain. My confusion at his actions was quickly replaced by rage when I saw what had happened.

A surviving werewolf had scrambled up and dug his claws into Orm's side.

Guilt that my inattention and arrogance had caused this burned inside my chest. My anguished scream lit the sky as the aether answered and lightning tore into the crippled beast, incinerating him before my eyes. My breath shuddered in my chest, and I turned back, looking into Orm's eyes.

'I'll call Vahin and take you to the castle. Please don't move. Alaric will fix it,' I was frantic, embracing him to support him before he placed a hand on my cheek.

'Shh ... Ani, I'll be alright. Dragon riders heal fast, and this was barely a scratch. Just another scar to add to the collection. I'll look after it when we're done here,' he said, slipping from my arms. His calmness caught me off guard, and all I could manage to do was stare at him. 'Fine, but are you sure everything's alright?'

'I am. Truth be told, I'm proud of what you've done, even if watching you fight was one of the most terrifying moments of my life. We need to talk—later, in private, because keeping you in the dark clearly isn't working. For now, we need to look after our men.' He pressed a hand to his bleeding side while he assumed command, directing soldiers and merchants alike.

More people poured from the castle, and in no time, the wagon was back on its wheels, the wounded taken care of, and we were walking back to the fortress.

'Please say something,' I begged when we were finally alone, walking through the empty corridors to my living quarters.

'What I have to say won't be pleasant to hear. But if you want to lead men, you have to think about them first. You are not fighting alone anymore. I know you thought you were doing the right thing, and yes, saving those people was right, but you didn't know what you were facing and led your men into battle without even informing the garrison officer or me. What if you needed backup? What if Vahin hadn't caught the group circling behind to ambush you?'

He turned to face me. 'You are an amazing mage and an excellent fighter, but at the moment, you are not a leader. That, thankfully, we can rectify because you have good instincts and rallied those rookies without hesitation.' I caught Orm's grimace as he finished and the trembling of his hand as he opened the door to my quarters.

His words stung because he was right, and although we suffered few injuries today, it could have been much worse, and it would have been on my conscience.

'I'm sorry,' I whispered. Orm nodded, placing a hand on the small of my back and ushering me inside. 'I know you well enough to realise that. Have I told you how awestruck I was when I saw you fighting those beasts?' He reached out to stroke my cheek before cursing when he saw the blood covering us both and dropping his hand.

'But you must be punished for your actions, and since Alaric is busy with the injured guards, you shall be required to tend to my battered body.' Despite his teasing tone, I noticed the sigh of relief when the door closed behind us. For the first time that day, Orm let a hint of weakness show.

I bit my lip and led him to the chaise lounge, cutting away his bloody shirt once he sat down. Without a word, I knelt next to him, cleaning and bandaging the wound. After a moment, Orm began smiling and I realised that I was humming an old folk tune from my youth. The blush that swept over my cheeks made the smug warrior smile even wider, so I tried to distract the annoying man.

'What are you thinking about?' I asked as I finished, and he sighed.

'That I should have told you this earlier. Maybe then you would have been more careful.'

'Tell me what?'

'That my brother thinks the Lich King, or even someone in our court, is hunting down conduit mages. You're the last we know of that's alive, and I want it to stay that way.' I frowned.

'Alright, I will be extra careful, but I can take care of myself,' I replied, tightening the knot harshly when he shook his head.

'I know you can, but—fuck, that's tight—but what if our enemy comes armed with your geas? How can I help if that happens?'

'How can you help if that happens? No one can help if they use that damn phrase. Thankfully, there's only one copy of the geas, and you have it.'

'But what if, Annika? I can't risk that. I can't risk ... you,' he elaborated. His voice was filled with tension and need as he leaned forward, brushing my lip with his thumb. 'Ani ... that kiss,' he started, frowning when I pulled away to busy my hands with packing the medical supplies.

I had to bite my lip because I still felt his touch and I wanted to feel it more, but not like this. Not when he was injured and I was angry about being blindsided by his secrecy. 'I always kissed Tal after we won. It was just the heat of the moment, and I forgot myself. I'm sorry,' I said, avoiding his eyes.

'I'm not ... but I understand.'

'If you do, you'll let me fight as I was trained to,' I replied, and he sighed heavily.

'I'll think about it.'

'Fine.' I finished my work in silence, but when I went to help Orm back to his room, he stopped me. 'Ani ... allow me to stay, please,' he mumbled, giving me a coy, almost embarrassed smile when I frowned.

'I know you are angry, but ... being near you helps me,' he added when I continued to look at him, surprised by his words. He exhaled slowly. 'No, I'm sorry, I know it's an unreasonable request.' Orm reached down to pick up the torn remains of his clothes from the seat, but I grasped his hand, stopping him.

'No, if it helps you, it is the right thing to do. Stay Ormond, be my guest tonight.'

It was the first time I'd seen him so timid, vulnerable. As angry as I felt at the tight-lipped, overprotective bastard, something in Orm's eyes had prompted me to agree. I helped him with supper when I saw him wince every time he moved his arm and even offered him my bed, willing to sleep on the couch, but he refused. *At least I tried,* I thought, as I slipped into bed.

'Goodnight, my fearless mage.'

I was grateful for the pillow as my cheeks flushed red upon hearing his soft-spoken words. Despite Orm being the one injured, I fell asleep first, so I expected to be the first one up. However, when I awoke, the chaise lounge was empty, and the blankets I had given him were folded neatly on the seat, leaving me strangely disappointed.

It had happened three more times since. The days were silent, both of us too stubborn to talk first, but every evening, I waited for the knock on my door, followed by Orm looking at me with that silent question in his eyes, then him slipping inside when I moved back to let him in.

I didn't know why Orm needed it, or what was disturbing him so much that he sought refuge in my presence, but from the hushed discussions he had with his men, I knew things weren't looking good.

I saw him conversing quietly with Alaric, who soothed Orm's headaches with his healing touch. But the damn man still wouldn't talk to me, and that was why I was going to go with him on the next patrol. I was determined to help him with whatever problem he might have and fix it before our disagreement fractured these budding feelings I had for him.

CHAPTER 22

ANNIKA

F our days. Four days without a word. When I finally cornered him, Orm had acted like such an idiot that I wanted to slap him.

Now I stood next to Vahin, watching Orm brief his men while I tried to control my frustration. The dragon nudged my shoulder, interrupting my thoughts.

'He will listen. Just give him time.'

'When? After the Lich King knocks down the doors? I get it. He's worried about someone coming and stealing away his precious conduit mage, but I've been cooped up in this fortress for so long that it's driving me mad. I may not have a dragon, but I'm a better fighter—well, ground fighter—than half his men. He saw me fight and knows I can deal with almost any human or demon, not just the ones breaching the Barrier.'

'Oh, but you do have a dragon, Little Flame,' Vahin answered with amusement, rubbing his snout on my hair. *'He knows you can fight but doesn't want you to. Orm has realised there's something he is afraid of losing. For him, you are the calm in the storm, somewhere he can feel the emotions he's bottled up for decades. It is all very new to him, so have a little patience with his fumbling attempts of showing you he cares.'*

'Well, good luck with that. Patience is not my strong suit.'

'Ani? I thought you would be working with Alaric today?' I looked up to see Orm in front of me and gestured towards my riding gear, paired with a fur-lined cloak. 'Oh, don't be dense. I'm coming with you. I know you're going to the Rift, and I want to see what's going on. I promise to listen to your orders and behave like a proper soldier,' I raised two fingers to reaffirm my promise, but he didn't smile back.

'I can tell you what's going on. The magic is fading and more creatures are passing through. I suspect they're tunnelling beneath the Barrier because the ground around the Rift is different every time we return. With the vjesci we captured in the mines, I believe what we see from the air is just the tip of the iceberg. All I can do is patrol the area and destroy anything that emerges.' Orm came so close that I had to raise my head to look at him.

He pulled my hood over my head when a cold gust of wind from the mountaintop blew in our direction. 'I'll be back this afternoon. We'll talk about you joining our patrols during dinner and share some wine together in the library afterwards. I would really like that,' he said after I was sufficiently bundled against the cold.

'And we'll reach the same conclusion we did during our shouting match at breakfast. No, Orm, this is my line in the sand. We are going together now, or I'll go alone on horseback.' I turned to climb onto Vahin's back.

It was interesting how Anchoring the dragon had stripped away my fear of heights, as well as the other feelings that had overwhelmed me before we bonded. It felt as if the old me had died that day, taking my past with her.

It bothered me, but there was no one I could talk to, no one who could explain why I felt like an observer of my own life.

'Not this time, Ani.' Orm grabbed my belt. The sudden jolt made me stumble and fall back onto his chest. His arms trapped me there while he dropped his head. I felt his breath caressing my earlobe when he whispered, 'Don't argue with me, Nivale. Please, not here. I will explain everything when I get back.'

'I'm not your prisoner; I'm your mage,' I snapped, wishing he could get it through that thick skull of his.

'You are so much more than that. This is the last time I'll refuse you, but we will have to plan your outings carefully. As much as I know you can hold your own, you are also a target, and that means the days of carelessly traipsing over the mountains are gone,' Orm insisted, and despite the goosebumps he caused, I turned around and jerked from his grasp.

'Why? Because you said so?'

'Yes, because I said so. Fuck, Ani, I understand. I don't want to do this to you, but letting you come is not a risk I'm willing to take. It doesn't matter how I feel; it never has. I'm your lord commander, and you will listen when I issue an order.' He clenched his fists.

Oh, you motherfucker. I'll show you, 'Lord Commander,' I raged internally, ready to tell him exactly what I thought about his orders when Vahin's voice in my head interrupted me.

'Please, Little Flame, stop. I know you are angry, but his men are watching. Don't undermine his authority in front of them.'

I looked past Orm, noticing the small crowd staring at us with interest. Vahin was right. I didn't want to undermine Orm by quarrelling with him like a fishwife. I just wanted him to see my point. I had to yield this time, but if he thought he'd won, he was sorely mistaken. I took a deep breath and exhaled until I was sure I could speak without anger.

'Of course, Lord Commander. As always, I am at your service. Please excuse me. Before you set off on patrol without me, however, I would like to request that you stay away from my quarters in future. I'm afraid you will find a less than cordial welcome.' I bowed to complete the effect.

Orm's face hardened into an unreadable expression. 'You don't mean that ...' He reached out for me, swallowing hard, but I stepped away, leaving his hand empty in the air. I wanted to be a source of comfort to him, a person he could rely on and trust, just as Alaric was. I wanted him to see me for who I was: a battle mage, not a child he had to protect and watch over as I slept.

'Yes, Lord Commander, I do. Now, do you have any more orders, or am I free to go?' I asked dispassionately. His hand slowly lowered, but the muscles on his jawline ticked rhythmically as he ground his teeth. 'You are free to go, my lady. I am sorry for disturbing your nights' rest.'

'That was cruel, Little Flame,' I heard Vahin's thoughts when I reached the castle. *'Orm comes to you because seeing you sleep calms his mind. He lives to serve, and you just took away the only indulgence he's ever allowed himself.'*

'What about me, Vahin?' I looked up, seeing the dragons rise into the sky. *'I'm not trying to be cruel, but I'm suffocating, and I don't want him to—no, I won't* let *him lock me in a tower like some fae princess,'* I screamed the thought, then, in sheer frustration, shielded myself from the dragon's mind.

As soon as Orm's squadron disappeared into the clouds, I marched straight to the garrison's stable. 'I need a horse and tack,' I demanded from the stable master, and the poor man paled under my stare.

'I can't, my lady. Yesterday when you said ... the commander ...' he stuttered, lowering his gaze.

I didn't know what angered me more: that Orm had thought to order his men to withhold resources in case I wanted to leave, or his soldiers' blind obedience. 'The commander can kiss my rosy ... dragon. Will you give me the horse or not?' I asked sharply. The man seemed to fold in on himself but refused to budge.

'My lady, please.'

I can force his submission. I can burn this entire shithole down, knock it down with a tempest, or destroy its foundations with an earthquake. Once I'd run through enough methods of destruction, I calmed down enough to think.

I was proud of myself; ten years ago, I would have just barged through, using my magic to get what I wanted—but I'd learned to target my anger at those who deserved it. I couldn't blame the stable master for following orders, even if those orders made my life difficult. 'Fine, I'll do without,' I said, turning around to storm off.

I went straight to my room. I was already dressed for travelling but now needed some supplies. I hadn't taken my falchion when I thought I'd be flying with Vahin, but I would need it if I'd be wandering alone. Together with a few healing potions—just in case my luck turned bad—I grabbed a bedroll and the food Agnes had laid out for me.

I was ready to go but slowed as guilt niggled at my senses. I would be in the mountains for at least two days, and I knew two men and a dragon who wouldn't appreciate my sudden absence. For a moment, I toyed with the idea of just letting them worry, but in the end, I decided to be a grown-up. Despite our argument, Orm didn't deserve the worry of thinking someone had kidnapped me.

I put quill to parchment and scribbled a letter.

To the Lord Commander,

I can only imagine the frustration you are feeling as you read this letter. It likely matches my own every time I heard 'maybe next time' when I asked you to allow me to do my job. I know there is danger out there, but you are risking your life flying without a mage when the spectrae have already crossed the Barrier. As we can't agree, let me take the decision out of your hands.

I will be back in two days with the heart of whoever tries to kill me, whether it be man or monster. Don't bother trying to find me.

Your always obedient mage,

Ani

P.S. Please tell Alaric I'm sorry, but I know he would've tried to stop me.

That should sort out the impasse we had reached. Two days should be enough to prove to Orm that there is no bogeyman trying to kill me, and after I returned, we could move on from the subject. I sealed the letter and pushed it under Orm's office door before heading to the fortress gates. I caught several covert glances as I walked through the town square, but no one dared to stop me.

'Does Lord Erenhart know you're going out hunting?' asked a familiar voice behind me, and I turned around, smiling at my friend. Katja looked at me with a raised eyebrow, waiting for an answer.

'What do you think?' I didn't bother to mask the sarcasm in my voice, and my friend shook her head.

'He won't be happy. Everybody knows our oh-so-illustrious commander and his dark mage are chasing after you like a pair of dogs in heat. They'd never let you go alone. So, little miss *Nivale*, how are you going to deal with his temper when you return?'

'I'll send for some of your calming tinctures,' I deadpanned, and she burst into laughter. 'If I'm capable of drugging you, I suppose it wouldn't be a problem doing the same to him, but you have to promise me one thing.'

'Oh ...?'

'Be careful, Ani. I quite like you the way you are. I'd hate to think what state you'll be in if the necromancer has to put you back together again.'

'Really, Katja. It's like you don't know me at all. When have I not been careful?' I asked, rolling my eyes.

'Oh, I don't know, maybe the time you got yourself stranded with an injured leg after chasing a bloody weregoat? Or the time you ended up puking all over the mayor's shoes after that undead water demon—the utopiec—bashed your head in while you were chasing him through the muddy river? Should I continue?'

I felt my cheeks burning, my face bright red, but that was Katja the Merciless, whose honesty took no prisoners. 'I'll be back soon,' I swore. She pulled me in for a quick hug,

'Remember your promise, you crazy lady, and come back in one piece. Otherwise, I'll send Bryna after you. Well, if I can drag her away from the garrison forge, that is. That woman is having the time of her life there.'

'Bryna's here?!'

Katja looked at me, then at my sword, and sighed. 'You need to come down from your ivory tower more often. Castle life—or the company of those two men—has left you witless. How do you think you got that sword? It grew wings?'

'I thought she just packed my stuff,' I mumbled sheepishly, and Katja burst into laughter. 'Oh, she packed your stuff—along with herself. Then came here, claiming the soldiers needed someone sensible to keep them safe with us two around.'

'And she thinks *she's* the sensible one?' I asked, roaring with laughter. Bryna, our lusty blacksmith, had only ever mentioned being 'sensible' when taking three men to her bed because—as she claimed—it was a perfectly 'sensible' use of sticks and holes.

Katja nodded, and when I finally caught my breath, I didn't feel a drop of this morning's anger. With Bryna's arrival, Varta Fortress felt like home, and I was more determined than ever to protect it.

'When I get back, I'll meet you both in the tavern. I need Bryna to instruct me on the most ... *sensible* way to deal with those men. Between Orm and Alaric, I feel like an uneven, wobbly table.'

'You've already bedded them?' Katja's eyes widened, and I frantically waved my hands. 'No, *no*, nothing like that, but ... you know.' I bit my lip. 'We'll talk more when I return,' I promised before turning around. 'Stay safe, my friend. I'll see if I can bring back some weregoats for Bryna.'

Katja nodded, a troubled smile on her face as I walked away, but the idea she'd planted in my mind stubbornly grew. *How would it feel to be between Orm and Alaric?*

I remembered my time with Talmund and Arno, the shared touches and nights we'd spent together ... Even if I couldn't feel that love anymore, I knew we'd been happy.

Gods, what am I thinking? There's enough trouble brewing without me inviting them both to my bed, I thought angrily as I rushed towards the gate.

CHAPTER 23

OR/AOND

I hoped this journey was worth keeping Ani in the dark because at the moment, I felt like the worst kind of arsehole. However, if my brother's informers were right, I could expect a messenger from the Lich King trying to cross the Barrier today; and the gods help us if that monster discovered Ani was alive.

I knew I'd been unreasonable, taking my precautions to the extreme, but I had my reasons.

Only a few days after I returned from Truso, I had received letters from court demanding Annika's return, and I knew I would have to talk to her about it. Worse, though, was my brother's warning of not only the growing unrest but also rumours of '*special means*' for bringing Ani back.

For a mage of her calibre, that could only mean that someone planned to use her geas. The royal mage had assured me he had given me the only copy, but could I trust him? Could I trust anyone in Truso except my brother?

This is the last time Ani, I promise. Alaric has almost finished checking the fortress for spies, and once he is done, we will hunt together, my beautiful Nivale.

Even now, I couldn't stop thinking of that fierce, caring woman who always had a smile for those she held dear, who was merciless in destroying those who targeted the weak. I couldn't wait to receive another *victory* kiss.

To feel the elation of her choosing me ... Except that she didn't choose me—it had become painfully obvious when I tried to talk to her. Reynard was right; Ani had demolished the years of rigorous training and walls I'd built around my emotions.

My thoughts turned to Alaric, and I felt my chest tighten as my hands gripped the pommel of the saddle. An emotion I couldn't identify made its presence known. I saw how he looked at my Ani—the raw hunger in his gaze matched mine. For the sake of this godsforsaken kingdom, *he* should be her Anchor; and I wouldn't stand against it, even if it killed me.

You have to let it happen. They share a powerful magical synergy, and that connection will only strengthen their bond. I thumped my chest, but the pain the thought caused didn't want to subside. The reality that the man I thought of as a brother deserved to be loved by Ani more than me was a bitter potion to swallow.

'Fuck!' I knew I had lost this battle. I should step away—a better man would ... but I couldn't. Not anymore.

The night I'd spent in her chair after being injured had been the most beautiful torture. My whole being demanded that I wrap myself around Ani and tell her how I felt—and hope that she would accept me and that no one would take her from me. I'd pushed the memory into the deepest recesses of my soul because it had shocked me that I wasn't repelled by the idea, but the reminiscence of the night I touched myself thinking of her and Alaric intruded on the moment.

'Orm, you're thinking too loud, and I really don't want to be imagining your hairy arse anywhere near Annika,' Vahin said in my thoughts.

'Do you think she hates me?'

'No, of course not. Why would Annika hate someone who refuses to reveal why he's so overprotective and acts erratic and confusing? Who fails to see that she is dying inside, suffocating in the golden cage he put her in?' I could feel his

sarcasm and anger, which only served to increase the guilt eating away at me. *The least you could have done today was explain why you refused her request.*

'I will apologise and explain everything, but she must understand that I wasn't doing it to spite her.'

'Must she? Even if you tell Ani about the letters, what other reason could you possibly give her? That you feel guilty for using her geas and swore you wouldn't let anyone do it again? Or that seeing her almost die awakened a fear you never knew existed? Of course, you could tell Ani you're harbouring a secret obsession with her, but I'm sure you'll keep quiet because you fear her having to choose between you and Alaric, thinking she will reject you.'

Vahin lashed me with his opinions, the anger and concern entwined with them making it even worse. *'You're trying to do the right thing, but in the wrong way. Don't keep her locked in a cage of your fears, assuming you know what is best for her. It won't work, my friend. Those born with wings die behind bars, even if those bars are made of gold and good intentions.'*

The image that Vahin shared with me was shocking: a beautiful dragoness, her kind eyes lifeless, and her wings—bound by a golden rope—withered and dry. It was the wake-up call I needed. Was that what he thought I was doing to Ani? Binding her wings?

I looked down at the squadron as we circled the Rift, swooping back and forth through the Barrier, but there was no sign of movement. No activity—human, animal, or monster. There was only the vast, bare, poisoned plain spreading out from the Rift.

I directed Vahin closer to Tomma, ordering him and two others to stay in position as a precaution. They signalled their agreement, and I sighed, feeling defeated. I'd argued with Annika for nothing. We were no closer to finding out who in the court was the Lich King's ally.

'Signal the return,' I said, and Vahin roared, relaying the information. *'What are you going to do?'* he asked, his attention focused on my reply.

'I will tell her the truth and let her decide what she wants to do. If she still wants to go on ground patrols knowing the danger, we will plan it carefully. You are right, but even if I put my feelings aside, this area is more dangerous than Zalesie, and it won't be only about her safety, but also about my men's. But I'll make it work. If I don't, she'll probably go out alone. I wish we hadn't argued. I just ... I keep messing it up,' I admitted to the dragon, which made him laugh.

'She agreed to help, so let her,' he said as we flew back to the fortress.

We arrived late in the afternoon, and I went straight to my office. I wanted to show Ani the letters, and I needed to gather my thoughts before meeting with her. Much to my adjutant's annoyance, I couldn't find them even after we scrutinised every document on my desk.

It wasn't that I didn't trust him; I just needed a sense of control with everything being so chaotic right now. Ani would probably be with Alaric at this time of day, and I wanted to come prepared with an apology and the information that would hopefully explain my behaviour.

A decisive knock broke through my thoughts, and after a moment, Alaric walked in with a deep frown on his face.

'I heard you'd returned early. Ani skipped our session today, and the only reason I'm not raising the alarm is that her friend Katja seemed calm and told me to ask you for an explanation. So, could you please explain? Because gossip around town says you had a spat with your little Nivale,' he said warily.

My confusion at the accusation in Alaric's voice made me frown, but I answered truthfully. 'And you came here because ... you thought I'd know why Ani didn't come to your session? I've been near the Rift most of the day with Vahin.'

I heard my adjutant mutter in the background, *'Typical. He pisses off a woman, and now the entire fortress has to suffer because she's avoiding them.'* Alaric had turned to him, having heard his muttering, but then his angry gaze snapped to my embarrassed features.

'What is he talking about, Orm? What did you say to Ani to make her avoid *me*?' Alaric demanded. His lips pressed in barely restrained emotion while my adjutant paled, likely realising he'd spoken out loud. 'Fuck, I'm sorry. That's not what I ...' the soldier wilted under Alaric's stare before I placed my hand on his forearm, halting his nervous attempts to clean my desk.

'Concentrate on finding those letters. It appears I have an angry mage to find.' I said, and he nodded vigorously. Ari ignored the other man as we headed for the door.

'So, where to start? Have you checked the garrison? Annika has become a regular there recently,' I asked, sighing when Alaric rolled his eyes. 'Yes, I did. Twice. It still amazes me how much they all love her despite you circling around like a bad-tempered lynx. It is a testament to how impressive she is.'

'I don't circle her like some horny wildcat,' I muttered, but he smirked. 'It's nothing to be ashamed of. I struggle whenever I see someone other than us touching my Domina.' He shrugged, and I sent him a sharp look.

'Did you—your Domina?'

'Why are you so surprised? I'm not just a mage. I'm also a male fae. Annika appeals to every aspect of my personality. Even if we didn't have perfect synergy, I would still want her. She is cunning, ruthless, and she made me bleed,' he grinned, and I gasped.

'Did you ... taste her blood, too?' I asked cautiously, and Alaric nodded before I continued, 'Does she know what it means?'

'No, and you won't tell her. She is not dark fae and doesn't have to adhere to our customs.'

'How the fuck did you let that happen? Was it on purpose?' I accused, wincing at the hostility in my voice, but I was at a loss. Dark fae took their blood rituals seriously, and Alaric had just claimed Ani as his domina. 'I didn't intend for it, but fate decided for us. You remember the mess we made after getting carried away duelling?'

'Yes, but Annika told me it was just horseplay and that she enjoyed it. Then she offered to cover the renovation costs.'

'We both enjoyed it, maybe a little too much. Although, in hindsight, I will admit that challenging Ani to a duel might have been a mistake,' he said with a crooked smile.

Gods, this is getting so out of hand, I thought, rubbing my neck. Even if Annika didn't know what had happened, *Alaric* knew—and in dark fae culture, he was now a bloodied contender, someone whom a dark fae woman was considering mating with. 'You have to tell her. Don't make my mistake; look where we ended up.'

'I will when she is ready. I want it to be her choice.'

I had no answer to that. Alaric wanted Ani to choose him, and I wanted the same. This was one massive fucking mess, but I couldn't argue or fault his reasoning, not when I felt the same. I could only grind my teeth in frustration.

We were exiting the central bailey of the fortress when a stern-looking soldier approached us. I recognised him as the sergeant in charge of the main gates and instantly focused on his grim expression.

'Sir?'

'Report, soldier,' I ordered, noticing the furtive look the man gave Ari.

'Lady Annika left the fortress and hasn't returned.' I felt the world darken around me.

'When did this happen?'

'This morning, sir. Just after you left.'

'You didn't think to tell Alaric about it?' I asked, tightening my fist. The sergeant paled, hearing the low, menacing tone of my voice.

'Respectfully, sir, there was no reason to stop her from leaving, and Lady Annika is more than capable of managing time outside on her own. I am bringing this to you now because it is almost nighttime and she hasn't returned.'

'You should've sent a message as soon as she left!' Alaric snapped from behind me, and I let him continue with the conversation as I struggled to calm my raging emotions. The bloody sergeant was reprimanding me. It might be indirect, but I saw his disapproval.

She fucking left. Why? Gods, did she head for the Rift alone? Did she want to return to Zalesie? I felt the weight of the world pressing down on me. *'Vahin? Ani left. Can you track her?'* The worry radiating through the bond made me shudder, and I felt the moment Vahin burst from his lair. To the solider I instructed, 'Bring my kirbai from the stables, and my hunting leathers. Now!'

When he took off, I turned towards Alaric. 'Ari, stay in the castle in case she returns. Take charge here until I bring her back.' It would take me time; kirbai weren't as fast as dragons, but they were more agile and versatile in the forest.

'I should go after her,' he contended. I could see he wasn't happy with my solution.

'No, she left because of my stupidity. *I* have to be the one to bring her back,' I insisted.

'She is my Domina, but I'll stay here, just in case. Orm—I know you love her; it is clear to anyone but you. So stop holding back. It's causing more problems than it's worth.' I took a step back, stunned by his words and the dark aura staining the air around him.

'Just find her and bring her back. Then we'll have the conversation you've been avoiding.' He walked away, the soldier returning with my kirbai and equipment. I dressed as quickly as I could while waiting for Vahin to reply. After what felt like an eternity, he sent a mental image of a female figure marching north towards the Rift.

'She blocked our thoughtspeech, but I still can see her. I will look over her. Nothing will touch her—but hurry,' came the dragon's thought, calming me a

little. Within minutes, I was galloping through the gates, led by the directions Vahin projected into my mind.

CHAPTER 24

ORMOND

The moon had been up for hours when Vahin informed me that Ani had finally made camp. I felt guilty pushing my kirbai so hard. His fur was now matted with sweat, and his breathing laboured. My mount was one of a race of magical, catlike creatures created by Cahyon Abrasan before whatever madness led to his transformation into the Lich King.

The kirbai were his first creation. No one knew if he'd abandoned them or if they escaped captivity, but they'd lived and bred freely in the mountains for several centuries. Rumour had it they were created to shelter the souls of warriors, giving them another chance to live on within a new body. I didn't know how true that was, but it took great patience and a gentle hand to tame the striking beasts.

They acted much like the cats they resembled, often using that strange sense their smaller cousins employed to select their riders. Once they made their decision, though, their loyalty was unquestioning, and it was well known that the kirbai fought to the death to protect their humans. They were also one of the most intelligent animals I knew, able to find their way home and understand complex commands. I often wondered if that was where the rumours came from.

Now, as the clouds drifted across the moon, my feline companion silently approached the small camp Ani had set up. The smile stretching my lips was predatory as we approached from the rear. I planned to surprise Ani and scold her for not being aware, but as I dismounted and took a few steps, my body froze, held in place despite my struggles to move forward.

'I'm willing to believe you weren't sneaking up on me to prove a point. My warning spell alerted me the moment you arrived. For a man so concerned about my safety, you didn't even notice the warning signs I left out.' She turned to look at me. 'Didn't you bother reading my letter? I asked you not to look for me, so what are you doing here?'

I would have answered, but her spell held me so tight I couldn't even blink, which was annoying because all I wanted to do was laugh at my carelessness. I had treated her like a simpleton from a backwater village and was now being served humble pie.

Ani must have noticed I couldn't speak because she smirked, muttering something under her breath, and the force holding me immobile disappeared.

As I stumbled forward, I nodded, acknowledging her talent for setting up such a cunning trap.

'I came to ask you to return to the fortress. I'm sorry for causing our disagreement. I made a mistake, and seeing how easily you caught me proves how wrong I was. You've made your point; no human can sneak up on you, and if it helps, you can tell everyone you captured Varta's commander without even trying,' I said, noticing with pleasure that her lips quirked when she looked at me. Seeing that coveted smile gave me such immense relief.

'I'm better in the wilderness than any of your men,' she responded, and I bowed my head. 'Yes, but please don't rub it in. There is only so much male pride can handle.' Ani snorted her amusement and her reaction gave me the courage to continue.

'Please come back with me. Returning to Zalesie makes no sense. We can discuss which patrols would suit you best, and you can join them as soon as you wish. Don't leave just because my paranoia got the best of me and I stupidly forgot how impressive you are.' Her frown was one of confusion as I came closer, and she took a moment to reply.

'I'm not leaving, you idiot. I just went hunting ... I thought it might draw out those threatening me. Once they're gone, there will be no reason for us to argue. I don't want to fight with you. I don't like it.' It was my turn to stare at her. 'You keep flying around, but some things you can only see while on land, especially if something's going on underground.'

'I didn't take you with me, so you went by yourself to act as fucking bait? Why didn't you tell anyone?' I dug my nails into the palms of my hands to control my temper. That was exactly what I was trying to avoid.

'I tried, but you didn't want to listen. I joined you at the fortress because my power could help, but our plans fell apart. I can still help, though. Look at what happened with the merchants. I can clear the roads. I can protect those fleeing monster attacks. But I can't do anything if you hide me away behind stone walls. Please, look around and ask yourself, was I really in danger on my own?' She bit her lip. 'I think you are right about the terrain and the vjesci. Something is moving underground, and I wanted to know what it is, preferably before it tunnels out and bites us in the rear.'

I ran a hand through my hair, now sweaty from the strenuous ride. It was my fault Ani couldn't talk to me. I was so absorbed in keeping her safe—partly from me—that I had forgotten to listen to her concerns.

'I'm sorry, Nivale. Still, you should have told someone. I thought I'd lost you. Ani, for the love of all the gods, was speaking to Alaric not an option?' I reached for her but stopped myself, willing my hand to drop before I wrapped her in my arms.

'If you want me to listen to your orders, maybe you should make them reasonable. You ordered the stable master not to give me a horse?' she challenged, rolling her eyes when I looked at her. 'Everybody seems to be under the impression that you and Alaric want to keep me locked up in my room, preferably chained to the bedpost. What do you think would have happened if I informed him? That he'd open the fortress gate for me and wish me good luck on my journey?'

'You have a point, but you should have told someone. Agnes, maybe?'

'Katja knew, and why do you keep saying I told no one? I left a letter in your room explaining everything,' she insisted. I frowned, trying to remember if I had missed a letter amongst the stack of papers my adjutant had brought me today.

'Orm, please tell me you got my letter. I slipped it under your bedroom door,' she said, observing my reaction before she sighed. 'You haven't been to your bedroom ...'

'No, I wasn't thinking straight. When I heard you were missing, all I could think of was finding you before anything bad happened.'

She shook her head and rolled her eyes so hard I had to smile.

'Let me guess, you jumped on Vahin and flew here as soon as you realised I'd left. So, should we sit by the fire, or are we expecting the dragon and Alaric to show up any moment now as the second half of your rescue party?'

'Vahin is flying back to the fortress as we speak, and Alaric stayed behind. I came alone on my kirbai. I wanted to have time with you alone, to talk—' I began, taken aback when she squealed.

'You have a kirbai?! Here? Why didn't I see it in the fortress?' Annika's smile instantly made every problem disappear. She grabbed my arms, steadying herself as she looked past me. I whistled quietly, and my mount trotted forward to stand beside me, hissing when Ani tried to stroke him.

I grasped her hand before it ended up in the stomach of the temperamental beast, gently placing it on the kirbai's neck, just like I did when introducing her to Vahin. I kept my other hand on his bridle, ensuring he wouldn't attack as Ani stroked his fur with wonder in her eyes.

'He is so beautiful and soft. What is his name?'

'He doesn't have a name. I don't like naming other beings,' I answered simply.

'You named me after a flower,' her voice was barely a whisper, but I felt it deep in my soul.

'And see where that got us? I grew attached to you.'

I slid her hand over the soft fur, letting our fingers entwine, feeling her body relax as she leaned towards me.

'Please … don't leave me like that ever again. I care for you, Nivale. I have tried to fight it, but I can't help how I feel around you. You bring peace into my mind and laughter into my life. I've even begun wishing I could be your Anchor. I can't stop thinking about how much I would give for it to be possible. I'm so afraid to lose you.'

Ani turned towards me and bit her lip before she finally nodded. 'You won't lose me. I want to make the fortress my home if you'll let me. After the year passes, I want to stay here. My friends are here. Katja likes the fortress and wants to settle there, and Bryna—well, she just arrived. Prolonged absence from Vahin is difficult … *would* be difficult, but you and Alaric aren't making it easy.'

'You want to stay? With me? With us? Even after the year ends?' I tried to stay calm, but the mere thought of Annika even considering it filled me with hope.

'W—well, in the fortress, yes. I'm not sorry for leaving today, but I do apologise for the way I did it.' As her words stuttered into silence, I let go of the kirbai and locked her in my arms. The world could fucking burn around us for all I cared. I had Annika here, leaning towards me, and that meant more to me than anything else I could imagine.

'Orm, what are you doing?' came the muffled query, and I felt hands pressing against my chest.

'Apologising,' I said, letting go of all reason.

I kissed her.

Ani tasted amazing, like honey mead that caressed your tongue before going straight to your head, leaving you dizzy. I felt arousal wash over me when she gasped, parting her lips and yielding to my touch. I was lost, drunk on her taste, and craved more.

Then I felt it, the sting of her magic, my skin shivering as it wrapped itself around me. I welcomed the feeling, hoping for more, *needing* more. 'Gods, you're perfect,' I groaned, her power lighting me on fire until Ani abruptly gasped and pushed me away.

'Could you apologise and let me breathe at the same time?' she said. Annika licked her lips, refusing to look me in the eye, and I had to use all of my willpower not to grab her again. A tentative smile ghosted over her lips as she smoothed down her braid, tussled from our passionate kiss.

I immediately reached out and wrapped my hand around the silk tresses, pulling her closer. 'Orm, no. That was very pleasant, but shockingly unwise,' she rebuked, though she didn't pull away from my touch. If anything, her breathing sped up. Cheeks flushed, she looked up and pulled the braid from my grasp.

'Not for me, Nivale. I want to do it again ... and so much more,' I said, her braid sliding over my palm.

'I can't,' Ani murmured, shaking her head and stepping away from me. I inhaled slowly, calming my thoughts, determined to find the reason behind her refusal. The pull was there. The desire I saw in her eyes was unmistakable. She wanted me, and I was ready to do anything to be with her.

'Tell me why, Ani, I ... I can't promise my nature won't get the better of me, but I'm done with sheltering you. I will happily employ you as garrison battle mage if you want.' She looked at me sharply.

'You would employ me as a battle mage? Even if I only have Vahin as my Anchor?' she asked. I nodded, pleased with myself as I sensed the hope in her voice.

'I would, although I think he'd be upset if he heard you say "*only*" Vahin,' I teased. As she smiled at me, I added, 'You can always add more Anchors, Ani. Alaric is eager ... and so am I.'

'I know, but I'm not ready. I need to be sure. I can't risk what happened with Vahin happening again. If I'd been conscious, maybe then I'd know what went wrong,' she pondered while playing with her braid. 'The way my emotions seem to have changed is unnatural. You can't just switch yourself off like the pain that dictated the last ten years of your life never happened. Without knowing how I truly felt, how can I know I won't reject Alaric? I can't risk anyone else. I can't bond with someone unless I'm sure I'd accept them.'

That was it—the key to Annika's refusal. I knew the moment we returned to the fortress, I would ask Alaric to help Ani; but before he could do that, she needed an explanation of what happened that fateful night. My reckless kiss opened my eyes to a simple truth: if I wanted Annika, I needed to come clean about what we'd done.

'Ani, the way you feel is my fault.'

She frowned, 'Your fault? You don't have that kind of power ...What do you mean?'

'The reason the past no longer bothers you is because Alaric used a spell to suppress your feelings, and I allowed him to do it. It was life-or-death, and you were being burned alive while you held onto the spirits of your Anchors. Your grief was preventing Vahin from controlling the fire and I used your geas to force your compliance so that Alaric could bespell your emotions.'

'You ... used my geas?' Ani pulled away from me, suddenly emotionless, a wall of distrust crashing down between us. The tears in her eyes almost sent me to my knees, but as much as I wanted her understanding, I couldn't regret saving her life.

'I had to! There were no other options. I would do it again if it meant saving your life. Every time I close my eyes, I remember my helplessness, seeing the flames beneath your skin as you slowly died in my arms. So yes, I used the fucking geas. I know I've been acting like a prick recently, but there is *nothing* I wouldn't do to protect you, even if you end up hating me because of it,' I argued with a vehemence that earned me a sad smile.

'I don't hate you. I never did. It's just ... this thing between us ... I like you, but I guess I forgot that I'm basically your slave,' she said in a monotone. 'You promised me you wouldn't use it, but your promise didn't even last a day. I fled the capital because they held that threat over me like an executioner's axe, and now, if I stay here, I know my choices will never truly be mine.'

'I *swear* I only did it to save your life.'

Ani raised her head to look at me. My dragoness with broken wings ... there was no light in her eyes—and I was the man who had crushed her soul.

'Tell me, if I said I wanted to return to Zalesie, or go somewhere those bastards from court couldn't find me, would you force me to stay? If I told you I was leaving for good and never coming back, would you promise never to use my geas?' I opened my mouth to deny it, but Ani shook her head. 'No, Orm. Think it through. If I can't have freedom, give me honesty. Please.'

Deep inside, I felt my answer would be the turning point for whatever future we might have. While I considered it, a gust of wind blew sparks from the fire, surrounding Annika with the light of a thousand dying stars. I couldn't offer her anything but my honour, even if that meant whatever feelings were budding between us would die like the sparks flowing into the night sky.

'I don't know. I know I would beg you to stay, offer you whatever you wanted, but ... for the people we're both striving to protect ... you are still my greatest weapon,' I whispered, knowing I might as well kiss my future with this remarkable woman goodbye.

To my surprise, she came closer and placed her hand on my chest.

'I hate it, Orm. I hate that you've been placed in this position, and I hate how it makes me feel. However, I really appreciate you being honest with me.

I don't blame you for saving my life, but knowing you own my geas ... it makes things difficult between us. We will never be equal. It is an unbreakable chain weighing me down. Even if I know you'd never want to use it to hurt me, the fact remains that it will always be there if circumstances force your hand. But I know that you're a good man faced with an impossible choice, and I don't blame you for any of this.'

Ani's answer, but more so the single tear that fell from her cheek, hit me like a hammer. Before I could do anything stupid, my kirbai headbutted me from behind. As I turned to rebuke him, Ani's eyes narrowed.

'Orm. My spell ... four Vel demons are heading our direction,' she stated, and I cursed because, whilst focusing on her, I'd forgotten we were still in a forest frequented by monsters.

CHAPTER 25

ANNIKA

The gods must hate me, I thought, trying to understand what had just happened.

Orm's kiss left me reeling and filled with a desire to hold the bear of a man closer and do it again. Then I learned he'd used the geas to save my life and failed to mention it, leaving me to worry that something was wrong with me and my emotions.

I hadn't even digested that punch to the gut when my proximity spell warned of an imminent attack. It also detected the frightening amount of foul magic the advancing creatures possessed, and it didn't look good. I frowned when, in answer to my warning, Orm stripped the kirbai's tack before grabbing the creature's muzzle. 'If we fail, run to the fortress and show the dragon what you saw here.'

'Do you think he understands?' I was curious despite the danger. 'He does, and he will fight with us. Get behind me, Nivale, and support me as much as you can.' I burst into laughter, pulling my falchion sword.

'No, Lord Commander. Without your wings, we are equal, and the ground is where I excel. Now, get behind *me* because I have some anger to vent and it's about to get messy.'

I stumbled a bit when I saw the pride and desire mixing in Orm's gaze as our eyes locked. *For a man who did everything he could to keep me in the fortress, he is far too happy to be fighting beside me,* I thought, trying to suppress the joy it brought me before I shook my head and started muttering a quick cantrip.

I felt them before I saw them. Two strigae, fast and deadly, burst into the clearing and rushed in our direction. My usual tactic, casting an arcane net to immobilise fast-moving targets, wouldn't work with Orm here—the net latched onto anything that moved—and I couldn't afford to lose his fighting skills.

This will be more fun anyway, I thought, trailing my hand over the sword, modifying my incantation. The runes etched onto the blade burst into blue flame. The advantage of being an elemental mage was that I could channel aetheric fire into almost anything, turning it into an arcane weapon.

Scholars often theorised the results of a conduit mage stripping the land of its magic, channelling aether until nothing was left. In theory, it was possible, but no one had ever come close to managing such a terrifying feat. Aether was like water: it flowed through the world, changing from one form to another—always there, sustaining, and renewed by, life itself. We could drain a lake of its water, but the rivers and rainfall would always refill it.

I was an elemental mage. My affinity for elements made it easy to cast basic elemental spells without the sigils or incantations that were necessary to use other forms of magic. I couldn't use my conduit abilities without my Anchor, but my own aether reserve was more than enough for such a fight—and these strigae were about to learn that it made little difference which of my abilities I used when the frustration of my situation burned within me like the heat of the sun.

Orm was left behind as I jumped between our attackers, fingers twisting to throw up a shield sigil to protect myself. At the same time, my sword swung in a deadly figure of eight. It cut the closest attacker's arm while I parried the other creature's claws. The sigil burned red but withstood the hit.

'Ani, for fuck's sake!' I heard from behind, but it only made me laugh.

I needed this. After what I'd just learned, my darkness, fear, worries, and unfulfilled desires demanded an outlet. I unleashed it on the monsters, lashing out with pure, unbridled violence. I lost myself in the sheer joy of combat. Fury blazed through my veins as I fought the monsters that Orm—with his heavy sword—was struggling to get a move in on.

I called upon the fire, creating a Morgenstern flail, its fiery chain spitting incandescent sparks as the ball of plasma crashed into one of the strigae's chest, setting her ablaze. The burning creature released a screech that almost made my ears bleed, and the earth shook beneath us. A massive shape, its head pushing aside the tree branches, emerged from the forest wall—a mountain troll.

What the ... why is there a mountain troll here?

The race had never before allied with the Lich King, preferring to remain isolated and only trading sporadically with other races. Yet here he was, charging at Orm, his thundering strides so heavy they shook the bones in my body.

When he passed me, I understood: the pall of death lay heavy on him, and whether it was wild or foul magic that animated him, his mind and soul hadn't returned from behind the Veil.

The fleeting glimpse of the decaying flesh was soon obscured by a set of claws slicing past my eyes. As I fell back, I saw Orm, motionless yet relaxed, with an intense focus in his eyes. I cursed, flicking out my fingers, creating another shield, this one a little different. I added a twist—an outlet for the magic that shortened its lifespan but propelled it forward at speed—and grinned as the strigae were knocked from their feet.

I looked back at Orm, another spell already primed to protect him.

My jaw dropped. No longer was the warrior standing still. He ducked the wild swing of the troll's arm, launching himself forward and cutting across his body with his sword. I watched as half the creature's hand sailed past Orm's head, falling to the ground at the kirbai's feet as it circled around, clawing at the monster's back. Orm rolled, and the sword licked out, carving more flesh from the troll's arm.

He was glorious.

I wished I could stop to admire his technique; efficient, deadly, no movement was wasted or unnecessary. Where I relied on dancing steps, Orm was pure, focused power: one move, one strike—resulting in devastating ruin. I couldn't drag my eyes away from the single combat; that is, until a striga's claw tore through my shield and sliced into my arm. It hurt, but it helped me focus.

The next time she tried to attack, I was already weaving the aether. My incantation created thorny vines that slashed through her torso, forcing her away. As my confidence grew, everything suddenly went blurry as a torrent of foul magic assaulted my senses.

I knew there was a fourth attacker, but I had forgotten about them in the heat of battle. The ground beneath us shook—once, twice, the earth suddenly moving and nearly knocking us from our feet. That could mean only one thing: an olgoi worm[1] was heading for the surface to devour its prey—and it was aiming to make Orm and me its next meal.

'Orm, get away from the centre!' I shouted to him as he stood within the rapidly growing hole beneath his feet. I could fight an olgoi if I had to, but the creatures were famously hard to kill. It usually took several battle mages *and* soldiers with axes to fell one.

---

1. **Olgoi worm** — a blind earthworm with rows of serrated teeth, famous for drilling tunnels in the dirt and rocks. They rarely hunt sentient beings, but during starvation periods, they may move to the surface and hunt for warm-blooded prey.

I felt conflicted despite the danger; olgoi worms weren't evil. They could be dangerous, but as they tended to live in isolated areas and mainly fed on carrion, it was rare for anyone to encounter them. This one must have travelled from Barren Lands; I could tell its energy had been tainted by the Lich King's magic—another testament to the fading barrier.

Orm looked at me then, before glancing at his feet as the hole he'd been standing in erupted, forced up by the giant worm as it burrowed its way to the surface. Uttering a heated curse, he threw himself to the side—but it was too late.

If I'd only warned him sooner, he might have stood a chance. A row of teeth burst from the ground, and the injured troll disappeared with hardly a sound, quickly followed by a twisting, snarling Orm. As the warrior's legs disappeared into the yawning maw, he thrust his sword into its glistening flesh and managed to lodge it firmly to halt his fall.

He was now dangling over the gullet of the worm, relying solely on the sword to not plunge to his death. To make matters worse, the worm was trying to pull back, and its mouth locked onto the wedged sword just as Orm gained his footing. The sound of teeth scraping over his breastplate was deafening as the worm fought to move backwards.

'Oh no, you fucking don't!' I swore, screaming out in my mind, hoping Vahin would answer my call. I dropped to my knees and scratched a glyph in the dirt, ignoring the strigae as they struggled to even stand. I tried snaring Orm or the worm with ropes of aether before the warrior could be swallowed completely.

'Run, Ani. Go back to the fortress. The kirbai will take you,' Orm grunted through gritted teeth, shaking his head when a piece of debris fell on his face.

'No,' I snapped, once again cursing an unfeeling fate. The only Anchor I had was too far away to help, and I needed him desperately. I knew with my distress broadcasting over our link he'd come eventually, but Orm didn't have that much time.

'Just run. My death will end your servitude to the Crown. You will be free, Annika. The parchment ... I burned it. I'm the only one who knows the incantation. Do it for me and live free, Nivale.'

Orm's words triggered something deep inside me. He'd burnt the damn parchment and was willing to die to set me free. I no longer cared if he held my geas or that he hid the truth from me. He'd made a mistake by not telling me, but so had I by not admitting that this grumpy, overprotective bear was *mine*, and I couldn't let him die.

'No!'

'Please don't make me use the geas to save you again,' he threatened while I felt myself being pulled inexorably forward by the magical ropes as I held onto them with all the strength I had.

'I can forgive you for using the geas when I was unconscious and dying, but not now. Now, I get to make my own choices, and I choose you. No matter what happens, *we do it together*.'

I saw the desperation in his eyes, the need to save me warring with what he knew to be right. As I slipped further towards the growing hole, I saw him smile as he seemingly made his decision.

He's going to let go.

I could see it in his eyes, in his calm acceptance. As he released his grip on the sword, I whipped a string of aether that wrapped around his wrist, preventing his fall.

'Don't you dare give up. Hold on to the fucking sword,' I hissed through clenched teeth, and to my relief, he listened. This lumbering bear of a man, whose gentle hand had shown me the proper way to stroke a dragon, frowned, but he listened, letting me focus on my next move.

'Trust me,' I said, digging my fingers into the soft forest ground. This time, I didn't reach for the aether but simply let it flow through me like a river. I whispered an incantation, gently shaping the primaeval power into a depthless void, knowing that I risked catastrophe with no one to stabilise me.

Magic funnelled through me like an endless vortex, an unholy amount of power penetrating the ground. A wave of frost spread from my fingers, all the warmth in the earth pulled into my spell. The magic delved deep beneath me, freezing everything in its path and destroying the strigae.

I felt the searing pain of frostbitten fingers that almost stripped me of my sanity, but I kept going. I needed to stop the olgoi from retreating underground and taking Orm with it. I opened myself to the wild, primal magic of the land itself, allowing it to course through me.

In an instant, the ground froze solid. I heard the kirbai snort anxiously in the background as it danced away. My eyes were on the olgoi, though, whose movements slowed before they stopped altogether, a thin sheen of ice moving up its body. I tore my hands from the ground when the ice came too close to Orm's body.

I watched the commander pull his arms free. *He is safe*, I thought, sitting on my heels. *He is safe.* That was all I could think of. My teeth clattered, and my entire body shook from the cold, slowly shutting down. I had saved him, but I was losing control.

Nothing I did seemed to affect the onslaught of magic pouring through my body. I was in danger of joining the giant worm in becoming a permanent feature of the forest. My vision blurred, but I could still make out Orm's form as he forced himself free from the olgoi's maw. He used his sword to break its jaw and clambered free, rushing to my side.

'Ani!'

'S-s-t ... s-stay a ... w ...way,' I bit out through clattering teeth, trying to protect him from the deadly cold. This was the fate of an unanchored conduit mage, and I knew it. My kind could cast spells at any time, but using our conduit abilities to channel the raw power of the aether without an Anchor nearby was almost always catastrophic.

Wisps of fog gathered around me, freezing the air in my lungs as I fought to detach myself from the wild magic. The air turned opaque, then utterly white, as it froze around me, encasing me in ice. Orm struck it with his sword, but I was too far gone to tell him to let me die before the spell I'd used turned into a never-ending winter.

I felt the ice shudder under his relentless attacks, but somehow, Orm's proximity helped. I gathered what strength I had left to end the disastrous situation. With my fingers shaking violently, I traced a sigil, redirecting a single thread of aether into heat, hoping I wouldn't create something worse than the blizzard that was killing me.

A deafening crack rang out as fire erupted from my chest, an agonised scream following straight after as I collapsed into unconsciousness. The shiver that awoke me shook me to the core, but the warm, muscular arms that held me tight drove it away, and I smiled, enjoying the wonderful dream.

'Stay with me, Nivale. Please. Open your eyes. You said we'd do this together, remember? You said it yourself, so don't you dare die now.' The insistence in the voice persuaded me to pry my eyelids open.

I was plastered against Orm's bare chest. My hands tucked firmly under his arms while the rest of his clothes were wrapped around us like a protective cocoon.

'There you are, that's my brave girl. Stay awake for me, Ani,' he murmured, rubbing my back as he held me. Despite my sluggish thoughts, being called a brave girl by Orm amused me. I wished I had the strength for a witty retort, but he was warm, and I could forgive him any ridiculous thing he wanted to say in the moment. I tried to tell him that, but my head felt too heavy, and I lolled, my cold nose bumping against his hairy chest.

'Warmmm,' I slurred, and his eyes lit up as if my words were a wonderful gift.

'And you are ice cold. Even your lips are blue. You should have run, Nivale,' he grumbled, and I tried to shake my head.

'No, you didn't use it ... m-my hero. My Ursus,' I stuttered, my teeth chattering.

'I will use it next time if you don't listen. Never hurt or sacrifice yourself for me again. When I tell you to run, run.'

Each moment in his embrace strengthened me, almost as if Orm was pushing his warmth into my frozen flesh. I squirmed a little, and he looked down at me with such tenderness that I blurted out the only thought I had in my head. 'If I'm hurt, you should kiss it better.'

Orm's pupils widened, but before I could retract my foolish statement, he bent down.

His lips touched mine in a featherlight caress, testing my resolve, and when I didn't push him away, Orm deepened the kiss. His lips were soft, and his tongue darted out, asking to be let in. With a soft moan, I responded. Warmth spread through me faster than a forest fire.

I knew I should stop, but after nearly dying, I felt alive and wanted to revel in the emotions the experience had awakened. I felt the magic in my soul reaching out, surrounding Orm's spirit, caressing it while I kissed him, too, knowing I had sealed my fate.

He would rather die than put me in danger—would rather sacrifice himself to protect my freedom. He was perfect, and I wanted him. The shadow of an old, half-remembered emotion surfaced, a brief glimpse of a man flickering in my mind—Talmund, my paladin mage.

If he had known the words to my geas, there would have been no hesitation. Tal would have shouted them to the heavens to save my life, even knowing it would break my heart. But Orm had learned that I would always choose freedom.

'Thank you,' I whispered between kisses.

Orm wasn't a mage, though he possessed what we called the *seed of darkness*, a potent kernel of wild magic that allowed him to connect with his dragon. The speed of my recovery told me that my magic, with its unique quest to be joined, recognised it and wanted to complete the bond.

It would be all too easy to whisper the Anchoring Oath, let the tendrils of aether dive into his chest and make him mine, but I wouldn't endanger his life by taking such a reckless step. Until I could feel my past, I would not take another Anchor.

Before I irrevocably entwined my spirit and Orm's, I pulled away, panting heavily, my lips still tingling from the kiss. I liked the taste of him on my tongue, and I had to fight not to lean forward and kiss him again. Orm must have taken my internal struggle as a sign of regret because he stiffened and tried pulling back further.

'If I crossed a line, I apologise. I thought you ...' He stopped, shaking his head. 'I could muddy the waters with excuses, but the raw truth is, I wanted to kiss you too much to hear the voice of reason. I understand if you ...' Orm had saved my life, yet he looked so remorseful for kissing me. I would have laughed if he hadn't been deadly serious.

'Does that mean you don't want to do it again?' I teased when he paused. When his brows drew together in confusion, I reached towards his face and smoothed his frown with my thumb. 'I knew what I was asking for. My magic recognised you as a potential Anchor, and that saved my life even if it took me a moment to stabilise it.' His eyes widened, something akin to hope flashing in them.

'You don't regret it?'

'You kept me from freezing to death. I'm warm now, or rather, I'm warm enough not to die, and I enjoyed the experience. Don't apologise for following my wishes. Next time I try to turn myself into an icicle, you are welcome to kiss me to your heart's content,' I offered, trying to relieve the tension.

The intensity of his gaze became almost frightening. 'I didn't kiss you to warm you up. I did it because I want you so fucking much that I can't think of anything else. Don't give me permission because I will use it, and one day, you may find me throwing you naked into an icy stream just so that I can kiss you again.'

'Orm … you don't need a stream.'

'Fuck! Don't tempt me, Nivale. Just don't. You need a proper mage, not a dragon rider who can offer nothing in exchange. I was close to begging to Anchor you, but with the greater Vella breaking through the Barrier—first the spectrae, now an olgoi worm—I can't allow my selfishness to damn this kingdom.'

A sudden roar from above made us both look up. 'I think Vahin is pissed at finding we were in trouble,' I mused because the feelings his words awakened were too raw to think about right now.

Orm smirked, shaking his head. 'If my dragon is here, it means we are still in trouble. You'd better brace yourself. If you think I'm an overprotective bastard, just wait until you experience a dragon's wrath.'

'Little Flame!' Vahin's voice roared, enhanced by the boom of his precipitous landing. His claws dug into the frozen ground with ease, preventing his large catlike body from slipping as he turned in our direction. I looked Vahin in the eye and gasped at the change I saw. My intelligent, compassionate dragon was gone, replaced with savage fury. For the first time since meeting him, I felt a tinge of fear.

'I almost lost you. I felt fingers of ice grasping my heart, and there was nothing I could do,' Vahin boomed as he circled me, unable to calm down. I reached out, stroking his head.

'I'm sorry,' I said, feeling a furnace burning under his skin as if he was trying to expel the last hint of ice in my veins. 'I'm fine, Vahin, I promise. Orm saved me.'

The dragon turned his head towards Orm, and as his pupils narrowed to mere slits, Orm gasped in response. Whatever Vahin projected during their silent conversation left the commander's face full of anger and worry.

'We need to return to the fortress. Vahin spotted a large group of remnant undead wandering towards Zalesie, and the dragons I left near the Rift reported a forest fire. I have to deal with it as soon as we get you to a healer.'

'I'll go with you,' I said, but both dragon and his rider looked at me as if I'd lost my mind.

I stood my ground; remnants were slow and mindless undead creatures, something akin to the university's first-year challenge to battle mage standards. 'Look. You can't be in two places at once, and I can lead the ground forces or simply support them if they have a decent officer. How about you deal with the forest fire while the soldiers and I head to Zalesie?'

Orm shook his head. 'The fire could be natural, and I won't waste my time on it unless it threatens someone's community. We will fly towards Zalesie tomorrow and exterminate the remnants. Those creatures move slowly and are unlikely to be much of a threat to the town.'

He pointed to Vahin's back. 'Get on, Nivale. Right now, we're flying to the fortress; my kirbai can find his own way home. We both need rest, and I have to make some plans because this event has completely changed our situation. You will go on patrol when the healers allow you to go. That is the rule for all my soldiers.'

'Come on, Little Flame. Your hunting trip is over for today,' Vahin said, a grumpy tone in his voice, and I turned, slapping my palm against his neck.

'My hunting trip eliminated two strigae, an undead mountain troll, and a bloody olgoi worm who would otherwise have been free to make new tunnels and drag down unsuspecting travellers or even people in the villages if they got too close. So don't you dare treat me like a wayward child because we all know it was an excellent decision.'

Orm gathered our belongings and secured them to the dragon's back, setting the kirbai free before he joined me. We flew in silence; I was sulking at the censure in Vahin's tone, and both males must have realised how I felt because, for a long time, not a word was spoken.

When we spotted the fortress in the distance, Orm whispered in my ear. 'You are an impressive fighter and saved me, again. You can more than hold your own, but you must forgive Vahin. You nearly died, and that worries him.

Whilst I could at least fight alongside you, he couldn't, and that's grating on him a lot.'

'You almost died as well, yet he didn't yell at *you*,' I said, refusing to let go of my grudge.

'I wasn't the one who gave his life meaning again. I love him like a brother, but he has had many riders and likely will have many more, while you ... You are his miracle, his only tether to a consciousness buried under the sands of passing time. Don't blame him for lashing out when he almost lost you.'

I didn't reply to that, but I did let myself relax and enjoy the ride.

'*I am sorry, Little Flame. Orm is right, losing you would be like losing my soul. But he is also wrong—I won't have another rider. Orm is the last one.*' Vahin said in my mind, and I welcomed the gentleness that had returned to his voice, even if his words troubled me.

My peace didn't last long, though.

As soon as Vahin descended, I saw Alaric rushing towards the landing area. The mage looked frantic and furious, grasping a piece of paper in his hand.

Looks like someone found my letter.

Purple magic curled around him like smoke, and if anything, showcased how close Alaric was to losing control. What was supposed to be a minor excursion to clear my head had turned into a complete disaster. I wondered how many people I had enraged today and whether I should start carving notches on my headboard.

'Annika, how courteous of you to leave us this *drivel*. *"Please tell Alaric I'm sorry?"* How very kind of you,' he seethed with worry. 'Hrae! What were you thinking? You want to sort things out? Fine! Tomorrow, you will spend the day in my workshop. It is time we start synchronising our magic. Be there at dawn.' I saw his nostrils flare as his hand tightened, crumpling the letter into a tattered mess.

'Ari ... I'm sorry,' I tried to say, but he shook his head while his eyes filled with crimson and pain.

289

'You're *sorry*? How do you think I felt when Vahin roared you were dying in a blizzard at the height of summer? You ripped out my heart. No, Annika, being sorry is not enough. I thought I'd lost you—I thought all I'd be left with was your body, and I was ready to bring you back just to hold you in my arms and say goodbye. No, you will have to try much harder to earn my forgiveness.'

He turned on his heel and marched back towards the castle. Alaric's outburst left me speechless, and I looked at Orm, searching for an answer. 'He'll be alright. Just give him time. Go get some rest, Ani,' he said with a sigh, and bent to kiss my forehead. The sweet gesture disarmed me completely, and, feeling utterly defeated, I dragged myself to my room.

CHAPTER 26

ALARIC

'Alaric'va Shen'ra, what the fuck was that?!'

Orm's voice thundered in the enclosed space, raising dust from old volumes and disturbing the ancient place. I loved the library with its high, arched crystal glass windows that filtered the harsh mountain sun during the day and allowed you to study the passage of the stars at night. It calmed me, and I needed to be calm right now.

I hadn't heard Orm use my full name for ... I don't think I'd ever heard him use it, and that best expressed just how angry he was. My friend was right to question my actions but facing the possibility of losing them both had driven me insane.

The plans I'd carefully crafted fell to pieces when I had heard Vahin's pained roar and saw him launch himself skywards, wrapped in flames. He projected his pain so strongly that even my weak psionic abilities caught the image of Annika dying, encased in ice.

I walked out from behind a large bookshelf, keeping my voice as calm and casual as possible. 'What brings you to the library, my lord?' Orm's eyes narrowed in annoyance before he covered the short distance that parted us in a few determined steps.

'Take a guess,' he said, taking the books I hadn't realised I'd picked up and slamming them on the table.

'There's something upsetting you?' I asked, looking at the priceless manuscripts whose spines had cracked from being manhandled.

'Upsetting? You berated Ani in front of half the castle. I know she made a mistake, and I know it's been difficult for you lately, but that's no reason to humiliate her like that.'

'You call that a mistake? You both nearly died from that *mistake*. Vahin was terrified at the thought of losing the two most important people in his life—he projected his fear across the fortress. Everyone with even a *hint* of magic had that image burned into their minds. Hrae! *I* was terrified, and so bloody helpless. My friends were dying, and I could only pray that the Dark Mother would spare you.'

I grasped the edge of the table, my purple necromancer's magic crackling under my fingertips. 'My sister is lost. You and Ani are the only semblance of family I have left. Do you even know how it feels? To be a man who thought he had lost everything only to realise he still has so much to lose? Then you go and act like it was just a stroll in the woods,' I snapped, unsuccessfully trying to rein in my temper.

My anguish seemed to take the wind out of Orm's sails and he sat heavily on the sofa nearby. 'It was a stroll in the forest for Ani. I thought I was protecting her against a potential assassin, but gods have mercy on the poor soul who tries to sneak up on her.' Orm threw his head back and snapped out a bitter laugh.

'She saved my arse. Again. Gods, that woman can fight. The way she dealt with the strigae ... she's perfect,' he finished with manic glee. As he turned to me, my friend's laughter died. 'Ani needs another Anchor. She used her abilities without one and that's why everything went to hell in a handbasket.'

'We both know she is unwilling. But ... I'll ask, even if it earns me a slap to the face,' I said, and Orm frowned.

'What if it was me? Could I be her Anchor?' he asked, and I approached him, looking at my friend in confusion.

'In theory, yes, but what would be the point?'

Orm grimaced, his lips tightening in a narrow line, and shook his head. Whatever internal dialogue was going on in that head of his, I'd have to wait for my friend to share the details. I observed the light dimming his eyes and his face returning to a well-known emotionless mask and sighed as he spoke.

'You're right; there's no point,' he said, his voice devoid of the usual warmth. 'I told Ani about her first night here—about the geas and your spell to suppress her grief. I want you to undo it.'

'How did she take it?' I asked, unable to believe he had actually done it. I warned him that a woman like Annika would not forgive him for taking her freedom. Yet, the way they had acted towards each other hadn't looked hostile.

'Better than I expected and certainly better than I deserved. Annika *thanked* me for saving her life. She's more reasonable than we gave her credit for—that's why you need to release her feelings. Ani is afraid that without them, she would subconsciously reject anyone who tried to bond with her.'

'I'm not sure I agree. There's a big difference between knowing what we did and having all that pain return,' I said, but the stubborn set of Orm's jaw told me he'd already decided. 'Fine, I'll do it, just not all at once. I will let them resurface slowly. That way, she will be able to cope with the strain.'

Orm smiled. I hadn't seen him smile with genuine happiness towards me in ages, but he was now. Then, leaping off the sofa, he came to me and locked me in a hard embrace. 'Thank you. Whatever troubles you, I will help you, brother. Now, go to Ani. I think she needs you.'

Calming down, I took a deep inhale. Orm smelled of leather, dragon skin, and verbena. The sharp metallic scent was masculine yet intoxicating when mixed with Annika's favourite flower. Before I knew it, I had placed my hand on his cheek, pulling him towards me.

'Ari?' There was a flash of uncertainty in his voice, but he didn't pull away. I promptly removed my hand. *Hrae, I almost kissed him.* I thought, as shocked as he looked.

'I'm glad you survived, my friend,' I blurted out, pretending that I hadn't wanted to lean in or seen the question in Orm's eyes. It wasn't uncommon for males of my race to share not only their mate but also affection with each other, but Orm hadn't seemed to have those inclinations. Until today, I hadn't realised *I* had them, as my thoughts were constantly drifting towards Annika.

The discovery that I wanted them both shook me to the core.

Orm's eyes widened. He studied me as if seeing me for the first time before his expression softened. 'Talk to Annika, then come find me. I'd like my friend back, so we'll talk about whatever it is that's come between us.' I nodded and turned to leave. I couldn't tell him the cause of my staying away wasn't the attraction I'd felt a moment ago, but the pressure I was under to kill the Lich King before he destroyed everything and everyone I loved.

I knocked on Ani's door, preparing myself for her anger, but it was her softly muttered *'Enter'* that made me flinch. I took a deep breath and entered the lion's den.

Annika was sitting in front of a small vanity, her shoulders slumped as she listlessly brushed at the tangles in her hair. She turned towards me as I walked in. I bowed and she frowned, reaching for a shawl and wrapping the soft wool fabric around her shoulders.

What surprised me was the lack of anger; Ani looked tired and sad. I would have preferred a thrown brush and curses or even a fireball over seeing her like this. 'I thought you were Agnes.' She pointed towards a pair of arm-chairs. 'How can I help you, Alaric? If you came here to scold me, it can wait till tomorrow.'

'I came to apologise,' I said, unable to drag my eyes away. Even exhausted and despondent, her beauty drew me in.

A white nightgown, the same one she'd worn on her adventure to Vahin's cave, flowed over the curves of her body, caressing them in modest reverence. Annika's hair, unkempt and wild, flowed down her back, but it was her eyes that captured my gaze. The vibrant green irises that now held a hint of wicked laughter at my mention of apologies made me wonder why I wasn't already on my knees, grovelling for forgiveness, all in the hope that she would grace me with a smile.

'Then apologise, fae mage. Let's see if your apology can improve on Lord Ormond's.' My shocked double take would have been worthy of the best mummers' play.

'*Orm* apologised? For what?'

'For being a stubborn arsehole who wanted to keep me locked away without even telling me why? I advise you to not follow his example ... in being an arsehole, that is.' I blinked in surprise, suddenly understanding Orm's question about Anchoring her.

I didn't remember moving, but the next moment, I was on my knee in front of Annika, my hands wrapped around the hairbrush, easing it from her grip as I pressed my lips to her wrist. She glanced at me, taken aback by my actions. Before she could say anything, I stood up, trailing my fingers through her hair and gently brushing her unruly tresses.

When our eyes met in the mirror, Ani smiled a little. 'Arno enjoyed brushing my hair—although he kept threatening to shave me bald if I continued forgetting to look after it,' she said with a chuckle. 'I remember laughing at that because, despite his threats, he was always gentle with me.'

Jealousy over her dead lover flashed through me, and my fingers tightened in her strands. 'I know Orm told you that we used the geas. Why aren't you angry?' I asked, just to avoid hearing that Arno was more to her than I would ever be.

'I wanted to be—angry. I wanted to blame Orm and you for everything that happened. I wanted to throw it in your faces and curse you because he had used the geas when I was at my weakest, but ... then I thought, what would I have done? What else could *he* do? Let me die when he thought I was the last hope of stopping the Lich King?' The smile she gave me was sad.

'It would be like blaming the sky for rain or a wolf for devouring its prey. Some things are inevitable. I am who I am, and Orm did what his honour and duty told him to do.' I hadn't expected that. Ani's understanding words, tinged with sadness as they were, made my quest for revenge feel reckless and childish.

'Did you forgive him?'

'Forgive him for what? Using the geas to save my life? Yes. Refusing to take me on patrol, locking me in the castle, and excluding me from any meaningful plans because he was afraid some bogus enemy might kidnap me? No. Just as I don't forgive you for yelling at me in front of everyone, even if you had a reason.'

She glanced at me. 'However, ... I can take you as my lady's maid; and maybe after three years of service, you might be allowed to redeem yourself.' I exhaled with relief at hearing her tease. *This* was my Ani, and I couldn't resist the temptation to tease her back just to coax the smile out a little more.

'I'd willingly take on the role. Especially if it meant I get to see you half naked and tend to your *every* need.' I grinned as Ani rolled her eyes.

'Agnes is more than adequate at the job. Go now and let me sleep. It's been a hard day, and some arsehole dark fae ordered me to his workshop before dawn.'

I took a strand of her hair, twisting it in my fingers, playing with it to prolong the moment. 'Orm told me you want to have your past feelings back. I can do it, but is that truly what you want? The pain and sorrow of losing your Anchors was a terrible torment to your soul.' Her hair slid through my fingers like liquid silk, and I waited patiently, letting her gather her thoughts.

'I want it all back. I know I'm calmer and less troubled now, but those feelings made me who I am, and the men who gave their lives so I could live deserve to be loved, not just remembered,' she whispered.

Pain blossomed in my chest, taking my breath away. How I wanted someone to love me like that, to be willing to go through hardship and pain because they thought I was worth it.

'So be it,' I yielded, putting the brush aside and sliding my fingers to her temples. Ani looked at me and then closed her eyes, showing me much more trust than I deserved. 'Thank you, Ari,' I heard her whisper before I wove the glyph. My fingers danced over her skin, creating patterns that shone like silver while I hummed the words of the incantation.

Annika's breath hastened before she regained control. I saw her inhale slowly, then release her breath each time the pulse of my magic eased the knot I had created in her mind. It would be easier to reverse the spell all at once, but timing the return of her emotions was a slow process, and I felt beads of sweat blossom on her forehead while I undid my spell.

Every now and again, Ani bit her lip, and I knew she was in pain, but not once did she ask me to stop. I could feel echoes of her memories resurfacing, and with them, the feelings of joy, love, and sorrow. Before it could reach her conscious mind, I built a dam, allowing only a trickle of those emotions to pass through.

When I was done, Ani slumped in the chair as if someone had cut the strings holding her up. Acting on instinct, I scooped her up in my arms and carried her to bed. 'Fuck, that was intense,' she mumbled, pushing her face into the crook of my shoulder.

I beamed. As ridiculous as it was, hearing her curse assured me she was okay and made me happy. 'Does this mean I'm forgiven?' I asked, placing her on the bed.

'No, but you are paving your way to atonement. I'm still considering taking you on as my lady's maid.'

'Annika Diavellar, you will do no such thing,' I pretended to frown, assuming a look of righteous indignation, and she burst into laughter.

'Of course I would, and you'd enjoy every second.' She grinned at me, and when I tried pulling away, she grasped my hand. 'Ari ... it will be all right. Yes?'

Annika was afraid, but I didn't have any way to offer her comfort. Instead, I lifted her hand, bringing it to my lips. 'I don't know. I hope it will. Your feelings will come gradually, but when they come, you will feel them as intensely as the first time. I will help as much as I can, but it will be a difficult process.'

I didn't know what she saw in my eyes, but Ani placed her other hand on my cheek. 'It's all right. I'm as strong as an ox, and I will survive this. Besides, I have Vahin if things become too much.' Her pupils widened suddenly, her face turning as white as the linen she rested on. 'Vahin? Will he feel it too?'

'I don't know. I know nothing about Anchoring dragons. I'm sorry, Ani.' My lack of knowledge shamed me, but no matter how much I had searched, there were no records of dragons bonding outside the of dragon rider bloodlines. I was walking blind.

'I don't want to hurt him. I ... Oh gods ...' I saw the shine of tears in her eyes, and I pulled her towards me, wrapping my arms around her and rocking her gently.

'Vahin is a powerful dragon. He was able to withstand a swarm of spectre. He will be fine. I promise.' I held her close to me, letting the warmth of her body seep through my clothes while her tears stained my shirt. She was struggling with her emotions while I basked in her touch, enjoying it without shame.

I didn't know how, but Annika was the end of my suffering, with whom I could breathe easily without the fear of daggers piercing my skin each time I took a lungful of air. Suddenly, I understood Orm and his need to keep her sheltered and hidden.

Dark Mother, this one time, have mercy on your lost child. Don't take her away from me, I prayed, holding my Domina until her quiet tears dried and she pulled away. 'Thank you for this. Today ... it was a lot, seeing Orm almost eaten by an olgoi worm, being shouted at by the men I care for, and this. I think I needed a good cry.'

'Any time you need it, I'm happy to lend my shoulder—and my shirt,' I said, and she smiled.

'I will remember. Now go if you want to see me in your workshop tomorrow. I need some rest, and the longer you stay in my room, the more the chance that Orm will come to join the crowd. You two are like twin souls; one always chases the other.'

I wished I could stay and hold her through the night. I knew the moment I stepped out of the room, my marks would flare up, searing my skin with aetheric fire. Still, Ani was right. She needed to rest, and I'd lived with my pain for too long to care if it returned. 'Sleep well, Annika, and come see me tomorrow ... at a reasonable hour. Let's not torment ourselves with a view of the sunrise.'

'Oh no, you wanted to see me at dawn, so dawn it is. Good night, Alaric, and don't be late.' I nodded, closing the door.

As soon as I reached my room, a wave of pain bent me in half, but worse was the voice that reverberated in my head, clearer than ever before: *'You're taking what's mine, young Shen'ra? Autumn is coming, and the Barrier has faded enough for you to pass. I won't wait forever.'*

'Get the *fuck* out of my head,' I snarled, clawing at my chest where the curse marks burned on my skin. Grim understanding dawned on me, and with it, the depth of my mother's betrayal. She hadn't just cursed me. She'd gifted me to an undead monster, forging a connection that had built up over time, and now ... now I could hear his voice in my mind.

Gods never listen to cursed men. Why did I think I would be any different?

I would have to abandon my dreams of ever being tethered to my Domina because—even if I entertained thoughts of revenge—I would *never* let him gain access to Annika through this perverted connection.

The Dark Mother has failed me again, I thought, and my world descended into whispers of darkness.

CHAPTER 27

ANNIKA

The soft, slow beat beneath my ear sent a shiver down my spine, and I smiled as I cuddled its reassuring rhythm. As consciousness slowly returned, memories of the previous day intruded on my peace: the freedom of wandering the forest, the argument and then the image of the olgoi erupting from the earth ... When I saw Orm fall, his sword piercing the worm's mouth, fear flooded my senses and I sprang up, screaming his name.

'Orm!'

'I'm here, Ani. Shh ... it's ok, you were just dreaming.' Only then did I notice the muscular chest beneath my hands, the gentle stroking fingers easing the tight muscles of my back. 'Deep breaths, Nivale.' I looked around in confusion, but apart from the mystery of Orm's presence in my bed, everything looked normal.

'Shouldn't you be elsewhere? In your own bed, perhaps?' He slowly sat up, and my eyes dropped to the rugged chest I'd just been cuddling. When my gaze trailed lower, following a narrowing band of hair, I sighed with relief, seeing he at least wore silk trousers. Still, it didn't explain why I was waking up splayed all over his chest again.

Orm noticed my wandering gaze and smiled. Then he stretched—the shameless man showcasing his muscles and letting the covers slide even lower, uncovering a sizeable bulge. 'I should, but you were calling for me in your sleep, asking me not to die.'

'And you couldn't just wake me up?'

'Oh, believe me, darling, I tried. But you pulled me onto the bed, calling me your Ursus, then went quiet after laying your head on my chest, so I stayed … I like it when you call me your bear.'

I just looked at him. His massive body took up far too much of the bed, and he wanted me to believe that I forced him to sleep with me? What a ridiculous excuse. I grabbed the pillow and smacked him upside the head with it. Orm jerked. His surprise lasted only a moment before he gave me a wounded, doe-eyed expression.

'You like it, hmm? Then get the hell out of my bed, you overgrown bear, or learn to lie better.' I continued my assault, and Orm roared with laughter. 'I didn't lie. You called me your Ursus and petted my chest. I'm considering asking Vahin to teach me how to purr.' He laughed, ducking under the pillow I kept hitting him with.

'Yeah, what else? I pulled you onto the bed? I would remember gaining the strength to lift a horse. Just admit it! You invited yourself, you bloody menace. Was the chaise lounge not good enough for you?' I gasped when he ripped the pillow from my hands. The soft fabric tore, releasing a cloud of feathers into the air right before Orm flipped me onto my back, pinning my hands over my head.

'Gods, you are a dream,' he groaned when I fought before his body tensed and his lips descended on mine. Our little adventure in the forest had changed so much between us, the cold commander having become a passionate man.

Orm wasn't gentle; I could taste his raw hunger when he nipped at my bottom lip, coaxing me to open my mouth, and I did. *Damn, this feels so good.* I'd clearly lost my mind when his tongue slid in, playing with mine.

'Nivale,' he moaned as our breath mingled. His hand dived into my tussled hair, crushing my lips to his. *I shouldn't be doing this*, I thought, arching under him, feeling the thin fabric of my nightgown between us and my peaked nipples rubbing against his chest, creating shivers of pleasure that melted my resistance. I wanted this man. Imperfect as he was, he was *mine*, and my body knew it.

Orm's kiss intensified, sensing my eagerness and his hips pressed against me, rocking gently. My moan was filled with desperate need as I felt his erection straining against the fabric of his trousers. His other hand slid between my thighs, and I cried out at the pleasure that threatened to overwhelm my senses.

Why does everything feel so intense? Was it because we almost died yesterday, or because Alaric had reversed the spell that had caged my emotions? Did it even matter? I was falling for Orm. It was bound to happen.

Even though I knew Alaric would likely become my Anchor, it was this delicious brute that drew me like a moth to a flame. It wasn't wise, but it felt so right ... I wasn't exactly known for making the best decisions.

'I love the way your magic slides over my skin,' he breathed, stretching under the caress of my power. He was eager to take it; no, he was *reaching* for it. His wild magic surged, wrapping around us beyond my control, and I responded. Just like with Vahin, I wanted him, wanted this soul-deep rapport. Before I knew it, my lips had started whispering the Anchoring Oath, and only then did I realise how far I'd gone.

'No. Please stop. Let me go,' I panicked. Orm growled—actually *growled*, like a feral bear—before instantly releasing my hands and backing away from me.

I saw the veins straining on his neck, fists clenching on the fabric as he fought with himself. There was magic dancing in his eyes, a dark inferno of primal power he fought to tame.

I cursed under my breath, shocked at what had just happened. The connection between us was so much deeper than I initially thought possible. As if the fates were staring me in the eyes, weaving the thread of destiny that linked us together.

And when I dared look at Orm, I saw a wild, ancient force gazing at me through the yellow glare of his eyes.

I felt a frisson of fear run down my spine, unsure if Orm could cage the power my careless touch had unleashed. 'Orm, I'm so—' I started, realising what I'd done, but he raised his hand, stopping me.

'I'm not losing control, but be mindful of what you do next,' Orm warned me when I reached out, wondering how to repair the damage I'd accidentally caused, and he backed away. 'Don't. If you touch me now, I don't know if I will be able to stop. The need to be with you is so … overwhelming. Just give me a moment, Nivale.'

'I didn't mean to cause you trouble,' I said remorsefully, but even as I spoke, I felt a perverse pleasure in knowing I had such an effect on him.

'I know, but you must … you had to suspect how I feel about you. Anchoring someone who's not a mage makes no sense. Alaric explained it to me yesterday, but I can't help it. After yesterday, I can't think of anything else. I want it so fucking much that it hurts. I keep coming here because seeing you sleep … I'm not explaining this right. You give meaning to my life, to this constant fight. My sacrifice is worth it if it brings just one smile to your lips. I didn't lie to you. You called my name, and I came. I will always come to you. I can't stay away,'

Orm's words carried so much hope, such desperation, that I was speechless. I don't know what he saw in my expression, but suddenly, he was pacing, a caged animal filled with frustration on the edge of violence. I studied the muscles of Orm's chest bulging under the strain he was under before he halted in front of me.

'Please say something. Am I making this up? If so, tell me you don't want this. Tell me it's just my imagination because I'm going insane. I felt your desire; there is something between us, I'm sure of it. It is not just your magic.

The way we fight together, the way you challenge me, make me laugh ... I may never have Alaric's magic synergy, but in everything else, we are one.'

He ran a hand through his messy hair before hitting his chest as if trying to push his wildness back inside. 'I wish you knew how much I crave you. I wouldn't kiss you otherwise. I wouldn't come here and impose myself on you like some wild animal. If this connection is all in my head, tell me to get the fuck away, and I will leave you. I swear I will leave you to Alaric and his magic; I'll never touch you again.'

Orm stopped, his fist so tight I swear I heard his knuckles creak. He looked towards the door, on the verge of bolting. He was waiting for my answer, holding himself back and letting me choose. I looked at him, this mountain of a man, lost in a passion that burned brighter than dragon fire.

I wished I could say yes, but yes to what? Just becoming my lover was no longer an option. Not after my power had almost forced me to Anchor him. I couldn't go through with it in this state, when my emotions were still a chaotic mess. I knew they would get worse before they got better. *If* they got better.

Orm was already unhinged by the touch of my magic, and I couldn't subject him to further strain. Having a dragon and his rider experience the pain of a broken bond could have devastating consequences. I didn't even know how I would take it myself. 'It's complicated ... I can't right now. The spell ...'

'That godsdamned spell!' I flinched at Orm's curse. I couldn't take my eyes off his bulging muscles, shocked by the power that he fought against. 'Could you please listen to me? I can't make this decision now; it's too early. Alaric just—' I tried again, but he startled me with a dark, menacing laugh.

'Alaric. I should have known. It will always be Alaric,' he said through clenched teeth, and I felt my own temper flaring. 'Yes, but this isn't about Alaric.'

'If it isn't, then choose me, be *mine*. Take all of my soul if you wish ...'

'I'm trying to tell you I can't right now—' I started, and he growled. Whatever my power had done to him, Orm's wild magic was now in control. I could see yellow flames overwhelm his pupils. There was no point talking to him until he calmed down.

He wouldn't hear anything except an enthusiastic *'yes'* followed by an immediate Anchor bond. We both needed time. I clenched my own fist, looking the beast in the eye. 'Oh, for fuck's sake. If you're too stubborn to listen, then leave.'

He looked at me with such pain and disbelief, then seemed to crumble into himself, one hand pressing against his heart. The yellow fire flared, and for a moment, I thought he would pounce, but Orm grabbed the bedpost, using its strength to force the magic back. When the eerie light in his eyes dimmed, then faded completely, I was once again looking at the stone-carved face of the lord commander.

He placed a trembling hand on his chest and bowed slightly. 'As you wish, my lady. I'm sorry for the misunderstanding.' I blinked as he spoke, his voice cracking and drained of emotion. When he turned to leave, I reached out, stopping when I saw him flinch.

I knew he thought I'd rejected him, but nothing could be further from the truth. As soon as Alaric's spell wore off, I was going to drag that man to my bed and Anchor the hell out of him.

I was still struggling to contain my frustration when I walked into the workshop much later.

It amazed me how much the place reflected Alaric's personality. The space was deep in the bowels of the fortress, with only one window on the northern side. It had little to no natural light but had candles and torches stuck on every wall or shelf to light specific areas, giving it a cosy feel. How he had managed it with stone benches carved from the mountain itself, I didn't know. There were even heavy oak shelves filled with vials and ingredients so rare, and often so toxic, that they made my eyes water.

There were few items of decadence, but next to the workshop's small fireplace, its mantle carved with intricate designs, was an oversized chaise lounge and a table where servants left snacks and drinks. It was kept filled under Orm's order because Alaric, lost in his work, often forgot the simple necessities of life.

Usually, I enjoyed coming here. The atmosphere reminded me of the university workshops, but today, even this space felt suffocating. Yet when I approached Alaric, I was glad I came. He looked like he hadn't slept at all, his chin resting on his forearm while he sat at his workbench with a bloodied quill in his hands.

'What happened to you?' I asked, placing my hand on his shoulder. He flinched as if awakened from a deep sleep, and the look he gave me in answer chilled the blood in my veins.

'An old foe reminded me of his presence.' Bitter laughter escaped his lips as he straightened. Only then did I notice he was lying inside a warding glyph drawn with his own blood.

'Who is it? Does Orm know?'

'No, he doesn't. He can't help, anyway. The Lich King tried to impose his will on me. Don't worry, though, Ani—I'm difficult to break. Just give me a moment, then we'll start working. Hah, it was a long night.'

I reached for him, simultaneously confused and worried by his words. 'I don't care about magic right now. How can you say the Lich King trying to reach you like that is no big deal?'

'Because it's happened before and will probably happen again.' He took my hand and pressed it to his forehead. The relief I saw in his features made me pause. I stepped closer and hesitantly embraced him. The earlier spat with Orm felt childish now, and I focused entirely on my tormented fae, determined to find the truth in all this.

'Is this helping?' I asked. In the back of my mind, hidden deep in memory, I remembered Arno's words. A conduit mage's presence could regulate the flow of the aether in others, either smoothing or disrupting it, affecting nearby spells. The way Alaric reacted to me brought the memory back to the surface, and I suspected I may have disrupted whatever connection he had with the immortal Lich.

'Yes,' he answered quietly, wrapping his arms around me, 'It helps a lot.'

'Tell me what's going on. Don't keep me in the dark when I know you're struggling.' Alaric pulled away, looking at me with a strange sadness before he reached up and unbuttoned his kaftan collar.

I'd never seen him undressed. All his shirts and kaftans were always tied up to his neck. Only on rare occasions had I seen a hint of his chest, and the view was unexpected. The skin was smooth, with a silk sheen covered with strange silver markings. I didn't recognise the symbols, but I still remembered the strange glow I'd seen the other night.

That must have been what was glowing, I thought, reaching towards them before I stopped, my hand hovering over his skin.

Magic tingled on my fingertips, awakened by my proximity to the symbols, but something felt wrong with the beautiful script. I let my fingers travel along the marks, noticing their otherworldly metallic feel, so contrasting with the warmth of his skin. 'They're causing me the pain you witnessed,' he explained in a low, husky voice.

'What are they? I know little about the dark fae. Is it some kind of family custom?' I asked, moving my hand higher and laying it on his collarbone. 'No, they are not, and I wish it were possible to get rid of them. If it would make any difference, I'd burn them from my skin with a red-hot poker,' Alaric said so vehemently that I gasped.

He placed his hand over mine, and I realised I'd been staring at the marks. His statement piqued my curiosity, and I took a better look. They were strange; with his torso fully exposed, I saw how unnatural they looked. It was almost as if someone had used molten silver as ink, the edges scarred and damaged. 'You can touch them again, Ani,' he whispered. 'I can see how curious you are.'

'But you told me they were painful.'

'Yes, but I'm a man who likes pain, remember?' I could see the tension written all over his body. My breath hitched when I looked at his golden eyes, crimson creeping in at the edges. I knew I shouldn't do it, but my curiosity got the better of me, so I let my fingers trail over the thin silver lines.

'Is it a spell?'

Ari closed his eyes, and a small moan escaped his lips.

'Yes, a spell of sorts. This is the reason you heard me that night and found me like this today. This is my curse, a link that my mother's power forged with the Lich King's magic.' He was so bitter that I removed my hand instead of sliding it lower, where the longest line slid down his stomach.

'Curse? Your mother cursed you?' I asked, struggling to comprehend how she could do that.

'I did it to myself, but the will behind each letter of this curse was my mother's. They are the symbol of the promise I made when her spirit possessed my body and a testament to the love she had for her misbegotten son,' he snarled.

Alaric tensed again when I scraped my nail over the silver symbols. It didn't feel like skin at all, but at the sudden intake of breath, I knew he could feel every touch. 'I need more than cryptic explanations.' I said, rolling my eyes.

Alaric grasped my hand and pressed it harder to the mark. The swirling crimson that had ghosted his pupils now threatened to overwhelm them. 'Don't stop. I told you they cause me pain, but not when you touch them

... they are silent when you are around me. You have brought me relief after centuries of agony. So please, please don't stop.'

'I won't, but we have to tell Orm. Knowing the Lich King can reach you ... it's dangerous, and not only for you. Is there a way to remove the curse?' I questioned, placing both palms on his chest. Orm's remark some time ago that Alaric seemed happier in my company finally made sense.

'We?' he asked, and when I looked up, I saw the first smile ghost his lips since my arrival at his workshop.

'What? You didn't think I'd leave you to face this alone, did you? Orm knows people in the capital. I know university mages are a bunch of arrogant pricks—well, most of them—but they know their craft, and if he can't force them to cooperate, I will. So, tell me, my beautiful fae, how can I help?'

'I've tried, Annika. I've spent hundreds of years searching for a so-lution. It is an unbreakable oath carved in blood and necromancy. It will only vanish when its conditions are fulfilled. When I find my sister Rowena ... And she's with the Lich King.'

'So that's why you wanted to go to the Barren Lands ... but Orm is right. It's a suicide mission, even if the Barrier would let you pass.'

'It will. If it's faded enough to let an olgoi worm pass, it will let me through, too. I know it is dangerous, but I may be forced to try it, anyway.'

'No, I refuse to accept that. I'm not losing you. There must be another way. Hell, I'll go to the capital myself if I have to, but we'll find a way to remove it. Also, you should have told me earlier that my touch helps you. I just remembered Arno saying something about conduits disrupting the flow of the aether.'

He looked at me with such disbelief that I had to chuckle.

'What are you trying to say?' Alaric asked cautiously.

'That you can touch me? When things get too much, even for a sucker for pain like yourself, just come to me, and I will hold you, touch your marks, no questions asked,' I said, and he took my hand, placing a long, soft kiss on my palm. 'You'll be the death of me.'

'Well, I hope not. I don't want to grieve for someone else with my old grief coming back around for a second time—which reminds me: I have a request. Speed up your reversal spell. I'm tired of waiting. And if I have to help you with this curse as well as the Lich King, I'll be needing more than just one Anchor.'

'It's dangerous, sweetheart,' he said, but I placed my finger on his lips.

'Just do it, I can handle it.' I just hoped I wouldn't live to regret the words.

CHAPTER 28

ANNIKA

One week later

D ragon fire surrounded me, the flames dancing before my eyes as Tal and Arno looked on in silent accusation, their bodies obscured by an impenetrable fog. I knew I loved them, had been willing to sacrifice myself to keep them safe, but something was missing, and I couldn't help but search for whatever that was.

A desperate sob shook my body. I wanted to burn away the fog and discover what I'd lost, to feel something, *anything* other than numb confusion. Two more shadows ghosted across my vision, and this time, I felt something: fear.

Fear that the emotions locked deep inside would break free and destroy those I'd begun to care for. As I looked down, I saw four threads lying in my hand, each one disappearing past the wall of flame. I pulled my hand back, gripping the threads tightly, but no matter how hard I tugged, nothing changed.

I screamed my anguish, and the flames surrounding me responded, leaping higher and hotter, blinding me. *'Little Flame, wake up! Wake up before you set the bed on fire!'* the voice in my head roared in command, and my eyes snapped open.

'Vahin?' I thought, feeling the warmth and concern radiating through our bond. Unfortunately, his voice was already fading, the distance between us too great. It was a miracle he'd awakened me from my nightmare.

Since Alaric had reversed his spell, there'd been glimpses of old feelings. Good and bad memories had stopped being a silent picture of my past, now filled with vibrance and colour, enriching my world with new sensations. The only things that hadn't fully returned were my emotions towards my Anchors, and that worried me.

It didn't help that Orm had been called back to Truso. I hadn't seen him since my messy rejection; he left almost the minute he stepped out of my bedroom, and I had no means to ask him to return or to tell him about Alaric's curse.

The fear of something happening to the dark fae gnawed at my insides so I tried to spend as much time with him as possible, hoping my conduit abilities would be enough to prevent any problems. If Alaric guessed the reason for my sudden closeness, he didn't comment on it.

A soft knock dragged my attention to the door. Agnes rarely knocked. She simply barged in, cleaning the mess my dreams always made of the bed before readying my clothes or bringing a tray of food.

'Enter,' I called, wondering who it was. I hoped Orm had returned, and we could finally discuss what happened when I had asked him to leave. I worried it was more than issues with the king that kept him away for so long; I hated this distance between us, and I missed his presence in my bedroom. I even decorated the chaise lounge by my bed with pillows and a soft, fluffy blanket in case he wanted to join me overnight to let him know he was welcome to stay.

'Good morning, Ani,' Alaric said as he entered. A single eyebrow rose when he saw me sitting amidst a circle of charred linen. 'Another bad dream?'

'How did you guess? Your reversal spell still hasn't settled, and Agnes is running out of clean bedding,' I grumbled, standing up and folding the destroyed fabric. 'Could you help me with this?'

He looked at the linen in my hands, and his other eyebrow joined the first as amusement lit his features. 'Did I just get my long-awaited promotion to lady's maid? Should I help you dress?'

'I am not letting you get your hands on me again. I still remember what happened after the duel.'

I chuckled at the disappointment in Ari's eyes. In Orm's absence, Alaric brightened my day, always making me smile. My spending time in his company seemed to improve his mood, and the mischievous smile that accompanied it looked good on him. Occasionally, when I noticed him frowning and clutching his chest, I stroked the back of his neck, soothing the magic of the marks until they went dormant once more.

'There goes my opportunity to see you naked again.' His sigh was so theatrical that I hit him with the pile of linen I'd been holding. 'Is this assault or an invitation?' he continued his tease with a smirk. 'If it's an invitation, you'll need to hit me a little harder. I can even show you where I like it most.'

'I will hit you where it hurts, and when I do, you definitely won't like it. Stop flirting with me, you incorrigible rogue.'

'Fine, bar me from all pleasure,' he grumbled with a huff before picking up the linen from the floor. 'What do you want me to do with this?'

'Whatever, just make it disappear. I'll find some replacements before Agnes notices and yells at me again.' I gasped when he tossed it straight into the fireplace. 'Oh, for fuck's sake. I didn't mean *burn* it. How will I explain that mess?' I said with exasperation before shaking my head. 'Why did you come here so early in the morning?'

'Would it be too awful if I said I just wanted to see you? Besides, Orm should be back today, and I wanted to let you know.'

'Are you sure?' Hope suddenly blossomed in my chest.

'Yes, the scouts have already returned. Orm made a quick stop to meet with some veterans and ensure the area around the Lost Ridge was cleared. The scouts told me they were expecting him today, though,' he said before coming closer and reaching for my hand. He raised it to his lips and kissed it.

'I know you were waiting for him. I would have to be blind to not see how much you care for that idiot soul brother of mine. Just ... don't forget I'm here—and if he behaves like a stubborn clod, come and talk to me. I can help in more ways than just hammering some sense into his thick skull.' The tension between us was sizzling, and I had the overwhelming urge to close my eyes and let him kiss more than my hand.

Why did it have to be so complicated? Why did I have to choose between Orm and Ari? I'd had a glimpse at Orm's wild magic, and I doubted he would accept me sharing a bed with another man. If I wanted to be with him, I had to accept the part of him he couldn't change; but deep inside, I rebelled against it.

I wanted Ari to be part of it, part of *us*. He wasn't as intense as Orm, yet sometimes, I felt such deep desire for him it left me gasping. Especially when he performed the little gestures I loved, like kissing the sensitive skin of my wrist.

'Thank you, Ari,' I breathed, feeling a sudden tightness in my chest. Dealing with feelings was difficult right then. I pulled my trembling hand back and walked to the window, opening it wide. 'The weather is really nice today. I think I'll head to town and visit my friends. I don't think I can sit in the workshop right now.' I licked my suddenly dry lips.

It wasn't my best attempt at changing the subject, and as I turned, I saw Alaric's beautiful golden eyes darkened by crimson.

'You think I'm interested in the weather when all I can see is the silhouette of your beauty before me?' The man looking at me was no longer the self-deprecating joker. He was a hunter stalking his prey and I felt myself freeze, realising I was standing there wearing nothing but a thin nightgown with the morning sun shining right through it.

As I struggled to draw breath into my lungs, I grabbed the nearest blanket and wrapped it around my shoulders before turning away from those mesmeric eyes. 'Erm, oh well. I'd best get dressed, so if you could leave ...' I asked—no, begged—because if he didn't leave now, I would end up doing something reckless.

'Yes, I should go ... but I don't know if I can.' Ari shook his head. 'If you ever desire my company, all you have to do is ask.'

I turned back to the window. The image of Alaric kissing my palm flashed before my eyes, sending a shiver down my spine, but I shook it off. No, not yet, not until I was back to normal and had talked to Orm. The loud bang of the door announced his departure.

Several shaky breaths later, I stood in front of the wardrobe, picking out a simple brown dress. I wanted to see Katja, and my friend had a tendency to make me work as we talked. I'd visit Bryna afterwards and maybe borrow a hammer or two in preparation for meeting Orm. Perhaps then the commander would listen to what I had to say.

Maybe he'd like to spar with me. Nothing cleared the air better between fighters than beating the hell out of each other on the training ground, then drinking a tankard—or three—of mead.

Tal had loved those discussions, and it still made me giggle, remembering how Arno grumbled and tried to patch us up afterwards. I felt the joy of those moments, the pain of the minor injuries Tal and I inflicted on each other. That single memory hit me like an avalanche, and my soul was buried by emotion.

My world went white, and I collapsed to the floor. Love, joy, then sorrow and the pain of my broken bonds flooded me, taking away my will to live. A wave of pain and grief, so overwhelming that I curled up to protect myself, tore apart my mind.

I knew; I finally knew why Orm had to use the geas, why I could never have accepted Vahin's Anchor. The love that I'd felt and the bonds that had been broken when the wlok took them away from me shattered my soul ... I was reliving the worst moment of my life, fighting to stay alive, to keep breathing, when all I wanted was to die with them.

Gods, if I weren't on the brink of death when the dragon had lifted me from the rubble, I would have taken my life to escape this pain. Violent streams of aether buffeted my body for a moment before I saw my falchion resting on its stand.

I could still do it. I could escape this blinding, heart-shattering torment threatening to crush my sanity.

'Vahin!' I screamed, desperate and heartbroken.

'I'm coming! Hold on, please. I will be there in just a moment.'

I gathered the last of my strength, crawling to my feet, and staggered towards the landing field. I needed my dragon. I needed my beautiful Vahin before my heart stuttered to a halt. A dragon's roar splintered the quiet, and Vahin's dark form plummeted to the ground like midnight lightning, cutting the deep blue of the summer sky in two.

I stumbled towards him, keening as grief poured from my broken heart. The stone beneath my feet melted as I passed. The aether surrounding me was a tempest of wild magic, leaving behind a trail of fire. Fearful screams echoed from the courtyard walls as everyone fled from the impossible conflagration.

I knew that if I fell, I would never rise again. The pain of the broken bonds reverberated through my soul and dragon fire erupted from my body, coating me with flames. I lost control, and chaotic elemental magic consumed me. I was in hell. The best and the worst moments of my life mingled together and burned me alive.

'Vahin!' I cried, desperate to hold on to the one soul that could save me from being entombed by pain.

318

Tal's body, torn apart by the wlok; the last shimmering touch of Arno's magic as he sacrificed his soul to save me. Then, finally, the rocks falling, suffocating me beneath their crushing weight. It all returned, and there was only one being who could end the torment.

'Vahin ...' I cried, collapsing, my world now wholly consumed by flames. The dragon leapt forward, uncaring of the rider on his back, ripping apart the ground as he forced his way to my side, wrapping his massive body around me.

'I'm here, Little Flame. Open your heart to me. Let me feel your pain. I can take it,' he crooned, his voice reverberating through my body when I clung desperately to his neck, pressing my face into the hard scales.

'I can't take it anymore. It hurts so much. Take my life, please. Let me die,' I cried, clawing at my skin, wishing I had a dagger to pierce my heart.

'No, my beautiful soul, your life is precious beyond measure, and I won't let you give up,' he soothed, his voice distorted by a purr that rumbled in his chest, and suddenly, the pain lessened. Only a little, but enough to end my pleas for death.

'Please, don't give up. Hold on to me, Annika. Hold on to my spirit.' I could barely focus on Vahin's words, but I could feel his emotions and the love that was pouring out of him through the bond. I was his everything, his light after the long, dark years of losing one rider after another, his spirit dimming with each death until his eyes had met mine when he pulled me out from under the avalanche.

'It was you,' I breathed, and a shiver rippled over his scales, along with blessed relief. I knew he was shielding me, sharing my emotions—my grief—so that I could breathe again. His touch was the only thing that kept me afloat in the sea of fire.

'Yes, Little Flame. Your soul burned so brightly it pulled me out of the sky. I knew you would find me again, and you did. I can't lose you now.'

My Vahin.

I needed him as much as he needed me. I pressed my face harder to his body, inhaling his scent, my eyes squeezed shut as I fought for control. This brilliant being, my rock, supported me, his strength allowing me to think and withstand the maelstrom of feelings, but something was missing. *Someone* was missing, and I gasped when I felt hands slide across my shoulders as a large figure embraced me.

'Nivale, I'm here; we are here,' Orm's voice rumbled next to my ear. He had come to me, despite the flames swirling around us, and now held me against his chest. I was unable to talk, but I turned around, wrapping my arms around his neck.

Orm stroked my hair while the dragon pressed against my back, crooning behind me. Tal and Arno stood before me in my mind's eye, and tears of blood trailed over my cheeks as I bid them goodbye. They'd want me to live on and be happy; I knew because I would wish the same for them. If one of them had survived, I'd want them to find love again.

So I spoke to them in my mind. Telling them about the dragon who had selflessly given himself to me when I needed him the most, about the warrior who fought every day for control over his wild magic and yet still managed to be gentle and kind. I told them about the mage who loved pain and made me laugh with his constant teasing, and whose heart was bright and loving despite the dark secret he harboured deep within it.

I talked for what felt like hours. Then, in the end, I told them that I loved them and that I always would, but that I didn't want to walk through life alone. Not anymore.

Eventually, the pain softened, slowly subsiding, as if my heart had finally accepted their deaths, and for the first time since the accident, I felt free.

'Gods, I should never have asked Alaric to reverse that damn spell,' Orm muttered, looking at my tear-streaked face. 'Ani, please talk to me. I'm so sorry,' he begged, and the sorrow in his voice made me open my eyes.

'Don't be, I couldn't go on living like that. Numb to the feelings deep inside me, throbbing like a missing limb. Now I've remembered how it feels to have been loved, and to lose that love. Even if it hurts, it was worth it,' I sobbed, but Orm shook his head.

'No, I've caused you nothing but anguish. You're shaking, Ani. I should have—' he started, but I placed a finger on his lips. 'Trying to decide for me again, Commander?' I teased.

He frowned. 'No, I just hate seeing you in such pain. All my life I've trained to protect my people, but when it matters most, I can't even protect the woman I lov ... care for. How could I ask you to be with me, to choose me, if my weakness caused all this? I'm sorry, Annika. I was a fool—an arrogant, thoughtless fool.'

'Yet you came through the fire to help me,' I murmured, before placing a hand on the dragon's neck. 'I'm so sorry, Vahin. It was my pain to bear. I shouldn't have dragged you into my bottomless pit of grief.' I felt the dragon move, and when I looked to the side, Vahin was directly above me. I could feel the sharp focus of his intense blue eyes.

'I waited for you to come to me through the streams of time, and I won't lose you to grief and sorrow. It was my honour to be with you when you said goodbye, and it is my privilege to offer my strength in your service. Never apologise for what you take from me because I'm yours, Little Flame. Everything I am is yours to take.'

Vahin meant every word; I felt it deep within my soul. I placed my hand above the symbol of our connection and bowed to the proud dragon who had chosen me before I ever knew I needed him.

With my spirit at peace, I finally noticed our surroundings. Of all the worst places it could have happened, I had to have my meltdown in the middle of the landing field, and now a crowd had gathered to observe the spectacle from a safe distance.

The tempest of flame and aether had dispersed with my last goodbye, but the damage remained. I heard raised voices gossiping, whispers of *the mage woman went mad* and *the dragon almost killed the commander* the most prevalent in the crowd. I bit my lip. I'd wanted to start a new life here; I hoped that after today, both my pride and my reputation weren't damaged beyond repair.

Vahin must have sensed my discomfort because he raised his head, wrapping his wings around me before he roared a warning, silencing the crowd.

'Get back to your lives. There is nothing to see here!' Alaric's voice carried such authority and threat that it made me swallow hard and tighten my grip on the dragon's body. He approached slowly, but as he came close, Vahin hissed viciously, and Ari halted, frowning before he cautiously came closer.

'Annika, are you all right?' he asked, and I exhaled slowly. Orm helped me stand, covering me with a cloak, and I turned towards the approaching dark fae mage. 'Yes. Your spell is completely gone. There will be no more burning beds,' I jested, trying to smile.

'What burning beds?' Orm's confused question made my lips twitch, but I didn't answer the question. I focused entirely on Alaric, whose haunted expression showed me how guilty he felt.

'Ari, it's not your fault. I'm grateful for everything you did,' I told him, opening my arms.

He fell into them, wrapping me in a tight embrace. 'I'm sorry, sweetheart. I should have known when I saw the linen. I should have stayed,' he whispered, but I shook my head.

'No, you're not a mind reader. Nobody could have predicted this. I'm just glad Vahin was close enough to help.'

All of a sudden, I was pulled back against Orm's massive body. 'What are you talking about? Why wasn't I told you were having difficulties?' he asked in a low voice that sounded more like a growl, and I tilted my head to look up at him.

'Seriously? You weren't here.'

I pulled away from both Alaric and Ormond. 'I need some time to recover, so if you'll excuse me, I'm going back to my room.' I wrapped Orm's riding cloak tighter around my body.

'Please talk to me when you're ready,' the commander grumbled, hand tightening on the fabric before he reluctantly let go. 'I'll be in my office or my chambers. Ani ... I'm sorry.'

I nodded, but before I could take a step, a loud voice rumbled across the plain. 'Annika, what the fuck did you do now?'

I would recognise that voice in the afterlife. I turned around to see Bryna, hammer in hand, and Katja, glowering next to her, holding bottles of what I strongly suspected was her special sleeping draught. The cavalry of Zalesie had arrived to save the day. The determination on their faces broke me, and I burst into cathartic laughter as I ran into their welcoming arms.

CHAPTER 29

OR☾OND

T he half-orc blacksmith and the herbalist gathered Ani into their embrace. How they could be so affectionate while still staring daggers in our direction was a mystery to me. I hesitated, feeling the urge to intervene. We'd come so close to losing her, and I was still processing my feelings. However, I couldn't interrupt seeing how happy Ani was in their company.

'*She isn't physically injured; her magic is calm now, and she wants to be with them,*' Vahin rumbled in my mind. I turned around to look at the two who'd hidden the fact that Annika had been struggling from me. Vahin hadn't been surprised by my reaction, but Alaric's entire posture radiated hostility and challenge.

'Is there a reason neither of you mentioned this?' I asked as calmly as I could. Annika had been whisked away by her friends, but the bravest of Varta's citizens and those too stupid to fear Vahin or Alaric's threats were still here, watching the spectacle.

'I only realised what was happening today. You took me too far away, and there was only one moment I sensed something was amiss.' Vahin's narrowing pupils focused on me in anger. 'Should I be asking you why you were so determined to postpone our return? Why you performed a task that could easily have been assigned to a low-ranking officer?'

I swallowed hard, but they both glared at me, and I felt as if someone had stripped me naked in the middle of the town square.

'Ani wanted me to leave, so I left.'

'Did she really?' Alaric huffed. 'You are such an idiot!' I looked at the dark fae, at his haughty expression, and my fist tightened.

'You think you have the right to berate me? You, of all people? Where were *you* when all this was happening? You knew she was struggling! And what the fuck did you mean by her setting the bed on fire?'

'I was in my workshop, pining after the woman I've been wanting to hold in my arms for ages while she spent every waking moment yearning for *you*. I only heard of Annika's firestorm when the steward alerted me. I came here that very moment, but you and Vahin already had the situation under control.'

I looked at the charred grass and melted cobblestones that had resulted from Annika's headlong rush to meet Vahin. He'd been so afraid for her. The terror overwhelming his thoughts had distracted me as we landed, and I'd been catapulted off his back, my bones rattling as I hit the ground.

'Did she really?' I looked at Ari, a spark of hope lighting in my heart despite the hostility aimed towards me.

'Did she what?' he snapped.

'Did she want me back?' I heard my voice, quiet and hopeful. Alaric's gaze softened.

'Yes, much to my sorrow, she did.'

It was my turn to study him. Alaric had changed since we had met Ani. She brought out the best in him, but without her presence, his morose side had become ever more prominent. He continuously oscillated between sarcasm and brooding anger, the dark mood seemingly consuming him.

I knew he spent most of his time with Ani, not just in his workshop but accompanying her in the evenings, reading together in the library, or just laughing and strolling along the fortress walls. It felt like he craved her company even more than I did, and for the first time, it occurred to me that it might be more than just about Anchoring the beautiful conduit mage.

'There's no limit to how many Anchors a conduit mage may take,' Vahin hissed out loud, and I looked at him sharply.

'Why did you say that?'

'Because I can see the speculation in your mind. You have enough wild magic to be her Anchor.'

I turned to Ari. 'Is that true?'

'Yes.'

Alaric's answer squeezed the air out of my lungs. When Ani had told me to leave, I'd been a mess of anger and rejection. She wanted Alaric, and I was going to accept it, but I needed time and distance to accept it because I loved her. It had become clear when she had mentioned Alaric while her lips were still swollen from my kisses, and a bottomless pit of pain had opened in my chest.

I ran away, using the patrols as an excuse, only to realise I couldn't run from what I felt. I returned, determined to tell Ani I would do anything she asked if we could be together. I would accept Alaric and acknowledge him as her Anchor. I only forgot to ask if she could have a third Anchor because I was a fucking idiot.

'In my office, now. We need to talk,' I ordered, and Alaric followed me with a knowing smirk.

'Of course, my commander. As ever, I humbly offer my service.'

I barely remembered the walk to my office. I had marched through the town and into the castle; one look at my face and the locals had stumbled out of my way. My teeth ground together every time I saw evidence of Ani's desperate flight; a melted stone where she grasped the edge of a granite gatehouse, half-burned tapestries, or the charred beams I glimpsed were silent testimony to how close we had been to disaster.

Gods, if we hadn't been nearby, how would this have ended? I knew Annika had powerful and volatile power, but wielding dragon flame at the same time? It was too big a threat. A threat that could be remedied if she only accepted at least one of us as her second Anchor. That way, I could arrange for someone to be close at all times, just in case she needed it.

As soon as Alaric closed the door, I turned to face him. 'Why didn't you let me know you reversed the spell? I would have returned immediately.' Alaric walked towards the desk and poured some mead into two goblets, passing one to me, but I refused with a shake of my head.

'Because Ani told me she tried to tell you, but that you had bolted, refusing to listen. That, and I wanted time with my Domina. I need her, Orm. I crave her touch in more ways than you can imagine.'

'You touched Ani? I thought she only had Vahin ...' I exhaled slowly to calm the erratic beating of my heart. 'You touched her ... but if she needed Vahin so badly, then you can't be her Anchor. Are you ... lovers?' Somehow, that thought hurt even more.

'We are not lovers, but we have become closer,' he said, and I wanted to strangle him for giving such an ambiguous answer. 'It is more that Ani touched *me* and discovered the ugly truth I'd hidden from everyone, even you.'

'Explain.'

'The day you left, Ani came to me, tense and angry. I ...' He unbuttoned his shirt, showing me the silver marks on his chest I had only caught sight of during our sparring practices. 'I know you've noticed them, but I never told you the truth about what they are. These aren't my family markings, but my curse. An incessant burning reminder of what I've become,' he started, before telling me about his mother and the blood oath her corrupted power had left on his body.

I had to sit down.

My hands clenched the armrest of my chair with a grip that made the wood creak and splinter. I listened, speechless, at the detailed story of the cruelty he endured. If Alaric had wanted to divert my anger, he surely succeeded because—despite the fury still burning in my heart—I wanted to embrace him. Fuck, he was a man—a dangerous fae—but the urge to wrap my arms around him, to tell him I wouldn't let anything else hurt him, was there, confusing my already troubled thoughts.

I saw him hesitate, and my jaw tightened. 'Just tell me,' I said, willing myself to breathe slower, to tame the wild beast that thrashed in the cage of my soul. My wild magic wanted to rip apart its prison to go after those who'd made Annika and Alaric suffer. 'I can't believe I was so *fucking blind* to your struggles, and Ani's ... Fuck! Just tell me everything, please.'

'Recently I ... I discovered they aren't just my torment, but a link to the Lich King. Just before Ani came to me, he tried to force my submission and fighting him off had left me exhausted. She saw the state I was in and helped me in the aftermath of the attack. Annika is the only thing that keeps the connection dormant, the only thing blocking his voice in my head.'

'And you want to Anchor her?' I was stunned by the revelation. How could I protect him without endangering her? The conundrum brought the anger back. 'That is ... What is wrong with you? I can't let you do it. I know she helps you but ... No, I will protect her, even from you. There will be no Anchoring, Alaric—not for you, not right now. Even if we had the crystal to replace the keystone, knowing this, I would not let it happen.'

I sank into the depths of hopelessness, but there was one more thing I had to clarify. 'When you first mentioned replacing the keystone, I spoke with the university's high mage,' I said, before bitter disappointment made me shake my head. 'He told me that all of the Barrier stones were carved from a single block of mountain crystal, that they are connected and that that's how they enhance each other's magic. He said they weren't replaceable. I didn't believe him. I trusted you. I thought you'd discovered something they hadn't, but we never stood a chance, did we?'

'No,' he answered.

I looked at the man who was like a brother to me, wondering if I knew him at all. 'Then why? Why did you have me bring her here? Did the Lich King force you to do it? Was our friendship a lie too? Help me understand because I don't want to believe you're my enemy.'

'I knew the Barrier was fading—it was only a matter of time until it was gone, especially near the Rift. I didn't plan it, but that chance meeting with Annika made me realise that with her, I might have enough power not just to pass through to the Barren Lands, but to kill the Lich King.'

'So you were lying when you agreed to abandon that idea?'

He looked me in the eye and didn't even flinch under my stare. 'Would you have brought her here and let me leave if you knew what I intended?'

'No, strategically, it makes no sense. You'd be killed the moment you made it past the Barrier, and she'd be captured and forced to serve that monster ...' I said, looking at his all-knowing smile.

'That's why Orm. Sometimes you just need to follow your heart, not your logic, and I wanted to be free.'

'Do you still want it? To Anchor her, to risk her life on the slim chance you might succeed?'

'No, Annika has become more to me than I ever believed possible. I don't need a reason to bind our spirits. I already belong to her, and I wouldn't hurt my Domina, not even for my freedom.'

'I want to believe you, but it's hard. You lied to me. You may have thought you had a good reason, but you've broken my trust, and I can't let you break my Nivale's heart,' I insisted, my voice hoarse with the hurt of his deception.

'I know, and I'm not trying to, but you have to understand something. Annika isn't mine or yours; Vahin has more right to that claim than either of us. If you want to Anchor her—and I can see that you do—you need to understand that she will never be just yours.'

'I know! I returned to tell her I would take whatever she offered, that I would accept ... Fuck, I should lock you in a cell or send you back to your empress. Why do I still want you around ...?' I rasped, my throat tightening before I leaned on my desk, hiding my face in my hands.

Alaric approached my chair and kneeled next to it. I frowned when he placed his hand on my thigh, but when I turned my head, I saw him looking at me with sadness in his golden eyes.

'That is your right, but what would *you* have done if someone who was supposed to love you tricked you into a curse that burns through your body day and night? I didn't know Ani would become so much for so many. I just wanted my freedom. Four hundred and eighty years ... I barely remember my life without pain and nightmares. What would you have done in my place?'

I jerked to my feet because he looked so ... vulnerable, kneeling like that, but I didn't want to think about it. I diverted my thoughts to the subject I knew best: war. 'You should have told me to prepare for war rather than chasing a mirage. I could have helped my brother build our forces. Even if I start now, I fear it is too late. We won't have an army ready to face the monsters.'

'We wouldn't have an army even if you knew. You can't prepare if the king you serve doesn't want to fight—look at the soldiers he sent you. Annika is our only chance and the best weapon you have. I brought her to you ... to us,' he said, standing up and giving me the space I needed.

I started pacing. Alaric's words came too close to the truth for my liking, and his following words brought my pacing to a halt.

'I can't change the past, Orm, but you have me, a necromancer, and even if Annika can't Anchor me, I still can help. We were working on a binding

331

glyph that would enhance my power. I can be your weapon too ... or I can go to Katrass ... alone, and try my luck with the immortal bastard.'

Before I knew it, my hand was locked on his throat. 'You are going nowhere!' I snarled before realising that the beast had slipped my control, and I loosened my grip. I swallowed hard, stepping away. 'As for Ani, I need a blood oath from you. I know you are fighting him, but if the Lich King ... I need your blood oath that you won't seek the Anchor bond until you are free of your curse.'

There was no hesitation as Alaric drew one of his deadly daggers and cut his forearms, letting the blood flow freely before he used the tip of the blade to draw a sigil. 'I swear on the Dark Mother's blood that I, Alaric'va Shen'ra, will not seek the Anchor bond with Annika Diavellar until I rid myself of this curse. Should I falter, may the Dark Mother take me to a world of eternal torment,' he swore with a bitter smile before looking me in the eye.

'You have my oath, Orm. I only ask that you not separate us. She is ... she means so much to me.'

'I couldn't keep her away from you even if I tried. I thought about it, Ari. I will not cause her pain and make her choose. I will respect whatever decision Ani makes.'

'Thank you,' he said, but I couldn't take my eyes from the fading mark my hand had left on his skin. 'I should take you to the training ground and beat you to a pulp for this,' I said, feeling less uncomfortable than I thought I would. The damned image of the three of us together returned, and I had to shake my head to dispel it. I wasn't ready for that thought, and I'd made enough concessions today. This time, when Alaric passed me the goblet, I accepted it.

As I gulped the mead down, I felt the sweet, burning liquid extinguish the fire in my heart. Somehow, despite the threat of an impending war, this moment did not feel as catastrophic as I'd feared it would. That Alaric had come to me with this information ... Yes, he'd withheld it for so long, but now there were no secrets between us, and the longer I thought about it, the more relief and apprehension replaced my anger.

I held all the strings in my hand, and I could start planning my next moves.

'I'll recall the units from the mines and build outposts near the border. Starting tomorrow, you will train with Annika and see what you can do without Anchoring her. I need you to send letters to the fae courts. Give them all the information about the situation here. I want them prepared and ready when my brother raises his banner to call them to stand with the Kingdom of Dagome. Then we will decide what to do next.'

Alaric nodded. 'I don't deserve your trust, but I can swear that I won't betray you. You will have my assistance in any way you need,' he said before coming closer, a small crease forming on his forehead.

He looked at me as if he was weighing a decision before his shoulder slumped. 'What is it?' I asked. This was not his normal behaviour, and Ari's body tensed in response. 'I need to tell you something else. The Lich King—'

His words were cut short by the doors bursting inwards, a pale messenger falling into the room.

'Lord Commander, biesy! Biesy have attacked Vodianka!'

'Fuck, what now?' I cursed, looking at Alaric.

Vodianka was a small village in a nearby forest. It wasn't a typical military target, and I hadn't expected it to be attacked. The people who lived there were mainly foresters and their families who provided wood and animal pelts to the Lost Ridge.

They could deal with a bies on their own. One horned demon—even if it were as big as a bison, with massive hooves, claws, and fur that resisted most weapons—could be killed by a few determined woodcutters. However, if many of them had attacked, the village was doomed. I couldn't even use dragons to fight them as the forest in the region was dense and high in natural resin, making it impossible to land.

'There hasn't been any movement reported on the border or across the Rift,' I mused, confused. If this was the start of the war, I'd clearly missed something.

Were we wrong?

My brother had built his support slowly. As long as the Lich King thought he had a foot in our court, there was hope he would stall long enough for us to gather a decent-sized army. We needed time, and right now, Vodianka needed a fucking miracle for us to get there on time.

'Get the kirbai and horses ready,' I commanded, turning to Ari when he tapped my shoulder to get my attention. 'I will come as well. It is time I stopped avoiding who I truly am. You will need a necromancer,' Alaric said before I could even ask.

'Annika, we should take her. It's just ...' I let my silent question hang in the air. She could be of great help but throwing her in the middle of a battle right now could be risky.

'No, let her rest. It is too early,' he answered after considering it, and I nodded. 'Let's go then, and hope our Nivale is too busy to notice our absence,' I quipped, remembering the last time I left her behind.

CHAPTER 30

ANNIKA

I was sitting in the forge wearing a pair of Bryna's breeches and a pockmarked tunic while my friends waited, staring at me expectedly. I looked like a child trying on their parents' clothes for fun, but as all my clothes were ash on the landing field, I'd been grateful for the loan.

'So ... what happened?' Katja asked. Instead of answering, I pointed to the anvil I was sitting on. 'Why did you bring me here? We could be sitting comfortably in my room.'

'Because you almost burned the town down, and I thought it might be safer to bring you somewhere where the fire is less of a problem,' Bryna said, and I felt a blush crawl up my cheeks.

'It was an accident. My magic became a little ... difficult, and I needed to reach Vahin,' I answered defensively.

'We're not blaming you,' Katja sighed. 'We just want to know what happened and what we should do if it happens again.'

'It won't happen again. It was a side effect of a spell reversal. Long story short, to defeat the spectrae that attacked us when we flew here, I had to bond with Vahin. However, I wasn't able to complete the process because I was still grieving for my lost Anchors. Alaric took the grief and some other feelings away, and today it all came rushing back.' I shrugged, the both of them staring at me in shocked disbelief.

'The fuck he did,' Bryna finally said, whistling through her crooked teeth while Katja pulled a small vial from the pocket of her dress. 'Here, this'll calm you down,' she said, and I laughed.

'Oh no, sister. You're not knocking me out again. Besides, I'm fine now.'

'Are you sure? You were never the sanest at the best of times.' Bryna was unyielding in pointing out my shortcomings, but it was Katja's silence that worried me.

'Last time, you needed two Anchors. Is the dragon enough?' she asked, and when I frowned, she added, 'I want to live here, Ani. There's this dragon rider, Tomma ... I like him. Besides, the commander offered me an apothecary position with a house and a workshop, and the men here—well, at least most of them—treat women with respect. I like it, and I don't want you to burn this place down if you lose your shit again.'

'Katja!' Bryna sent her a quelling glare, but I nodded.

'Need? ... Maybe? Want more Anchors? Yes. Two more, to be precise.'

'So, one will be that dark fae mage.' When I raised an eyebrow at her definitive statement, she chuckled. 'Don't deny it. He looks at you like a starved dog looks at a bone, but who else? One of the healers? There's that nice artefact master, but he's too old, I think.'

'Katja Laster, are you trying to push men into my bed? And no, it won't be a healer. I'm going to Anchor the commander,' I said, enjoying the moment their jaws dropped.

'Why him? He's not a mage, and he's been acting like a bear with a stick rammed up its arse,' Bryna was the first to comment, and I chuckled.

'True, but I like him like that, and when he pulls that stick out, the fire that burns inside him? *Gods*, that man can growl.'

'Soldiers have been gossiping that you've already had a little taste of that.' Katja's remark was met with a wide grin, and my friend sighed. 'Fine, just try to keep things together. This place is heaven for women.'

I didn't have the heart to tell her that soon, no place would be safe for women ... or anything else still living.

We chatted for a few hours, sampling Bryna's stash of orcish ale, and not only did my magic settle, but a pleasant contentment spread over me, as if everything had finally fallen into place.

A sudden commotion outside caught our attention, disturbing the peace. As I stood up to check what was going on, a red-faced soldier burst in and looked at Bryna. 'Do you have any blades left?'

'What for?' she asked, and he huffed.

'Just give them to me before the latawce drive more people insane.'

'Latawce?' Katja and I spoke in unison, and the man looked at me like he hadn't realised anyone else was there.

'Yes, Lady Mage. A flock of latawce have descended on the town, enraging people with their maddening song.'

'Get the commander and Master Alaric. Tell them to meet me in the town square. Katja, prepare more of your sleeping droughts. We may need to put people to sleep if they become violent,' I ordered, cursing the current predicament. My weapons were in the castle, and between me and the building was an entire town laid siege by an unknown number of wind demons.

'My lady, the commander and Master Alaric have already left the fortress. A group of biesy attacked Vodianka ...'

I exhaled slowly, trepidation tightening my muscles. Attacking the fortress while the majority of our soldiers were out dealing with another issue felt like too big a coincidence, and I knew only one person who could coordinate monsters on such a scale.

The Lich King was making a move, and the handful of soldiers posted around Varta and I were all the defence this place had left.

'*Vahin?*' I tried in my mind. I could still feel his Anchor, but not his thoughts. My magic should be temporarily safe, but we were too far away from each other to communicate and I wasn't able to speak with other dragons. Between the groups on patrols and the forces Orm likely took with him, I doubted there would be any dragons resting in the caves anyway.

'How many soldiers and dragon riders do we have left?'

'I don't know, my lady. I'm new. You'd have to ask an officer,' the soldier stuttered under my glare.

'Take this,' Bryna said, passing him a short sword—maybe not the sharpest, but still a weapon—and grabbing one of her heavy hammers. 'Ani, what do you want us to do?' I looked at my friends. I could see the expectation in their eyes. They saw me as a leader, but this wasn't Zalesie and I had no authority here. Would the soldiers even listen to me? Still, it was my home now—our home—and Zalesie's infamous trio always protected what was theirs.

From their grins, I knew what my friends were thinking, and my own grin slipped out as I stood up.

'Bryna, gather the remaining men and tell them I'm acting on the authority of Ormond. Lie, bully, or beat them into doing as they're told if you must, but bring them to the town. Katja, rally the healers. If the latawce are in town, we will have many on the brink of madness, harming themselves and others as long as the song lasts.'

'What are you going to do, Ani?' Katja asked, worry clearly etched in her eyes.

She's worried I'll lose control again.

It was a bitter thought, but I didn't blame my friend. I wasn't the most stable of mages, and I hoped Vahin was still close enough for our bond to keep me grounded. I had little choice unless I wanted to sacrifice the town while Orm and Alaric were away, but I felt the threads of the bond, and I hoped that would be enough.

'I will take the wind out from under their wings,' I said with a vicious smile, knowing exactly what I needed to do.

Latawce were wind demons. They floated on currents, their physical bodies like giant birds with sharp claws and colourful feathers, though they could never be mistaken for birds. They had human heads with faces so beautiful they left people mesmerised, and there was no sneaking up on the demons.

Like owls, they could turn their heads in any direction to capture their victim's gaze before they started their unearthly song. Once that alluring melody began, people fell to the floor, clawing at their own bodies, ripping away flesh to offer as tribute to their tormentors. Even worse was when they shifted shape, becoming the victim's most beloved, only to lure them to their deaths.

We left the forge, each of us heading to complete our tasks. I walked the steep path to the outskirts of the town, attempting to spot the demons and learn how many we would face. I heard the song as I approached and shuddered at its maddening beauty.

The soft melody rose and fell on a gust of mountain wind, caressing the mind, luring victims in, tempting you to let go of earthly constraints, then strip the flesh from your bones and throw it into the wind to finally be free.

Latawce didn't need their claws to feed—their victims did the work for them. I saw people running, senselessly tearing at their ears, but I didn't pause until I reached the town square. It wasn't big, but it didn't need to be.

One side led to the landing field, which in turn was connected to the high castle's courtyard. Shops, townhouses, the tavern, and the small but popular brothel stood next to the underutilised town hall. A little further on was the boarding house for indentured females, for those who didn't wish to live in the fortress—a place undisturbed by men. The latawce were there, flying around or perched on the rooftops, flocking, until another victim gave in to the melody and tossed a bloody scrap of flesh into the air.

When I entered the town square, every single demon turned in my direction, knowing smiles lighting their beautiful faces, and the song of the damned was blasted full force in my direction. The melody, however, had changed. It was no longer a wordless tune now, but filled with a tempting call to forget the problems of the world and leave, to leave and go to the Barren Lands. I was trained to detach my mind from worldly distractions as I concentrated on my spells, so their calls washed over me without gaining a foothold.

When it was clear their compulsion was having little effect, the song changed once more, promising to reunite me with Tal and Arno if only I would listen and go *now*.

This time, I did react, my concentration cracking, and an angry sob that held my outrage at them desecrating my lover's memories escaped my lips.

As I fought the compulsion, the biggest of the latawce flew down, transforming in midair. The man had a handsome, timeless face; dark hair slightly dusted with white on the temples; and grey eyes as tempestuous as a stormy sea.

'Lady Annika, thank you for coming to greet my servants. It is truly a pleasure to finally meet you.' With a tilt of his head, the demon studied my unwelcoming posture. 'What lies were you told about me that you look upon me with such anger? I am not your enemy, Lady Mage. In fact, I would like to make you an offer. Join me, and you will never have to worry about losing control.'

Seeing my features darken in anger, the latawiec's smile widened. 'Of course, that is not all I offer. I could reunite you with your lost lovers: your paladin mage and your fae healer. I can feel their restless spirits behind the Veil. They are waiting for their conduit to call them back, and I can return them to you. Unfortunately, I cannot do it alone. I would need you beside me, need your power to rip open the Veil for them to rejoin you.'

The demon's lips didn't move as he spoke, and as he reached out to me, I came so close to taking his hand ...

'Edoúru ta ere!'[1]

A single tear tracked over my cheek as I uttered the command.

A wave of aether distorted the demon's form, and the monster fought for control before he lost his shape, once again becoming birdlike. The rest of the flock rose into the air with a mind-shattering scream. I closed my eyes as sharp claws sliced past my face, so close that I felt the movement against my cheek. I fell back a step, shocked, but watched as the demons flew around me, not once touching my body.

Orm had been worried that an assassin would kill me, but our enemy didn't want me dead—he wanted me alive to use my magic. I smiled grimly and took advantage of that. I felt another breath of wind against my cheek, and my lips curved viciously.

The endless chaotic energy of wind, the power that gave the latawce their magic, was right there, at my fingertips. I spread my arms and took a deep, calming breath, releasing it slowly and letting the aether move through me, catching and moulding it to my need as I spoke.

'Vor'me.'[2]

The aether wrapped around me like a happy puppy eager to please, and I did what I promised Katja I'd do. I ripped the wind from under the demons' wings. They screeched and fell from the sky, feathers flying, their song forgotten, right onto the swords of the soldiers Bryna had rallied from the garrison.

It took some time to clear the town while I wove spell after spell, manipulating the wind every time a latawiec tried to escape. The spells were exhausting as I didn't reach for my conduit skills, but I smiled each time a vile

---

1. *Return to your nature!*

2. *Obey.*

creature fell from the sky, hitting the cobblestones like rocks, helpless before the soldiers' blades. Bryna and a young officer directed them with surprising efficiency, protecting Katija and her healers while they helped the injured citizens.

An enormous shadow moved over the ground, startling me. Raising my head, I saw a dragon gliding across the sky, its scales gleaming like pure jade in the setting sun. I followed his gaze: on the far end, near the landing fields, was a child.

A boy, maybe eight or nine years old, was sheltering his bloodied mother, hitting an injured latawiec with a broken branch. On instinct, I formed a fireball, but I didn't have time to release it before the jade dragon plummeted from the sky, incinerating the latawiec, then landing next to the child.

I knew from the awe on the child's face what had happened.

Vahin had told me about the Binding. In times of great distress, a human soul could call a dragon from the sky, binding them together. It was why dragon rider families left their male offspring in caves, scared, starved, and alone.

I felt tears pricking my eyes as I watched the child reach for the dragon, the massive beast lowering his head to let the small hand caress his eyelid. Amid the carnage, I had witnessed a miracle.

The birth of a new dragon rider.

Seeing a dragon pairing with my emotions working properly felt exhilarating. The fact that I was using my magic with ease made the experience almost euphoric, and I couldn't restrain my grin as I surveyed the battlefield.

As I felt that ease falter, I knew Vahin was drifting too far away, but with only a few demons left, I closed myself off to the tempestuous wind and used my favourite familiar fire. Despite my tiredness, it took little effort to burn away their feathers, sending the creatures to their doom. With the last notes of the maddening song dying down and the smell of burnt feathers making me sick, I sank to my knees, breathing heavily.

'My lady, drink this, please. You look tired.' The voice came from beside me and I raised my eyes to see the crippled man from the tavern. He passed me a tankard and I took the offered drink, raising it to my lips. I sighed with pleasure as the ice-cold fluid hit the back of my throat, the apple cider sweet and refreshing. When I turned to thank him for his kindness, the old soldier had already hobbled away.

'Ani, you bloody witch, you did it!' Bryna roared so loudly that several heads turned in our direction. 'She told me she would take the wind from under their wings, and she did exactly that. Cheer, you fuckers, cheer for our saviour!' she yelled at them, and a resounding roar rang out as the soldiers raised their swords.

I sat on the cobblestones, holding the tankard to my chest, forcing a smile while dread washed over me.

We had successfully defended against one attack, but how many more were there to come?

This had been a shrewd move, happening the moment I'd been at my most vulnerable. I felt a pricking sensation, as if I was being watched.

The Lich King.

I didn't know how he did it, but to lure Orm and Alaric from the fortress while attempting to take advantage of my raw emotions was a genius—and very cruel—scheme.

I was no longer hesitant to take an Anchor. Fuck, I would Anchor an entire army of mages if it would help, because witnessing the Binding, seeing my people fight together to protect each other? That was worth any heartache.

I was a bloody weapon. Imperfect, scared, and occasionally unhinged, but if this attack had shown me anything, it was that I could make a difference—not just for myself and my men, but for all of those too weak to defend themselves.

Sitting there on the cold cobblestones, dressed in singed blacksmith castoffs, I promised myself that if war was inevitable, then I would stand up and be counted. I prayed to the gods above and below that I wouldn't fail this time. I would rather die than let my home become a playground for monsters.

CHAPTER 31

ANNIKA

Three days had passed since Orm and Alaric went to aid Vodianka. I hoped they'd been as successful in their endeavour as we had been here. I spent most of my time in Orm's office, doing my best to assist with fortress affairs. I wrote a few letters to people I hoped I could trust at the university, detailing the attack and asking them to raise the issue at the next council meeting. We needed more mages and more protection at the border. It was about time they stopped sticking their heads in the sand.

When I wasn't busy writing, training, or talking to the citizens of Varta, I worried about the two men who held a special place in my heart. I tried to keep it under wraps, but my mood had noticeably soured and my brave front earned me concerned looks from Katja and Bryna. The only relief for my gnawing anxiety was drinking in the tavern, and with my friends both busy elsewhere, I was feeling less than pleasant.

'Mead—the strongest and sweetest you have,' I shouted to the barkeep, rolling a silver coin over the counter.

The old man always kept me well-supplied when I needed it. In reality, he was only a few years my senior; unfortunately, he looked as if life had rolled over him like an avalanche, then given him a swift kick when he was down. He was missing an eye and had a burn scar that covered the left side of his head and cheek, leaving only the semblance of an ear. The poor man was also missing two fingers and had a crooked leg that had obviously been caused by a badly set break, leaving him with an unsteady gait.

I quietly admired his resilience. I'd never seen him complain, and he worked tirelessly, fulfilling every order the rowdy soldiers threw his way, leaving their insults unanswered. There were plenty of both. The new recruits especially proved difficult, and without Orm's presence to keep them in line, they behaved as if they owned the place.

'As you wish, Lady Mage. Would you like to try some dried apple slices preserved in honey and cinnamon? They would go well with your drink.' I think he tried to smile, but the scars pulled, turning it into a painful grimace.

'Yes, please, and thank you. I need something sweet tonight.'

Regrettably, a group of newcomers overheard my words. 'Leave that crisper alone and join us, pretty lady. I can sweeten your time if you'd like,' said the bulkiest of the group, and I bristled at the cruel nickname they had given the injured man. I saw the barkeeper's shoulders sag, and he turned around, wiping the already spotless worktop.

Where the riders and veterans in the fortress were gentle and well-mannered around the females, the conscripted soldiers—especially those newly recruited—were the scum of the earth, press-ganged from the gutters and sent here to die in service to a kingdom disgusted by their existence. They were loud, obnoxious, and precisely the type of men any reasonable woman would avoid.

I, however, was not a reasonable woman, and I wasn't in the mood to deal with their attitude.

I turned towards the barkeep. 'What's your name?' I asked, doing my best to ignore the group. I should have asked earlier, especially since the man had been so kind to me, but I'd been too busy moping over the monster's words.

'Ian, my lady,' he answered, visibly surprised that I was still talking to him.

'How about this, Ian? Drop that rag. The worktop is clean enough, and nobody else is calling for a drink. I need some decent company, and you look like a man with an interesting story. Please, join me.'

He was utterly baffled. 'Me?' I knew why he had reacted that way; the lack of women at Varta Fortress meant most of them were already engaged, married, or counting the days until freedom.

Single females were wooed, cherished, and spoiled by every single man here. With a ratio of twenty-to-one, not counting conscripted soldiers, the ladies could take their pick from amongst the best mankind had to offer. Yet I had chosen him, and I saw the disbelief and suspicion on his face, as if he couldn't understand why.

'Yes, you.' I pointed to the conscripted soldiers. 'If I had any maternal instincts, I'd be over there changing their swaddling blankets, but seeing as I'm a grown woman looking for decent conversation, I want to talk to a real man.'

From the laughter in the tavern, I could tell I'd made my words clear enough for everyone to hear. The long-term residents of the town let me know they appreciated my biting wit by jeering and aiming various obscene gestures at the new recruits.

I knew I'd poked the hornet's nest, but I was strangely proud of myself, especially when Ian attempted to smile again. 'Please, my lady. Be careful. These men haven't been shown the way things are here yet,' he said, but I saw his posture straighten, and for the first time since I'd met him, the old soldier looked me straight in the eye.

'I'm Ani. I'd like to thank you for your kindness the other day.' I reached for my mead, sipping it slowly and pretending not to have heard his warning. 'I've never tasted such an interesting flavour. Where did you source it? It's delicious. Is that summer pear I can taste?' I rolled my tongue over the roof of my mouth to identify the ingredients.

'You have exquisite taste. There's not much for an old campaigner like me to do, so I brew mead and ale. In fact, I made this batch myself. It's summer pear and a little black pepper mixed into mead and left to ferment for six weeks. I can add a bit of water if it is too sweet for you.'

The pride in his voice made me smile before I shook my head. 'No, no, it's perfect as it is. You know, I think we're going to become the best of friends. If you make something new, can I try it?' I said, flinching when a heavy clay tankard smashed into the counter next to me.

'This beer tastes like horse piss and smells just as bad.' The soldier who'd tried hitting on me earlier clearly didn't know to never disturb a mage who's moping with a tankard of delicious mead. I turned, taking in the man before me, and he preened under my assessing stare.

'Did your mother drop you on your head as a bairn?'

He frowned in response. 'What?'

'Is that a yes?' I asked, and he bristled.

'Watch your mouth, wench. Where I come from, ladies know how to behave, but I'm guessing you ain't no lady.' He reached for my arm. 'Let me guess, you're one of them here to service the soldiers.' The snickers that came from his companions didn't mask the sound of falling chairs as the veterans leapt to their feet.

Thank you, All-Father, for those too stupid to know better. Your daughter needs to take the edge off, I thought, unable to hold back my smile. The wise god was giving me precisely what I needed—a distraction, in the form of an idiot who deserved everything headed his way.

I tossed back the last of my drink. 'Damn, that mead's too good to spill,' I said to Ian, and his pupils widened as I winked and tightened my grip on the handle.

That was the only warning anyone got before I unleashed chaos.

I didn't use magic. That would have been a low blow to the ordinary soldiers, beating them up with elemental power. Besides, I didn't want to put Ian out of business. Instead, in one swift move, I pulled my hand back and smashed the tankard on the soldier's head. He was strong, but he hadn't expected it, and when he slid to the floor, holding his bleeding nose, the rest of his group rushed towards me.

'Hands off our lady, you dirty bastards,' bellowed a veteran as he lunged forward and grabbed one man by the collar, choking the assailant as he threw him back against the wall. My laughter rang out as I leaned back against the bar and kicked my feet off my stool, catching another overeager fool between the legs.

As the man's face connected with the discarded seat, I landed on his back and launched myself into what was now a full-blown brawl. I grunted when my forehead connected with one man's nose. As blood sprayed across my face, a massive arm wrapped around my waist, pulling me off my current victim.

'What the *fuck* is going on in here?! Who dared attack my woman?!'

Time froze as the echoes of that roar died down. The silence was so deafening one could hear people's heartbeats stutter as everyone turned to look. At the centre of all the attention stood Orm, his armour still covered in blood, eyes glowing yellow like some terrifying god of war. His face was filled with such primal rage that even the veterans who knew him took a step back, lowering their heads, afraid to meet his gaze.

I hadn't noticed the commander's arrival, maybe because I'd been intent on beating up the arsehole whose ring had cut me above my eyebrow. Now, though, I was pinned to Orm's side, not quite touching the ground. He barely looked at me, but his tight hold left me in no doubt. I was going nowhere.

I wiped the blood flowing into my eye and leaned back to look at him. 'No need to roar, Lord Commander. We were just playing. Besides, my side was winning.' I gestured towards the veterans who were still standing as motionless as statues.

That ended up being a mistake because it allowed Orm to notice the cut and smeared blood on my face. 'Who the fuck made her bleed? Speak now, or you'll all hang.' The menace in his voice doubtlessly made it clear that he would carry out the threat. The soldier on the floor paled and attempted to hide his hand behind his back, but Orm noticed and his growl sent a shiver down my spine.

'You!' he roared. It was frightening how fast Orm moved. I was still stumbling to my feet after he released me, but as I looked up, my assailant was dangling from the commander's grip on his neck, legs kicking ineffectually as Ormond's bulging forearm lifted him higher. *Oh fuck, is he still worried about the assassin?*

I couldn't let Orm kill someone for brawling—especially since I had caused it—but I supposed his reaction made sense. He was terrified someone would attack me, and now that someone had, he had lost it. I stepped forward. 'Put him down.' Orm didn't react, fixated on the bloodshot eyes of the dying recruit. 'He is not the attacker you seek. *Put. Him. Down.*'

'Ormond! Lord Commander, restrain yourself!' I reached up to cup his face in my hands and forced him to look at me. His eyes were so full of rage and wildfire, I hardly recognised the stoic leader, but as my thumb stroked his cheek, his hand slowly lowered, and he threw his barely breathing victim to his comrades.

'You're alright? He didn't ...? Fuck, I thought ...' He pressed his forehead to mine as the yellow glint slowly disappeared from his gaze. When he straightened, I shook my head. 'No, it is just a minor cut. I'm fine. I promise I'm alright.'

'Take him,' he said to the veterans before turning towards the rest of the newcomers. 'As for the rest of you—since you've behaved like animals, you will not be permitted in the central city or the castle. You will stay in the barracks, and tomorrow, you will go on patrol at the Rift.'

The soldiers' faces went pale. The rift patrol was a death sentence for the untrained and was mainly carried out by the dragon riders as they had the best chance of survival. Orm was effectively sentencing these rookies to almost certain death just because of a little brawl in a tavern.

'Orm, no. We need men to fight, and even if these children are arseholes, you can still train them.'

'Then they will have the chance to prove themselves tomorrow. Let the fates decide. If they return, they will have earned their training. It was you they attacked this time, but what if it had been someone not as adept at protecting themselves? Few have your strength and courage, and none have your magic. That is the law here. Attacking a woman means death.'

'No. I started this fight. Blame it on me.' The realisation I may have condemned these people to death hit me.

'No, my lady. They were rude to you ... and handsy with the other women. It was bound to happen. The commander is right. That's our way, and they are being shown more mercy than I would've given them,' Ian said, and I looked at him before turning my head towards the veterans, but they all nodded in agreement.

'Come to the quartermaster tomorrow. He'll pay you for the damages,' Orm said to Ian, and the barkeep nodded, careful not to meet Orm's eyes. I wanted to protest again, but as the commander looked down at me, the words died in my throat. 'Are you well enough to walk?' When I nodded, he took my hand. 'We're leaving now,' he said, pulling me after him with such force that I had no choice but to follow.

We emerged from the tavern only to pause, surrounded by a large crowd. I should've known the brawl would attract attention, but I hadn't expected Orm to appear—and certainly hadn't expected to be dragged away in front of an audience.

He looked at the gathered people, and his jaw muscles ticked in annoyance. 'Do you need me to find you something to do? Because I will be more than happy to oblige,' he said, and despite a few sniggers from the gathered crowd, they dispersed quickly.

I moved closer, standing on tiptoes while grabbing his leather belt, both to stabilise myself and to get his attention. 'We need to talk, and you shouldn't scare the locals,' I whispered, but Orm cursed in response.

'If they're stupid enough to listen to my private conversations, they deserve everything that happens to them. I need Alaric to see to this cut first. Gods, I thought they had attacked you! And I wasn't even here,' he said, and I bit my lip as he continued. 'You knew about the threat. How could you let anyone come close enough to injure you? What if the blade was poisoned?'

'It was a *ring*, and I was just having a little fun.'

He rolled his eyes. 'Annika, your definition of fun baffles me. Now, let's go see Ari.'

'It's just a cut. Orm, please.' His face softened for a moment, and he pulled me into his arms, pressing my face to his chest and wrapping his cloak around me to protect me from the gust of wind blowing dust around.

'Fine, I'll take you somewhere no one can disturb us,' he conceded, reaching for me. I was blinded by the flying debris and so surprised at being picked up that I didn't realise he was carrying me towards Vahin, who—against standard practice—had landed in the middle of the street.

'You can't—' I started, but he stopped me. 'We can go to Ari or talk in private, but I'm not standing here just staring at the blood on your face. Your decision, Nivale: choose how you wish to proceed.'

'In private,' I whispered, feeling him hold me tighter as he climbed onto the dragon's back.

CHAPTER 32

ANNIKA

N o sooner had we taken off than we'd landed.

I was still trying to get my bearings when I caught sight of our destination: high in the mountains, the wide, flat plateau took my breath away. Granite walls crowded in on three sides, broken up by the misty cascade of an enchanting waterfall dancing over rocks to fill a small pool before making its way more slowly to a second, calmer pool.

A thin layer of soil held a mossy carpet of mountain grass and wildflowers, and the mist from the mystical cascade turned the rays of the sun into a magical display of colour. The air was bitter and challenging to breathe, but after I concentrated and took several deep, calming breaths, it became easier.

As soon as we dismounted, Vahin took to the air, leaving us stranded. He caught a passing updraft and disappeared into the clouds. I didn't mind. For a moment, I forgot about the world, drinking in the beauty before me.

'Annika ...' Orm's voice was raw as he spoke, grasping my shoulders to turn me around. 'Did I scare you?' he asked, then gently took my chin, tilting my head to see the cut. 'I should kill the bastard that made you bleed.' I couldn't help but smile.

'No, and no killing, maiming, or damaging your future soldiers. And make sure you provide them some dragon protection for that damned patrol—it should be a punishment, not a sentence. Please. For me?' He sighed.

'Fine. Now let me see your face.'

'It's just a scratch. I'll let you kiss it better if you'll relax,' I teased, and his groan was that of a man who could no longer withstand his torment. Orm's head dipped, but instead of the cut, his lips captured mine with a pained whisper.

'I thought you were in danger. I'd only just landed, and the first thing I heard was that the fortress had been attacked. Then a messenger bursts in, telling me you were fighting in the tavern. I fucking hate my life sometimes. I hate being away from you,' he ground out, peppering my face with little kisses. 'If you want those bastards to live, they will, but don't ask me to go easy on them because I'm going to beat the living daylights out of them until they understand no one touches my ... any woman.'

I gasped, melting into his possessive touch. The strength of his arms pressing my body to his turned the gasp into a moan, my skin prickling with goosebumps. I gave in to him, smiling when his short beard caressed my cheeks. My arms wrapped around his neck, pulling him closer.

'You taste so good ... like spiced, forbidden pleasure. Fuck, I can't think straight with you in my arms,' Orm murmured, and when I parted my lips, his tongue darted in, dancing over mine.

We stood in a field of flowers, alone at the top of a mountain, while he owned me with a single kiss, commanding me to submit, to take him as mine. My warrior was battered and bloodied, but so breathtaking; I wouldn't change him for anything in the world.

When our lips parted, and I could finally catch my breath, he refused to let go, as if touching me was the only thing that kept him sane. 'I can't believe I had to pull you out of a tavern brawl,' he grumbled with such an obvious eye roll that I chuckled.

'They needed to be taught a lesson.'

'And it had to be you that gave it to them? Next time, please, for the sake of my sanity, let me know when you're going to do it. I won't interfere, I promise.'

'Aww, you'll take away all my fun if I do that. No one will fight me knowing you are watching,' I joked before shivering at his thunderous expression. 'I didn't want to worry you. This brawl ... you know I could have wiped the floor with them if I really wanted to. I just needed to vent some frustration. These last few days have been hard, and ... I missed you.'

I smiled, seeing his eyebrows knitting together. 'I really missed you ... and your heartbeat.' I trailed a finger along his tightening jawline. He groaned as my finger slid down over his neck, hooking onto his breastplate, pulling him towards me.

My eyes widened as the hands on my waist tightened their grip in response.

'You beautiful vixen, you've turned me into a man possessed,' he said, hands sweeping up my arms. 'I was fighting biesy, and all I felt was regret that you weren't by my side. I want us to happen. Will you take me, Nivale? As you've regained your past, can we have a future?'

The heat in his voice flowed like molasses over my skin. I was lost in Orm's stormy green eyes, his fingers wiping the blood from my skin, but my silence seemed to bother him. 'Annika, I know you and Ari—' I cut him off, placing a finger on his lips.

'First, apologise for leaving without me. You took Alaric, but left me behind—I'd hoped our little adventure with the olgoi worm had taught you better. How can I Anchor you if you don't treat me as an equal?'

'You'd just had your heart ripped to shreds when we got the message. I didn't want you going from one battle to another. That's the only reason I didn't bring you with us. I won't leave you aga—' he paused. 'Ani ... did you say Anchor?' Orm stuttered into silence, and I saw his pupils widen in disbelief.

'You said you want us to happen. Don't you want to be my Anchor?'

Orm breathed hard, fighting with more than just the clasp of his breastplate. When he finally threw it aside, his eyes were ablaze with wild magic, but he held himself back—or so I thought until he dropped to his knees and pressed his face into my midriff. 'Gods, Nivale, *want*? I crave it. I thought you'd never ask,' he muttered, inhaling deeply.

'What are you doing?' I asked, taken aback by his actions.

Orm looked up, then took my hand and pressed it to his forehead. 'I, Ormond Erenheart, swear my life to you, Annika Diavellar. My mind, my heart, and my strength are yours to command. I will follow you in this life and behind the Veil; wherever fate takes you, I'll be there to protect you. May the gods above and below witness my vow. There will be no other for me but you.'

I knew Orm was from a ducal house of warriors and dragon riders, but I hadn't expected this. I stroked a stray lock of hair from his forehead as my eyes sought even a hint of doubt, but all I found was heartfelt honesty and love.

Orm had just recited the warrior's oath of marriage and fidelity; he had pledged himself to me, and it left me overwhelmed and awed. I swallowed hard, knowing he was waiting for my answer. 'Before I accept, there is one thing you need to know,' I said, and he frowned. 'What is it?'

'I ... you hold a special place in my heart, but I can't deny how I feel about Alaric and Vahin, too. I cannot choose one whilst denying the others. I'm sorry. I know that may be difficult to accept, and I understand if you want to take back your pledge, but I need you to know my heart.' I couldn't look Orm in the eye, feeling as if I stood on the edge of a vast precipice, but he reached up, capturing my chin to make me look at him.

The gentle smile that graced his lips melted my heart, but his next words? Nothing could have prepared me for them.

'You scared me half to death, my Nivale. I know how you feel about those two rogues. I was already planning to talk to you about it when I returned from my patrol. During my time away I ... I realised how unhappy it would make you if you had to choose. I can't change my nature, but I care for Alaric, and knowing it's him you want ... well, strangely, it eases my heart. I don't think I could share you with anyone else, but with Ari, I can, because, in a way, he is already a part of me.'

'There will be no one else,' I said firmly and was blinded by the brightness of Orm's smile. 'I accept your pledge, Ormond Erenhart, and I swear to the gods above and below to do all I can to be worthy of you.'

I meant every word. Since the moment I had met him, my magic knew Orm would become mine, even when I was too scared and lost in grief to acknowledge it.

I threaded my hands through his thick black hair. My warrior, bloody from his battle with the biesy, still knelt before me as I turned towards the waterfall, a mischievous grin lighting my lips as my gaze caught on the pools below it.

'Come,' I said, reaching for Orm's hand. He looked at me with confusion but let me take the lead. We reached the edge of the pool, and I turned around, placing a hand on his chest. 'Are you ready for a challenge, Lord Ormond? Will you let me command you for a short while?' I asked, biting my lip to hide my grin.

'I will, my lady. I am yours, am I not?' His eyes sparkled with joy as his fist hammered into his chest as if challenging me to try him.

I slid my hand into the basin, whispering a simple incantation to heat the ice-cold water. While my magic worked, I nodded towards the rest of his armour. 'Undress. I want to see what I'm working with. And before you complain, it's only fair since you've already seen me naked.'

Orm smirked, but undid the rest of his armour without comment. Metal and leather plates piled up beside him. My jaw dropped as he pulled off his shirt—he was perfect. The scar I'd noticed before was crisscrossed by several others, highlighting his ridiculous muscles. I also didn't miss his rich body hair, and I couldn't wait to trace the narrow band on his stomach with my lips. As if sensing where my interest lingered, Orm kicked off his boots, and his trousers soon followed.

'Oh!' my stomach muscles involuntarily tightened at the sight of his cock jutting out, fully erect and standing at attention. 'You were definitely blessed with all ... that,' I chuckled. A confident masculine smile bloomed on his lips before he slowly turned around, presenting himself without shame. 'Gods, you are such a tease. Get into the water,' I commanded, but he shook his head.

'I can't. My lady is too overdressed,' he said, gaze sliding over my body, caressing me with his eyes.

'You were supposed to listen ...' I started, but he chuckled.

'I wouldn't presume to disobey my lady's order. However, I would be remiss not to seek my lover's pleasure over mine.' He stepped closer, gathering the laces of my kirtle.

'But ...' I said, placing my hand on his chest, but before I could continue, he kissed me again.

'I have waited so long, sweet Nivale; I just want to see you ... touch you ... taste you. Do you know how many nights I've spent touching myself, imagining this moment? Wondering how you would taste when I finally buried my head between your thighs? I burn for you, Ani, hotter than any dragon's fire. Please, let me have you.'

With each word, the laces of my kirtle loosened until the garment fell soundlessly to the ground and I stood there in only a thin chemise. Orm smirked, then grasped the garment by the collar and tore it from my body. My breasts fell free, and he inhaled sharply as he captured them in his large hands. I gasped when his lips descended to my nipple, sucking it into his mouth.

'Divine,' he growled. 'You are a fucking goddess.' Orm's lips locked around my nipple again, sucking hard while his tongue lashed over the sensitive bud. I moaned, legs buckling under me, unable to support my weight. Before I knew it, I was in Orm's arms as he carried me into the pool.

'Better?' he asked when we slipped into the water. My magic had made the pool as warm as a hot spring, and I sighed in contentment. I turned in Orm's embrace, a wicked gleam in my eye.

'No, but you can make it better, can't you?' I moaned again, feeling heat rising inside me, a dangerous mixture of magic and desire, craving his touch. 'I was supposed to be in charge. You are such a naughty man.'

Orm gathered my braid and moved it over my shoulder, lightly grazing my neck as he did before he bent, kissing the soft skin. 'Hmm, I can be much naughtier. What will it be, Nivale? Will you let me take care of you, or do I need to fight for the privilege?' Before he finished, I had straddled him, climbing his rugged body like the mountain he was.

'Fight. I pick fight.' I rocked over his cock, letting the tip of it graze my sex. Just enough to tease myself, as my magic, so close to the surface, sent sharp biting tingles over my skin. It was so eager to unite with Orm that it took little effort to manipulate the energy into raising some water to splash over his back.

I scratched his chest, feeling the pleasure building in me when he arched under my touch. The warm water and cold mountain breeze raised goosebumps on his skin, and I wanted to lose myself in him. I loved his body. His skin felt tough, a little coarse even, and when I leaned closer, my breasts rubbed over his torso. Soft black hair gently caressed them, creating an intense sensation that set my mind on fire. My hand instantly slid between us, trailing blindly until it locked onto his long, hard shaft.

He nipped my shoulder, growling as he did. 'Fight? This isn't fighting; it's pure *torture*. I'm trying to take it slow, but you are goading me into taking you like a stallion in heat.' He grasped my hand, removing it from his member.

'Not a stallion. A bear, my Ursus. I want to goad you. I want you to lose control and unleash the beast whose eyes burn with yellow fire. You are mine, Ormond Erenhart. Accept my bond,' I moaned, lowering myself onto him despite his hold. His cock pushed inside when I rocked, taking him in deeply.

'Annika ...' His hips thrusted to meet mine. 'The way you feel ... Gods, your magic ...' he grunted, giving in to me. I kept rocking my hips, taking him in deeper, letting him fill me completely. A shiver of delight forced my back to arch. Orm's hands squeezed my waist in his vicelike grip as he lifted me up, only to slam me back down.

'You want a beast, then you shall have it, I can't deny you ... *fuck, Nivale*. It's never felt so good,' he growled, moving me up and down his massive length. He devoured my breasts, sending a flood of arousal down my spine, and I felt a tidal wave of primordial magic rise within me.

There were no doubts in my heart. I was finally ready. 'Just like that, my Ursus.' My abdomen tightened with my approaching climax. 'I'm going ... the Anchoring Oath ... it will hurt a little.' I panted, unable to hold my magic any longer.

'Su Aetheram, vede aligname faleter.
Me tuor, la'coren datro, sa fallorn.' [1]

I recited the ancient spell before my pleasure crested, and the power within me responded, spearing into Orm's chest. He gasped, and I felt his surprise through our new connection. 'Fuck, that is so intense,' he said with another tortured gasp, but I knew it would pass as the pleasure of our lovemaking eclipsed everything else. I felt Orm's spirit fracture as the pain burst within my chest, my soul splitting under the onslaught of magic.

'I accept you as my Anchor. Your life is mine, and my life is yours. I ... I bind us.' I opened myself fully and felt wild aether flood into my soul like an icy blade thrust into my chest. The world disappeared in an explosion of white light until a roaring inferno appeared, holding back the staggering

---

1. *With aether aligned in this world and beyond. Forever united with our Anchoring bond.*

power—Vahin's fire, his unique bond protecting me from the wild magic of Orm's soul. My breath shuddered in my chest, and the icy wind swirled around me, transforming the water droplets into tiny shards of ice before his magic settled, sinking deep into my soul.

'Nivale,' Orm hissed, bringing me back to reality as I fell forward, leaning against his shoulder, our bodies pressed together. 'I can feel you inside ...' His voice trailed off, replaced by a low growl. Then, without warning, he lifted me up and flipped me over, pushing me against the pool's edge as he held my hips, thrusting into me from behind.

His inner beast was in control, and gods, I loved it. My scream was drowned by out the sound of the waterfall as pleasure mixed with pain. He took me roughly, with primal desire, and I relished every second of it. My magic swirled around us, taking him in and sealing our connection while Orm pounded into me over and over again, each thrust marked with wild madness. My magic caressed it, and Orm roared, 'You're mine!'

'Yes, *gods*, yes.' That was all I could manage as another earth-shattering climax approached. The mountainside trembled, cracks appearing in the granite, my power slipping from my control. I was panting hard, blinded by the steam that rose from the surrounding water.

For a moment, I felt his thoughts, the absolute euphoria of our joining, the pride at my courage, and the concern that he wouldn't be enough, that I'd been harmed under his protection. Most of all, though, I felt his love. He saw me in a way I'd never seen myself, a woman of beauty and courage, a warrior and a lover. I was the goddess he would happily give his life and heart for.

His soulmate.

That glimpse of his mind was my undoing. Tears filled my eyes as Orm's body stiffened. I felt him filling me so completely that I didn't know where my body ended and his began as he once again roared, his pleasure pulsing inside me. It took us several moments to catch our breaths, but as I stirred, Orm kissed me between my shoulders and chuckled.

'Gods, Nivale, I think I died a little. I could feel your emotions, and this ... I've been with women before, but never like this. I will worship you in this life and the next. I may know your geas, but you own my soul,' he murmured before gently withdrawing and turning me around.

A soft smile ghosted his lips when he gazed at my chest. 'Is that how you see me?' I looked down as he lowered me back into the water and settled me onto his lap. The dragon mark on my chest was now entwined with a longsword, its sharp, clean edges covered with frost and surrounded by mist. They were a striking contrast with my skin.

'Yes, it looks like it,' I chuckled, stretching lazily, satiated by our joining. I trailed my finger over Orm's skin, enjoying the heat of his body wrapped around me. I felt power pulsing like a steady beacon, no longer unstable but blazing brightly within me.

'I feel like I could break another keystone just by raising my eyebrow. You were so wild,' I said, and he smiled, looking down at me.

'Let's avoid breaking any more of those for the moment. You certainly broke another mountain, though. Will this be an everyday occurrence, or is it the unexpected result of the Anchoring Oath?' he said with amusement.

When I frowned, Orm held up his hands in surrender. 'I'm not complaining. I'm just asking in case we have to be more careful with where we make love.' I looked over his shoulder. A crack ran through the field of flowers, uncovering the hard granite bed of the mountain itself, and I grimaced with embarrassment.

'If I hear you boasting that you gave me earth-shattering pleasure, I will fry that pert arse of yours,' I said, and he threw his head back, laughing.

'Can I at least tell Alaric, or even better, show him?'

Orm looked so relaxed and happy that I had almost forgotten the troubles that had brought us together. He was mine. Together with Vahin, I felt him deeply in my soul; and the gratifying soreness between my legs reminded me of how deeply he'd been in me.

As Orm sat in silence for a moment, stroking my back, I could tell he wanted to revisit our previous conversation. He didn't last long. 'Now, where were we with our argument? Ah, yes, care to tell me why you were bashing heads in the tavern? I hope you weren't looking for a companion there. And why you didn't send a messenger to tell me about the latawce attack?' he asked, fingers dancing across my arm.

'I can barely handle you three. I don't need any more hairy, scaly, or pointy-eared trouble.'

'I'm not that hairy,' he said before pulling me even closer and kissing me behind my ear. I acquiesced.

'I just needed to release some tension, and those new idiots were bullying Ian, so I decided to teach them a lesson. I like Ian. He makes a mean mead and truly cares for those around him. He helped me after the attack, and I found out that he had sheltered several families in his tavern ... What happened to him? Do you know?'

'He's a rider who lost his dragon. We were in the Barren Lands scouting when spectrae attacked his unit. His dragon fell, and he was caught in the crossfire of another dragon's fire,' he explained. 'When our dragons die, we lose their protection. It took him a long time to heal, but he insisted on staying here.'

'I'm glad he stayed. I like him. He reminds me that no matter what scars you bear, you can still keep living.'

'Careful, I'm getting jealous.' Orm wiped the droplets of water trailing over my cheek before he sighed with resignation. 'I need to revise our defences. I can't believe they lured us out in order to attack the fortress. Ani ... our lives may become even more dangerous soon. We are going to rebel against the king; my brother is rallying the nobles to dethrone the senile bastard as we speak. Please be careful and don't let any strangers get within arm's length.'

Orm's words took me by surprise, especially since I could feel his anger rising with each sentence. I slipped my hand into his hair, trailing my fingers through the thick, black mess.

'I will, but please don't worry. We will live or we will die. Life is never certain, but I will fight for you, Ormond. For you, for the fortress, and for all the people of the Lost Ridge. Still, I have to tell you something. When the latawce attacked the town, the Lich King sent his projection through one of them. He promised to bring Tal and Arno back if I went to Katrass. He knew I was here and knew my weakness. I was never in danger of being killed; the latawce didn't even scratch me. He wants me alive.'

Orm's face paled, and he rose slowly, lifting me from the water. His hands drifted to my face, cupping my cheek as he gazed into my eyes. 'Alaric told me he's connected to that undead scum. What if his connection goes both ways? If he sent his minions for you, he must know about your abilities. Fuck, if that's what's happening, the situation just got even more complicated,' he murmured, half to himself.

Orm helped me dress before he pulled on his shirt and trousers. He didn't bother with the armour, simply tying everything to his breastplate before we walked to the edge of the basin. After mentally calling Vahin, he moved behind me, burying his face in my neck and inhaling deeply while I stared at the vast, open vista in front of me.

The translucent barrier rose high above the peaks in the distance. It shimmered in the sunlight, distorting the view on the other side. A smooth magical curtain that appeared gossamer thin, it was an impenetrable barrier for those of the Foul Order—everywhere along it, except for the one dark scar near a jagged peak where the Barrier looked torn. But as I peered closely at the Rift, I saw oily black tendrils spreading from the centre, weakening and widening the gap. The void seemed to absorb magic ... It was no longer a mere tear, but a wide-open gap for the monsters to use.

'Oh gods ...' I whispered as the realisation hit me. The Barrier was broken—truly broken—the terrors of the Barren Land able to pour out into our kingdom at any moment.

'Shit. Look at me, Ani,' Orm said, turning me around. 'Don't think about the Barrier right now. Together, we can handle anything. But first, let Vahin take us home before Ari curses us for worrying him too much.'

CHAPTER 33

ANNIKA

The last few days had been eventful, to say the least. Since I'd Anchored Ormond, my access to the aether had stabilised, but not in the way I'd expected. I could weave it as usual, but whenever I held the skeins of aether in my hands, I felt a wild exhilaration flow through my body. I couldn't help but remember that moment on the mountain as the magic washed through me. It took a little getting used to, and after Orm caught me blushing a few times, he teased me mercilessly.

I loved the change in his attitude, and it became a ray of happiness during an otherwise difficult time. That it was Alaric's darkening mood that made those days difficult hurt me more than I cared to admit. I tried to spend as much time as I could with him, but between exploring my burgeoning relationship with Orm and the time spent training with the soldiers, I often felt distant from my dark fae.

Today, Orm was chasing another group of Vel demons. I stayed in the garrison, working through the spectrae strategy with a group of riders before we headed to the Rift on patrol tomorrow. It was immensely thrilling to work through various flying patterns, theorising which would best lure more of the vampiric ghosts to within my reach. After a few hours doing that, however, I was glad I could escape to the library alone.

Blissful silence descended when I finally made it there and closed the door. It was empty; apart from Alaric and me, few people showed an interest in the dusty room. It was exactly what I needed in the moment.

I looked up at the high, vaulted ceilings, inhaling the scent of leather and paper that made me feel at home. The afternoon sun, filtered by large crystal windows, highlighted the dust dancing in the air, eliciting a sneeze as I walked towards the reading area in the centre of the room. Unlike the university, there were no rows of tables with uncomfortable chairs; instead, we had a few comfortable armchairs and a large sofa where one could lose one's self in reading without giving up feeling in their backside. I loved how thoughtful that was.

I picked up the book I'd been studying recently, a rare manuscript detailing the violent creations of foul magic. After a moment's consideration, however, I put it aside. I didn't need to learn how to deal with these monsters; I needed something else.

I knew somewhere there should be a *Treatise on Immortality*. I'd discovered it in the library catalogue by accident and had been searching for it for the last two weeks. It was written before the Necromancer's War by a half-crazed mage and almost immediately after was entered into the index of forbidden books. Nonetheless, as with everything, Varta Fortress had its secrets, and I'd discovered one of them.

Since learning we couldn't restore the Barrier and that it was only a matter of time until the Vel demons descended upon us en masse, I hadn't stopped trying to find a way of undoing the spell that sustained the Lich King. I had no delusions about my own abilities. I couldn't create complex glyphs or cast multi-layered spells, but if I could siphon off the aether that prolonged his existence, then maybe I could kill the immortal Lich.

It was a dangerous thought and one I didn't want to share with Orm until I knew I could do it. He'd had enough of disappointments and failed hopes already. 'Can I do something that insane?' I asked myself, sighing.

I stood in front of a bookshelf on my tiptoes, stretching out to reach a dissertation titled *The Noble Undead*. The name suggested its subject might be helpful, but the book was too high up, and I was feeling too lazy to look for the ladder. I cursed quietly when the shelf I used as a step creaked ominously and prayed to all the gods for the ancient wood to support my weight a little longer when a deep voice called out behind me.

'Can you do what, Nivale?'

'Shit!' I yelped. My foot slipped from the polished wood, flinging me backwards. In a panic, I flapped my arms like a clumsy chick trying to fly, but a pair of muscular arms caught me as if I weighed nothing. After I felt his lips briefly caress my neck, I was suddenly spun around and found myself looking up into Orm's amused gaze as he spoke again. 'I sincerely hope not what you just exclaimed. So what you are trying to do, Nivale?'

Kill our enemy? And probably die in the process, I thought, inhaling deeply to calm my pounding heart. Orm smelled like autumn. I couldn't describe it any other way; the scent of ash and spices reminded me of nights cuddling in front of the fire with a loved one. I hadn't seen him since yesterday, and I had missed falling asleep to the sound of his heartbeat. With a content sigh, I embraced him, breathing in his scent.

'I like autumn,' I said out of the blue, noticing the dark shadow of stubble softening the sharp angles of his face. Orm's brows drew together, and he slid his fingers into my hair, poking and probing my scalp under the braid. His touch was gentle but unexpected. It was my turn to frown.

'What are you doing?'

'I'm checking to see if you hit your head on your way down. Why are you climbing the shelves in the first place? You know we have a ladder here, yes?'

'I didn't hit my head, you idiot. Your scent. You smell like autumn fires from my childhood, that's all. I climbed the shelves because I was too lazy to get the ladder. I would've been fine if you hadn't scared me, so you can let me go now,' I answered, half laughing because I couldn't blame him for misunderstanding my words.

'I'm glad you aren't injured as I need to ask for your help. I know you're not a healer, but we have several badly injured people and I fear it's too much for Alaric.' He stroked my braid. Only then did I notice his hand shaking ever so slightly and his usually radiant smile missing.

'Who was injured? Tell me what happened!' I insisted, frowning when I noticed the soot smeared on his cheek. 'Never mind. Tell me on the way to the infirmary.' He nodded, taking my hand. As we left the library, I watched the relief flicker on his face before the emotionless mask slid into place.

'We had to go fight a family of rarógs that had built their nest near the border. Do you remember the forest fire right after the worm attacked us? That was the cause. To make matters worse, the pesky creatures don't perish in dragon fire, so we had to fight with sword and claw ... and it ended badly for a few riders.'

Suddenly, I felt a tightness in my chest and sped my steps. 'How many are injured? Does Ari already know, or do we need to fetch him from his workshop? I can enhance his spells, even the healing ones, but I can't do complex healing by myself. Gods, I should have gone with you. I could have frozen those bastards in the air.' I almost ran before Orm pulled me to his side.

'Breathe, Nivale. Alaric's already there, and I came for you as soon as we had finished carrying in the wounded. I know you're no healer, but I also know you'd rip my head off if I kept you in the dark about this. Just please try to not overexert yourself. I need you on the patrol tomorrow. The unit stationed near the Rift sighted several spectrae.'

I whirled around sharply. 'Did you even consider it? Not telling me?'

'No, but as commander, I have to weigh every option. Alaric and the healers can help the wounded, but only you can deal with the spectrae. I need you combat-ready tomorrow if I don't want any more wounded. Ani, I'm sorry, but I have to ask: can you use your conduit powers safely? The situation is ... We're no longer able to keep the monsters back. Three other villages were attacked and decimated so completely that there was no one left to ask for help. It's almost a full-scale invasion. I sent letters to my brother and our allies, but until he's dealt with the king, we are on our own.'

'Yes, I can use my abilities. It would be even better if I could Anchor Alaric, but he's been avoiding me lately. If I could boost his foul magic, we could tap into the very source of the Vel.' I bit my lip, looking for signs of anger on Orm's face as we walked. 'I wish he'd open up to me.'

'He loves you, and I think he needs you now more than ever, but with the Lich King tied to his curse, I think he considers it too dangerous to Anchor you now,' he said, not looking at me, though I felt his hand briefly tightening on mine.

'Did you say something to him?' I was baffled by Orm's admission but relieved when he shook his head.

'My feelings won't change just because he loves you. When I first realised you were my soulmate, I was angry and possessive, but Vahin made me realise something: for him, you are his *Little Flame* who brought light to the fog that enveloped his mind. For me, you are my *Nivale* who gave meaning to a life that had become a never-ending battle. And for Ari? I think you may well be his salvation.'

Orm lifted me over a small stone wall as we took a shortcut through the rocky castle garden and briefly held me in his arms. 'He's been my friend for so many years. How could I refuse him the chance to be as happy with you as I am? There are things that prevent him from being your Anchor right now, but I'm not one of them, I promise.'

'Well, whatever his obstacles are, I will conquer them one after another, and once I'm done with the healers, I'm moving some clothes to your bedroom. No, scrap that. I'm moving in. I'm done sleeping alone, and this is your first and last chance to object. Just be ready—because Agnes, Katja, and Bryna will be strolling through your man cave, and most of the time, they don't even bother to knock.' His answering smile took my breath away.

'I would suffer greater torment to have you by my side,' he beamed.

We walked to the infirmary in comfortable silence after that. Orm still held my hand as we descended the many stairs to the encampment next to the landing field, and I shook my head, trying to hide my smile.

As always, my protective warrior ensured I was safe on the slippery, weathered steps. I wasn't sure if he realised how expressive he had become after we bonded. Even now, his thumb stroked the soft, sensitive part of my inner wrist, almost as if he wanted to comfort me or reassure himself that I hadn't changed my mind.

'You know I can fight monsters and even destroy half a mountain,' I commented when he lifted me up over another puddle of water.

'And what prompted that remark?' he asked without looking at me, focused on navigating through the small crowd of men gathered near the infirmary.

'I know that in your experience, every time I cast a spell I almost drop dead or fall on my arse if I try to grab a book, but I'm actually quite sturdy.' He stopped, turning towards me to study my face.

'Too much?' he asked with a sigh, and I nodded.

'A bit,' I said with a laugh, and he shrugged.

'I can't help it. I still can't believe my luck, but if it's too much, I'll stop,' he said it with such sad puppy dog eyes that I couldn't help but give in a little.

'It's fine as long as you remember it's for our pleasure, *not* because I need a knight in shining armour to fight my battles.'

'What a shame. I look *so* good in plate armour,' he said with a mischievous smile, but at my menacing frown, he continued. 'No, I promise, I promise. Please don't hex me.'

'Gods, you are impossible,' I sighed, chuckling slightly. 'You won't regret it.'

'Yes, I will. You like solving problems too much to stay away from trouble, but I know if I refuse, you'll just conspire with Vahin to do whatever you wanted anyway.'

'I would do no such thing!' I protested, trying to look offended, and he snorted a brief laugh.

'Oh, you would, but that's exactly what I love about you.'

'And here I thought it was because of my irresistible charm,' I deadpanned, and we walked for another moment in comfortable silence before Orm halted, suddenly serious.

'Annika, please remember that I need you tomorrow,' he said before pointing to the door, and we both descended into the cool, soothing interior of Varta Fortress' healing house.

CHAPTER 34

ANNIKA

The scent of burnt flesh assaulted my senses as soon as we walked into the empty antechamber. It was bad. Orm had downplayed the situation so much that I couldn't help giving him some very serious side-eye.

At least he'd come to get me straight away. But our relaxed banter on the way here felt completely inappropriate now. I was so close to scolding him that I took a deep, calming breath, regretting it instantly. Now wasn't the time to indulge in anger. Not when the suffering of so many threatened to overwhelm my senses.

The place was cold, with unglazed windows meant to reduce the stifling smell of open wounds. Unfortunately, that also made the wounded soldiers' moans sound eerily frightening. I knew one raróg could be challenging to deal with, but an entire nest? Those fire demons might be as beautiful as falcons, but being the size of a horse with flames issuing from their beaks, claws, and wings, they were more deadly than any bird of prey.

'Vahin, how are the other dragons? Should I send some healers there? Please tell me they are all right ... Vahin, answer me, you overgrown—If you don't answer, I will come to your lair and beat the answer out of your scaly arse right now!'

My thoughts were frantic and worried as it suddenly occurred to me that if riders were here, their dragons might also need help. I started freaking out when Vahin didn't respond immediately.

'They are fine, Little Flame. Some are a little battered, but we heal fast, and mostly, all we need now is to hunt and feed. You almost knocked me out of the sky, blasting me with your worry. Help your fellow humans and don't worry about me or any other "scaly arses." We have ways to heal our injured brethren,' came the amused thought. I inhaled deeply, thankful I could focus on the problems here.

The first issue was breathing. The further inside I walked, the stronger the stench grew. We stopped by a large oak door, and Orm opened it with one hard push. A few men and women in undyed linen aprons turned to stare as we entered but soon dismissed us, returning to their duties. I couldn't see anyone in green healer robes. That could only mean that they were elsewhere with the injured soldiers in their care.

I could smell the herbal paste often used by healers to prevent wounds from rotting, but this one had the distinctive smell that only Katija could achieve. Yet I failed to see the herbalist anywhere.

When my gaze swept to the furthest corner, I saw a man, marked by death, his eyes glazed by poppy tincture and body charred beyond recognition. 'Why didn't you tell me it was this bad?' I asked quietly. 'Orm, you need every pair of hands you can get.'

'I came to find you the moment I'd left the last man on a bed. I couldn't come earlier, Ani. I led these men, and it was my responsibility to get them help first. I failed and—' I turned, glaring at him, too exasperated to hold back.

'You didn't fail them,' I hissed. Orm's confession made me realise how broken he felt bringing back so many wounded soldiers. 'Go to the quartermaster and ask them for all their clean linen and healing paste. Find Katja. If she is not in the garrison, send her here to help with the wounded, then rest—and no, don't argue.'

'I sent the healers to the garrison, but not your friend. I will find her and bring her here.' His voice was uncertain, I took pity on him.

'Katja probably went with them, so leave her be,' I said, shaking my head when he opened his mouth. 'What did I say? Don't argue with me, not right now. Just do as I ask, please.'

'If you're sure you don't need me ... Is there anything else before I go? Fuck, I feel so useless.'

'Orm, we'll take care of your men. Just ensure we have the supplies we need,' I replied, and he walked away. For a moment, I observed his large back and slumped shoulders disappearing into the corridor's darkness before a cry for help woke me from my stupor.

I looked over the beds and noticed Alaric bent over the one in the far corner. He hadn't noticed our arrival, as his concentration was focused on a healing spell. I could see the aether move through the sigil as green light surrounded both him and his patient. I couldn't see the victim, but the silence was not a good sign, so I hurried over. 'Ari? How can I help?' I placed my hand on Alaric's shoulder, and he looked at me like a person awoken from a deep trance.

'The damage is too extensive, and my reserves are nearly depleted. He needs someone with plenty of power to maintain the high magic of the healing arcana sigil. That's the only thing that can heal him now. I barely have any aether left, and I can't sustain it.' The pain etched in his features mirrored that on the soldier's face.

'The only way I could do it is by using foul magic and a blood offering, and that doesn't work well with humans,' he explained, more to himself, and I knew he was using my presence as a sounding board.

Instead of working on his idea, I threw my solution into the pot. 'Or ... you could use me. I'm a conduit, remember?' His pupils widened, and he shook my hand off his back. 'You would have to Anchor me to do that, and I can't allow it,' he said sharply, but I raised my eyebrow.

'Ari, when I arrived here, we practised the tethering glyph. Draw it on my palm and let me touch you. You can channel my magic using it, and I will simply be a source of energy; I can be just that, a tool in your hands. That's why conduit mages are so valuable ... We are, in essence, a source of power.' I smiled when he looked at me with confusion.

'I hadn't thought about that, the fire when you Anchored Vahin ...'

'That was Anchoring. I was the channeler while he was the source. We'll do the opposite. I will be *your* source, and all you have to do is accept my help, create the bloody glyph, and let me touch you. You didn't have a problem with that before. You wanted my touch. What changed? It feels like you're rejecting me.'

Alaric's face went pale. I'd clearly struck a nerve, but my dark fae regained his composure without answering the question. 'Fine, but I will have to use my blood.' When I nodded, he pierced his forearm with a dagger and used its tip to draw a complex glyph on my hand. I watched the red runes disappear, almost as if my skin were a sponge absorbing the spell.

'My turn. All I need is your bare skin to place my hand on, so try to relax ... if you can.' I was still talking when Alaric reached up and untied his shirt, stripping it off his shoulders without a moment's hesitation. My breath caught at the sight, my fingers trembling as they made contact with his bare, muscled chest. I watched Alaric trace an incredibly complicated set of sigils over his patient, so fascinated that I forgot where my hand rested.

'I'm ready.'

That was the only warning I received before he started chanting a cantrip. I felt the pull of his magic and opened myself to it. Being a simple conduit for power was easy. It was so easy, in fact, that the skill could be used against my will if there was a mage strong enough to force the connection.

This time, however, I was willing. The sensation, the feeling of warmth that came with the aether flowing from my body into Alaric's, gave me an immense sense of satisfaction. I couldn't really heal others myself, but at least I was able to support a man who could.

As I had nothing else to do but stand there, letting him siphon my aether while Orm's and Vahin's Anchors stabilised the flow, I focused on the healing process. It was never too late to learn, and with all of the recent attacks, I hoped to pick up a skill or two.

The world around me was suddenly made from shades of grey as my eyesight adjusted to the aetheric realm. Alaric's sigils were exquisite. The visible parts were so complex that I didn't even know where they started, nor did I recognise the patterns.

What I saw when I opened my mind to the veiled world of the aether took my breath away with its beauty. Even Arno, skilled as he had been, couldn't have created as intricate a design as the one coating the burnt man's body in otherworldly light.

Alaric kept chanting a spell in his native language. I joined in, repeating the words I remembered, adding my will and power to the healing spell that glowed green over the patient. I saw the aether entering his body, filling every corner and lighting it from within, mending the charred skin and muscles shredded by a raróg's claws.

What Alaric did was nothing short of miraculous, and I knew it must have cost him dearly because he was taking energy from me faster than I expected. I closed my eyes, feeling the life force of every living being in the room, then further still until the entire building lit up in my mind like a summer bonfire. I siphoned energy from the surrounding area, careful to avoid burdening the injured.

When the pull stopped, I exhaled slowly. Alaric's hand was on mine, holding it to his chest. His muscles tensed when I tried to pull away, but he let me go and looked at me with a yearning that took my breath away. 'That was incredible. I felt ... you hide an addictive power, Ani. I understand even less why they let you walk away from the university and the king's service.'

'They didn't. I had to fake my death to break free, but even then they kept my geas.'

I looked at the patient. He was still injured, but he was no longer at death's door. His breath was now even, and I could see freshly closed scars instead of open, weeping wounds. Alaric turned his head, and I saw the amusement on his features as he said, 'I sometimes forget how resourceful you can be.' I shrugged, then changed the subject.

'Your skill is impressive. I don't think I've seen someone so well-versed in high magic ... What you did to his body, it feels like you could raise the dead without necromancy.'

'That's what a couple of centuries of practice will do. I cannot heal the dead, though. I could raise a soulless corpse with the foul magic in my blood, but I'm unwilling to pay the price for such an act.' The darkness in Alaric's gaze as he looked at me was shocking, but it disappeared as he continued, gesturing to the next cot. 'Are you ready to continue, or do you need a rest?'

Before I could answer, the door to the chamber burst open, revealing Katja and, to my surprise, Bryna. 'Gods, it stinks worse in here than the garrison's forge after the apprentice poured molten metal on his leg,' Bryna commented, wrinkling her nose before Katja elbowed her.

'You insisted on coming here, so shut your gob and help. We need fresh water and lots of it. Grab your soldier friends and make yourself busy,' Katja ordered, and the half-orc rolled her eyes.

'Fine, and good to see you again, Ani. Better late than never. These men need you more than the commander needs you in his bed,' she remarked, heading back to get some water. I looked at both women, baffled as to why the blacksmith was there.

'Bryna's helping the healers?' I looked at Ari as he ushered me to another cot.

'She came after the first victims arrived. Quite a few women volunteered to look after the wounded. Bryna decided that since she was the garrison's favourite blacksmith, she'd also be the soldiers' lucky charm—an unusually tall lucky charm ... with a hefty hammer,' he said with a smirk.

I turned towards Katija, giving her a tentative smile before speaking. 'Yes, that's our Bryn. I'm sorry that I didn't come earlier. When everything settles down, I need some female company to help deal with the recent overload of males. Lately, circumstances have been, well, *difficult*.' Katja rolled her eyes at my attempt at explaining.

'Yes, I know about your circumstances, all three of them. News spreads like wildfire here, and I'm telling you, this place is even worse when it comes to gossiping than our town square during market day. Let's help these patients, and you can share all the details later.'

I chuckled, watching Katija take over the care of those with minor burns, leaving the severe injuries to be magically healed.

After finishing up with a second patient, Ari and I found a good rhythm, and I even managed to repeat a few words of Ari's incantation without prompting. Not that I knew their meaning. But I repeated them anyway, trying to learn from the more experienced mage. We moved from one patient to another, repeating the process until all that was left were the soldiers whom Katija and the other volunteers had already patched up.

I washed my hands and walked out to sit in the fresh air. I hadn't noticed the passage of time, but the day had turned into evening. As soon as I sat down, the tiredness that always came with using my conduit skills hit me with a vengeance, and I felt my eyes closing.

I was half asleep when Ari walked out and sat next to me. He was quiet for a moment before embracing me and pulling me close. After an entire day of fighting death and pain, sharing the aether with a man whose skin felt like exotic silk made me feel close to him, and I welcomed his touch. With a deep sigh, I lay my head on his shoulder. It felt so right.

I could see several dragon riders mingling with the females next to the small lake while fae lanterns awakened to life in the falling dusk. 'I missed you,' I whispered, and he leaned over to kiss my forehead. 'I know, sweetheart, I'm sorry.'

Every now and again, a dragon descended to the landing field before heading for the caverns to rest. Crickets and owls filled the evening with their soothing melody, and even exhausted to the bone, I felt calm and at peace.

Home.

The thought made me smile, and I observed the citizens of the fortress wrapping up their tasks before they went to rest. Every one of them was unaware of my thoughts and the silent promise I had made to protect this beautiful, secluded place with everything that I had.

'We worked so well together,' I whispered, feeling the slow, languid stroke of Ari's fingers on my back. Alaric felt different, and I missed his mischievous smile and endless teasing. Still, he was here beside me and I cuddled to his side, enjoying the moment for as long as it lasted. Eventually, his soothing touch made me yawn and relax into him. I should have gone to bed, but I didn't have the energy even to keep my eyes open.

'You're tired, Domina. Let me look after you,' he whispered, almost too quiet to hear, but I was definitely too sleepy to understand. Lifting me gently, Alaric laid my head on his chest.

'I can walk,' I argued weakly.

'I know,' Ari answered, but didn't put me down.

He carried me to the castle, and I simply closed my eyes, my face resting next to the symbols of his curse. Ari's shirt was still open, hanging off his shoulders, and I touched the unblemished skin above the marks. Even though I was exhausted, my magic still responded to him.

I chuckled, brushing my lips over the figures, and Ari inhaled sharply.

'Annika, please,' he murmured, pressing me harder to him. His voice was so strained, and I could see he was fighting temptation.

How my life has changed, I thought, remembering how vehemently I had denied the idea of having another Anchor, and now I was contemplating seducing a dark fae to complete my bond. *Complete.* That word summed it up perfectly. I needed each of them for different reasons, but together, we felt complete.

With my mind on a flight of fancy, I smiled.

This is going to get complicated. I wonder how we'll make it work.

A vision of the three of them surrounding me as I twirled in happiness filled my thoughts. It would work; I knew it would. As the vision darkened and faded away, I felt myself slipping into slumber. I tightened my grip on Ari's neck and let my thoughts drift away, safe in the embrace of a cursed necromancer.

CHAPTER 35

ANNIKA

I *ndolence.*

I rolled the word over my tongue with a smile as I stretched, feeling a shiver run down my spine. The luxuriously soft sheets caressed my skin as I slowly opened my eyes, only to frown at the unfamiliar surroundings; I couldn't see much, with only a sliver of daylight escaping the heavy drapes over the windows. For a moment, I thought it must still be night, but it didn't take long to realise it was the sombre décor of the room that darkened it.

Above my head, the ceiling was painted with a mural depicting a scene from what must be the artist's idea of the underworld—a desolate landscape with monsters dominating the scene, their eyes replaced with gemstones that gave them an eerie semblance of life. When I turned my head to the side, I noticed black and silver curtains on the bed. They were luxurious but surprisingly lifeless, and the posts they framed were carved into strangely contorted female forms.

'Vel be damned, the owner of this room must have a lot of nightmares sleeping here,' I said, sitting up to lean on my elbows. In response to my outburst, a shadow rose from one of the chairs, and I instinctively reached for the aether, muttering a spell that formed a shield in front of me.

'There is no need for that, Ani,' Alaric said, stepping forward. 'And yes, I have nightmares, but not because of the décor,' he added, approaching the window to pull the curtains open.

At the sudden influx of light, I winced, closing my eyes, but not before noticing that Ari was almost naked, with only a pair of loose silken trousers riding low on his hips. At that, I opened my eyes slightly, shamelessly wanting to admire the view. His long white hair, unbound and flowing freely to the middle of his back, captured my attention, and I bit my lip in appreciation.

'What happened?' I asked, trying to distract myself from looking at him like he was an oasis in the middle of a desert. 'Did you bring me here?'

I vaguely remembered Ari picking me up at one point; I must have fallen asleep after helping in the infirmary. I lifted the covers, noticing I was in a similar state of undress, with only a white chemise covering my otherwise exposed body.

'You were so deeply asleep you didn't even stir as I carried you to the castle. My magic was so depleted that I was defenceless. I selfishly wanted to keep you close—just this once—and laid you to sleep here in my room. I asked Agnes to undress you. I promise nothing else happened,' he said, noticing my concerned frown.

'Come to bed. It is still early.' I patted the bedding. Alaric's resolve was crumbling if he'd admitted me into his sanctuary. He didn't even allow servants here. It was my turn to grasp the opportunity to be close to him.

'Annika, I can't. There are things you need to know.'

He seemed so distant that I reached out my hand, hoping he would take it. 'Then tell me. The man who takes the time to make me smile, tease me, and challenge me? I want him back. The world is falling apart around us, and I'm afraid and uncertain, but there is one thing that I am certain of. I want you.'

As the last word left my lips, Alaric moved. With inhuman speed, he captured my hands, pinning them above my head and caging me beneath his powerful body. 'You slept so peacefully, and I held back. I looked at you, wanting you, knowing I could never deserve you. I've done so many questionable things. I forced Orm to use your geas and forbade him from telling you. I wanted to use you as a weapon. To Anchor you and gain the power to destroy the Lich King. There was never any hope of repairing the keystone. I lied to Orm, and I lied to you,' he rasped.

'The man you are talking about ... doesn't exist. I did all of that to make you trust me, to make you want to bond with me. I knew it was wrong, and I still did it. All to rid myself of my damn curse. Then you stood up to me, refusing to bend to my will. You defended me in front of the envoy. *Gods*, woman. You trusted me. You let me touch you, and your magic soothed my pain while your heart eased my torment. I'm a monster ...'

'Ari? Shut up and kiss me.'

He looked at me in shocked disbelief, his gaze lingering on my face as he tried to assess my true intentions. 'Didn't you hear a word I said? I'm a liar, an evil necromancer who will only cause you pain ...'

I couldn't bear the anguish in Ari's voice, so I silenced him with a tender kiss. His stunned expression lasted longer than I expected, but once he'd gathered his wits, my dark fae leaned into the kiss, testing my resolve. Moments later, my hands were free and clasped behind Ari's neck, pulling him closer.

As soon as we came up for breath, Alaric looked into my eyes, stroking a gentle finger across my lips. 'Why are you doing this?' he asked in whispered awe, his hands not once leaving my skin.

'Because despite the incredible strain you've been under, you have integrity. Whatever your plans were, you never went through with them. You stopped because of me, choosing to suffer through your curse rather than betray my trust. You may see a liar when you look in the mirror, but I see a tormented man who told me the truth, sacrificing himself in exchange. I don't need a pure heart. I need a man who would burn the world for me, and you, Alaric'va Shen'ra, are such a man. I claim you. You are mine.'

I scraped my nails over his marks. The guttural moan that Ari made sent shivers down my spine. His body shook with raw need, his touch growing more insistent, and when he kissed me this time, his tongue explored my mouth with a passion that I couldn't help responding to. I didn't care about the world anymore. I wanted this man, his bright mind, his magic. I craved it all, and my body reacted in the most primal way.

My hand trailed over the hard muscles of Ari's abdomen, threatening to disappear under the soft fabric of his trousers before he stopped me. 'Ani, I will do whatever you want, but I cannot Anchor you, not right now. You said you had to feel ready to accept me, but now I am the one who cannot accept you. *Hrae!* I want you so much, but I cannot do it.'

There was a finality in his words, but it couldn't disguise the desire in his voice. I knew he felt he didn't deserve me, but I refused to let his despair take this moment away from us.

'Ari, I understand. I would welcome you as my Anchor, but this isn't about magic. I can't let you wallow in the guilt of your deception so let me give you what you need. Redemption through the pain you enjoy so much. Will you accept the agony of my touch and be mine?'

He shuddered under my scrutiny. In some strange way, I understood him. Alaric was a good man, but deep inside, he was a broken soul overcome with a guilt that he felt he needed to atone for.

'I ... Yes,' he breathed. Despite his hesitation, I saw the flicker of something in his eyes and felt the press of the bulge in his trousers. He was aroused by the mere suggestion of my offer.

'Release me, Alaric.' As Ari took a breath, I could see the struggle he was under, but he fell back. My smile turned almost vicious as I followed, pushing him back until he fell, helplessly staring into my eyes. The hand I laid on my prey's chest was open and gentle, but as I maintained eye contact, my fingers curled. I pressed my nails into his flesh, drawing them down over the marks of his curse, scoring his flesh.

Ari cried out in response, and my lips moved, calling on magic. With a twist of my wrist, I released my power, forcing it into his body, and his outcry became a moan. I slid my other hand down a hairsbreadth above the delicious muscles of his abdomen, watching them tense and shiver as he strained for a single touch until I stopped over his cock.

Ari's back arched in desperate yearning, but I laughed and moved my hand away. 'Kneel,' I said, and his response was instant.

'Yes, Domina,' he breathed, and I gasped at hearing the dark fae term of endearment.

'Good, now you understand.' I bent forward to kiss him.

I teased Alaric with tenderness, feeling his reaction before releasing lightning from my fingertips. The flash as it arced to his body made him flinch, but I deepened the kiss to swallow his scream. Another gesture and the magic disappeared. I didn't stop there, though.

As Ari gasped in relief, my teeth bit down on his lip and blood flowed over my tongue. When his eyes flew open in surprise, I deepened the kiss and nicked my tongue on his fangs. It hurt, but when my blood mixed with Ari's and flowed over his tongue, I felt him almost melt in ecstasy. When I drew back to end the kiss, Alaric pushed forward, his magic blossoming and surrounding us, trying to keep me close.

The slap I delivered to his cheek rocked him backwards, and as he swayed, I grabbed his throat with uncompromising strength. The response was immediate, my dark fae lover freezing beneath my hand. I had no means of physically overpowering him; he was stronger and had proved to be a much better mage. Yet, at the very core of his existence, he was dark fae, and their men never disobeyed their domina. I was walking blindly into the role, but his voluntary surrender flooded me with arousal.

'What do you want, Alaric?' I asked, almost purring at the hunger I saw in his eyes.

'You, my Domina, I want to follow your every command and please you in any way I can.' His voice was so hoarse and filled with desire that I gestured for him to rise. He was fully erect and as beautiful as the gods themselves. With a gesture, my magic blew across his trousers and the material unravelled, falling to the ground. I grasped the base of his exposed cock and gave it a harsh tug.

'Like this?' I asked, already knowing the answer.

'Yes, my ... Harder ...' he stuttered into silence as I knelt down and took his length into my mouth, sucking so hard my cheeks hollowed. 'Dark Mother! Annika, please,' he cried as I continued to move my hand and mouth. He was mine, and I wouldn't let this end with such simple pleasure. I felt Alaric's fingers tangle in my hair, but after savouring the salty liquid gathering on the tip of his cock, I stopped.

'Ani!' My name was a guttural half-growled protest from a man at the end of his tether, and I chuckled, giving him one last lick with the tip of my tongue. 'I promised to make you suffer,' I purred with a wicked smile, and he grabbed the nearest bedpost, panting heavily and looking like a wounded animal.

'You are a cruel mistress, Annika. Beautiful, but cruel. Gods, you're fucking perfect.'

I teased my magic into wrapping around Ari without him noticing. Then I muttered a short cantrip and the aether solidified, turning into thorny vines that pierced his skin with thousands of tiny needles.

'Tell me all your secrets. If you want to taste me, to take a bite, you will tell me all the dark, vile thoughts you are harbouring.' I moved to the middle of the bed and slowly spread my legs, letting him see everything as he stood there powerless.

Alaric's eyes were pure crimson, his breath ragged as he struggled against the magical restraints. 'I want Orm to join us in bed. I want us all to be together. I want to feel him fucking me while I feast on your cunt.'

I gasped, surprised at Ari's confession, my mouth falling open at the image his words painted in my mind. I had been with two men before; Tal and Arno liked to share my affections, but they never touched each other intentionally. I wasn't sure if Orm would even agree, but as my power surged, almost Anchoring Alaric without me uttering the oath, I realised how much I'd love it.

Alaric noticed my surprise, and I caught his vulnerable expression before he looked away. I wanted to slap myself for making him doubt me. 'No?' he asked, refusing to look me in the eye, but I wiggled my finger at him, dropping the restraints.

'Yes, but only if Orm agrees.'

Ari stalked towards me until I stopped him with a push of my foot to his face. This time, however, it seemed my wily fae was done following my orders. He took my foot and planted a kiss on the ankle, then another and another, moving up and caressing my skin. I bit my lip before asking the question I needed the answer to.

'Was that the reason you pulled away? Because you wanted us both?'

'No. I stayed away because my mother's curse connects me to the Lich King. He speaks to my mind, and he wants you, Ani. I made a blood oath to not pursue Anchoring you until I'm free of him. He may kill me, but I will never give you to him.'

I gaped, my skin suddenly freezing under his touch. Alaric raised his head and looked me in the eye. He was so bitter, so resigned to his fate that he must have assumed that would be the last straw; that I would reject him.

My powerful, broken fae. Little did he know how much he meant to me.

The Lich King could fuck himself if he thought I'd let him have my necromancer.

'Now you know why I can't Anchor you. I won't subject you to his influence, his voice ...' Ari pulled away, but I stopped him.

'I understand, but this changes nothing for me. Come to me, my darkness. Show me how much you want to be mine.' I crooked a finger, leaning back. Alaric's eyes widened before he gulped and gave in to my siren's call.

He seemed to flow forward as his lips trailed over my calf and thigh, and as his lips parted, I felt the edge of his fangs tease my skin. I shivered and whimpered, then moaned as he kissed my sex. I slid my hands downward, but as Ari's tongue slid through my folds, my back arched, and I grasped the sheets instead.

'My sweet, cruel Domina. I've waited so long for those words,' he murmured, feasting on my body, and I fell back onto the pillows, giving my wicked lover free rein.

Ari's hands were gentle, and the cool touch of his fingers added to my excitement, especially when his thumb brushed over my pearl. I whimpered again and the sound seemed to please him because Alaric redoubled his efforts, enticing a stream of delightful responses until I felt my body tense in anticipation of the upcoming release. 'Stop,' I commanded as I fought for control of my body and the magic that so wanted to take him.

He did, but when Alaric looked at me, there was nothing gentle left in his gaze. Those burning, crimson eyes looked at me with the inhuman gaze of the elder races. He looked feral, and I gestured him closer. Ari glided forward with predatory intent, and I couldn't look away. As the soft caress of his silken hair brushed over my body, I reached up and captured Ari's lips, pulling him into my embrace. The press of his shaft to my entrance made my eyes flutter closed, and I couldn't help rubbing myself all over his cock.

'I need you,' he said through the clenched teeth.

'Then take what you need,' I challenged, using my nails to pull him closer, and he pushed forward, breaching my entrance.

The room became bathed in crimson light as Alaric's curse lit up, his teeth bared in a tortured grimace. I bit Ari's chest, feral in my need to protect my lover, as he drove his cock into me over and over again. Perspiration covered his body, his breathing uneven as he drove me wild with his harsh, punishing pace. My conduit magic wrapped itself around us, the aether dancing to my heartbeat as I felt my pleasure cresting.

'I love you,' he cried out, his body tensing in approaching climax.

'I forgive you,' I whispered.

I pushed my magic away before pleasure overwhelmed all thought. Alaric groaned and I felt his release filling me while I held him tight, floating on waves of bliss. He collapsed, his head resting on my chest while I stroked his silver skin.

'I can't accept it ... your forgiveness,' he said after a few moments, but I heard the hope in his voice. He craved pain because he thought he deserved nothing else, and I barely held back my tears, realising his spirit was even more broken than mine.

'You have to if you want my love, but that's the last time you hide something important from me. I believe it was fate and not your deception that brought us all together. You saved me from an empty life locked in grief. I love you, Ari. I love you, my beautiful fae.'

I embraced him, stroking the white strands of his hair. The man who had always held his head high and faced the world with a sardonic smile just buried his head in the crook of my neck, a silent sob shaking his body. He held me as if his life depended on it. And maybe, in a way, it did ... because I doubted even Orm knew the pain he kept inside. I held him for a while, and when he raised his head, I saw something that had been missing from his face for too long.

Hope.

'Rest a little longer,' he said, stroking my cheek with a smile. 'I will send someone with breakfast, and once you are ready, I would like you to come to Orm's office. He needs to know what's happened between us, and I want us to tell him about it together.'

My answering smile faltered when the door to Ari's quarters burst open. Alaric threw himself in front of me, shielding me from the sudden intrusion. Orm strode in, his face thunderous, only to stumble to a halt when he caught sight of me peeking out from behind Alaric's naked body.

'Ari, please leave us.' I looked at the dark fae calmly, and to my relief, he didn't argue.

'Call me if this overbearing idiot gets to be too annoying,' he said before grabbing a robe from the chair and, with an uncertain smile, walked towards the door. When he passed Orm, he bowed his head. 'With your permission, Commander.' There was too much sarcasm in his voice to take his words seriously.

As the door closed quietly behind Ari, Orm frowned before turning back to me. We stared at each other, and the silence weighed on my nerves so much that before I knew it, my temper exploded. 'If you stormed in here to give me a lecture or express your jealousy, think again because I won't take it kindly.'

'Did you Anchor him?' Orm asked, worry etched on his face. My face must have given away my confusion because his next words were not what I was expecting. 'Oh, you thought I was jealous? I told you—I've accepted your feelings for him, but I won't accept him putting you in harm's way.'

'I didn't. We made love, but he stopped me from going further.'

Orm's eyes opened so wide I nearly laughed. 'You stormed in here like a savage because you thought I Anchored him? Ari was worried it would expose me to the Lich King's influence. I agree with him. Besides, in the state he's in, his spirit would likely refuse anyway, and we both know how that would end, but you should have told me about his oath and ... what exactly did he swear?'

Orm sat down beside me. 'I was worried. I ... I felt your pleasure, only for a moment, but I knew you were with him. Ari swore he wouldn't pursue the Anchor bond as long as he's cursed. Nothing else, nothing permanent. It is just a precaution ... I made a fool of myself,' he said, taking my hand and looking at me with a strange expression. 'How was it ... with him?' he asked before shaking his head and grumbling under his breath. 'No, forget it. I shouldn't ask ...'

I place a hand on Orm's cheek, forcing him to look at me. 'It was amazing, but so different from what we have. Ari is a male of the dark fae. He likes me to be dominant, even a little cruel, and I never thought I would, but I like it, too.'

Orm gazed into my eyes for a long moment before his lips curled into a contented smile. 'I'm not giving you much chance to be dominant in bed, am I? Maybe it's good he can give you what I can't.'

I chuckled. 'No, you aren't, but I wouldn't have it any other way,' I said, embracing him. I wasn't happy about this blood oath, but I understood their reasons, and I admired Orm for adjusting to our ever-changing bond. 'Give me a moment, and I'll meet you down at the landing field.'

The Anchor bond flared to life as I kissed him, and I felt his emotions wrapping around me like a comforting blanket. Orm was confused and uncertain, but he wasn't jealous, and I couldn't help but smile, intending to show him just how much I appreciated his new attitude.

CHAPTER 36

ANNIKA

I rushed to the landing field only to find Ormond talking to Alaric. The riders greeted me with knowing smirks as I walked past and I gave them a confused look, wondering at their expressions, until both of my men turned around with smiles that could light up the entire valley.

'I told you she'd forget.' Alaric smirked at Orm and I blinked in surprise. 'Forget what?'

'A cloak. It may be warm down here, but up in the currents, you will be cold,' the dark fae said, wrapping a fur-lined coat around my shoulders. Orm turned to me.

'Are you ready, Ani? The reports say there is a large swarm of spectrae gathering near the Rift, and I had to recall the patrols because of it. I'm hoping the Lich King isn't using it to sneak more creatures out of the Barren Lands.'

I felt fingers of trepidation squeezing my heart—the last time I dealt with the spectrae, I'd almost died. Now I was heading straight for them, knowing exactly what we were about to face.

Alaric, the more sensitive of the two, must have noticed the change in my mood because he embraced me before kissing my forehead. 'I know you can do it, Domina. You have your Anchors and your magic. I'm already proud of you.' I took a deep breath before Orm pulled me out of Alaric's embrace and lifted me onto Vahin's back as he spoke to his friend.

'We need to go. Please ask Agnes to move Annika's belongings to my bedroom and prepare the castle for the king's envoys. We need to keep them ignorant of the upcoming rebellion, so make us look like the Crown's humble servants.'

I saw Alaric's expression darken.

'Why am I moving your things there?' He looked at me, but it was Orm who answered.

'Because Annika told me she wanted that and ... you are welcome to join us,' he said curtly. Alaric's throat bobbed while he looked back and forth between me and Orm. I smiled, reaching out from my space on Vahin's back.

'It would make me very happy.' We leapt into the air, leaving Alaric behind with a baffled expression, and as soon as we were beyond earshot, I asked, 'Are you sure?'

'No, I'm not, but we are heading into a war. I may lose men today, and I thought that if fate doomed me to die tomorrow, I wanted to make sure I at least tried to make us happy. I hope it will work, but I can't guarantee anything.'

'I don't want you doing something you aren't ready for,' I said, leaning back against him, and he sighed, kissing my cheek.

'I won't know if I'm ready until I try. All I ask for is a little understanding if things don't go as we hope.' I nodded, and we spent the rest of the flight discussing the formation patterns I'd worked on with his riders yesterday before we drifted into a comfortable silence.

I welcomed the change of scenery that riding Vahin brought. As I admired the mountain views and enjoyed the wind in my hair, Orm organised everyone into formation. We were closing in on the Barrier, and I could see the complex weave of its construction, including the strange purple lightning intended to prevent foul magic from crossing. However, the normally opalescent and semitranslucent curtain was so dull that even if it was still working, there was no doubt its magic was fading faster than any of us were willing to admit.

I'd never been so close to the Barrier and seeing the ancient creation of the archimages, even in such a state, was awe-inspiring. My gaze drifted to the wound in the fabric of the Barrier; the rift I'd created by collapsing the mountainside onto the wlok had so clearly sped up the deterioration of the spell. Then I noticed a golden dragon flying towards us—and I didn't like his rider's grim expression.

'Sir, we need to abort this patrol. The swarm has doubled in size since yesterday and more are coming in from the other side of the Barrier. Two of our dragons barely escaped trying to assess their numbers.'

'Doubled?' Orm's body tensed behind me, and I felt him tilt his head as he planned a new strategy. 'Did any of the swarm try to move further towards civilisation?'

'Yes, a few, but their drift patterns suggest they are waiting for more to arrive. The area they cover has already widened, and the Rift is essentially inaccessible, but we burned the few strays that headed towards the villages.'

'We may need to break up the swarm and tackle them in smaller groups.'

'Orm, you can't break up the swarm unless you sacrifice dragons,' I said, and he nodded behind me. 'I know, but I can't let the spectrae move deeper into the kingdom. People in the villages have no protection and no weapons to fight the greater Vella. Fuck, I'd hoped I wouldn't lose men today.'

He shook his head, and I remembered how distraught he was after the rarógs' attack. 'I think it is time to see if I'm as good as you think I am.' I said it with a bravado I didn't feel and I was proud that my voice didn't wobble. Inside, I was terrified, but it wasn't the time to show it.

'Whatever happens, Little Flame, we will get through it together, and I will help you with my fire.'

'I'm scared, Vahin. Last time I didn't care. I was ready to die. But now I'm not and if I can't control it ... if I lose my grasp on the aether ...' I shivered before

a wave of calm washed over me. *'Stop calming me, you big dolt. I have to learn how to handle this,'* I told him, but Vahin didn't listen.

'You need clear thoughts, unmuddied by fear. I can help in more ways than just safekeeping a shard of your soul. Trust me to keep you safe and help kill those abominations.'

'Ani, what are your thoughts? If you have a plan, I will follow it.' Orm's voice broke through my conversation with Vahin, and I noticed several riders circling around us, creating a perimeter. Vahin turned towards me, the unblinking stare of his vertical pupils leaving me slightly concerned.

'We can deal with it, Little Flame. Be careful using my fire; protect my flight mates, but don't leave yourself vulnerable.' I nodded, removing my gloves and placing my hand on his scales. 'The plans stay unchanged. Vahin agreed to take the risk, and I ... I can handle this.'

'Alright, you heard our mage. Move into formation,' Orm bellowed. Vahin added a strange, modulating roar that made the other dragons turn towards him. It was as if a silent conversation passed between them, but I didn't have time to ask him about it.

I could feel the potential of the dragon's fire coiling inside him; Vahin's flame formed when liquids from two special sacs inside his body mixed and were expelled from his mouth, exposure to the air igniting them to create an intense blaze. I didn't need to access the physical part of it; that potential—the primal core of the dragon's soul—was a deep well of magic, and that is what I connected to. I felt my hands on Vahin's scales warm up once the link was established.

It didn't take me long to whisper an incantation meant to reduce the toll the flow of the primaeval aether put on my body ... in theory. If it worked, the amount of energy I could safely access would increase; unfortunately, the spell had been abandoned centuries ago after only two conduit mages had survived its use. The only restriction to the limitless spells a conduit could cast was the finite endurance of the human body; and if the spell failed, I wouldn't be the first conduit that had burned in the flames of raw aether. I'd never intended to use it; I had studied it after I found it in Varta's library simply because it caught my interest, but I didn't have a choice now.

Cold sweat pooled in the small of my back and I hoped Orm wouldn't notice how my hands trembled on Vahin's neck. I couldn't let Orm's feelings for me impact his decisions as commander.

Once I felt the link stabilise, I turned to him with the bravest smile I could muster.

'I'm ready. Signal the riders and ask them to distract the spectrae. I need to get closer before they attack,' I directed, surprised at the budding excitement for the upcoming battle beneath my terror. If I was ever to take on the Lich King, I needed to test my limits.

Vahin glided along the Barrier, heading towards the Rift while the rest of the squad followed, keeping their distance. We hovered close enough to see the tendrils of corruption spreading from the edges, draining the rest of the Barrier. The land below was desolate, with dry husks of diseased trees marking the terrain where a once lush forest had covered it.

'Hold formation,' Orm commanded as he turned Vahin away from the Barrier.

Moments later, we observed the tail end of the swarming spectrae as it moved towards the Lost Ridge. I couldn't help but look at the damage I'd caused all those years ago as we waited; its eerie darkness was mesmerising. The gap itself looked strange for another reason, though. It appeared almost alive, changing shape, twisting and narrowing as I stared. There was so much purple lightning here that I was sure it was the only reason we didn't have more Vel demons breaking through.

I concentrated on my magic. I closed my eyes and inhaled slowly, then reached for the energy of the aether, letting it fill me. As we closed in on the swarm, it changed direction, heading for the dragons. Orm's arm tightened around my waist, and I realised how tense he was.

Vahin, are you afraid? I asked the dragon in my thoughts. I didn't want to say it out loud, and the massive dragon rumbled in response. *'No. I don't like the pain, but I know you will protect us. I will endure for the pleasure of seeing the swarm burn under your touch.'* His steadfast faith in me helped strengthen my resolve.

I watched the dragons swooping past dangerously close to the swarm, distracting the demons, but the bulk were still heading for Vahin. He was so calm even as the first tendrils shot forth and hooked into his chest. I felt his pain and wanted to lash out and destroy the parasitic leech, but we had to wait. In a moment of inspiration, I diverted the primal power from my surroundings and into the dragon.

'Little Flame, you don't need to ... that feeling ... I've never felt so drained yet so powerful. That is an interesting sensation, almost as if I'd been struck by lightning.'

Helping Vahin as I prepared my attack put a strain on my body, but without my support, the sheer numbers of spectrae draining him would send us crashing to the ground long before I could destroy them. My breathing grew laboured, and I leaned down, plastering myself to the dragon's neck while Orm directed his riders.

'Annika, stop. Your body can't withstand such a torrent of magic,' Vahin said, distressed and filled with pain. 'I can't let them harm you,' I replied. My voice was so hoarse I barely recognised it myself. 'Orm, tell the riders to disperse.'

Orm's body radiated such tension that he felt like a coiled spring ready to explode. He didn't discuss my order; he simply gestured to the riders, and they flew in the opposite direction, leaving only us on Vahin's back. The unsated ghost vampires instantly flocked towards the aether-fuelled dragon, latching greedily onto his core.

'Little Flame?' I heard the tone of desperation in my dragon's words, and we dropped several metres as he struggled to keep us in the air, but almost

all of the spectrae had regained corporeal form. I sank deep into both of my Anchor bonds.

Vahin and Orm gasped when I dropped all restraint, fully opening myself to the raging aether. It shimmered over my skin like a desert mirage, and they felt it. This impossible power, able to create or destroy, was mine to wield, and I shaped it into coils of dragon fire, directing the flames with a soft-spoken command.

'Išātum.'

Magic erupted from me, rushing through the spectrae's tendrils, setting the greater Vella demons ablaze as they screeched, falling away like burning cinders. They couldn't escape. The tactics we'd spent hours perfecting were put into practice as the riders returned and fought the stray spectrae with a fury that set the sky ablaze. When the burning demons drifted too close, almost colliding with Vahin, I instinctively latched onto the aetheric fire and thrust it at them, turning the screeching ghosts into smoking ruin.

Gods! That was far too easy.

With Vahin's fire and Orm's ironclad control, manipulating the aether felt like child's play. I'd never felt so elated and so frightened at the same time. The power I controlled felt absolute.

Could I kill the Lich King with dragon fire?

I looked at my glowing hands on Vahin's scales. I'd felt a pain in my chest for some time but had ignored it; now, it blossomed like a firebird, and my heart stuttered. The human body was not built to withstand the power of creation, but if I could hold on for a little longer ... if I could do it, Alaric would be free and my people would be safe.

I just need more time, more power ... I could do it, I thought.

'No, Little Flame, close the gates! Disconnect from the aether before it changes you—do it now, Annika! Do it before it destroys you,' I heard Vahin's thoughts, his soul pulling away, taking the fire with him.

I can do it. The aether ... if I can take a little more, it will be enough to kill the immortal bastard; it must *be enough.* I was losing myself in the power of creation, but the thought of saving my Ari, of freeing Orm from the burden of fighting any longer, kept me pushing past the pain. I barely heard my dragon's voice before an ear-splitting roar shook the skies.

'Ormond, stop her!' Vahin shouted. I felt a hand on my cheek, turning my face away from the Barrier, and I looked into the deep emerald eyes I knew so well. Eyes that had recently been filled with the dancing yellow flames of wild magic. Calm and ironclad control filled the bond, helping me to see I'd drifted too far and letting me emerge from the addictive pull of the aether.

'There you are, Nivale. Come back to me, I can feel how hard it is, but you are the strongest woman I know,' he muttered, stroking my face. The tether to his soul pulled at my core, demanding attention, and slowly, I closed myself to the immense power.

I vaguely noted several riders cheering, their dragons roaring in triumph. A few more spectrae came from behind the Barrier, but the dragons hunted them down and I was astonished to find that my intervention had turned the deadly experience into a playful game. From the distance, it almost seemed as if the dragons and their riders were frolicking in the air.

'Never scare me like that again,' Orm whispered in my ear before kissing the bare skin on the back of my neck. 'You saved a lot of good men today, but we need to work on your control. There will be more spectrae for you to battle, more monsters to kill. You can't burn yourself out like this each time,' he added, and I turned my eyes back to the Rift.

'Can we fly there?' I asked, pointing to the ugly scar in the Barrier. It didn't matter that I was exhausted; while I was immersed in the raw aether, I had felt the wrongness radiating from the place and knew I had to check it out.

Orm nodded, 'If you wish. Tomma can deal with the rest here. We should see what the spectrae were guarding so fiercely.'

Vahin grunted in agreement, and soon we were gliding down towards the Rift. The closer we got, the worse it looked. I hadn't returned since Tal and Arno's untimely demise, and even feeling Orm's embrace, I couldn't shake off the deep, aching sadness.

'I'd like to land, please,' I said, but Orm objected. 'We're too close to the Rift. The foul magic has made the soil unstable, so landing will be dangerous; besides, you are tired. If you want a ground expedition, we can come back another time.' I huffed with frustration.

'Please, I need this,' I insisted. Orm finally nodded, his eyes stormy.

'Fine. Vahin, find a place to land. You, my insistent rebel, stay by my side. I haven't been on the ground here for weeks and don't know what dangers await us.'

'So you'd better stay close to me,' I ribbed, preparing a shielding spell glyph.

As soon as we'd dismounted, I set off to investigate. The dirt was loose and felt like the sand dunes near the sea. We trudged towards the chasm, and I was glad that instead of a dress I was wearing riding leathers as my boots kept sinking into the ground.

Just as I'd noticed earlier, the place was devoid of life; only rough dirt and mountain rocks with scattered, gnarled remains of dead vegetation surrounded us. The closer to the crevasse we were, the more I felt the pressure of condensed aether on my body. Finally, it grew so oppressive that I stopped and turned towards Orm.

'Something is terribly wrong here. This place feels like a void ... and it's filled with foul magic. I just—I can't identify the source.' I whispered a revealing spell. The area lit up with purple magic, and as I suspected, most of it came from the chasm itself, but not all. The entire field around us was soaked in swirling aether, almost as if we stood in the middle of a gigantic vortex of energy. I knelt down, digging my hands into the dirt while Orm stood beside me.

'Can you tell me what you feel, Annika?'

I closed my eyes, letting my senses drift into the soil. Part of my training had been in detection and identification. I could use the elements to determine the unique signature of the creature I was about to hunt, but what I felt here didn't make sense.

The place was *empty* but filled with so much corrupted aether and signatures of monsters that I thought tiredness was affecting my magic. The only other explanation was an unseen danger under our feet.

'I think there's something underground. I don't know what exactly, but it feels similar to the olgoi we fought in the forest.' I frowned as an idea formed in my mind. 'I need to go to the fissure. If I'm right, the danger is greater than we thought.'

Orm started laughing—until he realised I wasn't joking, and his face hardened into that emotionless mask.

'No, that's out of the question, Annika. Are you *trying* to turn my hair grey? You just destroyed a massive swarm, and don't think I've missed how much you're trembling after that—now you want to go to the Rift? No one's ever returned from there. No, I'm not sending the woman I love to her death.'

I didn't know if Orm realised he'd just told me he loved me, but I felt warmth spread through my chest. I stood up, brushing the dirt off my hands before reaching for him. When I stroked his cheek, my fingers left a smudge of dirt on his face.

'I'm not asking for permission, but for your help,' I said, and he frowned, grasping my hand and holding it to his chest. 'I've dealt with the spectrae, and I appreciate you're worry for me, but we need to know what is tainting the soil. This is my job. You command the army—I use my magic to help you in whatever way I'm needed.'

'No! You are right, and we will go there; but you need to rest first, and I need to organise your protection. Going alone is suicide.'

'The more people we bring, the greater the chance we'll disturb whatever's down there. I have a better chance of sneaking in undetected if I go in alone.

We have an envoy coming from the king and the gods only know what problems he'll bring with him. We may not be able to return here for days, and then we'll have to repeat today's *fun* with the spectrae all over again. Just wait for me here. I should return shortly.'

'The fuck I'm letting you go alone,' he swore, giving me a quelling look, daring me to argue. It was inconvenient, as I wanted someone outside in case something went wrong, but I couldn't command him any more than he could command me.

With a deep sigh, I shrugged. 'Fine, I concede. Just make sure to follow my lead.'

The trek was slow and perilous, the rocks and soil loose and unsteady. We spent half the journey sliding down near vertical slopes on our rear ends, desperately trying to slow our descent, not knowing what dangers awaited us.

Before long, I was panting, out of breath, and covered in a thick layer of dirt, which left me looking like one of the mythical golems. When we were almost halfway down the mountain, I noticed a tunnel to my right that seemed to pulsate with foul magic, so I changed direction, gesturing for Orm to follow. A few moments later, we were in a large, ominously smooth passage, its walls glistening with moisture.

'Remind me to bring rope next time,' I said when I finally caught my breath.

'A rope? I want climbing gear, a squad or two of soldiers and a unit of dragons. And what's this about *next* time?' Orm sneezed, then almost gagged. 'What the *fuck* is that smell?' he gasped, pinching his nose. The tunnel stank like a rotting corpse floating face down in a sewer.

'I don't know.' I shook my head. 'I don't think I *want* to know either.'

Trying to breathe as little as possible, I conjured a bright spark and bound it above my shoulder to light our way. 'Let's go. The sooner we find out what's going on here, the sooner we can get back to the surface,' I said, pretending not to hear Orm's muttered curses.

The tunnel was large enough to let us walk upright and I had a sneaking suspicion about what had created it. The question was *how* an olgoi this size could have passed through the barrier that had seemed strong enough to hold back most of the Vel. Still, it certainly explained the creatures we had fought in the forest, the ground near the Rift that looked freshly ploughed, and the carnivorous demons that kept multiplying in the mountains.

'I think the spectrae were sent to distract you and the other commanders,' I ventured as we walked deeper into the underground.

'Well, it worked. We were so focused on fighting them in the air that we haven't patrolled the Rift for weeks.' He looked at me, and I saw the tension in his eyes. 'You think it is an olgoi, don't you?' I nodded.

'Fuck!' Orm hit the wall so hard that the skin on his knuckles broke, and I instantly covered his hand with mine. 'No bleeding here. Vel demons can smell it from miles away, and we don't need a horde of monsters chasing us,' I reprimanded him, concentrating on my limited healing skills to seal the wound.

'You said you weren't a healer,' he commented, and I rolled my eyes. 'I'm also not a cook, but I can boil water for tea. These are just scrapes, so try not to get your guts spilt or you'll have to carry them to Alaric yourself.' He smiled a little at that.

'Sassy wench. Any other commands for your superior?'

'No bleeding, screaming, or running away. Also, if anything happens, hide behind me. I will protect you. Follow basic battle mage procedures while on a hunt,' I ordered, and he shook his head, smirking.

'Let's go, Nivale, before I give in to the urge to spank you for those brazen words.'

I knew we were in danger and that the Lowland Kingdoms were in dire straits, but in that moment, I felt ridiculously happy bantering with Orm. *I love him.*

It wasn't just the Anchoring bond, an infatuation, or plain desire, although I admit I would happily spend every free moment in bed with him. I loved him, flaws and all.

The thought came so unexpectedly that I gasped, and Orm turned towards me with a drawn sword in his hand. 'No, it's nothing. Let's go,' I said, hiding my blush. We continued on in silence.

I don't know how long it took; it felt like an hour, maybe two, but I finally noticed a faint light at the end of the corridor and heard a rustling and screeching sound that *almost* resembled human voices. I gestured for Orm to let me lead.

After a silent argument, during which we waved our hands like lunatics, he finally agreed. I couldn't cast an illusion spell. That kind of magic was beyond my capabilities; Arno had always taken care of that whenever we fought. However, I could confuse the senses of those nearby, blurring our form using the mud caked to our bodies to blend into the background.

We quietly approached the end of the tunnel and entered an enormous cavern. Grey, sickly tree roots spread out above us, creating a shadowed canopy that was broken up by a few crevices that allowed a little light to filter through. What the weak glow revealed, though, sent icy shivers down my spine in horror.

Foul magic creatures filled the cavern. It was like some twisted vision of horror made reality; hundreds of corrupt bodies writhed across the floor, their hideously content sighs churning my stomach. Strigae, ghouls, and the undead remnants of humans were piled on top of each other. I saw several creatures that weren't created by foul magic but of wild aether, like biesy and vile[1] and beings of nature that inhabited forests or marshlands, harmless to those who didn't seek to harm them. These, however, looked tainted—as if their very essence were rotten to the core.

'There's an entire army waiting to be awakened right here, and no one knows about it,' Orm whispered before laying a hand on my shoulder. 'That's what the spectrae were guarding. Gods, they're already in the kingdom. The Lich King is pretending to negotiate while staging an army for invasion. We need to go back. I need to inform my brother and the other commanders as soon as possible. Fuck ... the envoy is coming today.'

'I'll help. I contacted some friends while you were away, and I'm expecting an answer any day now. I also still have some contacts at the university; one or two of them may even be councillors by now. But right now, we have to go up there.' I pointed to the ceiling where a ray of light fell down through the gap. 'I can feel something ... Gods, I hate I was the reason for the Rift.'

'Stop blaming yourself for what you did to survive. If anything, it alerted us to the failing magic. The Barrier was already fading, and your unit stopped the wlok; that's all that matters,' Orm said, embracing me. And just like that, I found peace in his arms.

I raised my hand, placing it on Orm's cheek. His stubble scratched at the skin of my palm, but all I could do was look at those green eyes. Even if I had to fight the Lich King himself for this man, I would. If there was a light in the world worth fighting for, Orm was the embodiment of it.

He smiled at me, unaware of my thoughts, and I gestured to the crumbled rocks above before telling him my plan. 'We'll have to climb up. Vahin should be still above the Rift, soaring the skies, and we can call him whenever we get to the surface. I can't see any other way there. The Vel will probably sleep until sunset, and if we're careful, we should be able to get there unnoticed.'

Orm sighed heavily before grasping my waist and lifting me to the first gnarly root. 'Off you go. At least this way, I'll have something nice to look up at,' he teased. His words confused me at first, but as we slowly climbed, I noticed his eyes were firmly attached to my backside, and if the situation weren't so dire, I would have laughed.

It took a while to reach our destination. We had to stop several times when falling debris caused several monsters to stir in their sleep, and when we finally made it up, the crack in the ceiling was too small to squeeze through. After a few whispered prayers, I drew a sigil, using the aether to carefully scour away the fractured rock with a mix of air and earth magic to widen the gap.

After forcing our way through, we emerged in a smaller but still spacious chamber, its walls so high the ceiling was bathed in darkness. I could feel a faint breeze coming from above, but it didn't fully register as my attention was captured by the sight before me.

We were in the Barrier crystal's chamber. A pulsating crystal floating in midair and I struggled to believe what I was seeing, but the dull glow, the crack, and the shards littering the floor convinced me it was real. There were two tunnels leading from the chamber on opposite walls and a large complex set of sigils in the centre of the chamber. The crystal wasn't the only thing damaged. Several lines of the diagram were missing, cracked, or smudged, and Orm swore as he pointed towards it. 'Is this what I think it is?'

'Yes, and it is clearly damaged. Still, at least the diagram's an easy fix. You know, since you told me Alaric wanted to replace the crystal, I couldn't stop thinking about it. I wanted to try fixing it. Now I'm here, and I don't know what to do. It all feels overwhelming, but ... I want to try.'

I crouched down, and Orm placed a hand on my shoulder while I lay mine on the ground. I studied the writing intently, then closed my eyes, picturing it in my mind, adding what was missing and repairing the damaged parts. My connection with Orm was firm and steady, and I leant into his strength as I sought the primal energy of the mountain.

The breath in my lungs froze as I connected with the vast power. It rushed through my body, lighting up the diagram with blinding white light, mending and filling the glyphs with magic. Something changed in the air, and I felt the old spell rising like a tide.

'Orm ... the crystal, I can feel its power. Please help me focus. I need to control the aether, but I feel so tired.' Not waiting for a response, my hands danced in the air, creating the pattern Alaric had taught me. The shards vibrated on the ground, and a vortex of energy followed my stream of consciousness. I saw the small pieces leave the ground and fuse with the main crystal, but something felt wrong, tainted.

The crystal was being drained of its aether, weakening it, but I didn't know how to break the link. I couldn't get a grip on it, though I still tried yanking the thread of magic while it resisted me. Worse still, the aether defied my manipulation, and even with Orm's help, my concentration slipped, my power erupting in a blinding burst of energy.

The chamber trembled, loose rocks and dirt falling around us as a wave of magic rolled through the air. Then the magic died down, and the crystal above me dulled. 'I can't,' I murmured as Orm caught my shoulders, preventing me from falling. 'No one can fix it.'

'You tried, my love, but some things are beyond even your control. We will try again, maybe with Alaric, but right now, we need to go home.'

We chose the corridor that didn't smell rotten, but it was a slow journey. Initially, I was too weak to stand, and Orm had to carry me. The further we went, the more damage we encountered. Roots punctured the walls, dry husks of once majestic trees. Many of them broke when Orm, with his bulky muscles, forced his way through several times. After an hour, we reached a rockfall that blocked the passageway; only small gaps remained, letting in little light and fresh air.

'Now what?' he asked, finally putting me down. 'Now you'll see what elemental magic can do,' I told him with an exhausted smile, feeling like I'd aged a century in a single day. I dug my hand in between the roots and soil and the aether flowed through me as I reshaped the ground around me. The rocks shifted, following my unspoken command. Then, the light grew bright as the broken roots and rocks began disintegrating.

Soon, the debris gave way, dust streaming past us as I funnelled it behind us. I raised my face to the light, enjoying the rays of the evening sun that kissed the horizon before I stepped through the hole.

We were free, but the feeling of utter failure was overwhelming. I'd harboured hopes of fixing the Barrier, but now I knew nobody could. Even if it wasn't my fault, it didn't make me feel any better.

'Vahin? Where are you?'

I hoped he wasn't too far away to answer. We were much further west than I'd expected, but I could see the Rift and hoped the dragon could hear my thoughts. When a roar shattered the silence, I winced.

Orm sighed. 'I'm blaming it all on you, my love. I will crawl through mud and worm shit for you, but I am not listening to the cranky old bastard tell me off.' I sighed, knowing exactly what to expect, and as soon as he landed, Vahin didn't fail to deliver.

CHAPTER 37

ANNIKA

Vahin berated me all the way back to the fortress. We learned that the other riders had returned after dealing with the spectrae, and during our time underground, Vahin had stayed close to the entrance and flew above it to keep an eye out for danger. He hadn't worried at first, but when he'd been unable to warn Orm of a small landslide near the chasm, he'd landed and begun searching for us.

After that, Vahin had soon realised that the tainted aether and thick layer of earth blocked his thoughtspeech. Once he was done roaring to the heavens that I was an irresponsible woman with a death wish, he decided that if I worried him like that again, he would never take me anywhere or, even better, lock me in his lair until I grew wiser.

Orm was as silent as the grave during the entire exchange, only squeezing my hand in sympathy and smiling when I bent to press a kiss to my scaly Anchor's neck.

'I'm sorry. You know I love you and would never worry you on purpose. The situation just got a little out of hand,' I said with complete honesty because, although Vahin's berating was slightly amusing, the genuine fear hidden in the dragon's heart was not.

'Our connection will increase your lifespan. It's difficult to extinguish a dragon's flame, but none of that matters if you continually throw yourself at monsters, begging them to eat you.'

'I know, but I had to try, especially when I saw the Barrier crystal. It was *right there*. To not try would have been criminal. Vahin, I was so close. If I'd had the right—' I stopped, realising that nothing would have changed the outcome, and leaned in to kiss his neck again. 'I'm sorry.'

When we approached the landing field, I could see Alaric pacing back and forth. His relief was evident on his face when he saw the landing dragon, and as soon as Vahin had folded in his wings, Ari rushed towards us.

Before he had a chance to speak, I placed my hand on his chest. 'Please, don't. Vahin already told me his thoughts on my actions. Can we meet in my room later? In about an hour? We need to talk, but first I have to get this worm shit off me.' I shuddered with disgust.

The dark fae turned towards Orm with a deep frown on his face. Unexpectedly, my tired warrior embraced him, pressing their foreheads together. 'What the hell happened?' I heard Ari ask, but I was moving away too quickly to catch the rest of the conversation.

'Sweet mother of gods, what happened to you?' Katja's voice focused everyone's attention on me. The passersby had already been sneaking looks, but my friend's shout gave them an excuse to openly stare.

'You should see the other guy,' I said, hoping she wasn't stopping me for long because my knees were threatening to give way, leaving me to sleep in the middle of the path.

'What other guy? Were you wrestling in the mud? You look half dead.'

'Katja ... it was just a rough day on patrol. I'll be fine as soon as I wash this crap off.' I sighed, but she already had me by the elbow, dragging me off to the castle baths. I didn't have the energy to fight her. With Agnes' help, she had me naked and neck-deep in bath water before I had time to even open my mouth.

'Katja, you are a miracle worker,' I moaned, half asleep as the pain in my tense muscles dissolved. I could finally think clearly, even if my thoughts were a little sluggish, thanks to her dainty fingers massaging my scalp. 'You don't have to do this. The bath was more than enough. Whatever you mixed into the water is far better than any magic,' I murmured with my eyes closed. When her fingers stopped, I smiled in gratitude.

'Would you deny me the pleasure of making you feel good, Domina?' a decidedly *non*-feminine voice asked.

'What the—how did you get in here?' I turned around to mock glare at Alaric, ruining the effect with the biggest grin.

'Katja was needed in the infirmary, and Agnes ... I kindly asked her to leave,' he said, resuming the sublime massage.

I lost track of time, drifting off into the sensual pleasure of Alaric's fingers as they melted away every thought and care in my mind. I moaned quietly when his hand slid down my spine, pressing into a painful spot that suddenly eased under his touch. 'Do something that wonderful again, and I will Anchor you on the spot. What did you press on? My body suddenly feels all tingly.'

'Do you like it?' he asked quietly, and I sighed.

'I love it.'

'Good, my Domina, then I have a purpose and the means to make you happy even without an Anchor bond.'

'You know you don't have to call me Domina. I'm not a dark fae. I don't see you as inferior. If anything, you are much better than me. Stronger, faster, a better mage,' I pointed out, and he tilted my chin.

'Is that what you think it means? I don't call you Domina because I feel inferior. I like certain things, but it's not about pain and submission. Calling you Domina gives meaning to our relationship. You are the woman I crave to belong to, the woman ... who loves me.' The slight hesitation in his voice made me turn to look at him.

'Yes, Ari, I love you. I love you so much that, if not for your objections, the Lich King could kiss my taut arse because I would take you as you are and Anchor you while I'm naked, tired, and in the bath. Call me what you wish, and I will do what I can to be worthy of the title, but even without it, I will always care for you.'

Alaric's eyes burned with crimson fire before he abruptly turned away. 'I will call Agnes. Please prepare for the evening. We were only expecting the royal mage's envoy, but he brought the chancellor and an entire entourage of sycophants with him. Orm ordered a late-night banquet, which you are expected to attend. News of your presence here has spread throughout the court, and all of them are determined to see the legendary conduit mage.'

I sighed deeply, pursing my lips. The last thing I needed today was to be shown off like a mare at the farmers' market. 'Fine, I will try to be on my best behaviour.' He bent to kiss my forehead, whispering, 'That's what I'm afraid of.'

He left, and Agnes appeared to help me dress, carrying my battle mage uniform, Anchor pin, boots, and medals. I looked at the reminder of my past with wide-open eyes, and my maid shifted uncomfortably under my stare. 'I can bring a different outfit if you want, but I thought this one suited the occasion.'

'No, you're right, it's perfect. I just wasn't expecting you to know I had it.'

'Master Alaric mentioned it would be the best choice for the evening.'

'All right. Well, if he said so,' I answered with laughter, muttering a *'bossy bastard'* before letting her wrap my damp hair in a towel. Half an hour later, I was dressed and my hair was in an elaborate peasant's crown held together by an intricate golden rope Agnes had seemingly produced from thin air.

I walked to the dining hall, pausing at the entrance to take in the room's pageantry. Alaric had done an incredible job. The place was large but cosy, in the hunting lodge style. Tapestries with battle and hunting scenes covered granite walls, protecting the diners from any draughts, while arched crystal windows filtered the night glow of the sky. Massive wooden beams held brass candelabras, the melted wax giving them an otherworldly look.

In the middle of the room, tables were set out in a large rectangle. On each table, a variety of food—meats, cheese, and vegetables—had been placed before the gathered guests. In the seat of honour was Orm, with his back to the fireplace. Next to him were his military and administrative seconds-in-command, Tomma and Alaric, while the visiting party was seated directly opposite him. I counted at least fifteen people gathered for the late meal, and every single one of them was now staring at me.

'Lady Annika, it's a pleasure to see you again. I couldn't believe it when Ihrain told me you were alive and thriving here in the fortress.'

The man who spoke rose from his chair. He looked vaguely familiar as I dredged through my memory, trying to recall where I'd seen him before. He was a plain-looking but expensively dressed nobleman with a sparse beard and receding hairline. I also didn't fail to notice how his eyes shone with dangerous intelligence.

That was the moment I remembered—Felarian Haerne. He'd been the senior advisor to the chancellor when I was finishing my studies, and as the old man had died three years ago, he must have taken his place.

'Thank you, Sir Haerne,' I acknowledged his presence with a curt nod before walking to the only free space at the table. I could see the aristocrat didn't like my brief reply, but before he could say anything, Alaric rose from his chair and approached me. 'Please, allow me, Domina.'

He took my hand, leading me to his seat next to Orm. As I settled in the chair, Tomma moved down to the empty space. It all felt too staged for a casual changeup, and I guessed Alaric did it on purpose to show everyone I was an equal, second only to Ormond.

When I sat down, Ihrain asked with a sarcastic smile, 'Domina? I didn't know you liked to indulge in perversion. Wasn't it enough that you Anchored him?'

I was surprised by how proudly Alaric used the title. Dark fae males reserved it for the lady of their household, but he had never voiced it out loud before. Still, I'd done an excellent job of masking my shock. Ihrain's remark not only silenced all conversation but irked me immensely. Before I could say something, Orm placed a hand on my thigh.

'I'd have thought after your last visit that you would have learned by now not to offend my family. Court etiquette may bind me, but not my dragon. One of the unfortunate consequences of living in such a lawless backwater,' he warned with a cold smile before pointing to the tables. 'Please, eat and be merry. There will be plenty of time later to hear what brings you to this desolate place, though it's clear you didn't bring the reinforcements I asked for.'

'Thank you, Lord Ormond. Our mission here is simple. First, I'd like to take this opportunity to inform you that our negotiations with the ruler of Ozar are nearly complete, so your need for constant reinforcements shall end. You can deal with the remaining Vel demons still in the mountains with the forces currently at your disposal,' Ihrain said. Orm's eyes flashed yellow as he fought to hold in his temper.

'What exactly do you mean, envoy?'

'Only that there will be no additional reinforcements for any of the fortresses. With the few Vel demons left, you can use your riders and the soldiers already here to dispatch them. Our king denies your request, especially since the high nobles of Dagome seem to think that sending their soldiers here is to the kingdom's detriment.' Ihrain gloated like a fool as he looked at Orm.

'You mentioned two missions?' Orm asked, deceptively calm.

'Yes, since you don't need additional support, His Majesty asks for the safe return of his conduit mage. I'm sure the Lady Annika will be delighted to see Truso again, especially after her sudden departure. If she refuses to return, I'm entitled to deliver His Majesty's request using her geas.'

Orm and Alarick jerked from their chairs, and several men from Ihrain's entourage reached for their weapons. I, however, remained seated and smirked at my former colleague. 'Sit down, please, and sheath your weapons. I'm hungry and want to eat in peace.' After a moment of tense silence, the men of the fortress obeyed.

'Y-you ...' Ihrain stuttered when I reached for the fruit before Alaric took it from my hand and started peeling it with his dagger.

'Look around, Ihrain. You can't take me from here by force. Not only because the men would end you, but because I would sooner demolish the palace than serve under the geas.'

'No one is using force here,' the chancellor said, placing his hand on Ihrain's shoulders. He must have used significant pressure because the mage actually winced. 'My colleague has misinterpreted the king's words. It was a simple invitation. You are welcome to reject it, though I think it would be unwise not to make a brief visit.'

'I thought my reputation for unwise decisions was well known.' I shrugged off the topic and made sure I had the chancellor's attention. 'Tell me, does the king not know of the army hiding in a cave under the Lost Ridge, or are the countless demons there all part of His Majesty's plans?' I asked, and he had the decency to look away.

'Erm, well, let's not dwell on His Majesty's plans right now. As the lord commander said, it is time to eat and enjoy the company of the bravest warrior in the kingdom.' I felt Orm's grip tighten as if he were telling me not to continue with the conversation, and I sighed, putting on the friendliest smile I could manage.

'Of course. Have you tried the local wines? Our makers freeze the grapes before they press them, which gives them a delightful and very deceptive complexity. The wine can easily trick you into drinking more than you can handle.' I paused, pointing towards the bottle on the table. 'I recommend you try it in small quantities. It is not only refreshing, but it also can help with certain ... digestive problems.'

'I see, my lady,' he said, raising the glass to his lips and barely wetting them. 'Indeed, certain indulgences have to be given due care and attention.'

Alaric smirked and bent to my ear. 'You're playing a dangerous game, Ani. I doubt our friend Ihrain understood the meaning of your words. However, you should not be so careless in telling the chancellor we can be persuaded, but not forced,' he whispered.

'I know, but Haerne is well aware. He dropped the geas subject quickly and put Ihrain in his place, so I want to see where he stands. If my guess is right, he may not be as loyal to the king as the rest of them.' I placed a kiss behind his ear, giving the gathered men the impression that we couldn't keep our hands off each other; not uncommon for conduit mages and their Anchors. 'I will need to talk to him ... in private. Help me make it happen?'

'In private, yes, but not alone,' Orm interrupted our conversation. 'I don't trust them. You are both staying in my quarters tonight. I burnt your geas, but if the royal mage made a copy before he gave it to me ... I don't want you alone until this circus leaves my fortress.'

He paused briefly before adding, 'I'm not trying to cage you again, but if they attempt to use the geas with us around, we can overpower you to keep you safe. Between Alaric's magic and my strength, it should work. Then maybe your bond with Vahin can overcome the compulsion, just like he did with your fear of heights?'

Ari's eyes widened at Orm's words, and I felt a shiver run down my spine at the thought of having them both with me tonight, even if all I was planning to do was sleep. Today had stripped me of energy, and all I wanted to do was fall into bed and close my eyes to the world.

After our brief exchange, we focused on the meal as the tense atmosphere at the table grew strained with each passing silent minute. I ate my fill, and with the flames warming my back, I struggled to keep myself awake. When I failed to stifle the latest in a series of yawns, I stood up from the table.

'My apologies. Fighting the spectrae and my attempt to repair the keystone has left me feeling drained. I intend on heading to bed. If you'll excuse me?' I said, and before I knew it, Ihrain rushed towards me, grasping my wrist so hard I hissed.

'You touched the keystone? What did you do to it?'

I knew I was tired, and that it left me sluggish, but in my defence, I hadn't expected to be attacked. Orm, though, already had the envoy's wrist in his grip and twisted it so hard that I heard the bones creak, tearing Ihrain's hand from my arm without a struggle.

'If it wasn't already clear enough, anyone who touches my lady with malicious intent will lose their hands, eyes, and tongue before I grant them the mercy of death.' Orm's words were iced fury, his tone quiet and controlled, but what truly chilled my blood was Alaric's follow-up, his gentle voice filled with deadly intent.

'And when Lord Ormond has finished with them, I will revive their corpses for the sheer pleasure of watching him do it again. He may damage their bodies, but I will take my revenge on their very soul.'

Ihrain backed away, as if he faced the Lich King himself, cradling his injured arm to his chest. As if on command, Vahin roared, his dark silhouette flying so close to the castle that the crystal windows shook to the beat of his wings.

'On that note, I shall leave you to chat amongst yourselves. We can talk about our findings and my magic tomorrow, hopefully in a more civilised way,' I said, turning to leave. Alaric took my arm before I could take a single step.

'May I accompany you, Domina? Our friend from the capital can find a healer in town if he needs assistance. We wouldn't want the taint of my foul magic touching his precious skin.' With a smirk, I let him lead me away.

We walked through the long corridors, lit by more torches than usual. Their existence was obviously the dark fae's doing, so I let Ari's concern for my safety ease my tense muscles, entwining our fingers and smiling. 'You called me your Domina in front of everyone,' I said, and he smiled, pulling me closer.

'Because you *are* my Domina. To my kin, I'm the untrustworthy son of a traitor. To humans and the light fae, I am darkness incarnate. Most people worry my touch will taint them. Only you—and perhaps Orm—think I'm a man worthy of affection, worthy of fighting for. How could I not call you by the title you deserve?' Ari finished when we stopped in front of Orm's chamber.

'Come. Commander's orders,' I insisted when he hesitated, and my gentle teasing made him sigh.

'So be it.'

I undressed quickly, throwing my clothes on the chair and sliding under the covers. Alaric soon joined me, keeping his trousers on, and I promptly snuggled up to his naked chest. I was half asleep when Orm joined us, sliding into the bed on my other side. I instinctively turned towards him and felt his chest rumble with laughter as I combed my fingers through his body hair. Alaric then tried to leave the bed, so I whimpered in protest, and Orm reached over, placing a hand on Ari's shoulder.

'No, Ani needs us both. I want you to stay.' There was only a slight hesitation in his voice. 'Please, it would mean a lot to me.'

'Are you sure?' Ari asked, but I already felt him settling back down beside me, his body pressed to mine. 'Yes. We all need the rest. The meeting tomorrow will be brutal, and I want us all to have clear heads to deal with their demands. We need a way to get rid of them without bloodshed. However, if it comes down to it, I'd rather that than let Ani travel to the capital alone,' Orm whispered over my head.

'What's your plan?'

'I don't know yet, and I don't trust the chancellor, despite his compliance. Do you think Ihrain's been bribed by the Lich King, or is he just a pawn of someone stronger in court?'

Ari's hand, which had been stroking my back, paused for a moment. 'I don't know. Do you want me to arrange an accident so I can talk to his corpse? For how he treated Ani, I have no objection to helping fate find the right ending to his life.'

'No, that would look too suspicious.'

I let the quiet murmur of their voices send me to sleep and an almost forgotten feeling of warmth and contentment spread through my chest before I drifted into my dreams.

I could feel Vahin in my thoughts as he circled the castle, guarding our sleep while my men cocooned me in their love. I'd failed to fix the keystone, and war would surely come to our kingdom, but in that moment, I just felt happy, safely enveloped in their arms.

CHAPTER 38

ANNIKA

S omething—either the heat from the two bodies wrapped around me or a noise from outside—had woken me up, but when I opened my eyes, only the reddish hue of the rising sun greeted my tired mind.

Orm and Ari were still on either side of me, but their hands were now clasped together on my hip. I couldn't help but smile at that, a special place in my heart filling with tenderness.

I loved them both.

I knew deep in my soul that they had become a part of me, even if Ari had yet to Anchor himself to me. *He will. Not even the Lich King can stop me from claiming him,* I thought, stroking their hands.

A sudden thundering on the door made me flinch, and I gasped when Alaric instantly covered me with his body while Orm jumped out of bed, pulling two daggers from gods knew where.

'Commander, there's an emergency,' sounded a panicked voice from the outside.

'Enter and report,' Orm was furious but professional while I still wrestled to extract myself from beneath my dark fae shield.

A dishevelled man burst in, and with him, the putrid smell of smoke. 'The boarding house is on fire. We rescued most of the women, but we need more men to tackle it ... and the mage,' he said, and I finally recognised Tomma, Orm's second-in-command.

'And you waited how long to tell me?' Orm snapped his question to the rider, but Tomma couldn't answer as his body was wracked with a hacking cough. I winced at Orm's pounding of his subordinate's back, but it seemed to help, and Tomma straightened. 'It didn't look like much initially, but the fire wouldn't die down.'

I struggled out of bed, yanking my dress off the chair. 'I need you both outside with me. Now!' I ordered. My battle mage uniform was designed for ease of dressing, and I was ready in no time. Sprinting towards the door, I looked at the men, who frowned at my words. 'Now! Someone is playing with fire in my fucking castle. I can douse these flames, but someone has to look after our people.'

I bolted outside without giving them a chance to answer, cursing up a storm as I ran. What I'd thought was the glow of sunrise was, in fact, light from the fire engulfing the female boarding house and threatening the town. '*Vahin!*' I shouted in my thoughts, and the dragon's roar answered from above. '*Here, Little Flame, tell me what to do.*'

'*Stay nearby. I will have to counter the spell and douse the fire. I need your Anchor.*'

His reassuring presence was all I needed, especially when I entered the town square and saw the scale of the disaster. The boarding house burned fiercely, and the nearby buildings were already smouldering, giving me very little time to think. I heard Orm shouting to the soldiers, commanding them to further evacuate people, but I ignored him as I tried to concentrate. I cleared my mind, tuning out everything but the beating of my heart.

Then I felt it—a spell of the High Order that had used a small amount of aether to combat any attempts at smothering the flames. I needed to find the glyph controlling the energy and erase it while preventing the fire from spreading.

Think, Annika. No man can enter the female boarding house, so it has to be nearby.

I reached for the aether, and its power flowed through me with ease, grounded by the presence of my two Anchors. I took a deep breath and exhaled, slowing my heartbeat, letting more and more magic filter through my body until I reached a hand out towards the lake.

'Hoc ta mae.'[1]

Water answered my call, rushing through the streets, flowing uphill while the citizens leapt from its path. I condensed the stream, forcing it into a tighter, smaller jet that turned and twisted into a spiral surrounding the boarding house. As the water scoured the walls, the flames and smoke cleared enough for me to spot the complicated diagram drawn on the side wall.

'Motherfucker!' I cursed, unable to stop myself. Whoever had done it had tied the spell to a fire elemental, and the poor creature was burning everything it touched as it attempted to flee.

I drew in the water, spinning it faster and faster, moulding it into a raging torrent. I aimed its entire power at the offending glyph, grinning in triumph as the diagram was obliterated. I felt the joyous cry of the elemental as its shackles shattered, and the fire whipped and jerked, suddenly less intense.

'Annika, we need more water directed to the front,' Orm shouted, and I heard screams coming from the building.

Alaric rushed inside. I felt a shift in the air and saw something flicker around him. The dark fae had shielded himself as he entered the burning building, but I almost panicked when I realised he wouldn't be able to breathe. Meanwhile, Orm focused on protecting the town, directing the soldiers to drag the burning debris away from the other building and beat it with wet blankets. At the same time, the dragons small enough to fit in the

---

1. *Come to me.*

narrow area were holding their wings out to protect the soldiers from falling wreckage as they worked.

I'd solved one problem, but I still needed to deal with the *ordinary* fire. 'Move back, everyone!' I shouted, and the people who were still on the street next to me ducked for cover.

I weaved the elemental power of the water within my grasp, exhilarated beyond measure. My mind called to Vahin, and the image of torrential rain so heavy even a dragon's wing would struggle to withstand it was his answer. Vahin understood my intention, expanding the vision to include the image of a cloud heavy with water drifting slowly over the mountain peak.

The aether in my hands weighed me down as it gained substance while the euphoria of channelling its power nearly lifted me from the street. The only steadying forces were my Anchors, their strength holding me in place as I wove magic into the vision, with the dragon's deep understanding of the sky helping to recreate the natural order.

This has to be enough, I thought, unwilling to repeat yesterday's experience. I reached my hand to the sky, releasing the magic, and thrust forth the vision and my intent behind it with one powerful word of command.

'*Das'an!*'[2]

The skies opened and water crashed down upon the ground with the sound of thunder. The dragons protecting the soldiers huddled together, supporting each other as they kept their charges safe, while everyone else sheltered beneath the nearest doorway. The fire that had raged like an inferno just moments ago hissed and stuttered, falling back from the relentless deluge, filling the air with the smell of soot and burnt wood. I kept the spell going until its light was completely extinguished, holding the waterlogged clouds above the damaged building.

---

2. *Rain!*

'Little Flame, it is done. Any more and the building will collapse.' Vahin sent the message with an image of the town from above, and I worked on releasing the raging aether.

That was the most challenging part of being a conduit—it was easy enough to call on a power so vast it felt infinite, and only a little more difficult to shape it into a spell you wanted to use. Closing yourself off from the onslaught, however, was next to impossible without an Anchor.

It felt like I was trying to stop a raging river with a pair of curtains, and I called out to my Anchors, begging them to join me and offer their strength.

I heard the roar of a dragon at the same time that a heavy hand dropped onto my shoulder and let my gratitude flow through our bonds. Laughter burst forth as I felt their spirits meld with my own, our bodies glowing with power as I closed myself off from the vast energy of the aether, dispersing the residual power into them.

'That is an interesting sensation, Little Flame. It feels so primal, like the day I was born from the mists,' Vahin rumbled, gracefully landing next to me. The halo of my power subsided, but his scales were glowing blue and lightning crackled over their surface.

'You don't say,' I said, nodding my thanks to Orm as he rushed back to his men. My head was still spinning from the euphoria of channelling so much power, but the fire was out, and that was all that mattered. 'I've never channelled so much and with such ease. Thank you for helping me with the clouds.'

'I am always at your service, Little Flame. Now, go help our dark fae. He doesn't look well.'

I looked to where Vahin gestured, seeing a coughing Ari stumbling from the boarding house. He was arm in arm with two women from Zalesie, and it was impossible to tell who was holding up whom.

'Ani, are you all right?' Alaric gasped as he approached while two healers led the sobbing women away. 'Yes, I'm fine, just tired. Some bastard started the fire. I think we both know who, but you ... what happened?'

'I'm depleted and ...' Alaric hesitated, and I pursed my lips when he continued. 'I created a shield using a basic glyph, but keeping it up around three people was tasking.'

He swayed and I had to grab his arm to keep him upright. He was swaying so much, in fact, that I instantly knew he'd used all his magical reserves and more, taking from his own life force to sustain the spell when his aether ran out. That's why he had looked like he'd gone through a month of starvation and aged overnight.

'Orm!' I shouted, but he was standing in a circle of his officers, commanding the scene and the townsfolk, and my voice wasn't loud enough to reach him. I turned. 'Vahin, please tell Orm I'm taking Alaric back to the castle. He's of no use here, but I'll come back to help as soon as I'm able.'

The massive dragon placed his snout over my shoulder. 'Go, and don't worry, Orm can handle this. Look after our fae, Little Flame.'

I wrapped my arm around Alaric's waist and lurched unsteadily towards the castle.

I knew we'd have to confront Ihrain, but Alaric was my priority at the moment. I was going to rip the royal mage's apprentice to pieces for what he'd done; I'd even let my men lose on him. We'd see how much that bastard enjoyed Orm's fury and the art of pain the dark fae were so famous for once we'd found him.

When we finally arrived at Alaric's room, I was covered in sweat. He was dragging his feet, half asleep as we weaved back and forth, and I had to use all of my strength to keep him upright. I placed him on the bed and covered him with a warm blanket. I knew he needed to eat, but there was nothing in the room I could serve him. Every servant would be in town helping with the aftermath of the fire, so it was up to me to provide water and some sustenance for when he awoke.

I sighed heavily, my back protesting, and left the room, heading for the kitchens. It was still the middle of the night, but I was hoping to find some fruit, bread, and—if I was lucky—possibly even mead for myself.

I felt weak and dizzy and had to resist the urge to open myself to the aether, its energy still pressing at my senses. I wasn't sure if I could risk creating even a small light without my magic getting out of control. Instead, I strolled along, keeping one hand on the wall as I tried to recognise shapes in the surrounding shadows.

Maybe it was the lack of light, or maybe how tired I was, or even the safety I'd come to feel in the fortress, but I didn't sense the danger until it was too late.

At first, I only felt a quick, sharp pain in my neck, and when I reached up to probe the area, I pulled a tiny dart from my skin. Whatever poison it contained, it had already entered my body. I stumbled, my knees buckling despite my mind screaming at them to work, and slammed into the wall shoulder first.

In my panic, I called for my Anchors, only to find them gone, missing from my mind. I attempted to stay upright, using the wavering structure to support me, when I caught the sound of footsteps echoing behind me.

Ihrain, that bloody fool, was walking towards me with a slimy, triumphant smile on his face. I tried to reach for the aether, but much to my surprise, I was cut off from that, too.

'Don't bother, Annika. The poison was concocted especially for mages, its purpose specifically to subdue someone with unstable talent or those too volatile to control. The effects are temporary, but they will last long enough for our journey to court.'

I could barely stand now. I still swung my fist in a weak attempt to defend myself, but Ihrain easily caught it and smirked. 'Feisty as always, but don't worry, you won't be feisty for long. I knew my little fire would distract you and leave you vulnerable. You are so predictable—always there to help the needy, even if it means getting hurt. Well, you had your fun playing peasant queen, but as soon as the king speaks the words of your geas, you will do what you are told, just like every other conduit in the country.'

I looked my enemy in the eye and was tempted to tell him that the king didn't even have my geas. That the royal mage had given it to Orm, making him the only person who could bring me to my knees, but the sudden thought that they could have made a copy made me gasp, and the quiet sound made Ihrain smile even wider.

He must have taken it as the sound of my fear, and he revelled in it. I didn't correct him and didn't bother resisting when his servants carried me down the stairs to the small carriage waiting in the courtyard. I had to conserve my strength, so I curled into a ball when they threw me inside. I landed like a sack of turnips right under the chancellor's feet.

'Lady Annika, how nice to see you again, and so soon,' the chancellor said politely, his eyes betraying a coldness as they studied me with indifference. 'Ihrain, I told you she must be unharmed. Our lord wants her intact in body and mind. Did you at least confirm she didn't lie about being Anchored?'

'Yes, the only way she could call rain from the peaks was through her conduit abilities, and both Ormond and the dragon felt the brunt of it when she closed the circuit.'

My eyes narrowed in anger. I studied them both as they casually discussed the fire that had almost destroyed the town while the carriage drove down the road towards the fortress gates.

'What about the necromancer? You assured me he was Anchored to her.' The chancellor kept asking questions, and I started to suspect they weren't taking me to the king, that there was more going on than just a frightened old man retrieving his conduit mage.

'I don't know. He was inside when she used the Anchor bond, and I couldn't see, but when I was here before, he stepped forward, claiming to be her Anchor, and you saw yourself that he called her his Domina during the meal.'

The conversation was interrupted by the fortress guard questioning the coach driver. I breathed slightly, bracing myself to scream when I heard the heavy steps approaching, likely for an inspection.

'No, my dear, keep that pretty little mouth shut. If you try to alert them, those men will be dead before you finish speaking. No one can save you—not even your dragon,' Ihrain warned me, covering my face with his hand while the king's advisor stuck his head out through the window.

'Haven't you heard, good man? About the fire? It is not safe for us anymore, and the commander is too busy dealing with this tragedy to sign our paperwork. I need to report what happened to the king immediately.'

I silently cursed. The man knew how to play people. His tone sounded so sincere and convincing, and his reasoning was persuasive. I couldn't blame the guard for letting him pass. As soon as we left the fortress gates behind, the driver cracked the whip, and the horses shot forward, rocking the carriage.

'They will come for me, and not even the gods themselves will save you when my dragon finds you,' I croaked past my tight throat.

'By the time they realise you're gone, we'll be close enough to the capital that they won't be able to catch us. I have to admit—the necromancer surprised us by running into the fire, but that only worked in our favour.'

'Who is your master? And don't try insulting my intelligence by saying this has anything to do with the king.' As soon as I said the words, the chancellor threw his head back and laughed.

'Yes, you are right. The king is old, and his mind is filled with desperation to prolong his life. Still, we are taking you to him so he can give you to our true master, the one your ilk calls the Lich King.'

'You serve him? How did he contact you?' I was so baffled by the discovery that I sat up, looking at the envoy with disbelief.

'Oh Annika, you are so easy to read. Only the tainted cannot breach the Barrier. You all forgot that, and it will be the downfall of the Lowland Kingdoms.' He reached down and stroked my cheek with his thumb, looking at me with a knowing smirk.

'We are not touched by foul magic. The Barren Lands is a place where humans still live and often thrive. None of the dragon patrols enter deep enough to encounter the humans or Moroi who escaped the initial purge when our lord took his rightful place. I know what the riders see when they come to patrol. A desolate land full of undead, a useful distraction for them to see before the spectrae chase them away.'

'What?' I asked, shocked. Here were two people that not only were from the Barren Lands, but who *served* the Lich King and held influential positions in the country. 'And the living serve him? Why?'

'Why are you so surprised? What is the difference between serving a king who controls his country with necromancy and one who uses bloody torture to obtain a mage's geas? At least with our lord, you know what to expect. Those who serve him well are always rewarded. Those who fail serve him in another way.'

'So when you tried to Anchor me all those years ago ...' I asked, looking at Ihrain.

'Yes, Annika. That was the reason. Mages like me can easily pass through the Barrier.' He glanced at the chancellor, and the older man smiled.

'We knew the Barrier would eventually fall. It started fading a hundred years ago. At first, it was a slow process, but as time passed, the cracks in the crystal unravelled the magic holding it together. Not to mention a certain powerful mage accidentally drawing energy from the keystone to defeat a wlok. That was the moment we knew the Barrier's deterioration had reached the point of no return.,' he said before gesturing to Ihrain to pull me onto the seat.

As he dragged me up, the high mage's apprentice couldn't help joining in the explanation. 'Our liege is not infallible. He has learned a lot since taking over Ozar. Ruling over the undead is not as satisfying as he thought. He wants the Lowland Kingdoms and their people as his subjects, not as walking corpses. That's why he has spared the remaining humans and Moroi, letting us thrive unbound by fear. Now, we have infiltrated every court in the Lowland Kingdoms. You are the final prize our lord desires before the Barrier falls, and your king will deliver you, along with your geas.'

Then Ihrain smiled at me with such superiority, as if he were explaining it all to a toddler, and I had to turn away to stop myself from spitting in his face. 'This is your fate, Annika. There is no sense in resisting. Soon, you will be bound to the most powerful mage on our continent, giving him the power to rule all. As long as you serve him with your skills, nothing bad will happen to you. If you resist ... well ... many have tried, but in the end, he broke them all.'

I *should* have spat on the little toad, but the only thing on my mind was how Alaric's curse had broken him, and I believed every word Ihrain said. I wondered how long the poison would last because, at the first tingle of my magic returning, I knew I needed to free myself and run away to somewhere the Lich King couldn't find me.

I refused to become his weapon. I couldn't let him use those I loved to break me. 'I will never submit to him. I'd sooner kill myself than become a weapon in that madman's hands,' I threatened with vehemence. Both men looked at each other, snorting with laughter.

'Don't wish for death ... The dead don't rest in peace around him; they serve him even better than the living. You, too, *will* serve him, one way or another. Because our lord has already decided that in life or even death, you are his and only his, so ask yourself which you would prefer. To be his as a living mage ... or a walking corpse,' Ihrain answered, murmuring an incantation. I recognised the words, but I was helpless to stop it. Sheer panic choked me as I fought the mind-numbing spell, but in the end, I lost ...

And everything went black.

GLOSSARY

Aether— live giving-force. A power that created and sustains life, also being the source of magic. Aether is produced and stored by every living being, with mages having access to the aether stored by the bodies. Conduit mages can access called wild aether, a force that exists in unanimated objects and non-sentient beings.

Amare—he title given to a secondary male in a dark fae household. It means 'beloved' and shows a meaningful bond between males, contrary to the term 'servus,' which shows a submissive, subservient role.

Biesy(plur)/Bies(sing)— a personification of all the undefined evil forces in nature. Once, they are placed amongst the most dangerous and oldest demons in Central and Eastern Europe. They were massive bison-like beasts with horns and hooves that were hostile and resistant to most types of weapons.

Borovio—one of the seven dukedoms of the Dagome kingdom, governed by the Erenhart family.

Dagome— one of the kingdoms participating in the Lowland Kingdoms coalition

Domine—the official title of the primary(alpha) male in a dark fae household responsible for the protection and external affairs. His authority is almost equal to Domina's.

Domina(sing)/dominae(plur)—a lady of her own domain. Dark fae title for the head of the household.

Falchion—abroad, slightly curved sword with a cutting edge on the convex side

Geas—a form of magical compulsion, curse, or obligation. Those under a geas are required to follow certain conditions or orders, risking death for disobedience.

Ghoul—minorWel demon. A male with pale bodies, sharp fangs and poisonous claws that feasted on dead bodies, preferably freshly killed.

Jarylo—god of fertility and spring, exceptionally well endowed.

Kirbai—a hybrid of the horse and snow leopard created by Cahyon Abyasa before he was corrupted by foul magic. The animal is known for its intelligence, fierce nature, and loyalty. It can survive in the harshest environments and climb almost vertical walls.

Kirtle—adress similar to men's tunics. They were loose and reached to below the knees or lower. Slits on the sides were pulled tight to fit the figure. Kirtles were typically worn over a chemise or smock and under a formal outer garment or surcoat.

Lanara poison—is a potent poison invented specifically for the mages. It suppresses the ability to connect with aether and, therefore, cast the spell.

Latawce(plur.)/Latawiec(sing.)—shapeshifting demons. They fly in the currents; their physical bodies are similar to large birds with sharp claws and colourful feathers, with human heads. They could shift into any human to tempt the victim with their song, and when they sang, those who heard it clawed their bodies, ripping the flesh as an offering for the ravenous demons.

Mamuna—a female swamp demon in Slavic mythology known for being malicious and dangerous.

Morgenstern—otherwise known as Morning Star flail - mace with a chain ended with a spiky ball.

Olgoi worms— are blind earthworms with rows of serrated teeth. They are famous for drilling tunnels in dirt and rocks. They rarely hunt sentient beings, but during starvation periods, they can move to the surface and hunt for warm-blooded prey.

Peasant's crown—a traditional crown-like braid for women

Ragróg(sing)/Ragógs(plur.)—fire demons coming in the shape of horse-size falcons with beaks and claws made of burning embers and wings that start fires while they fly.

Skeins—length of thread or yarn, loosely coiled and knotted, oftern refered by mages as skeins of aether

Spectrae—major Wel. Ghost-like creatures created from tortured and fractured souls. They feed on the life force of other beings attempting to regain their solid shape and restore themselves. Particularly attracted to the life force of the dragon.

Striga(sing)/Strigae(plur.)—MonorWel demon, A female demon born from violent death. They hunted those who wronged them, and once their vengeance was completed, they hunted for any human. They looked like skinny females with two rows of teeth, large claws, and leather-like hair.

Truso—the capital of Dagome

Utopiec(sing)/Utopce(plur)—spirits of human souls that died drowning, residing in the element of their own demise. They are responsible for sucking people into swamps and lakes as well as killing the animals standing near the still waters.

Vambraces—forearm guards are tubular or gutter defences for the forearm worn as part of a suit of plate armour that was often connected to gauntlets.

Vjesci—(originally from Polish folklore adjusted to the lore) An undead demon that preserved the thoughts, personality, and body of the person. After death, the body would cool closely, and the limbs would remain limber. The lips and cheeks would remain, and spots of blood often appeared under the fingernails and on the face.

Vyraj—an afterlife paradise for those who deserve it and warriors who have fallen in battle.

Wlok—a major demon that looks like a tumbleweed made of bones. It rolls over the roads and fields, killing any living creature that has bones inside to include them in its existence in the constant need of growing.

CLASSES OF MAGIC USERS:

HIGH MAGIC ORDER

Healer

A mage uses the aether to alter the natural processes in the body. This is usually applied to healing but can also cause alterations and mutations in natural beings.

Enhancer

A mage is able to take the power of objects and other mages and weave it into patterns that enhance the effectiveness of what spell is being used.

Illusion

A mage. who manipulates light to create realistic images but can also sense the surface thoughts of a person to trick them into focusing on it and not their surroundings

Psychic/Psionic

A mage is able to discern the Aether within a person's soul and can interact with it on a base level, influencing emotion and thought to various degrees depending on their ability to relate and empathise.

Artificer

A mage who can create artefacts that perform magical spells by altering the flow of Aether through an object. These artefacts often require various stages to construct, with many glyph diagrams infused, melded, or etched into them.

PRIMAL MAGIC ORDER

Paladin

A mage of the warrior class well versed in classic fighting techniques who applies magic in conjunction with his fighting style.

Elemental

A mage who uses primarily elemental force in his spells or is able to direct elements. Mages can be specialised or versatile in their use of elements.

Animage

A mage is able to communicate with animals and shapeshift into animal form. Minor talents are used in husbandry. Those with major talents often communicate with animals marked by aether, like dragons, gryphons, and manticores.

Seer

A mage able to foresee future events and recall the past from a person or object. This class is often used as advisors or investigators pending individual affiliation.

FOUL MAGIC ORDER

Necromancer

A mage tainted by foul magic who can manipulate the flesh of the dead, extract the spirit of a living being, and manipulate the life essence through nefarious means. As a subclass, blood mages use blood rituals to bind the aether and transform both living and dead flesh into undead creatures.

Summoner

Often outcasts in the mage community, this mage uses Foul and wild magic to break through the veil and draw Vel demons from the plane of existence, often cooperating with necromancers to corrupt the aether of the dead bodies, creating a Vel demon.

Cursegiver

Cursegiver mages that are weak in Aether manipulation but have a talent for disrupting the Aether of objects and people, which causes what seems like bad luck but is, in fact, their inherent magic running wild. Often known for creating objects that cause similar effects (fetishes)

Dreamwalker

A controversial branch of magic. in order to be a dream walker, the mage needs to have Foul magic in their blood. However, dreamwalking itself is looked upon as a subset of psychic magic as the mage influences the unconscious person's emotions and thoughts whilst in a dream state

ALSO BY

Epic Romantic Fantasy (4 books in the series)

In the land where the Old Gods still walk on earth, the antihero, the harbinger of Chaos, and the daughter of the Autumn, lady Inanuan of Thorn have to face her magic and choose between power and the life she always wanted.

For many, known as Striga for her explosive temper or Royal Witch for her role, she is just Ina, a woman of many colours, craving to live her life free and without too many expectations.

With a rare Chaos magic, she becomes the centre of a power struggle between those who desire to rule the world with her hands. And when her life gets tangled with Marcach of Liath, and Sa'Ren Gerel, her heart have to choose between them even if her magic has already claimed them both.

Do you know the place where your nightmares exist, the Nether? Realm shifted in time, a shelter of those hunted to almost extinction by iron and silver, a place where the gods rule and monsters thrive. The place where magic flows freely.

No? I thought so. It was separated from a mortal plane for a reason, but it is still there. This hidden world that lurks in the shadows, caught in the periphery of your vision when you speed your steps, afraid of the darkness.

What you saw in your dreams is real. What you see in your nightmares is even more because now the Gates are open, and danger no longer hides but barges into your life, demanding nothing less than your soul.

Walk the cobbled streets of Gdansk, where the living stone - amber measures the magic of time and the guardians of the Nether ensure unsuspected humans don't discover the existence of those for ages considered a myth... unless they are tonight's prey.

Amber Legends is a series of standalone books inspired on Slavic mythology and the legends of Pomerania. Dark Paranormal fantasy with mature themes, including graphic violence, swear words, and on-page intimacy. For mature 18+ audience.

ABOUT AUTHOR

Olena Nikitin is the pen name of a writing power couple who share a love of fantasy, paranormal romance, rich, vivid worlds and exciting storylines. In their books and out, they love down-to-earth humour, a visceral approach to life, striving to write realistic romances filled with the passion and steam people always dream of experiencing. Meet the two halves of this Truro UK-based dynamic duo!

Olga, a Polish woman, has a wicked sense of humour with a dash of Slavic pessimism. She's been writing since she was a small child, but life led her to work as an emergency physician. While this work means she always has stories to share, it often means she's too busy to actually write. She's proud to be a crazy cat lady, and together with Mark, they have five cats.

Mark, a typical English gentleman, radiates charm, sophistication, and an undeniable sex appeal. At least, he's reasonably certain that's what convinced Olga to fly across the sea into his arms. He's an incredibly intelligent man with a knack for fixing things, including Polish syntax in English writing. If you give him good whiskey, he might even regale you with his Gulf War story of how he got shot.

Olena Nikitin loves hearing from their fans and critics alike and welcomes communication via any platform!

For other books please check our website: www.olenanikitin.uk